GW01186158

FLOOR 68

Jack Probyn

CLIFF EDGE PRESS

 Published by: Cliff Edge Press Limited, Essex.

ISBN: 978-1-912628-17-9

eBook ISBN: 978-1-912628-15-5

First Edition

Visit Jack Probyn's website at www.jackprobynbooks.com.

For You.

Dear Reader,

While every effort has been made to ensure the events and sequences and procedures in this novel are factually correct, the world of counter terrorism and covert surveillance is a dark and tricky and mysterious place. The production of this story has been assisted with the use of some experts and guides in the fields. Meanwhile, in some instances, I have exercised creative license to suit the needs of the story. I hope this does not in any way detract from your reading experience, and that you enjoy the work as it is meant to be – a high-concept thriller with life-altering stakes.

Until next time.

Jack Probyn

PROLOGUE

A Friend From The Past

August 1, 2017, 22:17

Charlie Paxman was going to change the face of humanity. Forever. It was dying, and he was the cure. He had been for a long time. He just needed a little longer.

The smell of chemicals smacked him in the face as he entered his small, nondescript one-bedroom flat in Greenwich. The stench clung to his nostrils and the inside of his throat and lingered there. He coughed and convulsed. Chucking his bag on the sofa, he removed his hand from his mouth. It felt moist.

Blood.

Lined with something else Charlie had never seen before. An internal fluid he didn't know existed. *Strange.*

Creating the virus was beginning to have serious

detrimental effects on his health. But soon it would all be over. His work would be complete, and it would be ready for release.

Charlie wiped the blood from his hand onto his trouser leg. He moved around his flat, taking off his coat and placing it on the back of the chair in his office, before undressing to his boxers. Feeling his bladder press down hard on him, he went into the bathroom. The tension in his body relaxed as he pissed into the toilet, ignoring the splash back on his feet and legs. Leaving small droplets of urine on the seat, and with the stench of chemicals and poison rising through his nostrils, he decided it was time for his second shower of the day.

The first was in the morning. The second was when he got home from work, to remove the smell of greasy food and salt from his skin and hair. The third was just before bed, to rid himself of the outermost layer of chemicals in his pores.

Charlie stepped into the shower. The steaming water hugged his body and loosened the tense muscles in his back and shoulders. It had been another stressful shift. His manager had been on his case again, chastising him for serving food to the wrong table. It wasn't his fault he hated his job. It wasn't his fault he had been kicked out of a dream career he had yearned for since he was a child. It wasn't his fault the world's problems were taking immediate effect.

But it was his responsibility to fix them.

He switched off the shower, stepped over the lip of the bathtub and dried off, wiping the condensation away from the mirror so he could look at himself.

The man he saw was different to the one he had been a few months ago when this entire process began. The messy, unkempt blond hair receding at the temples. The high, hollow cheekbones that made him look malnourished. The lines on his forehead. The bushy blond eyebrows nestling above deep-set eyes, which held a haunted look that reflected the fluorescent bathroom light overhead. The five-day post-shave stubble that lined the sharp angles of his jawline. The thin frame, small shoulders, skinny waist and legs miraculously supporting the weight of his torso. The sinewy forearms, skeletal fingers and bony wrists.

It hadn't been long, and his body was already suffering. The coughing. The bleeding. The vomiting. The fatigue. His immense exposure to the virus had weakened his immune system beyond repair. And when the time came for it to be ready, he hoped he would be in a fit enough state to see it through — he hoped he'd be alive.

A lot had changed since he'd begun. And he had sacrificed even more. But it was necessary. The world needed to change. Humanity didn't know it yet, but it would thank him later. Even after his death, his name would live in infamy, forever written in the history books. Adored by many. Abhorred by more. But he didn't care; he believed that what he was doing was right, and he had the technological and scientific know-how to succeed.

Nothing was going to stand in his way.

Charlie dressed, shoved the towel in the wash bin, and returned to his desk. He started up his computer and played static noise to help him focus. To his right, quietly humming away, was a large metal cabinet with one glass vial inside, rotating. The glass was green, his favourite colour. He moved to the cabinet, pulled aside its small metal hatch, and peered in. The machine's harsh pool-blue light almost blinded him at first, but his eyes had long since adjusted.

Charlie inspected a timer at the top of the machine. Two more hours until today's incubation period was finished. The device had been running all day, silently building the world's most powerful virus. Fifty millilitres of clear, genetically engineered liquid. He felt proud. His life's mission in one small container.

Satisfied for the time being that everything was in order, Charlie slid across to his desk and opened the BBC News homepage. Breaking news articles about the worst terrorist attack London had ever seen littered the page. He read through them. Shook his head in disgust. What Adil and Moshat Hakim had done was nothing compared to what he could do. What he was *going* to do. The attack was minor, insignificant – the needle of destruction amongst the haystack of chaos.

His work was going to change the world.

Quickly bored with the images of burning train wreckages and an auto-playing interview with a police officer and victim – a man called Jake Tanner, whom the media and public adored – Charlie turned his attention to another article. It piqued his interest more than anything else.

He scanned the page. The story was about the World Health Organisation – the agency he had once been a part of and that had started this entire project. Their annual conference, usually held in Geneva, had been moved, and would now take place in The Shard, western Europe's tallest building, on December 2, seven months later than it was supposed to have been held.

A smile grew on his face, sending a strange tingling sensation coursing through his body. Charlie checked his calendar and noted the virus's completion date would be

December 1. Four months away. The day before he would be reunited with old colleagues, old friends, and old enemies.

Time to get down to some serious work.

Pushing himself away from his desk once more, Charlie began his secondary preparations. Inside the wardrobe by the office door was an AK-47, an explosive vest, a saw and a handgun, surrounded by crumpled wads of aluminium foil, all wrapped up in some clothes and thin sheets of copper inside a duffel bag. The weapons, vest, and copper sheets were purchased earlier in the year through a contact he made by chance one night at the restaurant. Untraceable. Undeniable. Nothing would ever lead back to him, and by the time it did, he would be long gone.

Charlie placed one final item – a nine-millimetre handgun – in the bag and sealed the wardrobe shut with a padlock.

The countdown had begun, and he couldn't wait. He looked one last time at the article's featured image that filled the computer screen – a man and woman, side by side, waving to the camera, smiling, happy – and then began the rest of the work that needed completing.

Five metres away, hanging from the wall inside his flat, was another image of the same man. Except this time Charlie was with him, and they both held an award, grinning fervently.

The man was a friend from the past, soon to be seen in the future.

1

Appointment

November 28, 2017, 14:11

Adrenaline and endorphins surged through Jake Tanner's blood. The music in his ears blocked out the rest of the world while the gym's air conditioning set the hairs on the back of his neck and arms on end. The boxing gloves hugged his fists. He jabbed the bag again and again, feeling his body vent its anger on the big sack of sand. After releasing one final heavy right hook, he stopped to remove his gloves and wipe his forehead with the palm of his hand. A thin layer of sweat slicked off his skin, and he dried his hand on his shorts. He looked out of the windows as he grabbed a bottle of water. At the city of London. At the autumnal grey sky. At the pouring rain. At the droplets descending the windowpane. It was just after lunch, and the gym inside New Scotland Yard was empty. Nobody could afford to spare the time to come down here.

Except for him.

Over four thousand personnel hours had been logged for everyone in SO15, the Metropolitan Police's counter terrorism department, since the attack on 01/08, and Jake's hours were less than ten per cent of that. The investigation had even stretched into other departments within the Met's Specialist Crime & Operations division. Jake had been allowed to come back to work on the proviso he shorten his shifts and carry out a reduced workload. Which meant the numbers would only increase for everyone else. And yet they were still no closer to finding Moshat Hakim, the terrorist responsible for the attack, or uncovering any affiliation he had with any terrorist organisation, either domestic or international. To make matters worse, investigations had been impeded by Adil Hakim, Moshat's brother. It had taken the cyber security team months to hack into Adil's seized computer hard drive, and when they were finally able to, it was blank. Adil had placed a fail-safe on it that wiped the contents after weeks of inactivity. Adil Hakim had won, and he was still fucking with them even though he was dead.

Just the thought of him annoyed Jake. Throwing his water bottle to the ground, he picked up a rope and began to skip. In recent weeks, he had been training hard, improving his physical fitness while allowing his mental health to fall by the wayside. Most of his time in the gym was spent working, preparing, and imagining the day he would reunite with Moshat Hakim. The day he would defeat him - sending him to prison for the rest of his worthless life. Or even better - and completely off the record - the day he would kill Moshat

Hakim. It was a day Jake looked forward to.

'Supersonic' by Oasis played in his ears. The guitar riffs spurred him on. He breathed in and out rapidly through his mouth as he jumped to the beat.

The door at the end of the gym opened. DCS Mamadou Kuhoba, Jake's boss and one of his closest friends within the service, stepped through. He was a wide-set man with a large stomach, and his short, tightly curled hair was shocked silver. Jake stopped at once, dropped the rope to the floor next to his bottle, and removed his earphones.

'What's going on in here, then?' Mamadou asked, advancing towards Jake.

Jake looked around him. 'Petting animals at the zoo. What does it look like?'

Mamadou's face dropped. 'Funny. I was just wondering if you were all right.'

'Yeah.' Jake shrugged. 'Why wouldn't I be?'

'I've not seen much of you, that's all.'

'I've been busy.'

'So you keep telling everyone. I feel like I haven't spoken to you properly since that day. I'm glad you stuck with us in SO15 and didn't join MI5. I couldn't see you as a spook.'

'It would have been too much physical and mental strain. Elizabeth and I decided it was best I turn it down. Not just for me, but for the family, too.'

'I'm glad. Although I wouldn't want to be working there right now. Lot of backlash.'

'Why?' Jake frowned.

'While you were signed off, Director General Brockhurst declared that Moshat and Adil had been on their radars. They investigated but found nothing of any worth, so they stopped. It was his decision,' Mamadou said.

'Wouldn't be the first time they've let someone slip through the net, would it?' Jake said. He was referring to an attempted attack that had taken place in a shopping centre last Christmas that both he and Mamadou had thwarted.

Mamadou smiled, avoiding the comment. He reached into his back pocket and produced his phone. He stared at it a while, hesitating, as if afraid to speak about something on his mind. He cleared his throat. 'IT sent me the logs for your computer the other day.'

Jake froze.

'And?' he said, trying to act as nonchalant as possible.

'It made for interesting reading.' Mamadou looked to his left and gestured to the row of benches by the weight rack that ran along the wall. 'Shall we?'

Jake didn't respond. Instead, he found himself a seat and looked up at Mamadou as he sat opposite. The synthetic leather was uncomfortable, and he could feel himself sweating even more.

'We need to talk, Jake. Are you sure you're OK?'

Jake sighed. He hated being babied liked this. It had been constant ever since he'd returned from the hospital following the attack. Mamadou, Elizabeth, Frances, his mum – they all wanted to show him that they cared, that they were there for him. They acted like they knew how he felt. But they didn't. None of them did. How could they? How could he ever let anyone close to him know what he was feeling when he didn't understand it himself?

'What did you see on the log?' Jake asked. He found himself gripping the bench's edge until his knuckles whitened.

'Your internet searches, mate. PTSD. Symptoms, signs, treatments. Why didn't you tell me you were suffering from it?'

'I thought it would have been obvious,' Jake said, grinding his teeth. He chided himself for forgetting to delete his browser history. It was a rookie mistake, and now he was suffering the effects of it.

'Well, sure. It's assumed. But I'd not had any confirmation. That stuff is above even my pay grade.'

'How can it be? You're my supervisor.'

Mamadou leaned closer, resting his elbows on his knees. 'I thought you were having meetings about it.' He spoke softly, the quietest Jake had ever heard him. For a moment, there was no employer–employee divide between them. They were just two friends, having a chat.

'I was,' Jake said, looking to the floor. In the months succeeding the attack, Jake had had multiple counselling and therapy sessions with the in-house psychiatrists. But he was still no closer to finding peace, nor to finding the time, let alone approval, to chase Moshat himself. Jake had to live with the harsh reality that he had let the man go. That's what played through his mind every time he looked at Elizabeth, or lay next to her in bed. Every time he looked at his own wife, he was reminded of Martha, Elizabeth's mother, who had fallen victim to Moshat. Some nights he lay awake recounting the events of that day, reliving them, trying to think of what would have happened if he'd acted differently.

'Why did you stop going to the meetings, Jake?' Mamadou's face contorted as his concerns for Jake grew.

Jake fell silent.

'Come on, Jake. You can tell me. We've known each other

a long time, and this is the first time you've shut me out. I can't help you if you don't let me. No one can.'

Jake opened his mouth to speak, but the words wouldn't come.

'I've been busy,' he said defiantly.

'With what? Don't tell me it's because you've been in here all this time.'

'Elizabeth. She needs me. I've had to reschedule most of my meetings with the psychiatrist because she's worried about the baby. She's been dealing with a lot of stress. Her mum. Me . . .' Jake hesitated. He hated lying to his friend, but it was necessary. The simple explanation for it was that he didn't want to discuss his problems with anyone. Not even himself. Every time he searched on the internet for symptoms and signs of PTSD, he feared himself – worse, he hated himself – even more. The thought he could be susceptible to it, that he had let everyone down by suffering from it . . . It made him feel weak and vulnerable.

'When was the last time you saw someone?' Mamadou asked, touching Jake's leg, bringing him back to the present.

Jake searched his mind. 'September.'

'September? Bloody hell, Jake. That was over two months ago. A lot's happened since then. Has your PTSD been getting worse?'

Jake didn't respond, which was encouragement enough for Mamadou to continue.

'Why haven't you spoken about it with anyone else?'

'Because it's hard, all right? Admitting defeat like that.'

'Admitting defeat?' Mamadou rose. 'You can't be serious? Nothing about what happened on that day was normal. Nobody blames you for anything. Nobody went through even a tenth of what you did. Nobody.'

Jake looked up. Stared into Mamadou's deep, dark eyes. 'You did.'

'That's different. I've learnt how to deal with these things.'

'Have you been speaking with someone about your mum?' Jake asked.

Mamadou paused a beat, reached into his pocket and produced his mobile. 'Right, listen up. I'm not going to send you back to the shrink here; they'll get pissy about you lying to them and trying to get out of so many meetings for so long. I'll appease them for you. What I'm going to do instead is send you to the specialist I saw. She's an expert. Even if her methods are . . . unconventional. She helped me loads. Whatever she prescribes, I want you to consider trying. I did, and it went against everything I stand for, but I have to admit it helped. It's only a short-term solution. The moment it becomes long-term, you speak with me about it.'

Unconventional. Short-term. Long-term. What does he mean? Dozens of questions and concerns floated about Jake's brain.

Mamadou extended his hand. 'Give me your phone.'

After removing the earphones from the jack, Jake passed his mobile to Mamadou.

'I'm adding her details to your address book. Her name's Kim Olson. Just make sure Elizabeth doesn't see it. She'll start to think something's up,' Mamadou said. His eyebrow rose and the sides of his mouth flickered.

'That's the least of my worries,' Jake said, finding himself smiling. It was a long time since he'd done that. In the months following the attack, he had ostracised himself from the rest of the team, and it felt good to have a chat with someone he cared about, and to find something they could laugh about.

Mamadou returned his phone. Jake stared at the name and number on the screen.

'What are you waiting for?' his friend asked, clearing his throat. 'I'm not leaving until you book an appointment.'

Jake stared at Mamadou in disbelief. 'Come on, Mam. That's not necessary.'

'Yes, it is. I'm not having you flake out on me. You're making that call. And if you don't, I'll make it for you.'

Sighing, Jake stepped to the side and dialled the number, so that Mamadou was just out of earshot.

The person on the other end answered on the second ring.

'Dr Olson speaking.'

'Hi, Doctor. My name's Jake Tanner.'

2

Therapy

November 28, 2017, 15:06

Dr Kim Olson was an attractive woman in her mid thirties, with brown hair and even more vibrant earthy brown eyes – the colour of the leaves on the ground outside. Her high cheekbones and pursed lips made her look as if she were constantly posing in front of a camera. She had been born and raised in Norway. She was forced to study at a top university in Oslo, chosen by her parents. The only thing she had any control over was the subject she studied, and in the end, she'd settled for psychology. She had focused on the consequences of dealing with psychological trauma for members of the emergency services, and after two months of searching, had found counselling prospects in Norway slim, especially in the policing world. When she graduated several years later, she decided she would emigrate to England in search of a better career.

'And that's when I decided to consult freelance for high-profile cases – and individuals – in the UK.' Kim removed her glasses from her forehead and placed them on her nose. 'Enough about me. Let's talk about you. After all, that's why you're here.'

She was wearing a grey blazer with a white shirt underneath. The top two buttons were undone, revealing a small patch of skin just underneath her collarbones that still left everything to the imagination. She sat to the side of her desk, left leg folded over the right, with a small notebook resting on her knee.

'Thanks for meeting me on such short notice,' Jake said.

'This isn't how my clients usually arrive,' Kim said, nodding at his sodden top.

Jake looked at his chest and sniffed. His sweaty odour slapped him in the face. He hoped she couldn't smell it. 'Sorry,' he said. 'Blame Mamadou. He sort of sprung this on me.'

'How is Mamadou?' Kim asked.

'Shouldn't I be asking you that? Considering you're the one seeing him.'

'*Was* seeing,' she corrected. 'He cancelled our meetings a couple of days ago. He didn't tell me why, but I think he sorted everything he needed to. Although, in our meetings, he mostly seemed concerned about you.'

'What did he say?' Jake asked, his curiosity getting the better of him.

The sides of Kim's lips rose. 'Come on, Jake. You know that's confidential between myself and DCS Kuhoba. Much like this conversation between you and I.'

Jake stared at her. He didn't know what to say. He always hated these meetings, especially his ones with the resident shrink at the Yard. He was more suited to being the one on the other side of the chair, asking the questions, probing deeper into a suspect's life, diagnosing.

'From what I hear, Jake, you're something of a hero,' Kim began.

No, I'm not, Jake thought. He hated being called that. At first, he thought news tabloids printed that word for attention and sales. But the longer the investigation into the 01/08 attack, code named Operation Tightrope, continued, the more prolific and infamous Jake became. Journalists and members of the public would wait outside his house, stop him in the street, disturb him in a coffee shop or in his local Tesco, and ask him about his version of events. They all wanted to know the same thing: What really happened?

'I'm nothing of the sort,' Jake replied. 'I was just doing my job.'

'Don't be so modest. You saved thousands of lives. The death toll could have been far greater if it weren't for you.' Kim looked at him with open admiration; he returned her gaze with a scowl. He wanted to move the conversation forwards but didn't want to be rude about it.

'What else have you heard?' he asked.

'Mamadou tells me you're a psychology graduate.'

Jake prepared himself for a barrage of questions. 'How much more do you know?'

'Enough. So, I know how difficult this is for you. He also told me your previous psychiatrist prescribed medication for your PTSD. Is that right?'

Jake bowed his head.

'How long have you been on them for?'

'A few months.'

'Does your wife know?' Kim nodded at Jake's wedding ring.

'Nope.'

'Do you think she deserves to know?'

'I don't want to worry her.'

She scribbled something down on her pad. 'Why did you start the meds?'

Jake swallowed before responding. He was cautious about how much to tell her. How much was safe? How much was confidential, and how much would be relayed back to Mamadou at the end of it all?

'Night terrors.' A lump formed in his throat.

'Night terrors? Tell me about those.'

Jake looked at the ground, then at Kim, then back to the floor. Finally, deeming it a safe place to talk, he began. 'I'm still seeing him. Moshat. I'm still re-experiencing everything, again and again. That night. The explosion. The gun. The blood.'

'Has the medication helped in any way? Have the night terrors abated?'

Jake shrugged. 'It's not doing anything.'

Dr Olson nodded as she continued to write on the paper. 'And how frequent are these episodes?'

'Almost every night. The last one was today. I woke up in a puddle of sweat.'

'Is that a regular occurrence?'

Jake nodded.

'And what happened in this particular vision?'

'Moshat's face appeared. I was working at my desk, filing a report from years ago, and he was just there . . . at my desk, lingering in the background.'

'What case were you working on?'

'I can't remember.'

'Can't, or don't want to?'

'I don't know. It was something to do with Operation Tightrope.'

'But I thought you said it was a case from years ago?' Kim asked, constantly making notes on her pad as she spoke.

'I did. It was. It seemed like years ago. But it was 01/08. I could see the images of my mother-in-law and Tyler on the documents, but it was dated 2012. I don't know why.'

'Is there anything that happened in 2012 that you might be repressing?'

He shook his head. 'Nothing that's even remotely related to this case.'

Kim fell silent as she made a final note on her paper. She pressed the pen to her lips and chewed the top. 'How much of this have you told your wife? Do you discuss with her the nature of your terrors?'

Jake hung his head low.

'You need to tell her, speak with her about it. The more you shut people out, especially your family, the more they'll separate from you. I can only do so much. I can only offer you a certain amount of help. The other fifty per cent you have to find yourself.' The hum of Kim's computer monitor seemed to reverberate around the room. 'If you can't confide in your wife, then there must be someone you can trust.'

'Tyler,' he said, surprised to hear himself say it. He hadn't referred to his friend by name for some time, and whenever

Tyler came up in conversation with relatives or family friends or strangers, Jake always referred to him as just 'him'.

'There you go,' Kim said. 'Mamadou tells me you see him on the first day of every month. That's good. Your coping mechanisms are different to anyone else's. Completely different to Mamadou's. He doesn't visit his mother.'

'I thought that was confidential.' Jake's eyebrows rose.

'That bit isn't. So, tell me: What do you do when you see him?'

'I speak to him. That's it. Sometimes I make sure his grave is OK. Sometimes I leave it up to the staff – but they do a shitty job of maintaining it. He gave his life for me, and I'm not going to let the memory of him be ruined by some lazy people who aren't willing to do their job properly.'

Kim nodded as she made another, final note on the paper on her lap, underlining it.

'Here's what I want to happen. I'm going to prescribe you something, but before I do, I need you to tell me what Mamadou told you about me.'

'I'm not sure I understand.'

'When Mamadou referred you, what did he say? Anything about my methods?'

Jake hesitated as he considered, replayed the conversation in his mind. What was it he had said? 'That you were unconventional.'

A smile formed on Dr Olson's lips. 'Good. He's already managed your expectations.' She tore the top-right corner of the paper and handed it to him. On it was a mobile number and a name: Mark. 'Right there is someone who will help you further. I need you to stop taking the antidepressants your psychiatrist gave you for now and try a different prescription.

Our next meeting will be on December fourth, a couple of days after you've been to visit Tyler. There, I want you to tell me if the new medication has made a more positive or negative impact on you than the antidepressants. With this particular form of treatment, however, it is up to you whether you wish to share the fact you're taking the new meds with your wife or not. Sound good?'

Jake grunted as a way of response. His eyes remained fixed on the shred of paper he held in his hands. The sound of Kim rising from her chair startled him. He joined her, and they wandered over to the door, the meeting adjourned.

Kim opened the door. As Jake left, staring at the name on the paper again, she said, 'From what I hear, you and he have had a relationship in the past.'

He stared at her, and then at the piece of paper once more. Mark. *Mark?* Did he know anyone by that name?

As Jake exited the office, he ignored the door closing behind him, removed his work phone from his pocket and dialled the number. The internal memory of the phone populated the name. In his address book, Jake had only one contact under 'Mark.'

An informant, specialising in gang crime and drugs.

3

Coffee

November 29, 2017, 07:37

The following morning, Jake entered New Scotland Yard an hour earlier than usual. The night terror had been bad and he hadn't been able to fall back asleep. He had skipped the previous night's antidepressants on Kim Olson's orders, but hadn't yet been able to bring himself to give Mark a call. His night terror had been made worse by the constant thoughts of Mark and Kim in his head as he lay there awake, unable to return to sleep. Why had she given him Mark's number? How was Mark possibly going to help combat his PTSD?

Jake wandered to the canteen, ordered his usual breakfast of two pieces of toast and a yoghurt, purchased a coffee and, once the food was ready, headed upstairs to his desk. On his way, he was greeted with muted stares. As people passed him, he felt like they gave him derisive looks, as if they were unsure whether he was real or just an apparition, a figment of their imagination. He hated that – feeling like an outcast, an invalid, someone who shouldn't be there. But he had every right to be. In fact, he had more right than anyone.

As Jake entered Room 1430, the name given to the operation control room of SO15, the office fell silent. It was the first time in months he had been there this early. Before Operation Tightrope, he'd usually been one of the first souls in the office, making the most of the silence and the extra time to complete the day's tasks. It had been a while, but today was no different.

He had his own investigation to continue.

Picking up where he left off, Jake loaded the CCTV archives the Met had been able to access of the industrial park next to the location where the Heathrow Express had been taken hostage – the exact location from where Moshat Hakim had fled. A road ran parallel to the small, enclosed woodland area where Jake had last seen Moshat, and nearby where Tyler had died. Jake found the correct date and time he was looking for – the numbers were stained in indelible ink in his mind – and changed the camera angle with a few clicks. The road was empty, save for plastic bottles rolling around on the pavement in the wind.

Jake leaned closer to the screen as he sped up the playback. He had seen the footage multiple times, but still there was nothing that gave him any inclination as to where Moshat Hakim had disappeared. It didn't stop him from replaying it again and again, hoping each time that he might learn something new. He never did.

As the numbers on the bottom left-hand side of the screen

climbed higher, the sun lowered in the recorded sky, casting great shadows on the ground. Jake finally gave in and switched to a different angle. In the hours of the recording he had been watching, there had been no signs of movement in or out of the industrial park.

All except for one. A single van, driving into the park. It continued through without stopping and turned right down a small alley. Jake pressed 'Pause', 'Rewind', and then 'Play'. Moments before the van arrived at the centre of the screen, the bottle rolling on the ground disappeared, and then reappeared as it shot off the bottom of the footage. He had paid little attention to it before, yet it had been so simple, and such a tiny movement, it was easy to overlook.

Jake enhanced the image of the van, ran the number plate through the ANPR and cross-referenced it with the delivery routes obtained by the company that owned it. ANPR stood for Automatic Number Plate Recognition and was the intelligence service's way of monitoring and tracking vehicle number plates. From the simple seven-character alphanumeric code written on both the front and back of every vehicle registered in the country, the police could gather as much intelligence as they needed. It was the perfect way to track fugitives and criminals and terrorists. And it was completely legal.

A few seconds later, the system popped up with a hit. The car was registered with Reliance Autos and had travelled through the centre of London to Essex on the other side of the city, despite its delivery route saying it should have travelled to Hertfordshire.

Excited by the discovery, Jake put the remnants of his breakfast in the bin beside his desk, grabbed his phone and dialled a number. He just hoped the person on the other end was there.

After the fourth ring, a voice answered, 'Hello?'

'Lucy?' Jake asked, suddenly overwhelmed with happiness at hearing her voice.

'Jake? Is that you? I thought you weren't supposed to be back until the new year?'

Fucking rumours, Jake thought.

'I don't know where you heard that from, but it's not true. I've been back since September—'

'Wait,' Lucy interrupted, 'you've been working all this time and you haven't even bothered to come and say hello?'

It was true, Jake hadn't visited Lucy. But that didn't mean he hadn't wanted to. They had, after all, experienced the same things on the day of the attack, when Adil Hakim summoned Lucy as Jake's hostage. The day after the attack, she had been offered a position as a legal representative within Scotland Yard and, unsurprisingly, she accepted the offer on the spot. Working for the police had always been what she wanted to do, in any capacity. That was three months ago, and now they were back to reality, things were different. What could he say to her? How would their relationship change? How had she been affected by Tyler's death?

'I guess I've just been busy. You know how it is,' Jake said. 'You're only a few months into the job, and I can already guess you're swamped.'

'I am. But that's not the point. You should have mentioned something.' She hesitated. 'You owe me a drink, or a coffee. Something.'

Like Tyler said he'd take you out for one, but never had the chance. Jake smiled. 'I'd like that.'

'Now, how can I help you? Did you want anything in particular, or were you just ringing to let me know you're alive?' There was a hint of sassiness in Lucy's voice. It was one of the reasons he liked her.

'I was wondering if you could help me with something.'

'Sounds ominous. What is it?'

'I need to get a warrant through by midday.'

'Right – what do you need me for?'

'Your expertise. It's for a small company based outside Heathrow called Reliance Autos, near where Moshat disappeared. We checked them out after the attack, but I think something's been overlooked. I think someone may have overwritten the CCTV footage they sent to us. And one of their vehicles went the longest way possible through London to get to Essex when it should have gone round the M25 to Hertfordshire instead. Seems suspicious to me. I just want to get in, look around the place, and if I can find anything then I'll get a proper warrant for arrest.'

Lucy paused before replying. 'You think he's there, don't you? You think Moshat's been hiding in an industrial park all this time?'

'I don't know,' Jake said. 'But I think there might be someone who knows something.'

'How can I help with this specifically?'

'I need you to draft an all-premises warrant.'

'What for?'

'Anything. Make it up.'

'Why can't you do it?'

'Because I want to place a bug in there. I need you to draft only the all-premises warrant – and not the warrant for the surveillance. That'll take longer. You and I both know the Investigatory Powers Act fucked that up for us last year. I'll handle the bug on my own.'

Lucy hesitated for what felt like a lifetime. 'I don't know, Jake. Can you not wait?'

At that point, Jake pleaded with her. He kept his voice low, lest anyone in the office or in the work stations nearby overhear him.

'I'm going out of my mind here, Lucy,' Jake said in a final attempt to convince her. 'I've been on antidepressants for weeks and speaking with another shrink to help me. I'll go mad if Moshat isn't caught soon. This has to happen.'

Silence.

'Jake . . . I didn't know . . .' Lucy trailed off, as if there were no more words to say.

'Why would you? So, please, could you do this for me? For Tyler? We all need Moshat found. Soon.' Jake hated guilt-tripping people, but if it was the only way he could get what he wanted, then so be it.

A long pause. 'Fine,' Lucy said. 'Just this once. And I swear to God, Jake, you're responsible—'

'I know. It's all on me,' Jake said.

He thanked her profusely and put the phone down on the receiver, a smile as wide as his ears stretching across his face.

Jake left his desk and headed down to the lockup where the service kept their technological equipment. Using his ID card, he pretended to sign out a stun gun and kept the bug he'd picked up discreetly hidden in his back pocket. After he returned, he hid the stun gun in the top drawer of his desk and continued to sift through the video footage of the industrial park. He found nothing more. By the time Lucy showed up with the search warrant folded in an envelope, he was growing increasingly impatient.

'Thanks,' he said, rising out of his seat. He looked up at her. 'I owe you two coffees now.'

With that, he smiled and thanked her again before he left the building.

The drive to Reliance Autos was long and monotonous, but it gave him ample time to think, to consider his actions. He was onto something, and he knew it. Soon, he hoped, the world's most wanted terrorist would be caught.

4

Reliance Autos

November 29, 2017, 14:59

Anthony Baldwin was sat in the reception area of Reliance Autos with his feet resting atop the desk, a mug of tea in his hand, and his gaze fixated on the horse racing on the television on the wall to his right. Now and then, a draught blew in around his ankles as the November breeze buffeted the building's door. He was enjoying himself. There were no customers, and all the mechanics had left. It was just him and Rachael, who was out back.

So it was understandable that when a man proclaiming to be a police detective from the Metropolitan Police's Counter Terrorism Command appeared in front of him with a search warrant, Anthony was miffed.

'What?' Anthony asked. He eyed the piece of paper that

was held in front of his face, but paid little attention to the words written on it.

'I'm leading the investigation into the disappearance of Moshat Hakim, the terrorist responsible for the 01/08 attacks,' the detective said.

'You got some ID on you?'

The detective fished inside his blazer pocket and produced an ID card. Anthony leaned forward to read it.

'Detective *cunt*stable Jake Tanner,' Anthony said, nodding, his lips pursed. 'Impressive. But what's it got to do with us?'

'We believe you or someone within your company was involved with his disappearance.' The man stood nonchalantly, his shoulders pressed back and his chest raised. He looked like a cock, and like he constantly had a finger – or several – shoved up his arse.

'How is that possible? You had guys come down here a day after the attacks. They cleared everything. Went through it all. Bastards misplaced some very important documents. And will I get compensation for the business I lost that day because of the four bloody police cars outside my building? No? I didn't think so.'

Detective Constable Jake Tanner shifted uneasily. 'Sir, it was vital we examine every company in this park. Now it would appear other evidence has come to light, the likes of which I am not at liberty to discuss with you. If you don't mind, I'd like to begin. The sooner you allow me to, the sooner I'm out of here.'

Anthony didn't like this. Firstly, there was a copper on his premises, albeit lawfully. Secondly, there was yet another police car stationed outside his reception. God only knew how much business that would turn away.

'Don't have much of a choice, do I?' Anthony said, swallowing his pride. The detective shook his head and smiled facetiously. 'But I'm coming with you wherever you go.'

The detective nodded, and Anthony stepped aside to allow him through a back door to their right.

Jake entered the door first, ignoring the obese man beside him. He had looked up Anthony Baldwin on his phone when he pulled over at the entrance to the industrial park. Anthony had been convicted of a car theft in his early twenties, which he had served time for. It wasn't long, but it was obviously enough for Anthony to change his outlook on life. Since then, he'd been nowhere near a police station. And Jake got the sense he wasn't about to change his ways now.

'What is it you do here exactly at Reliance Autos?' Jake asked, scanning the factory floor in front of him. A row of desks adjoined a car garage in an open-plan space. Workbenches and tyres were left on the side of the building; meanwhile in the centre was a large vehicle lift, which was empty.

'We deal with the re-customisation of dilapidated vehicles. Owners bring their old motors in and we modify them. Bring some of 'em into the twenty-first century,' Anthony said. He suddenly spoke with passion in his voice.

'Where is everyone else? Or is it just you today?' Jake asked as he looked around the garage. In his pocket, he rolled the tiny recording device that would eavesdrop on every conversation within the premises between his fingers. All he had to do now was find a secure place to leave it.

'They're all out with clients. As part of our service, we offer them a free test spin at the local racetrack off the M25, courtesy of an old friend.'

'So, it's just you?'

'No,' Anthony said. He looked over to a wooden door to Jake's left. 'Rachael's here. She's filing some paperwork.'

Jake nodded. 'What's her position here?'

'Secretary. Deals with all my admin and everything. Never met a girl as organised as her. She's a hard worker. Sometimes doesn't know when to stop.'

'May I speak with her?'

Anthony rolled his eyes, huffing. 'Sure.'

Anthony left Jake where he was and wandered over to the door. Jake used the brief moment he had alone to stick the recording device on the underside of a nearby desk. It wasn't original, but it would suffice, given the circumstances. A few seconds later Anthony reappeared, his body only just able to squeeze through the small hole in the wall. Behind him was a petite woman who was half Anthony's size in every respect – and about half his age. Jake estimated she was in her mid- to late twenties. She had brown hair and powerful, striking eyebrows that looked as if she were frowning at him, judging him. Her legs and arms were skinny, but she carried an air of power and intimidation about her that said she knew what she was doing and she wasn't going to be told differently.

'Hello,' Rachael said as she approached Jake. She held out her hand and Jake shook it; her grip was firm. His, on the other hand, was doused with a thin layer of sweat – the nerves of placing the bug on the table getting the better of him.

'Nice to meet you. I gather from Anthony here you're in charge?'

Rachael smiled, revealing all her teeth. Two strands of hair delicately dangled either side of her eyes, and they lifted as her cheeks rose.

'He's basically right. I run this place. He's just the not-so-pretty face at the entrance.' Rachael glanced at her manager, smirking. Turning to Jake, she asked, 'How can I help?'

The way she looked at him was intense. 'I was wondering if I could access your CCTV footage from the day of the 01/08 attacks, and check your records pertaining to any business conducted on that day,' Jake explained.

'Don't see why that would be a problem,' Rachael said calmly. She stared into Jake's eyes, not once breaking contact with them to ask Anthony Baldwin for approval.

Maybe she really is the boss, Jake thought to himself.

She turned on the spot and started towards the office behind the factory wall. Anthony and Jake followed.

The three of them entered the small room. Compared to the reception, it was spotless. The desk was tidy, the remnants of lunch the only thing that seemed out of place. Along the wall were filing cabinets. Written on them were letters of the alphabet. Jake wondered if there was anything buried deep within the mountain of paper and if it would uncover some corrupt irregularities. But that would be for another time and another department.

'Told you,' Anthony said, shutting the door. 'Tidy as fuck. And not just in that sense of the word, either.'

In the corner of Jake's eye, he saw Rachael rotate as if she were about to say something back to her boss, but she moved away after looking towards Jake meaningfully. He didn't appreciate sexual harassment in the workplace, and he could only imagine how Rachael must have taken it and how frequently Anthony made such comments.

Jake turned to Rachael, who continued to stare at him. What was that look about? 'Seems like you run a pretty tight ship here.'

'I do what needs to be done. This lazy prick isn't going to do anything, so I will instead.' The sides of Rachael's mouth flickered up slightly, bearing the tops of her teeth.

Just as Jake was about to say something, his phone vibrated in his pocket. It was Mamadou.

Fuck, he thought, already fearing the worst. He held his finger in the air and stepped outside Rachael's office.

'Yes, boss?' Jake said.

'Where the fuck are you, Tanner? Do you know what I've been hearing around the office? I suggest you apologise to the staff at Reliance Autos for your incompetence and get back here now.'

Mamadou hung the phone up before Jake was able to respond. *How could he have known I was here? Did Lucy say something?*

And then he realised: the phone call. Internal calls were recorded. *How could I have been so stupid?* Jake would have to worry about that on the way back to the Yard. He pocketed his phone and stepped back into the office. He was met with awkward glances.

'Sorry about that,' he said, 'but I have to go. Urgent matter's come up. Thank you both for your time. I'll be back soon with another warrant. Here's my card if you need to give me a call about anything in the meantime.'

Jake placed a card on a nearby table. It had his email address and mobile number on it. Neither Rachael nor Anthony seemed bothered by it. Brushing his blazer with the palms of his hands, Jake nodded to Anthony and Rachael, thanked them again and headed towards the exit. As he jumped into his BMW X5, only one thought was on his mind: the bizarre looks that Rachael kept giving him. Was it flirting? Was she trying to tell him something? Or was she trying to hide something?

Or was he just imagining the entire thing?

On the radio, the hit song 'Despacito' was playing, and as soon as it started, Jake couldn't help but think how he'd like to get to New Scotland Yard slowly. He was in no particular hurry to be berated by Mamadou. During the drive, his thoughts turned to Lucy. She had only been in the job a short amount of time, and he would hate to be the one responsible for jeopardising her career.

By the time Jake arrived back at his second home, it was late afternoon, and the atmosphere in the office was getting a little relaxed. Jake wandered along the fourteenth floor, stopped outside Mamadou's office, heard his boss talking to someone on the phone, and knocked.

There was what felt like a long silence before Mamadou responded.

'Enter.'

Swallowing hard, Jake twisted the door handle and stepped inside.

5

Leave

November 29, 2017, 16:22

Mamadou was angry. A vein throbbed on the left side of his temple. And Jake knew, from experience, that whenever it appeared, Mamadou became a tyrant, insufferable, an absolute pain to work with.

'What were you thinking?' he shouted as soon as Jake had touched down on the seat. 'Getting Lucy to sanction a search warrant for you so you could go gallivanting around the city. It's not on, Jake. What were you expecting to fucking achieve? I thought I told you to stay away from Moshat Hakim and everything to do with his disappearance. It's not good for your mental—'

'I can't, boss,' Jake interrupted, feeling the overwhelming desire to defend himself. 'He's out there somewhere, and I need to find him. For Martha's sake.' Jake swallowed. 'For Tyler.'

'It's got to stop. You can't break protocol like this.'

'Mam, please. Lucy had nothing to do with it. It was all me.'

'I know it was. I've listened to the phone conversation. Which is why I'm taking control of the situation, Jake,' Mamadou continued. 'Effective immediately, I'm ordering you to take time off.'

'What?'

'I want you to take the week off. I'll deal with things here. It won't be easy, but so long as no one finds out about it, you'll be OK. And if they do, I'll just explain you've not been of sound mind recently,' Mamadou said. By now, the vein in his forehead had disappeared. Something different was going on inside Mamadou's head, and Jake didn't have the courage to object.

He didn't respond. His mind was spinning. What was he going to do? What was he going to tell Elizabeth and the kids? That he had let them down again?

'I just don't understand why you did it, Jake. Well, I know why, but I don't know why you didn't feel like you could come to me beforehand. I thought we'd agreed you'd let me help you.'

'I knew you wouldn't let me.'

'That's not true. I want to catch him just as much as you. Trust me, I do. All of us do.' Mamadou paused a beat. 'Was it worth it, though? Did you uncover anything?'

Jake shook his head and looked down at the floor. 'I didn't get a chance. You bloody rang me at the wrong time.' Jake could feel himself returning to normal. Then a thought crossed his mind. Did Mamadou know about the bug? If he'd listened to the conversation on the phone then he must have done. And if he did, then why wasn't he saying anything about it? Jake decided it was in his best interests not to find out.

Mamadou smiled. 'Good. Better to get you out of there and find nothing than for the owner to find out you were there illegally and file a complaint. Then you would have really been up shit creek. And I'd only be able to do so much with my paddle. Now, I want you home. Take a few days off. You're not going to get any better here. And it's probably best for everyone else if you're not. I don't want to be dealing with more hassle.'

'Nothing's going to happen to Lucy, is it?' Jake asked, eager to find out her fate.

'No. She'll be fine. Don't worry about her. Just get yourself home to Elizabeth and the kids and spend the weekend with them, not thinking about Moshat Hakim, Operation Tightrope, or anything else for that matter.'

'We're going to The Shard,' Jake said, stepping out of his chair, taking his cue to leave. Elizabeth and Jake had decided to take the girls to London for the day to visit the impressive skyscraper, their first day out as a family in a long time. 'It's our way of rewarding the kids for being so good throughout this whole thing with their gran.'

Mamadou had stood and was walking him out. 'That'll be nice.'

Jake stopped by the door. 'Yeah. We're going for a meal in the restaurant up there as well.'

'I thought you hated heights?'

'I do.'

'Let's hope that's the worst thing on your mind,' Mamadou said as he shut his office door behind Jake.

6

Little Moments

November 29, 2017, 19:48

The restaurant was busy. Busier than usual for a Wednesday. Charlie Paxman checked the floor plan to see if they were fully booked. They were. Right until closing at midnight. That meant he wouldn't get home until one in the morning. Which meant there would be no time to continue his preparations.

And in eleven hours' time, he'd be back here, ready for yet another thirteen-hour shift. He couldn't call in sick. Not so soon to his big day; he was running out of warnings with his manger. No, it was vital he find the time elsewhere. The countdown was ticking, and soon the hour would pass and everyone on the planet would understand. Everyone would realise what good he was bringing to the world. How he was saving them.

Charlie stopped for a moment to absorb his surroundings. There were customers everywhere. All dressed nicely. Smart. Authentic. Rich. Wealthy. Arrogant. He was looking forward to being treated like scum, like he was beneath every single person he served tonight; it would make the second of December even sweeter.

'Charlie!' someone called behind him. He turned to face the owner of the voice. It was the head chef, his Scottish accent sending shivers down Charlie's spine. 'Wake the fuck up, you daft bastard. Steak is ready for table fifteen.'

Charlie grabbed the plate from the metallic surface and contemplated sneezing into it. He wanted to see if there was enough of the virus in his DNA that would spread to others.

No, he thought. *I must contain it and wait. No one will know my name if it breaks out now.*

Charlie wandered over to table fifteen. A family of three were dining: a mother, a father, and a daughter. The parents were deep in conversation, while the child was engrossed with a tablet in her hands, her face illuminated by the blue light from the screen. None of them paid much attention to the view of London at night. The thousands of lights that flickered in the distance. The ominous glow of St Paul's. The sparkling Ferris wheel of the London Eye.

Charlie placed the food on the table.

'How is everything for you this evening?' he asked in his politest voice possible, placing his hands together by his crotch.

'We've been waiting a very long time for our food. We ordered drinks from another of your colleagues almost five minutes ago, and we've still not seen them!' the father barked in Charlie's face. A piece of spittle landed on Charlie's finger.

'I'm sorry, sir, but we are short-staffed today. We're doing our best. I will make sure those drinks are on your table in the next two minutes.' Charlie smiled facetiously. Behind the stretched facial muscles, he was swearing at the man and his family, berating them for wasting his time.

The man said nothing. Charlie glanced over to the woman to smile at her. To his surprise, she reciprocated. She was good cop.

'It's fine, honestly,' she said. 'He's just had a busy day at work. He doesn't mean to take it out on you.'

'I understand,' Charlie said, nodding. 'We all have days like that.'

It's still no excuse.

He apologised again to the family for the delay and then continued on with the rest of his shift. The few remaining hours went by quickly; they were made easier by the renewed vigour he had after dealing with that father. The man was an arrogant bastard who deserved to suffer. He reminded Charlie of someone – someone he had once called a very close friend – and it made him hate that family even more for it.

He enjoyed having little moments that reminded him why he was doing this. They meant any doubt he had about his operation was completely removed.

7

The Darkness

December 1, 2017, 03:37

It was dark. And then light. Dark again. Jake's surroundings spun in a carousel of orange and brown. Intense, searing heat blasted him from behind, burning the hairs on his back, the backs of his legs, and the side of his head. A huge fire roared behind him. He landed hard on the ground and his shoulder caught on a small rut, disjointing it slightly. A wave of pain consumed his body.

His ears rang with a deafening sound, and his arms and legs felt weak as he tried to lift himself up. To his surprise, the only noise he could hear was the sound of train wreckage raining down over him. Pieces of glass, chairs, suitcases, clothes, shoes and metal components cascaded over him in a fiery downpour. A small piece of debris landed inches from his head with a heavy thud.

What happened? he thought as he clambered to his elbows, nauseous and dizzy, as if he were intoxicated. Jake stumbled to his feet, wincing as he aligned his back into a normal position. The sudden rush of blood to the head set off a blinding pain in his skull. His vision blurred, and his balance faltered.

As he collapsed to the floor, he felt something hard across his shoulders. Was it Tyler? Or was it worse – Moshat coming to finish the job off?

Jake looked up and relaxed as he saw it was Tyler helping him to his feet.

'Tyler,' Jake whispered.

'Come on,' Tyler said. 'Get up!'

Willed by a new sense of urgency, Jake rose and steadied himself as he scanned his surroundings, taking in all the carnage around him. What had once been a train, a forty-tonne machine, was nothing but a burning wreckage split in half.

'Where is he?' Jake asked Tyler, glancing into the woodland area to his left before returning his focus to his partner.

'Gone, Jake. Come on, we need to go back. We can't chase after him. He's got a gun, and we're unarmed.' Tyler pulled on Jake's shoulder, but Jake remained firm, despite his body's overwhelming desire to topple like a collapsing building.

Remaining silent, Jake turned to face the woods and stepped forward. Right foot. Left. Right. As soon as his body began to regain control over itself, Jake felt more confident. And with each heavy breath and blink of his eyes, he stepped further, longer, wider, hunting for the terrorist who had killed his mother-in-law, determined to capture the son of a bitch before he got away.

Jake ignored Tyler's cries for him to stop and head back and continued deeper into the undergrowth. He was going to stop at nothing.

For the next few minutes Jake searched the rows of trees and bushes for Moshat. Until—

The world went black and then all Jake could see was blood. Was it his? He didn't know. He touched his chest, his forearms, his body - praying it wasn't his own. Then Jake looked down at his feet. Tyler lay on the ground. A flower of red spread across his chest, staining his white shirt. Blood sputtered from his mouth as he took his final breaths.

Jake's mind couldn't process what he was seeing. He was frozen for a split second that felt like hours. Consumed by dread, Jake bent down to his side. As his hands touched Tyler's chest, the pounding heart beneath the rib cage stopped beating and Tyler's body went limp.

'No!' Jake screamed, clutching Tyler's shirt, heedless of his partner's blood on his hands.

In that instant, Jake awoke, chest heaving. His body was covered in a thin film of sweat, and it had formed a darkened patch on the bedsheets.

'It's all my fault,' he whispered, finding himself clutching the duvet.

The bedroom light switched on and he saw Elizabeth in the doorway. She rushed over to him with a glass of water in her hand. She ripped the duvet from his body and perched herself on the edge of the bed.

'Oh, Jake,' she said, placing the glass on the bedside table. 'Are you OK?'

Jake didn't respond. His heart raced too much.

Elizabeth leant in and embraced him. Her soft skin and delicate touch relaxed him a little.

'Just a bad dream. Nothing to worry about,' Jake replied. He looked over Elizabeth's shoulder at the time on his small digital alarm clock. It read 3:37 a.m. Later than any of the other nightmares had been.

Elizabeth pulled away and scowled at him. She placed the back of her hand on his forehead. 'Didn't sound like just a bad dream. You were thrashing again. And look at you – you're covered in sweat.'

Jake felt ashamed, sorry he had woken Elizabeth and placed an increased amount of stress on her and their unborn child. He hated what was happening to him. He hated how he had allowed his thoughts and stresses to plague his mind like this. They were like a cancer, spreading through his body, impacting him in every aspect. And there was no cure. He still hadn't called Mark, and he was beginning to regret stopping the antidepressants – at least they alleviated some of the violence he experienced in the attacks.

'What was it this time?' Elizabeth asked, distracting him from his thoughts.

'The usual. The explosion. Then chasing after him. Then Tyler . . .' Jake trailed off.

'You kept whispering something as well.' She passed him the glass of water. He took a sip and handed it back to her. She placed the cold glass against his cheek and forehead. Beads of condensation ran down the side of the glass onto his face.

'It was all my fault,' Jake whispered.

'What was?'

'Tyler. Your mum. I should have . . . I could have stopped them . . .'

Elizabeth sighed, looked at him, and then kissed him. A sudden rush of warmth spread throughout his entire body.

'How many times, Jake?' she asked, pulling herself away. 'How many times have I told you it is not your fault? And it never will be.'

'It is, Liz. It is. I couldn't protect them. It was all for nothing.'

Then, for the first time in a long time, Jake cried. The tears rolled down his cheeks, like the beads of condensation on the glass; they grew in density as their frequency increased. Elizabeth pulled him into her chest and cradled him like a baby. She ran her fingers through his hair until his breathing returned to a steady pace, and his body felt heavy against hers.

Jake was exhausted, and a few minutes after placing his head on the pillow, he was asleep. The darkness had enveloped him.

For the next twenty minutes, once Jake's snoring had started and she knew he was finally under, Elizabeth sat on the bed, her eyes unable to break away from his body. She continued to stroke his hair and run her knuckle gently over his cheek and neck.

What is going on inside your head, Jake? she wondered.

She was worried about her husband. Throughout this entire situation, he had been acting as if his condition weren't an issue. As if she didn't know what was really going on. *And it's affecting us both. I feel like I don't know you anymore, Jake, and it scares me to think about what might happen if things don't get better . . .*

She was six months pregnant. Her stomach had swollen in size, as had other aspects of her body. Her back ached. Sleeping was difficult. Moving was difficult. Controlling two other children was difficult. And the pressure was beginning to build. She could feel herself resenting Jake for his inability to let her in. She was his wife – they were supposed to be going through this together. In sickness and in health. But they weren't. He was trying to deal with it all himself.

She wouldn't give up on him. She loved him. And their love was worth fighting for. But she just hoped he would get better soon and that things would go back to normal. She had her own grief to conquer – there wasn't a day that went by where she didn't think about her mum – and where was his support for that? It had been non-existent.

Elizabeth was willing to make their marriage work, so long as he was.

Their lives had changed, and she knew nothing would be the same ever again.

8

Graves

December 1, 2017, 11:11

Apart from the innumerable corpses that lay six feet beneath the ground, the graveyard was empty. Just the way Jake liked it. During one of his earlier visits – the first month after Tyler's and Martha's deaths – there had been several elderly couples and widows wandering the grounds, disturbing his monologue to Tyler.

Now, however, it was just him and the dead. Him and Tyler. Him and his thoughts.

Bizarrely, Jake liked it there. It gave him a chance to clear his mind, express himself, and get everything off his chest.

Jake walked up to Tyler's tombstone. In his hand, he held a mug with the words 'You're a P____ sometimes' on it. When the contents of the mug filled with boiling water, an image of a cactus would appear, and the letters *R*, *I*, *C* and *K* would fill in the blanks. Tyler had found it one afternoon internet shopping while they were both supposed to be working and had loved it. Jake brought him a new one every time he visited. It acted as a constant reminder that Tyler had been a prick, but he wasn't all that bad. Jake didn't mind shelling out the couple of quid it cost to replace. It was the least he could do.

He set the mug down on the ground and crouched before Tyler's grave. He placed one hand on his knee and the other on the grass.

'All right, bud,' he began, plumes of water vapour expelling from his mouth. 'How you doing? You've not been missing much. Mam's still being Big Mama. I met a new shrink the other day, Dr Olson. She seemed all right. Except she gave me an old informant's number. Mark's. I can only assume what that was for. She also told me to stop taking the prescribed antidepressants, but the night terrors have been even worse . . . But anyway, enough about me – how have you been? How's life up there? What are the girls like?' Jake paused, waiting for a response he knew wouldn't come.

'This morning's night terror was bad. Woke up in a sweat and everything. Elizabeth was there for me as usual. But I wasn't. I kept thinking about everything. I shut her out. I don't talk to her about what's going on up here anymore, Ty.' Jake prodded his temple. 'And it's not fair on her. I know it isn't, but I'm too far gone to do anything about it.

'I know she loves me unconditionally. And I love her the same, but there's something inside me that's keeping it from her. It's keeping the darkest bits from the therapist as well. The only person I can tell is you, mate. How sad is that? I know what you'd say – you'd tell me to stop being a little bitch and own up to it. "Girls love a sensitive guy." I can hear you say it now.' The thought made Jake smile.

'I don't know what to do, though, Ty. Moshat is still out there and it's been months since he disappeared. He could be anywhere by now. I tried to chase a lead on my own, but it didn't work. Mamadou found out and now I'm suspended – unofficially – while he sorts it for me. I spend yesterday with Liz and the kids. Suppose it's a good thing, really. Get the attack out of my head somehow and occupy it with something different for a short while.

'We're going to The Shard with Alex and his family tomorrow, you know. We've been keeping in touch with them ever since the attack. But don't worry, he won't replace you. He could never replace you. And we thought it would be nice to go on a family play date.'

Alex Tough had let Jake use his mobile phone on the Golden Jubilee Bridge during the 01/08 attack. Jake had lost his and needed to get in contact with Tyler. Since then, Jake had stayed in touch with Alex and his wife, Karen, who also had two children, Ellen and Ethan. He and Elizabeth had even met the couple for a few evening meals without the kids whenever Jake could come home at a reasonable time.

'It should be a nice day out. At least, I hope it's not shitty weather, otherwise we won't be able to see anything. I don't want it to be a waste of time, and money – it cost a fortune! You know how tight I am. Although I was surprised to find out you didn't put me in your will . . . I'll be having words with your mum and dad to see what I can swindle,' Jake continued. He rose to his feet, looked around the grounds and then down to Tyler's grave. 'Anyway, enough about that.

I'll keep you posted. See you next month, mate. I miss you.'

Those last three words were the hardest for Jake to say, and as he said them he felt a lump swell in his throat. He had never missed anything as much as he missed Tyler's banter, his camaraderie, his personality, his presence. It was a lot for Jake to take in.

That was when an idea floated into his head. What if he could find something that would take his mind away from everything and transport him to another land? What if he could find something that would release all his inhibitions and anxieties in one go? What if it helped reduce his anxiety and stress and the effect of the daily memories haunted by Moshat? And what if he could find that source of something in the next hour before he got home to Elizabeth?

Jake pulled his work phone from his pocket. It was a classic Nokia 3310; every staff member of the Metropolitan Police Service had been given one for emergency use. They contained different processors and SIM cards that encrypted messages and calls. It had cost the service millions of pounds, but it had been money well spent.

And Jake was beginning to see why.

He opened the address book, scrolled down to the name he was looking for, and dialled. The receiver answered on the fifth ring. *One more than usual,* Jake thought, taking a mental note of the information.

'Hello?' the person asked, their tone unassuming and, to Jake, different.

'Mark, it's DC Tanner. Can we meet? Usual place?'

9

The Beaten Bush

December 1, 2017, 12:07

Mark Hayford was already waiting when Jake entered the Beaten Bush, a small pub on the corner of Portsmouth Road in Kingston. He lounged in a chair, with one arm resting on the edge of the seat and another on the table, spinning a half full glass of Guinness in his hand.

The air inside the pub was filled with the smell of grease and alcohol. A bartender, a woman over sixty, pulled a pint for a man in a bomber jacket slumped against the bar watching a foreign football match. On the screen beside it, Sky News played. He slurred his words as he attempted to make conversation with the owner. Jake and the bartender exchanged glances and gave each other a curt nod. During his time in the Criminal Investigation Department, the Beaten

Bush had been a regular haunt of his. He would often schedule covert meetings with drug dealers and other informants there. No matter the situation, the owner of the bar always turned a blind eye.

Jake took a seat without saying anything. He looked at the man opposite him. In the time since they had last seen one another, Mark appeared to have lost a considerable amount of weight, and the lines on his face had deepened.

'Jake,' Mark said, nodding.

'Mark.'

'Drink?'

'No. I can't stay long.' Jake shifted in his chair uneasily. 'Do you have it?'

Mark gasped, holding his hand to his mouth. 'It's been this long and all you want to talk about is business? I'm offended.'

Jake sighed through his nose, trying to stifle his frustrations.

'Come on, Mark,' Jake said, keeping his voice low. 'You know I can't be seen with you. At least not for too long.'

'You've still upset me. I thought we could have a little catch-up. How have you been?'

Jake looked around the bar, made sure no one else was paying attention to them, sighed, and returned his attention to Mark. It was pointless trying to argue with him. Jake had tried it many times in the past and knew Mark had the upper hand, had the information and resources that Jake needed, and if he was going to stand any chance of getting his hands on it, he would have to play ball.

'Shit,' Jake replied. 'You?'

'Shit.'

'Not much has changed there, then.'

'I saw you on the news.'

'As did half the country, I imagine.'

'Looked fucked up. I'm surprised you didn't die.'

Jake didn't respond. He couldn't tell whether Mark was inflicting his usual banter, or if he was just being obnoxious.

'What have you been doing since we last worked together? Still dealing? Still stabbing people in the back?' Jake asked.

Mark dipped his chin an inch. 'When I've not got you lot breathing down my neck.'

'Just doing our jobs.' Jake shrugged.

'So am I.'

Jake felt the left side of his mouth flicker into a smile. 'I noticed you didn't answer my call on the fourth ring. You becoming more cautious?'

'Christ, you pay attention, don't you?' Mark said. 'If you must know, no. I answer the phone when I answer. That was the old me.'

'And who's this in front of me – the new you?'

'In broad fucking daylight.'

'Interesting,' Jake said. He checked his watch. He would have to be home soon. He had told Elizabeth he would only be at the graveyard for a few hours. 'Do you have what I asked for?'

'Have I ever let you down?'

'You really want me to answer that?'

Mark fished in his pocket, produced something that looked like a ring box, and placed it on the table. He slid it across the surface to Jake.

'Everything you need is in there,' he said. As Jake

stretched his hand out to grab the box, Mark's hand fell on top. 'Now, you don't need me to tell you some dos and don'ts, do you? Or tell you how to roll it up? This is some of my strongest stuff. If you take too much, it'll knock you out for hours. Especially on your first time.'

Jake gave him a stern look. In the background, the pub door opened and a dog and its owner wandered in. 'No. I've been around long enough to know what I'm doing. You told me everything I need to know back when we first met, anyway. From what I remember you seemed to get a kick out of telling people how good you were at rolling.' Jake made inverted commas in the air with his fingers.

Mark reclined in his chair. 'Ah, yes. The good old days. So, what's a man like you doing with some herb? Time's getting tough? Or you and the missus looking for some excitement?'

Jake tucked the box into his blazer pocket, a hint of marijuana climbing up his nostrils. It would be a task in itself keeping it from Elizabeth and the kids.

'That's not important to you right now. What is important is that this stays between us, yes?' Jake said, leaning closer to Mark. It was more a statement than a question.

Mark nodded.

'Good.' Jake stepped out of his chair, thanked Mark, shook his hand and left the pub. Mark stayed where he was. Jake strode purposefully to his car. He didn't want to be home too late.

Jake entered the car, strapped himself in, and stared out of the window, his hands firmly planted on the steering wheel. The smell of marijuana lingered in his senses. What was he doing? What was he thinking? Was he seriously going to take drugs to help combat his stress? Elizabeth would kill him if she found out. No, he was being stupid. Ridiculous. Idiotic.

'I'll get rid of it at home,' he said aloud as he started the engine, half believing what he was saying.

The only other problem was where he was going to keep it until he could dispose of it properly. Ellie and Maisie were always searching for things they'd either misplaced or lost. And Elizabeth spent most of her time at home – she would know if he had put something new where it wasn't supposed to be. And not to mention the smell. That would give him away almost instantly.

Jake put the gearstick into first and pulled away. When he arrived outside his house, he switched off the engine, opened the glove compartment, and placed the small box of drugs inside. No one would look in there; no one had for the past year or so.

As Jake entered his home, Elizabeth was waiting for him in the hallway.

'What time do you call this?' she asked.

Jake checked his watch. 'What's wrong?'

'Nothing. I missed you, that's all. I've got used to having you home these past couple days.' Elizabeth walked up and kissed him on the cheek.

After dinner, Jake undressed and sat on the sofa cuddled against Elizabeth.

'Looking forward to tomorrow?' he asked.

'Yeah. I just have to mentally prepare myself. It's been a while since the four of us have been out. I almost forgot what that was like.'

'You and me both,' Jake said, looking out the living room window to where the small box of marijuana sat twenty yards away.

10

Undisturbed

December 2, 2017, 02:49

Jake couldn't sleep. He had spent the whole night lying there, eyes wide open, staring at the ceiling, thinking about the small box in his glove compartment. Should he try it? Shouldn't he? He didn't know. He hadn't taken the antidepressants. And he was too afraid to sleep, lest another night terror wake him. But if he tried the weed, then he would let everyone down. Elizabeth. The kids. Tyler. Martha.

Himself.

But he was an adult. He could control himself. One joint wouldn't hurt, would it? Jake rolled over to look at the clock next to his head. 2:49 a.m. There was still another four hours until he needed to be awake, and at this rate he wouldn't be sleeping at all.

Heaving himself out of bed quietly, Jake put on a pair of slippers and a coat and started towards the car. It was cold outside, and his nipples stood on end in protest. Jake opened the car door delicately, so as not to disturb the still, silent air around him. He reached inside, took out the box of weed and placed it in his jacket pocket. Then he headed back through the house to the garden, grabbing matches on the way.

Standing outside in the cold, Jake rolled half the cannabis into a joint and ignited the end. The flame flickered and danced in the late autumnal night, illuminating his face a deep orange. Whispers of smoke climbed into the sky, and as Jake took his first drag, embers of red and grey crept closer to his lips. As Jake inhaled, ash dropped to the floor, and the smoke descended his throat, clinging to his lungs. He coughed. Hard. Covering his mouth with his hand, he stifled the sound, but it was still audible. He hoped he hadn't woken the girls.

After he'd finished coughing out the smoke from his lungs, Jake took another drag. This time it passed through easier. He still coughed, but it was muted, like a dog whimpering behind a closed door. For the next few minutes he stood still, inhaling deeply, allowing the end of the joint to reach his fingers before he eventually stubbed it out on the patio floor and threw the remains into his neighbour's garden.

When he returned to bed, he felt no different, save for the tingling sensation swarming his body. He didn't know what he had been expecting, but it wasn't this. The house remained undisturbed, and Elizabeth was in the same position he had left her in. As soon as his head hit the pillow, he was asleep.

11

Different

December 2, 2017, 09:02

The following morning Jake woke peacefully. He wasn't covered in a layer of sweat. He wasn't out of breath. Instead, he was calm, relaxed, rested. His body still tingled. He rolled onto his other side and faced Elizabeth. She was sat upright reading a book, a cup of coffee steaming beside her.

'You're up early,' he said, rubbing the sleep from his eyes.

'You're up late.' Elizabeth closed the book and drank. 'Sleep all right?'

Jake yawned. 'Better than ever.'

'What caused that, then?' She stared at him meaningfully.

'Don't know,' he lied. He licked his lips and swallowed. His mouth was dry, and he needed water. He lifted himself to his elbows and kissed her cheek before attempting to move off the bed. She frowned and quickly pulled away. It was only then that it dawned on him what he had done. Betrayed her. Gone behind her back and broken the promise they had made to each other when they were younger: that neither of them would do anything stupid if things got too bad – and if they did, then they would each tell the other.

They had been too distant since the Hakim brothers' attack for him to tell her much of anything. Did she know about the cannabis? How could she? He had covered it well; he had been silent in the garden and made sure the weed was hidden in his jacket pocket downstairs.

Then he realised.

The coughing. Was that what had given him away? No. It couldn't have been. There must be something else going on.

Jake yawned again and stretched. Inhaling deeply, feeling his body and muscles relax, he noticed the remaining stench of cannabis on him. The smell! He stank. Shit. He was going to have to play it off as if there were no issue.

'You excited for today?' he asked, rolling to the other side of the bed. He placed his feet on the floor and twisted to face her.

Elizabeth nodded without looking at him. 'I think it'll be nice to get out for a change.'

'Is that it? I thought you'd be bouncing off the walls. You nagged me every month for a year when it first opened.' He laughed, ran his fingers through his hair and rubbed his eyes.

'Still would have made a nice anniversary present.' Elizabeth sipped from her coffee again. 'You going to be on your best behaviour today?'

'What's that supposed to mean?' He grabbed his phone and scrolled through his emails.

'Karen. She was all over you last time. And you didn't seem to mind.'

'Come on,' Jake said, turning to face her again. 'You know they've been having a few issues.'

Before Elizabeth could respond, their bedroom door burst open. Ellie charged in. She was in her pyjamas and her face beamed with excitement.

'Morning!' she said, jumping onto the bed.

'Someone's in a good mood,' Jake said.

'We're going to The Shard today!'

'Thanks for reminding me, I almost forgot.' Jake winked at her. 'You looking forward to it?'

Ellie nodded. 'It's going to be the best day ever.'

'Try not to get your hopes up too high, Ellie. You've never been that high. You might not like it.'

Ellie sulked and left the room.

Once Jake was certain she was out of earshot, he turned to face Elizabeth and said, 'What was that about?'

Silence. Elizabeth threw the bedsheets from her and walked to the bathroom. The sound of the shower starting filled the background. Jake lowered himself onto the bed and rested his head on the pillow, his thoughts wandering. Was he still high? He didn't know. Ignorance manifested itself in inexperience.

After Elizabeth finished in the shower, it was Jake's turn, and by the time he was done, the last remnants of the tingling sensation in his feet and hands had subsided. The effects of the drug had worn off. Except for one.

Jake dried himself with the towel, wiped the condensation and steam from the mirror and stared at himself. Looking back at him was a man with red, bloodshot eyes.

'Oh shit,' he whispered. It was impossible for Elizabeth not to have noticed. How was he going to get himself out of this one?

Deny, deny, deny, he told himself. A motto he'd never thought he'd have to use. He started digging through the cupboards for some eye drops.

'Jake!' Elizabeth called to him from outside the bathroom.

Stunned, Jake flailed for his bathrobe, wrapped it round his waist, and opened the door. Elizabeth stood on the other side.

'Yes?' he asked, stepping out of the room.

'Hurry. I need to do my make-up. We need to leave soon.'

'You don't need it – how many times have I told you?'

'Enough for me to stop paying attention to it.'

'Why's that?'

'Because I know when you're lying.'

Jake stopped. Face-to-face with Elizabeth. Her breathing brushed his upper lip. 'Never. I wouldn't say it if it wasn't true.'

'If you say so.' Elizabeth barged past him and entered the bathroom.

Jake grabbed her arm gently and pulled her back. 'Hey,' he said, 'are you OK? You seem different this morning.'

'I'm fine. I'm glad you got a good night's sleep.'

Jake smiled awkwardly. 'My snoring keep you up?'

'Yeah. That's what it was. Now come on, let me go. I need to put my face on. Need to cover the bags under my eyes. And you need to get dressed. Karen and Alex are expecting us in thirty minutes.'

'They won't mind if we're a little late, I'm sure. I'll just tell them I had some errands to run.'

By the time ten rolled around, the Tanner clan were ready for their exciting day ahead. As they left the house in a rush, Jake wrapped his jacket around his body, forgetting the weed was in there, and gave one last look at himself in the hallway mirror. He felt ashamed at the sight he saw. Jake closed the door behind him, got into his X5 and started the engine. They were meeting Alex, Karen, Ethan and Ellen at the train station. From there it was a thirty-minute train trip to London Bridge, and Jake had a feeling it would be the longest journey of his life.

12

Safe

December 2, 2017, 10:14

Charlie Paxman breathed heavily. A thin layer of sweat covered his back, and his palms felt greasy. He was forty-five minutes early for his shift, and he stood at the security gates in the lobby of The Shard. He had already scanned his employee pass at the turnstiles, and now a guard on the other side of the metal detectors waved him through.

Charlie removed his heavy gym bag from his shoulder and placed it on the conveyor belt. He swallowed hard as he watched it disappear into the X-ray machine. This would be the most difficult part of his entire plan. If the scanner detected anything in there – if the copper sheets and crumpled aluminium foil he had placed around the weapons and explosives to confuse the machine didn't work – his mission would be over before it had even begun. The sweat across his back intensified.

Charlie heard a voice. It was calling him.

'Sir!' the guard said. He was new, unfamiliar - someone filling in from a different department, someone Charlie hadn't spent months building a rapport with. The man gesticulated with his hands for Charlie to advance towards him.

Charlie stepped forward, his moist armpits already forming dark crescent moons. He let out a little sigh of relief as the metal detector remained silent. He waited at the other end of the conveyor belt, his eyes transfixed on the small hole his bag would appear from. He checked his watch. It was 10:15 a.m. He didn't start until 11 a.m., and neither did the World Health Organisation conference.

Charlie's bag appeared from the X-ray machine and rolled closer to him. Just as he was about to grab it, the bag stopped. He looked up. The security guard, a small, unassuming man, placed his hand firmly on the bag.

'Is this yours, sir?' the man asked.

Of course it is. There's no one else here. Charlie nodded.

'Do you mind if we take a look inside?'

Charlie shook his head. He swallowed hard and clenched his fists. This was it. This was when everything was going to go wrong. This was when he was going to be caught and sent to prison, where he would spend the rest of his life wishing he had done everything differently. Wishing he had released his virus sooner. Wishing he had come face-to-face with old enemies earlier.

The security guard pulled the zip. The bag was open halfway when a scream sounded from the entrance to the building. Both Charlie and the man darted their gaze towards the source of the noise.

A woman had collapsed on the floor. She fell on the hard, shiny marble, gripping her chest, and another woman kneeled beside her, attempting to help her.

'Help! Please!' the kneeling woman cried hysterically. 'She just collapsed. I think she's having a heart attack.'

The security guard next to Charlie rounded the metal detector and rushed over to the dying woman. Charlie didn't need to be told twice this was his only opportunity to pass through security with no one second-glancing him. He had been given a lifeline, and he was going to use it.

Charlie zipped the bag up to the top so it was perfectly sealed, slung it over his shoulder and disappeared around the corner of a giant pillar. He stopped by the lift, pressed the up button and waited. Screams and shouts filled the reception area behind him. His breathing and pulse raced. He tapped his feet on the ground, anxiously waiting for the lift to arrive.

He took a step back and dared a look at the scene. It was at that moment a crowd of people in smart business attire entered the foyer. Charlie froze.

It had been a long time since he had last seen the esteemed members of the World Health Organisation. They hadn't changed. None of them had. They hadn't aged the way he had. Of course they hadn't – it had nearly been a year. And what had they achieved in that time? Nothing. Whereas he, the man expelled from one of the greatest organisations in the world, had decided he was going to change it.

And today would be that day.

Ten seconds later, after what felt like an eternity, the lift sounded. The metal doors parted, and Charlie stepped inside, pressed the button for the thirty-second of sixty-eight available floors in The Shard and waited. As soon as the doors had closed, he relaxed. He rested his entire weight on the railing on the side of the elevator and ran his fingers through his greasy hair.

He was safe.

The weapon in his bag was safe.

The explosives were safe.

And, most importantly, the virus was safe.

13

Chills

December 2, 2017, 10:18

The Oblix is the second-highest restaurant in The Shard. Split into two sides - a casual lounge area in the east, and a formal sit-down area in the west - it offers diners perfect views of the city of London. And over the past few months, it had been like a second home to Charlie. Not because he adored spending his time there, but because his job as a waiter was demanding and required he spend most of his waking moments there.

At first, the views had been spectacular. The way the sun bounced off the surface of the River Thames, and the deep orange, purple, red and blue hues cast across the sky as it descended at the end of the day. When he first started his job there, Charlie had loved it. But then, as the days wore on and the work demanded more from him, and his aspirations for success grew, he resented the views and everything else that came with them. Now, however, as he was going to be reunited with the World Health Organisation once more, he felt himself paying closer attention to the microcosm of life several hundred feet beneath him. The red double-deckers. The taxicabs. The pedestrians wandering the streets. The cyclists. The police cars. They were all contributing to the death of society and to the death of the world. And none of them cared. It was going to take something destructive to make them wake up and realise what effect they were having on the planet.

The human race was in an incredible amount of danger, and the World Health Organisation insisted on solving the problem with words. *All bark and no bite,* Charlie thought to himself. *Well, I'll show them some bite. And we'll see how much they bleed.*

Charlie entered the staff room on the south side of the thirty-second floor. It was empty, before the mad rush of the afternoon, which was good, because it meant he could store his bag in his locker in peace. Inside his gym bag was a smaller rucksack. There he had hidden the explosives and other necessary equipment. He pulled it carefully out of the larger bag, placed the rucksack over his shoulder, shut the metal door and left the room, leaving the gun and virus protected in his locker.

'Where are you going?' a voice called from behind him as he walked down a corridor. 'I've been meaning to talk to you.'

Charlie turned. It was a colleague, dressed in their black-and-white uniform. An apron hung over his crotch.

'Fuck off, Jim,' Charlie said. 'I don't start for another forty minutes.'

'What's your issue?'

Charlie sighed before replying. 'Nothing. You're an amazing person. I'm sorry I shouted at you – can I go now?'

Jim opened his mouth to speak, but Charlie was already gone.

Charlie arrived at the nearest set of lifts in the centre of the building and pressed the button to take him upstairs. As the doors closed, he felt more relaxed than he had done five minutes before. He was past security. He was in the safe zone. And no one had any reason to suspect him of anything.

Charlie pressed the button labelled 68. The highest indoor floor. He had been invited up there on his first day, as part of the company's welcome induction. He had hated it. Heights were never his thing, but over the last few weeks, as his preparations for today intensified, he had grown accustomed to the height, and his body had become numb to the nauseating sensation that crept up on him every time he was up there.

The lift doors opened, and Charlie stepped out. The sixty-eighth floor was densely populated with bodies. Families, tourists, students, elderly couples – they had all paid to come and see the view. A family of five ambled in front of him, breaking his stride as he rounded the corner. Charlie skirted them, cursed their insolence, and headed to the bathrooms. There were eight toilet stalls in a row along the north side of the building.

Charlie rushed to the cubicle on the furthest left and unzipped his bag. Light flooded the small room. He ignored the floor-to-ceiling windows that offered brilliant views of the

River Thames. On the wall opposite the toilet was a row of long, thin tiles, running from left to right at eye level. He removed a screwdriver from his bag, pried one of the tiles from the wall, and revealed a small hole approximately three inches wide, two inches tall and six inches deep – the result of two weeks' meticulous chipping away at the rubble behind the tile during his lunch breaks, like he was Andy Dufresne.

As he removed the small pipe bomb from his bag, he heard someone coughing outside the cubicle. He stopped. Held his breath. Once it was safe, he inserted the small package into the hole. It was a snug fit, crafted to perfection. He activated the countdown timer and watched the numbers spin round.

03:39:54.

2 p.m. detonation.

A knock on the door disturbed him. Charlie froze, holding his breath. 'Occupied,' he said. His eyes scanned the bottom and top of the door, afraid someone would try to peek through the millimetre-wide gap.

'Come on, man. You got to hurry. My son's about to be sick.'

Good. 'I'm busy, mate.'

The man knocked on the door repeatedly. 'What are you doing in there?'

Charlie's patience was running out. He hefted the heavy tile off the ground, keeping the sound of his exertion to a minimum, held it in place against the wall, removed a battery-powered glue gun from his bag, and squeezed.

'What do you think I'm doing?' he asked, struggling to focus his entire attention on the glue. He ran the gun along the edges of the ceramic tile as best he could, keeping it firmly back in its silhouette. 'There are more cubicles, you know.'

'They're busy.'

'You'll just have to fucking wait. Sorry.' Charlie finished applying the glue to the tile; thick globs of mixture ran down the dark ceramic. It wasn't perfect, and he wasn't happy leaving it that way, but it would have to do if he was going to get rid of this incessant bastard outside.

As Charlie returned the gun to his bag, he heard the door handle move up and down. Panicking, Charlie flushed the toilet, zipped his bag together, and opened the door. The man fell through, stumbling atop Charlie.

'Watch what you're doing' Charlie said, shoving the man against the sink.

He left the bathroom without washing his hands. By the time the father and son entered the cubicle and locked the door, Charlie was already inside the lift on his way back downstairs to his locker.

Adrenaline surged through his body, raising sudden doubts in his mind. Had he glued the tile in position properly? Had he blown the entire thing before it had even begun?

He inhaled deeply, trying to relax. Things were falling into place, and soon he would be able to take control again – by force.

Soon, he told himself. *Soon.*

14

Mirror Reflection

December 2, 2017, 10:36

Large groups of people occupied the East Croydon platform, and as they stepped onto the train, Jake felt an overwhelming sense of claustrophobia leap onto him, like a voracious tiger pouncing on its prey. He felt light-headed, and visions of darkness consuming him in the underground tunnels returned.

He needed to sit down.

He looked around him, up and down the length of the carriage. There was nowhere to sit. He could feel himself getting hot. Since Operation Tightrope, Jake hadn't set foot on a train. The memories of the attack were too raw.

'Jake? Are you OK? You've gone pale,' Alex asked next to him. He touched Jake's arm.

Breathing deeply, Jake replied, 'I'm fine. Just a mild panic attack. Nothing to worry about.'

Pretending his PTSD wasn't a problem was one of the defence mechanisms he had formed over recent months. *I'm bigger than this,* he thought to himself. *I won't let it beat me.*

The journey from East Croydon to London Bridge was over in just under thirty minutes. But for Jake, it felt like a never-ending series of twists and turns, light turning into dark, dark into light. As soon as the train came to a stop, Jake and the rest of the group stepped through the doors. He held Ellie in his arms, hoping she would provide a distraction from his disturbing thoughts. They climbed the stairs at London Bridge station.

'Daddy, look!' Ellie said as they breached into the open air. The harsh adjustment to the light, combined with the pounding sensation in his head, blinded Jake. Ellie pointed into the sky.

'It's high, isn't it, darling?' Jake said, feigning excitement.

He placed Ellie on the ground and held her hand as they wandered up the escalators, through The View From The Shard shop, and up to the security gates. Jake emptied his pockets of his wallet, keys, police ID, spare change, watch and two mobile phones onto a tray for the guard to inspect.

'What have you got that for?' Elizabeth asked, tapping him on the shoulder.

Instantly, Jake knew what she was talking about. His work mobile. The one he had told Elizabeth he would leave at home.

'Sorry,' he said. 'It's just a force of habit. Muscle memory. I put it in my pocket every day for work, and I guess I forgot.'

He wasn't lying. He'd forgotten he had promised

Elizabeth the other night he would leave anything work-related at home for the day. The only problem would be convincing her he was telling the truth.

'You promised.'

'I know, and I'm so sorry, Liz. Look, I'll turn it off and put it in my back pocket. If I use it, then I'll sleep on the sofa tonight.'

Elizabeth scowled at him and brushed past his shoulder as she wandered through security. *I've got some making up to do,* Jake thought.

The two families headed towards the seventy-second floor, which was a glassed-in, no-ceiling space at the top of the viewing gallery. Gentle music played in the background, and there was a bar on the south side. Waiters and staff and photographers patrolled the small perimeter, offering advice and answering questions at every turn.

'You going to be all right?' Elizabeth asked, holding Jake's sweaty hand as they climbed the final step.

'Me? I'm a trooper. You know that. A little height won't faze me,' he said, winking at her.

Elizabeth smiled at long last. 'You're such an idiot.'

Just as Jake was about to lean in for a kiss, he felt a tug on his leg.

'Dad, I don't like it,' Maisie said. Her skin went pale, and she hugged Jake's waist.

Stroking her hair, he said, 'It's OK. Daddy doesn't like heights, either. How about we have a look together? I'll make sure you're safe.'

Maisie hesitated, looked up into his eyes, and nodded. Jake grabbed her hand, smiling at her, and then together the two of them started towards the glass barrier that made up the perimeter of the gallery. There was no escape from the view. They were eight hundred feet up in the air and could see the whole of the city. It was a view of overwhelming and terrifying beauty. Jake inched towards the edge, keeping his feet as rooted to the floor as possible, feeling as though a heavy step out of place would send the building into a wobble. Maisie squeezed his hand.

'Don't worry,' he said to Maisie, 'everything will be fine. These buildings are very safe.'

Saying nothing more so as not to disturb the internal foundations of the building with his deep voice, Jake stopped a foot away from the glass. There, with his body frozen to the spot, he could hear everything: his galloping heart, the sirens blaring seventy storeys below, the cheers of excitement coming from other children in the venue, and the scripted discussions from The View's employees.

'. . . there are ninety-five floors in total, of which seventy-two are habitable. The remaining floors are structure and glass. There are forty-four elevators in the building. Some of them are double-deckers, and they can travel up to sixteen miles per hour – or six metres a second.'

No wonder I feel sick, Jake thought, intrigued by the useless information the employee continued to reel off: 'The building is comprised of three segments. Office. Leisure. Apartments. The first twenty-eight floors are occupied by company offices from across the globe. Up to the fifty-second are the restaurants and hotel. The final segment of The Shard features its apartments, reserved for the most influential patrons. The penthouse is situated a few floors beneath our feet, although it has remained empty for some time.'

He had seen on the news just how much the ten

apartments in The Shard cost: fifty million each. Fifty million British pounds. An amount Jake would never earn in his lifetime. For a moment, Jake couldn't help but wonder what it would be like to live in someone's wealthy shoes for the day. Even for an hour. How different it would be. How hollow he would feel inside to have all the material possessions in the world and to run out of new things to experience. How he would become bored of having everything he wanted, without ever having worked for it.

'Hey.' Elizabeth wandered over to him and tapped him on the shoulder. 'What are you doing?'

'Learning for free.' Jake nodded in the direction of The Shard employee, who was now moving over to the west side of the building.

Elizabeth rolled her eyes and told him to follow her towards Karen and the rest of the Tough family. Karen and Alex were standing together, staring out of the window, a child in each of their arms. Jake thought they looked like the perfect family. And then he looked back at his own and realised how wrong he was.

'How is everyone?' Jake asked as he cast his eyes towards the London Eye. The sight disturbed him. The structure held painful memories. Less than four hundred yards from the wheel was the apartment building where Adil Hakim had masterminded his plan. And where he had met his untimely demise.

'Enjoying ourselves, I'd say,' Karen replied. Her brown hair danced in the air as she flicked her head to face him. 'Beautiful. We were lucky with the weather.'

Jake felt nauseous. His intense vertigo made the room spin, and he needed a drink. He needed to sit down, allow the blood to flow away from his brain. He needed to get out of there. He placed his hands in his pockets, and his fingers fumbled over the box Mark had given him the day before. Shit! He had completely forgotten it was in there.

'Hey,' he whispered to Elizabeth.

'What's wrong?'

'I'm just going to the toilet.'

Jake let go of Maisie, smiled, and turned to the centre of the floor, heading down the four flights of stairs towards the toilets on floor sixty-eight. He wandered straight into a cubicle on the furthest left. Shut the door. Gasped at the few layers of glass in the floor-to-ceiling windows that kept him from plummeting to his death, undid his belt buckle and then urinated, releasing the pressure on his bladder. He held onto the sink beside him for support as he could feel his legs shaking.

Before flushing the toilet, he stared into the murky yellow water and dug his hands into his pockets. The fingers of his right hand closed around the box. Did he want to get rid of it? The weed had helped his sleep last night. And he didn't want to throw it out if it was going to work. But Elizabeth. The girls. Alex. He didn't want them to find out. What would they think of him? What would he use as an excuse?

He glanced at himself in the mirror and scarcely recognised the man who stared back at him. The two-day unkempt stubble. The dark shadows hanging under his red, bloodshot and tired eyes. He thought he looked skinnier, as if the stresses of the past couple of months had had an adverse effect on his body, despite the effort he had been putting in at the gym.

He was suffering, and he couldn't ignore it for much

longer. In the end, he made his decision.

Grabbing the toilet roll from the handle built into the wall, Jake wrapped the box in toilet paper and returned it to his pocket. He hoped it would mask the smell.

Conscious of the time, Jake flushed. As he bent over, watching the yellowy liquid disappear, something in the mirror caught his eye. Something glistening in the light. What was that? He leant closer to the wall, inspecting the milky liquid that descended a singular tile. Almost instantly, he grimaced. He didn't like to think of what some people got up to in the bathroom in the privacy of their own home, let alone in a public stall. He convinced himself he was being paranoid. It was probably soap. Or hand sanitiser. Or dirty water. Nothing to worry about.

But he couldn't deny the fact there was a certain chemical smell in the air that just seemed off. And he was certain it wasn't the smell of the weed in his pocket. It reminded him of Elizabeth's craft projects with the girls, though he couldn't say why. Shaking away the paranoia, he determined it was down to cleaning supplies.

Jake washed his hands in the sink. He splashed water over his face. The cold was refreshing. Water dribbled down his forearm, and he wiped it clean with a paper towel. As he left, another man was stood waiting to use the toilet after him. Jake gave him an awkward nod and exited.

A few seconds later, Jake returned to Elizabeth and the rest of the group, with his hands firmly in his pockets, protecting the box from exposure. Lingering at the back of his mind were the overlapping smells of cleaning chemicals and craft glue.

15

Hero

December 2, 2017, 11:28

The 2017 World Health Organisation's annual meeting was finally getting underway. Benjamin had been informed there had been an initial hiccup with someone at the reception desk. Apparently, a woman had had a minor heart attack just as he and the rest of the committee were entering the building. But it hadn't delayed them too much, and the rest of the attendees were only a few minutes late. Since then, bodies filtered into the Ren, the largest private room in The Shard's resident five-star hotel, the Shangri-La.

The room was large, capable of accommodating almost 150 people. Not that the WHO needed that much space today. A magnificent blue cloth draped the table that ran the length of the meeting room. At the head of the venue was a small stage that reminded Benjamin of something he had performed on in primary school, and overhead hung a series of gold crystals, sparkling in the light.

The venue was hardly up to his usual standard, despite the breathtaking views of the River Thames and the city of London. If he were director general of the World Health Organisation - which he would one day become - he would have chosen somewhere of a higher calibre. Somewhere with a more sublime view. Perhaps a castle buried deep in the mountains. Or a palace beside a lake. Not a tall building overlooking a grey and dreary city. He had seen it all before.

The WHO's reputation had diminished since Marianne had taken charge. Everyone could see it. But nobody was brave enough to say, or do, anything about it. It would be Benjamin's job to change that. With the right team behind him, and with the correct amount of brown-nosing, he would be where he wanted within a year.

Marianne Evans, director general of the World Health Organisation, stood tall by the podium on the platform at the head of the room, one hand outstretched, the other holding an award. She had just called his name for some prize he'd been nominated for. Applause soon echoed around the Ren.

'Many congratulations, Dr Weiss,' the DG said when he made it up to the podium.

Benjamin took her hand, squeezed hard, felt the tendons in her hand wriggle and move under her saggy skin, and gave her a kiss on both cheeks.

'Thank you, Marianne,' he said, taking the small trophy from his boss. It was a large *O*, with the letters *W* and *H* inscribed inside and the distinctive WHO globe logo and caduceus below them. This was the third such trophy

Benjamin had won. And the third he would discard. They meant nothing to him. They were pieces of metal - and sometimes plastic - that held no place in his heart. They bore no significance, and they would only collect dust on whichever shelf he left them - most likely the shelf in his shed.

'Wow,' he began, as he moved to the microphone, 'what can I say? I'm honoured to have received another award for Outstanding Contribution to the Field of Human Genetics. For years now, the world has been obsessed with technology that simplifies our lives. Robots. Drones. Self-service technology at supermarkets. The things you see every day on the news.

'But these are superficial. What if we could use technology in a better, more humanitarian way? What if we could use technology to replicate and genetically engineer DNA so it is possible to live longer and eradicate disease? Cancer. AIDS. Malaria. The common flu would become extinct. Countries would save billions on vaccinations and be able to invest those funds in agriculture, security, climate - a plethora of sectors.

'That's what my team and I have been working on in recent months. It's been a tumultuous time, what with the absence of a dear colleague of mine earlier in the year, Charlie Paxman, who sadly had to leave the team due to personal . . . difficulties. But we have still made a considerable amount of progress, and I am pleased to say that two days ago we made a breakthrough. On the thirtieth of November, my team and I uncovered a method to alter genes HERC2 and OCA2, thus allowing us to change a person's hair colour from the nucleotide polymorphic level outward.

'Now, that may not seem like much. But it really is a huge leap in the right direction. And soon - we're estimating by the end of 2019 - we will be able to completely recode someone's genetic makeup to make them immune to disease. We can save billions of lives. We can even create superhumans. Imagine: We can adjust a man's muscle growth, his bone density, his ability to cling to the outside of buildings by the tip of his fingers. We can create our very own modern-day Spider-Man. Exciting times lie ahead, ladies and gentlemen, and the world had better be ready for it all when it comes. Thank you.'

Another burst of applause erupted around the venue. Benjamin tilted his head forward humbly, raised the award showcasing his immutable excellence in the air and strolled back to his chair. The speech had gone better than planned. He had ad-libbed the entire thing, and it had worked. Those around him slapped him on the shoulder, further congratulating him, further fuelling the fierce ego that burned inside him. It was hungry, and it was being fed. But it wouldn't stop there. There were still those remaining few above him whom he would chew up and spit back out again.

Just like he had done to Charlie Paxman. And no one had a clue.

The thought made him smile.

At the podium, the director general returned with a card in her hand.

'Marvellous,' Marianne began. 'What a truly marvellous intellect Benjamin has. He is a testament to everything we do at the World Health Organisation. I wish him many more successes during his career.'

I'll be taking them from you.

Marianne glanced down at Benjamin and smiled. There was something else there as well. A wink? No, surely not! She was a married woman in her sixties. Nevertheless, Benjamin eyed her up and down, unafraid of who might see. He would sleep with her if it meant he could get what he wanted easily. He wasn't afraid to battle it out until he had complete autonomy over one of the most powerful organisations in the world.

'It has been a turbulent year,' Marianne began after sipping water and clearing her throat. 'Population rates are still increasing, but as a result, we have directly increased our presence in developing countries, delivering contraception and education on the practices of safe sex to reduce the number of new pregnancies. Not only this, but we have stepped up our projects in developed nations. The UK, the USA, China, France, Germany and Australia, among others. We are working together to combat this global problem.

'In addition, combining our efforts with various instrumental worldwide organisations to counter the effects that waste and global warming are having on our planet will be a major focus for us in 2018. The world's water levels are rapidly increasing, and the water itself is becoming more and more toxic. We plan to eradicate and remove all plastic waste from the world's oceans by the year 2021. There is nothing we cannot do, ladies and gentlemen. Human beings have been put on this planet for a specific reason, I believe. And that is to respect it, use it but not abuse it. We can enjoy it, sustain it, preserve it, and nurture it for generations to come.

'Together, we can make that future a reality. No longer will we have to worry about the stress our consumption is having on the planet.'

Everyone in the room clapped. Reluctantly, Benjamin joined in. He placed his thumb and forefinger inside his mouth, on the edges of his teeth, and blew. The whistle caught Marianne's attention almost immediately. He had hated her speech; it was pretentious, boring, and impossible. *There's no way we can achieve any of that success,* he mused. *But I can. I will be one of the most successful scientists and philanthropists to have ever lived. A hero who cursed the world with prolonged life.*

'Now,' Marianne continued, 'we just have a few more matters to discuss before we take a lunch break in the Oblix downstairs. I hear the food there is wonderful.'

16

Lunch

December 2, 2017, 12:07

The two families were sat at a round table for eight in the east wing of the restaurant, looking out at the northern part of the city. A waiter who went by the name of Miguel had greeted them. Miguel offered to take everyone's coats. Jake had declined; he wanted to keep it with him at all times lest he lose the weed in his pocket. After he had finished hanging everyone else's up in a nearby storage cupboard, Miguel showed them to their table. To Jake's left was Karen Tough, and to his right was her son, Ethan. Karen had requested he sit between them; she wanted to get to know him better, and Jake, being a gentleman, couldn't refuse. The last thing he wanted was for the atmosphere to become awkward. Even if he knew how much Elizabeth was resenting him for it.

The Oblix restaurant was at a comfortable height for Jake. From his seat, he could see the Tower of London, the Walkie-Talkie, the Gherkin, and the Cheesegrater. In the background of the room's ambiance, amidst the noise of conversation and laughter, a piano played. He liked it. It relaxed him. Helped put his nerves at ease.

Everything was fine.

There was nothing to worry about.

Jake looked down at the menu.

'Jesus,' he whispered, without realising he had spoken.

'What?' Karen asked.

'Didn't realise it was this pricey. Does everything come with a piece of twenty-four carat gold or something?'

Karen laughed and touched his leg. 'You're so funny,' she said.

Jake looked down at her hand on his knee, and then his eyes fell on Elizabeth, who glared at him.

'Stop your complaining,' Elizabeth said, a hint of bitterness in her words. 'Why don't you take your coat off?'

'I'm cold. It's a bit chilly in here.'

'Maybe you're getting sick,' Karen said before coughing and removing her hand from Jake's thigh. 'Alex and I came here last year, and the food was superb value for money.'

'I think I'll have the steak.'

'We haven't even ordered drinks yet!' Karen said.

'I like to be prepared. Know exactly what I'm doing before I've even done it.'

'Is that because you're a police officer, or because you're a control freak?' Karen raised her eyebrow.

Was she flirting with him again? Whatever was going on, he found he enjoyed it. It felt new, refreshing, exciting. To be wanted again. To enjoy new company – especially a woman's. It had been so long since he'd last felt a touch like that from Elizabeth. He had almost forgotten what it was like. He knew that it was his own fault, but that didn't stop it from feeling nice when Karen did it.

'I think it's more about being a creature of habit.'

Before Karen could speak again, a man appeared behind her shoulder. He wore a white shirt and a black apron pulled tightly around his waist. He was unlike the other waiters and waitresses Jake had seen, who wore their uniforms limply. However, the man's hair was dishevelled, and Jake thought he looked tired.

'Good afternoon,' the man said brightly. 'My name is Charlie, and I'll be your server today. Can I get you started with any drinks?'

The Tanner and Tough families made their way around the table, ordering their drinks. Jake was last to go, and when he did, he was interrupted.

'Daddy – look, it's the man from the bathroom,' a child's voice called.

Jake twisted round. A young boy of similar age and size to Ellie was standing with his father, hand in hand. The dad looked aggrieved.

'Oh, you're right, it is.' The man spoke with animosity in his voice. He wandered up to their table and pointed at Charlie. 'Sorry to interrupt, folks, but you – you were rude. I can't believe they hired you here. Do you not even have your own staff toilets, or do you have to use the ones upstairs?'

Charlie stuttered. 'I – I don't know what – I don't know what you're talking about. I think you must have me confused with someone else.'

'No, mate. I don't think I do. Unprofessional. If you have kids, I hope you raise them correctly, and not the same way you've been brought up.'

A moment of tense silence as Charlie's face lost all colour. The restaurant had quieted and people were staring.

'Don't worry,' he finally said. 'I won't be having any soon. Now, if you wouldn't mind, I'd like to get back to serving my customers.'

The man stopped, looked at Jake and the rest of his family and friends, and said, 'Right, sorry.' With that, he turned away and disappeared.

Charlie spoke first. 'Please accept my apologies for that little outburst. Now, what can I get you, sir?'

'Foster's.'

'Coming right up,' Charlie said, making a note of Jake's order on his notepad before speeding off towards the bar, sidestepping a waiter who carried a large plate of filled glasses.

'Well, that was weird,' Jake said, addressing the table.

'Tell me about it,' Karen replied.

Jake turned to face her and asked, 'So, how are things with you?'

'Brilliant. We're coming up to the end of term and we can't wait to finish.'

'What year do you teach again?'

'It's a secondary school, so all ages from eleven to sixteen.'

'That'll be Maisie soon,' Jake said. Shit, the thought scared him. In a couple of year's time, his firstborn child, their first little miracle, would be attending secondary school, and both he and Elizabeth would enter a foreign world.

'They grow up fast, don't they? Although you don't look

old enough to have a child Maisie's age.'

Jake flushed red. 'Thanks,' he said, distracted. He smiled as he stared at Maisie, who sat next to Ellen on the other side of Karen. The two children were busy talking. Jake looked to his right, at Ellie and Ethan. They were both playing games on their tablets, a generation lost to the digital age. Meanwhile, Elizabeth and Alex were mid-discussion. Jake saw, every now and then, her scowling at him, monitoring his conversation with Karen. Either that or she was giving him snide looks because she knew about his betrayal last night.

Before Jake could contemplate it for too long, Charlie returned carrying a large tray full of glasses and multicoloured liquids in his hand. He wandered round, placing the drinks on the table.

After he'd finished, he asked, 'Now, what can I get you all for food?'

Everyone ordered, and Charlie left. Jake watched the man leave. The detective instincts in him brought him back to the patron's outburst minutes earlier. What had Charlie been doing in the bathroom? Why was the man so irate? It was something, he knew, that would fester in the back of his mind like mould growing in a fridge.

Jake felt a tap on his leg. It was Ethan. The young boy looked up at him with curious blue eyes and a handsome face that Jake knew would flourish one day.

'Do you have a gun?' Ethan asked, pointing to Jake's hip.

Jake laughed.

'Ethan!' Alex interjected, overhearing.

'No, no. It's fine.' Jake bent down to Ethan's level and said, 'I don't carry one of those, but many of my friends and colleagues do. Perhaps one day you could say hello to them if you see them on the street?'

Ethan nodded, and Jake ruffled the child's hair. The boy made him smile. That was the one thing he was missing from his life. A son.

A son he could take to football practice on the weekends. A son he could take on adventure holidays. A son he could watch grow up. A son he could love unconditionally. Soon he and Elizabeth would be celebrating the miracle of birth for a third time. And soon he would be able to hold a baby boy in his arms for the very first time. He couldn't wait.

'Have you ever been shot?' Ethan asked.

'No. But I have been stabbed. It hurt a lot.'

'Can I see the scar?'

'Ethan, that's enough!' Alex said, grabbing his son by the forearm, leaning across Ellie.

Instinctively, Jake defended the young boy by clutching his right shoulder and pulling Ethan closer into his body.

'He's all right,' Jake said, looking deep into Alex's eyes and grinning disarmingly. 'I don't mind.' He turned to Ethan. 'But I can't show you the scar, I'm afraid, buddy.'

Minutes later, while the discussion around the table ebbed and flowed, a large group of individuals entered the restaurant. Jake could hear them from the entrance twenty feet behind. He glanced over his shoulder and watched as fifteen men and four women dressed formally in suits and ties sat in the three booths to his left.

Jake didn't know who the rest of them were, but he recognised one of them from the news a few days back. Benjamin Weiss, the acclaimed geneticist – the David Beckham of the science world – was sitting inches away from him.

17

Old Friends

December 2, 2017, 12:22

Upon first impressions, Benjamin Weiss hated the Oblix restaurant just as much as he had hated the Ren room. It wasn't the most lavish restaurant he had found himself in these past ten months, since his career skyrocketed thanks to Charlie Paxman's departure. And there had been a fuck-up with the tables. They were in the wrong section of the restaurant – the cocktail lounge, the peasants' area – when they should have been on the west side, the formal side, the wealthy and high-end side. But it would do; there was no alternative. The chairs and table were clean. The floor was polished. The cutlery and glasses were unblemished, and the vase in each of the three booths were large enough to satisfy him. He appreciated the floral arrangements, a personal requirement of his. They added a level of class to the day, thankfully, because so far, nothing had lived up to his expectations.

He was seated next to Marianne in the middle of the three tables. Directly in front, beyond a table of two families, were the views of London. He should have enjoyed it, but there was a much better view beside him.

His boss.

For one particular reason.

He really wanted that promotion.

'Wonderful view,' he said.

Marianne cast her attention out over the city. Boats idled up and down the Thames. Buses and cars and bicycles and pedestrians inched along the streets, caught in the furore of the busy month of December.

'It certainly is,' Marianne said, turning to face Benjamin.

'I wasn't talking about that view.' He allowed the edges of his mouth to turn, letting Marianne know he wasn't joking.

Her cheeks flushed red, and she slapped his hand gently. 'Stop it. You can't say things like that here. You're less than half my age. You know that. You're just being silly again,' she said.

'I don't say things I don't mean.' Benjamin eyed the menu, playing hard to get now. He searched for something that might pique his interest. 'What are you having, Mar?' he asked, using his nickname for her. It was a nod to her Spanish heritage; *mar*, meaning sea, reflected her character: deep, powerful, and incredibly intimidating.

'I'm leaning towards the lobster.'

'Expensive taste. I like it. I'll join you.'

Benjamin stared ahead, his curiosity getting the better of

him as he observed the group in front. He always liked to see who his fellow diners were. Fortunately for him, the two families were respectful and kept the noise down. There was nothing Benjamin abhorred more than obnoxious, insolent diners disturbing his meal.

As Benjamin returned his attention to the wine menu, a team of three waiters arrived at their tables. A male and two females. Each to a table.

'Good afternoon,' the male waiter said, stopping in front of him.

Listening but not paying attention, Benjamin looked up, and was immediately taken aback, as if he had just seen someone he presumed to be dead.

'Well, I'll be fucked,' Benjamin said, before the man could finish introducing himself. Those around his table turned to face him, a look of confusion sprawled across their faces. 'Charlie Paxman. I never thought I'd see you again. And here, of all places.'

Benjamin rose, shuffled in front of Marianne's legs, grabbed the waiter's hand forcefully and embraced him. Their bodies came together with a loud thud. Benjamin slapped his old friend on the back and released him.

'Fancy seeing you here,' Benjamin said.

'What are the odds?'

'You tell me – you were always more statistically minded.'

Charlie Paxman smiled but said nothing. His expression gave nothing away.

'How have you been? I hardly recognised you there. You've lost a lot of weight.' Benjamin inspected the other man's face.

Charlie had changed drastically since Benjamin had last

seen him. His former colleague's complexion had been coloured with vibrancy and energy and youth just last year. But now, all that remained was a skeleton with skin. Charlie's eyes looked out at Benjamin from deep inside his skull, and his Adam's apple yo-yoed up and down every time he swallowed. Being sacked from the organisation had clearly had a profound effect on him. *I'm surprised they let him work here, the state he's in.*

'It's all the work,' Charlie said. He was shy, reserved . . . almost afraid. Unlike the Charlie that Benjamin had once known. 'And the stress.'

'Waiting on people too difficult for you?'

'Only when they're assholes.'

Both men shared a look that insinuated they were thinking the same thing: *Like you, then.*

'You'll be all right. It can't be that difficult!' Benjamin laughed and slapped his old friend on the shoulder again.

'What's that supposed to mean?'

'What? Nothing. I was just saying.'

'Well, perhaps you shouldn't, Ben. Perhaps you shouldn't.' Charlie paused, looked at the ground, then around the table, and said, 'What brings you all here, anyway?'

'Annual convention.'

'A little late in the year, though, isn't it?'

'There were unforeseen delays,' Benjamin said.

'What happened?'

'A virus.'

'Oh?' Charlie's eyebrows raised.

'A terrible virus hit almost all of us.' Benjamin turned his chest to face the table. 'Poor Marianne – she was bedridden for weeks.'

Charlie looked down at Marianne. His face remained placid, the years of personal history between the two of them hiding behind his hollowed-out cheekbones.

'Marianne,' Charlie said, 'it's good to see you.'

'Likewise, Charlie. Likewise. How have you been?'

'The rest of us got ill as well,' Benjamin interrupted. He wasn't going to let Charlie steal the limelight. He wasn't going to let Charlie get all the attention from Marianne. Not again.

'Sounds terrible,' Charlie said.

Benjamin looked at him. Was that a smile on his face? Was there a glimmer of enjoyment in Paxman's eyes?

'Yes,' he said. 'It was. Everyone is better now, though. It's taken time, but everyone's mended.'

'I'm glad to hear.'

A moment of awkward silence descended on the two old friends, lingered, stuttered, and then disappeared as Charlie said, 'It's quite a change of view, no? London is slightly different to Geneva.'

'Again, delays and unforeseen changes were responsible. Think of this as a pre-celebration for the seventieth anniversary next year. I must admit, the hospitality you and your team have shown us has been wonderful so far.'

'My team?'

'Oh, wait. No? I didn't mean to . . . I'm sorry – I thought you were managerial.' Benjamin darted his glance to his colleagues beside him; he could see them laughing behind their hands and napkins. 'Even after all these months, you still haven't got a team of your own? It's OK. You're young – you'll find one.'

'That's enough, Ben,' Marianne said.

'Piss off,' Charlie retorted.

'That's enough from you as well, Charlie,' Marianne said, rising up and coming between the two men.

Charlie's expression dropped. He stepped back, away from Benjamin, and away from any further altercation.

'That's right, listen to Mummy.' Ben smirked.

Before Charlie could open his mouth to respond, the waitress who was serving nearest to the building's windows arrived and pulled him away.

'What are you doing?' the girl said within earshot. She was taller than Charlie, and Benjamin could tell that intimidated him.

'Nothing. Sorry.'

'Do you want me to report this to Callum?'

'No.'

'Do you need to go home again?'

Charlie hesitated, looked into Benjamin's eyes, and said, 'No. Definitely not today. Myself and Ben here have got some unfinished business to attend to.'

Jesus, Benjamin thought. *What the fuck does that mean?* He had known Charlie Paxman for many years; they had been at the same university and in the same student accommodation block. And in all those years, he had never seen so much hatred nor fury in his old friend's eyes, like there was a blazing forest fire rapidly spreading throughout the man's body. It seemed like Charlie would soon be consumed by rage, and Benjamin didn't want to be there when he was; he knew what Charlie's dormant temper could be like.

'So long as you don't spit in my food, we'll be all good,' Benjamin said. Laughter erupted from around the table.

'That's the least of your worries.'

18

Shot

December 2, 2017, 12:29

Charlie stormed out of the restaurant, experiencing a new, potent combination of feelings.

He was pissed – pissed at Benjamin for embarrassing him in front of everyone. Again.

He was excited – excited that soon, in a few very short minutes in fact, the entire world would turn on its head. And they would all be calling him a hero, a miracle, a genius – amongst other, more derogatory and cynical names.

He was concerned – concerned that he might not be able to pull it off, that he might not be able to release the virus into the air before anyone, or anything, stood in his way.

All he would need was an hour or two, maximum. So long as he stuck to his timeline.

In fact, he didn't even need that.

He just wanted the extra time so he could play around with everyone in the restaurant. Instil fear into them. Convey his modus operandi. Let the entire human population know who he was, how he would save them all, and how his virus would protect them from themselves. And how, in two generations' time, when he was long dead, they would thank him.

Charlie passed the walls that led to the toilets, rounded the corner past the kitchen, charged into the staff room, unlocked his locker door with such force it slammed against the wall, and then grabbed his duffel bag. He left the room, slinging the bag over his shoulder. A colleague called after him, but he ignored them. He didn't even see who it was; they had become a blur, a disturbance in the clarity of what lay ahead.

Returning to the restaurant, Charlie made a left turn towards the exit. As he scanned his key card to leave through the emergency exits, one person caught his eye and he stalled. It was the man sat at the table opposite to Benjamin's. He had got up and was now at the bar, ordering another Foster's. He looked familiar. But where had Charlie seen him before? An image from months ago popped into his head. He had seen him on TV. Yes, that was it. Or was it on his computer? The news?

Focus! Charlie lambasted himself for becoming distracted. He didn't have the time to allow his thoughts to migrate to other places.

Charlie scanned his key card again. The small control panel on the side flashed green, and he descended the stairs. They would be his only mode of travelling through the building for the next sixty minutes. Lifts and machinery were not to be trusted.

Taking the steps two at a time, Charlie arrived at the thirtieth floor, where the entire building's electrical components and generators were stored. The Shard's thirtieth floor was its beating heart, its organ that fuelled everything. And Charlie was about to sever its arteries.

The only problem was the man standing in his way.

'Excuse me, sir,' a man dressed in a black suit said. He had a radio cable tangled around his ears, and his hands permanently crossed in front of him. 'You can't be here. You need to leave.'

Charlie laughed internally at someone's poor attempt to dress the man up as security personnel. To be honest, he felt a little disappointed with how easy this whole operation had been. During his time at the World Health Organisation's headquarters in Geneva, he had needed multiple key cards. And even then, his permissions had been limited. Now, however, in the tallest building in England, he was able to waltz straight through, only to be deterred by a man whose efforts at exuding authority and intimidation were hampered by cheap cologne and a bad haircut.

'Oh, I'm sorry,' Charlie said, feigning ignorance. 'I'm new here. I'm lost. Would you be able to help me?'

'Sure.' The guard wandered towards Charlie.

Six steps separated them.

'Where do you need to go?'

Five steps.

Charlie reached inside his bag.

Four steps.

'I was wondering if you could tell me where the company

called OP is?'

Three steps.

Charlie felt the handgun. His fingers caressed the grip while his forefinger found the trigger that dangled from the main body.

Two steps.

Charlie removed the gun from the bag. The man froze, overcome with a fear so tangible Charlie could sense it prickling his own skin. Before the man could reach the radio on his shoulder, Charlie pulled the trigger twice. The guard collapsed to the ground as a mist composed of blood and internal organ fragments burst into the air, landing on the windowpane behind him.

The security guard never made it to the final step.

Charlie pulled the trigger again. Again. And again. Until the barrel jammed and the weapon misfired. He had plunged five bullets into the man's body. It had felt great, invigorating. It made Charlie feel alive, invincible, like there was nothing on this earth that could defeat him. It was just a shame it had come to an end so soon. He tried the trigger one final time before throwing the useless weapon to the ground. He had no further need for it.

The sound of the nine-calibre bullet blasting from the gun still echoed, leaving a tinny ringing sound in Charlie's ears. He wiped his face. Specks of blood had sprayed onto his mouth and cheeks, yet missed his forehead.

He had to move quickly, in case someone had heard the gunshots. Stepping over to the security guard's lifeless body, Charlie bent down, reached inside the man's breast pocket and produced an ID card. *Rik,* he repeated in his head, reading the name on the badge. 'Sorry we had to meet like this,' he said aloud, patting the dead man on the stomach.

Charlie moved towards the door of the electrical room to his right, flashed the card, and relaxed as he heard the satisfying sound of the mechanisms unlocking on the other side.

Charlie pushed the door aside and stepped forward. He had done it! He was in. But it had only cost him one casualty; he had been looking for more of a fight. Something a little more exciting. *Add him to the total tally,* Charlie thought as he entered the control room. Pipes ran along the walls, containing the thousands of cables and wires that powered the building's electrical circuits. There were three large vaults, each containing servers that provided the building with its internet and business services. And a large control panel, sweeping across the back wall of the room, glittered and sparkled in front of him.

Charlie had no idea how any of it worked, but he didn't need to understand. He wasn't there to alter the mechanisms and functions. No, he was there to be heavy-handed, to create as much disturbance and destruction and mess as possible.

Charlie placed the bag on the floor; it landed with a metallic clatter. He reached inside, grabbed a bottle of acid and poured its contents onto the power centre's control panel. All the buttons and knobs, dials and switches, levers and touchpads sizzled and sparked like a barbecue. Within seconds, acrid smoke filled the air as the liquid corroded the control panel.

Wasting no time, Charlie bent down and reached for something else in his bag. After fumbling about for a moment, he found what he was looking for and advanced towards the rows of pipes that ran across the wall. In his hands he held a small circular Dremel 4000 saw. Thirty-five thousand revs per minute. A 175-watt motor. And it had cost him only eighty pounds from a consignment sales website. Damage it would cause: irrevocable.

Absolute bargain.

Charlie stopped in front of the pipes, looked down at the saw's circular head that was the same size as his big toenail, and engaged it. The device buzzed and vibrated in his hands as the blade spun mercilessly, blending into a blur of whirring silver. It produced a little noise that reminded Charlie of a remote-controlled car he'd had as a child. His dad had bought it for his ninth birthday. It was just about the only thing his parents had ever bought him, and it had lasted all of a couple of hours until it got run over in the street by a speeding car.

Sparks ejected from the pipe as the saw churned through the metal. It didn't take long for the Dremel to slice its way through the piping and disconnect hundreds of wires that ran along the wall. As soon as he'd severed the final pipe, the lights in the control room went out. Everything went pitch black, and he felt the room's air temperature drop slightly. Consumed by the blackness, Charlie pulled out his phone and turned on the torch, illuminating everything in front of him.

Almost immediately, the backup generators, which were situated underground, booted up and engaged the lights. Charlie had committed the blueprints of the building to memory and knew where everything was. He had purchased the plans online, on the Dark Web – it had cost him almost everything he owned to acquire them.

They were worth every penny.

Charlie dropped to the floor and placed the Dremel back inside his bag, being careful not to damage the vial containing the virus. He zipped up the bag and left the control room. He skipped over the dead man lying slumped against the glass. A pool of blood that reflected the flickering light above had formed around the body, and it was rapidly spreading towards the door.

While climbing the stairs two at a time, Charlie could hear confused voices coming from deep below him in the stairwell. There was little time to waste; if he was delayed for any reason, the diners at the Oblix would pack up and leave their things, despite the protocol the waiting staff and managerial team would follow.

'There's nothing to be alarmed about,' they would say. 'It's just a minor power outage. Please remain calm and return to your seats. You are perfectly safe.'

Charlie had taken the monotonous emergency training module on mass panic and how to combat it during his initial training at the Oblix. And he had hated every single minute.

He reached the thirty-second floor and burst through the doors into the kitchen on the south side of the building. He knocked a chef over, who collapsed in a heap, spilling the contents of a plate to the floor. Charlie's blood was pumping. His heart rate had rocketed, and his mind was focused. His muscles were taut with adrenaline and euphoria.

The Oblix was relative calm. When he'd first conceived his plans, he'd believed the power outage would reduce everyone inside the restaurant to their primal state: survival of the fittest. But there was no animosity in the way people moved about the restaurant. No fury and aggression, no pushing others over to get to the lifts first.

Soon there will be. And everyone will fight to stay alive.

Charlie stopped in front of the bathroom stalls, the perfect position. To his left was a fire exit, and to his right a small seating area. No one in the immediate area could get in or out. Just how he had planned it. He reached inside the bag, removed the assault rifle, and held it in the air.

He fired one burst, the deafening sound reverberating around the open expanse.

By the second shot, everyone inside the restaurant was up on their feet, screaming, shouting, crying out for their loved ones.

It was time to begin.

19

Up

December 2, 2017, 12:33

When Tim Keane started work that day, he was hoping for yet another uneventful shift. Not that much to do, just like every other day. People coming and going. Some giving him shit, some treating him with respect. He could deal with that.

But so far, he had experienced a catatonic elderly woman who had collapsed after a heart attack, and just now a homeless man had tried to break into the building, desperate for somewhere to stay for the day as the bitter chill of December crept along the streets, searching for its next victim.

'Thanks for all your help,' the homeless man said as Tim escorted him out of the lobby.

'No problem, mate,' Tim replied, smiling. 'Have a good

day.'

Tim watched the man leave. As soon as he stepped outside the revolving doors, Tim wiped his hand on his shirt and made his way to the bathroom. He felt dirty. He wandered up to the bay of sinks and washed his hands. Stopped. Felt a knot in his stomach tighten.

'God's sake, not again,' he said, rushing into a cubicle.

He slammed the toilet seat down, pulled his trousers to his ankles, and let the contents of his body flow right out of him. His skin turned to gooseflesh. No matter how many times he told himself eating spicy food was a bad idea, he preferred the taste to any of the consequences. Even if it meant it would flare his IBS.

A few minutes passed. He spent the time scrolling through his Facebook feed on his mobile phone, procrastinating, hiding away from doing his job.

Suddenly, the lights went out. His only source of illumination was the blue light cast from his phone screen.

'What the—?' he said, his hands fumbling for the toilet roll. Using his sense of touch, he cleaned himself. And when he was done, he washed his hands and made his way to the reception area. It was crowded, and as he stepped over the threshold, the natural light flooding in from outside blinded him.

'What is going on?'

No one answered, too caught up in the panic of the situation. Tim looked to his left. The revolving doors had stopped spinning. Whenever there had been a minor technical fault in the past, the systems always rebooted. Except for now.

He wandered over to the lift, pressed the button and

waited. When none of the lights on the button or at the top of the lift doors flashed, he became concerned. Something wasn't right. There was no monotonous drumming coming from behind the doors. There was no light. There was nothing.

He made his way to the reception desk.

'Cassy, what's happening?'

'I don't know. My computer just stopped. It went dead. And now it's not turning on.'

'Is it a power cut?' a girl beside Cassy asked.

'No, I don't think so,' Tim said. 'The technological infrastructure supporting the building combats that sort of thing. It would have to be a massive power surge to cause something like this. Besides, if it were, there would be some sort of backup power coming into play.'

'Are you sure?'

Tim smirked. 'I was an electrical engineer a long time ago – I should know what I'm talking about.'

As he finished, the radio strapped to his hip bleated. 'Tim. Tim, you there?'

'Yeah, Vince. I'm here. What's going on?' Tim replied. Vince was another member of the security team. He was stationed at the entrance to the Shangri-La hotel. He and Tim had worked together for the past two years upstairs in The View From The Shard, although Vince had been there since the building's construction finished in 2012.

'Complete power outage. All the systems have gone down, including the emergency and staff exits. Oh, wait. Hold on – I think the backup must be kicking in.' Vince hesitated. 'Yeah, we're back up and running, but only at minimal capacity. Some of the doors will be working now, but not all.'

'What's caused it?' Tim asked. He confirmed to Vince that the computer monitors, lights and printers were now working.

'I don't know,' Vince said. 'Have you heard any word from Rik?'

Rik was on the thirtieth floor, where all the building's electrical components were situated, and he was their boss. Recent budget cuts had meant the number of personnel manning the floors was significantly reduced. Which was why when Rik had told Tim last night he would be working more hours, Tim had requested the ground floor; it was slightly less dull and made a change from being a thousand feet in the air.

'No,' Tim said. 'Maybe he's fallen asleep. If he has then he owes me ten quid. Want me to check on him?'

'We'll both go. Something might have happened to him.'

And you're too chicken shit to go on your own.

'Meet you there in a second,' Vince said.

Tim rang off, clipped the radio back to his belt and headed up the stairs.

20

Lift

December 2, 2017, 12:37

The lift shook as it stopped. Christina Klepf hated lifts at the best of times, but when they came to an abrupt halt for no apparent reason, that was when the claustrophobia kicked in. That was when she wanted to scream, break down, crumble to the ground and cry, beg to be somewhere else. Anywhere. In the middle of the desert. A rainforest. A civil war. A place better than these four walls that felt like they were closing in around her, a millimetre every passing second. The childhood trauma of getting inside a beach cave still haunted her. Cold. Dark. Damp. Alone.

Except this time, she wasn't alone.

'Great!' the man locked inside with her said. From what she could see of him, he wore a suit and had short, thick brown hair.

In the outage, they had been plunged into complete darkness. Almost a minute later, a dim safety light flickered overhead, illuminating the cabin somewhat. It wasn't brilliant, but it would be enough to settle her nerves a margin.

'Come on,' the man said, slamming his fist on the side of the lift. 'Open up!'

Christina watched him. Why was he doing that? Why did he feel the need to make such a noise and cause a disturbance? What if the slightest movement sent the lift plummeting to the floor?

Christina forced the idea from her mind and dismissed it as ludicrous. It was just her paranoia teasing her. She needed to calm herself down. Fast.

The man slammed his fist on the side again.

'Stop it!' she snapped. 'Please.'

The man turned to face her, his handsome features accentuated by the low light. It cast an almost mysterious aura over him. He opened his mouth, about to protest, and then closed it again.

'Sorry,' he said eventually. 'I didn't mean to scare you.'

'You should be,' Christina said, sliding to the floor and sitting down. 'I don't like being in lifts.'

'You and me both,' he said. He moved to the doors, stuck his fingers in the thin slither of metal that separated them both from the outside world, and began to pull. Nothing happened. The doors remained where they were, frozen solid, mocking them.

The man stopped and sat next to Christina.

'Looks like we'll be here for a while,' he said. His words

weren't helping.

'No shit.'

He extended his hand. 'Neil.'

After a moment's hesitation, Christina took it. 'Christina.' His hand felt warm and strong. Reassuring. Protective. Something she hadn't felt from her husband in a long time, and something she needed in her life, now more than ever.

'Nice to meet you,' he said.

Christina let out a hollow laugh. 'Don't have much choice.'

Christina closed her eyes and breathed. In through the nose, out through the mouth. Like her husband, who was also her yoga instructor, had told her. The man she loved and had had an affair with. He had been off limits when they first met because he had a wife and two kids. And yet he'd still seemed so eager to come over to hers for their weekly private yoga sessions. And then there was the session that changed everything: the one where they had slept together for the first time. It was a Sunday. The eighteenth of June. She remembered it well. They had been together for three years now. Married for two. And she had never looked back on her decision, until recently.

She was sure Sebastian was cheating on her. Coming home late from other private yoga lessons. Always going to rescheduled appointments later in the day. Never in the mood to have sex with her when he got home. Their marriage had stagnated, and so had she. And then there was the news she had received recently that had turned him away even more . . .

'You all right?' Neil asked.

Christina opened her eyes, shocked back to reality. 'Why?

Was I bothering you?'

'No.' He hesitated. 'I was . . . I was just asking.'

'If you must know, I was thinking.'

'About?'

'Life.'

'Sounds deep. I don't think you need to worry that much. Things like this happen all the time,' Neil said. He shuffled against her so their shoulders touched one another. He radiated heat against her nervous and shivering body.

Christina placed both her hands between her legs. Interlocked her fingers. Found her wedding ring. Twisted it, rotated it, slid it up and down her finger.

Removed it. Returned it. Removed it again.

'I hope you're right,' she said, placing the ring inside her sock.

21

Hiding Places

December 2, 2017, 12:41

Jake's ears rang with the deafening - and unmistakable - sound of bullets firing. At first everything went quiet, faint, as if someone had stuck his head deep underwater. Then, moments later, as the initial sound wave moved past his ears, screams and cries filtered through his ear canal. It took him all of one nanosecond to react. Acting on instinct, he cowered his head down to the table, spreading his arms like a bird, bringing both Karen and Ethan down to the ground with him. In situations like this, finding shelter and getting out of the way was the best option. He moved round the table to Ellie, grabbed her from her chair and clutched her tightly against his chest. On the other side of the table he saw Elizabeth and Alex yank both Ellen and Maisie from their chairs to the floor.

Around them screams echoed. The group of scientists beside them erupted out of their seats, spilling to the ground. One of them knocked into Jake, but he didn't take heed. He was too focused on protecting the ones he loved, the ones he would do anything for. Jake made a mental note of where the gunfire was coming from: the same entrance he and the girls had used. On the east side of the building near the bar and toilets, less than twenty feet away.

Jake glanced over the lip of the table, still protecting Ellie in his arms and Ethan by his side. His heart raced, and his body shook with adrenaline. But then something came over him, and straight away he knew what it was. A blanket of darkness. Of fear. Fire. Flames. Explosions. Moshat. He was having another terror. His PTSD was bringing on an episode, unlike any he had ever experienced before. He didn't know what to do. He had his family to protect, and he wasn't about to let his imagination defeat him.

Pushing the images out of his mind, Jake forced himself to ignore the sensation of being strangled by Moshat in the darkness. He became immensely aware of how many seconds he was wasting and how much he was endangering his family by his inactivity. Blinking hard, he looked around the table. All eyes were on him. He was the only one with the knowledge and experience to handle this situation. Everyone he loved and cared for was relying on him to save them, to protect them from whatever danger lay ahead.

And he was going to do exactly that.

'Over there,' Jake whispered. He pointed to the bar behind him that rounded the internal structure of the building. It was no more than ten feet away, but Jake knew it would feel like forever trying to get everyone there safely.

Keeping his knees bent and his body low, he grabbed Ethan by the shoulder and dragged him and Ellie to the bar, pushing the table that lay in his way to the floor. There was no time to do it nicely; if he had bruised the boy's arm inadvertently, he would apologise afterwards. Their lives were at stake.

After pushing Ellie and Ethan out of sight, Jake turned to face the table. Next thing he knew he was forced to the ground. His right shoulder and the right side of his face ached. Someone had just sprinted past and tripped to the floor. They howled in pain but quickly got back up on their feet.

Jake steadied himself, focused on what was important, and gesticulated for Ellen and Maisie to follow next. They both looked scared - horrified, in fact - and were rooted to the spot. Neither of them could move. Just as Jake was about to reach them, Elizabeth and Alex grabbed one of them each and sprinted over to him, Elizabeth struggling, holding her stomach as she ran.

Then everything went silent. The screaming stopped. The gunshots stopped. All Jake could hear was the sound of his pounding heart in his head and ears.

Jake held his breath. Everyone and everything remained still, their fears paralysing them. What was going on? Jake didn't want to hang around long enough to find out.

Whispering, so that his voice was barely audible over the sound of his heartbeat, Jake ordered Karen to join the rest of them. She was the only one left by their table, and she was positioned on all fours. She leaned to the side, peering round the bar and overturned tables, her gaze fixated on something out of Jake's line of sight.

'Karen!' Jake whispered.

She didn't move.

'Karen!' Jake tried again. By now, the screams had ceased completely, and Jake felt as if his words were being conveyed through a series of stereos and surround sound speakers like he was performing at a concert.

At that moment, he decided calling out to her again wasn't worth the risk, so he crawled over to her, keeping one eye on her and the other on the direction she was staring, grabbed her by the arm and shook her a little to bring her out of her trance. Eventually, after what felt like an age, she turned to face him.

'It's the waiter,' she whispered to him, her eyes wide with horror.

Jake didn't need to ask any more questions. He already knew who she was referring to. He had suspected there was something amiss about the way their server, whose full name he'd overheard, had stormed out of the restaurant, carrying that oversized bag. But he had ignored his instincts; he had promised Elizabeth there would be nothing work related about today. Now he was going to pay the price.

'Come with me,' Jake said, grabbing her other hand with his.

Karen held on tightly as he pulled her in front of him and thrust her towards the bar. Before he followed, he gave one last look behind him at the table where, moments from now, they would have been enjoying a lovely meal together, socialising, relaxing, not thinking about work – not thinking about anything. Jake searched the ground and table for an object that might be of use, or anything they had dropped in the mad scramble to save themselves. A phone. A knife. Fork. Spoon. Box of weed. Broken shard of glass. Anything he would be able to use to defend himself if the time came. There was nothing there.

A second later, Jake overturned a napkin, saw his steak knife concealed beneath it, and slid it into the waistband of his jeans. He kept it wrapped in the napkin. It felt tight against his skin, and as he moved one knee in front of the other, he felt the blade's edge graze against his backside.

'All of you!' a voice screamed. It was Charlie. Jake recognised him at once. 'Get up and move against the window. Now!'

Jake froze. He could see a group of hostages coming near him. There was no time for him to scurry across the floor to Elizabeth, the kids, and everyone else. It was too far. He would be seen for certain.

Slowly, with fear visible in the way they walked, the hostages inched closer to the window beside the piano. To Jake's right, one of the scientists tried the fire exit door directly next to the bar, but it was no use. It wouldn't move. In the power outage and the mad frenzy of escape, the door had jammed. The man returned to the rest of the cowering scientists hiding in their booths.

'Get moving!' Charlie screamed. 'If anyone thinks about doing something stupid, I'll pull the trigger.'

Shit. Jake had very little time to react. If he didn't move now, he would be swept into the crowd like a fish caught in a trawler's net. And he presumed the only way to escape was in a body bag.

He scurried beneath the table, but it was no use. He was in plain sight, and he knew it. There was no other option. There was no going back.

The murmurs and cries and groans coming from the people being herded like cattle stopped. Nearly everyone in the restaurant had been rounded up and moved against the window near to the piano. Jake didn't dare think what was going through Charlie Paxman's mind. It would be easy for Charlie to shoot the glass with his assault rifle and for everyone leaning against the window to fall through, plummeting to their deaths.

He made a mental note to tell his family when, and if, he was reunited with them to stay as far away from the windows as possible.

'Stay perfectly still,' Charlie called to his hostages.

Jake peered through the chair and table legs to catch a glimpse of the attacker.

'There were families here. Where have they gone? Has anyone seen them?' Charlie asked the crowd. He swung the weapon from left to right; cries and gasps sounded.

Silence. No one responded.

Charlie walked over to Jake's table. His legs were within a few feet of Jake.

Jake retreated his hand to his backside and gripped the handle of the steak knife, ready and waiting.

Charlie's feet came to a stop. There was a moment of hesitation. Jake held his breath. Then Charlie squatted and came face-to-face with him.

'There you are.'

22

The Other End

December 2, 2017, 12:43

Jake squeezed the steak knife's handle so hard it bruised the inside of his palm. In the second he stared at Charlie, he keenly observed the man's face. The blank expression, the lack of remorse, the unnerving air of calm about him. Only minutes ago, the same man had been upset, embarrassed and bullied in front of a group of people, and now he looked as if it had never happened

'What are you doing hiding down there?' Charlie said, smiling at Jake, baring his yellow-stained teeth. 'Come on out.'

Charlie waved the gun at Jake, motioning for him to crawl from beneath the table. Tentatively, Jake inched forward, keeping his eyes on Charlie's. There was no point arguing;

the waiter had already proved he wasn't messing around as soon as he fired the bullets into the air.

'Well done, sir,' Charlie said as Jake rose to his feet. 'I'm sorry about this. I bet you were looking forward to your steak, weren't you?' Charlie laughed while Jake remained silent, stern. 'So, where is everyone you were with? Have they all run and left you to suffer as last man standing?'

Charlie raised the gun and pointed it at Jake's chest, holding it inches from his skin.

'They ran away as soon as they heard the gunshots,' Jake said, keeping his voice calm and steady. Even the slightest slip-up would show that Charlie was the one in control.

Charlie looked behind him, at the emergency exit door that had been jammed shut, and then returned his gaze back to Jake. 'I'm not stupid. They're here somewhere. It's best for you to tell me now, and I'll spare them. But if you don't tell me and I go looking for them, and find them, then I'll have no other option but to shoot them all. Imagine that, those poor little girls and boy, dying so young. They were so cute.'

While Charlie was talking, Jake began formulating a plan in his head. It wasn't much, but it was a start. For now, though, Jake would have to concede defeat. He didn't want to risk the lives of everyone he loved.

Jake glanced at the bar at his twelve o'clock. Charlie followed Jake's gaze and smiled.

'Thank you. Get them out of there. I want to see all of them. I remember how many there are.'

Swallowing deeply, and keeping his body facing Charlie so as to conceal the steak knife in his waistband, Jake backed towards the bar. The first person he saw was Alex. His friend looked afraid. His chest was heaving, and he seemed unsteady on his feet. But Jake admired the fact he was protecting Elizabeth and the girls, and for that he would thank him. After all of this was over.

Jake nodded to Alex and to everyone behind him, inviting them to stand up and walk out from behind the bar. They rose to their feet slowly, and then, with their arms raised in the air, they moved over to Charlie and the rest of the hostages against the window. Alex and his family went first.

Jake bent down and picked up Ellie, who had been walking side by side with Elizabeth and Maisie. Jake grabbed Elizabeth's hand and squeezed it, hoping it conveyed the message that everything was going to be all right, and that he was going to take care of it all. He was relieved to feel her hand tightening around his. Her soft, warm, delicate skin. The wedding ring around her finger that dug into his. It was bliss.

'What's your name?' Charlie asked, putting a hand out to hold Jake back. Charlie's grip felt weird on Jake's arm, and he twisted so he was facing the other man front on, hiding the weapon in his waistband.

'Jake.'

'Nice to meet you, Jake. You've been most cooperative. Now, take a seat.'

Jake joined the rest of the family on the north side of the building. They were seated in front of a row of other people, nearer to their table than anything else. Jake's pint of beer was fizzing away. After Charlie ordered Jake to sit down, he found the scientists hiding under their tables in the booth and forced them to join the other hostages. It was cramped, and there was nowhere for any of them to go. Jake tried to develop the plan in his head, but as he watched Charlie saunter up and down the length of the bar, he saw his chances of success deteriorate with every passing second.

The main priority now was to alert someone. Anyone. Mamadou. Frances. Simon. Susanna. Edwards. Carmichaels. The list went on. But how? If he were caught . . . He didn't want to know the outcome.

'Here's what I want you all to do,' Charlie said, his voice loud and clear, commanding the attention of every hostage in the room. He was no longer the shy and innocent waiter who had served them less than twenty minutes ago. He was a crazed, cold-hearted gunman whose breaking point was unknown. 'Throw all of these tables and chairs to the floor and build them in a wall so they keep you cooped up here. No one's getting in or out. It's going to be a tight fit, but I'm sure you'll all manage.'

Neither Jake nor anyone else in the restaurant could tell whether his instructions were sincere. There was something in the way Charlie spoke, something articulate, pronounced, that made him sound intelligent. And Jake knew from experience that that could only mean one thing: Charlie had planned this entire thing, and he knew what he was doing.

'Come on!' Charlie screamed, raising the gun in the air, incentivising his hostages to do as he wanted. 'What are you waiting for?'

As soon as the weapon was raised, men, women and children screamed, cowering behind one another. Some lifted their hands in surrender, some in protection. For a while, though, nobody did anything. Nobody took it upon themselves to be a leader, to oversee the fight against their captor.

Jake sighed heavily. He rose to the centre of the small

enclosure where everyone was being kept, moved to a table, planted his feet firmly on the floor, grabbed the edge, and lifted using his leg and back muscles. Glass and cutlery and crockery smashed to the floor and echoed around the restaurant. He repeated that multiple times until eventually there was a series of six tables that separated the hostages from Charlie. That separated life from death. That separated freedom from uncertainty. The wall stretched from the edge of the booth on one side to the piano on the other. Jake made a quick estimation that there were approximately forty people locked inside Charlie's trap. After he was finished, Jake wiped his hands on his jeans and stared at the gunman, waiting for a reaction. Waiting to see who would be first to break.

'Well done,' Charlie said. 'You're the only who listens around here.'

'You should consider yourself lucky.'

Charlie scoffed. 'Why's that?'

'I never do as I'm told.'

'Fighting talk. I like it. Perhaps you and I are going to get on,' Charlie said. 'Now sit back down.'

Jake remained where he was for a moment, determined not to retreat under the pressure.

Charlie raised the gun. 'I said, *sit down*.'

Jake looked into Charlie's green, cavernous eyes. They reflected so much light, yet behind that, there was so much darkness . . . It worried Jake. He wanted to know how far this man was willing to go.

Then he had his answer.

While Jake sidestepped to the right, face-on with Charlie, a woman to his left, at the far end of the window nearest to the piano, jumped to her feet. She sprinted towards the table, hopped over it, and then fell to the floor. The bullet had travelled through the right side of her head and out the left, burying itself deep in a beam that ran up the height of the window. The impact of the bullet sent a flower of blood up the wall of glass. The woman's body slumped against the window, looking like a rag doll.

Screams ensued. Chaos erupted. Fear struck.

Jake looked on in horror. Now he knew how far Charlie was willing to go.

Pulling his gaze from the lifeless body on the floor, Jake retreated to his seat, stepping over plates and glass and cutlery. He felt for his work phone in his front left pocket, and in particular, the on button. Holding it down, he felt the mobile vibrating to life. As he carefully lowered himself to the ground, Jake removed the device from his pocket and passed it to Elizabeth, shielding her from view. He left it up to her and hoped she'd know what to do. As Charlie moved around the room, Jake cautioned a glance at the phone in her hand. It was open on Mamadou's contact details in his address book. He gave her a nod. It was all she needed. A moment later, she dialled.

Within seconds the person on the other end answered.

23

999

December 2, 2017, 12:44

Tim met Vince on the stairwell of the thirtieth floor. He was out of breath and his thighs ached.

'Seems like you need to exercise more, you fat shit,' Vince said as Tim lumbered up the final few steps.

'Fuck off. You need to stop wanking every night. Your right forearm's huge. Doing it too much isn't good for you.' Tim stopped at the top of the landing and doubled over, his chest heaving, trying to catch his breath.

'Asshole.' Vince shook Tim's hand. 'How is it in the lobby with all the cretins? They giving you any shit?'

'Nothing I can't handle. What about up here? BAU?'

'Boring as usual.' Vince nodded. 'Come on. Let's see what all this fuss is about.'

Tim stepped through the door first, took a detour towards the lifts, repeatedly pressed the buttons to see if they had started working since his arduous climb, and left, disappointed. The lift doors showed no signs of life, save for the creaking sound as the wires suspending them swayed in the wind descending through the top of the building.

Vince took the lead and rounded the corner into the control room.

'Jesus Christ!' he screamed, his voice echoing around the hallway.

Concerned, Tim turned and sprinted ten metres before skidding to a halt behind Vince. Rik's dead body was sprawled across the floor. Blood was pooling inches from Vince's feet, reflecting the overhead lights, looking almost demonic in the phosphorescent glow. Rik's eyes were open, dark and empty, staring into nothing. A thin dribble of blood trickled from a bullet hole in his forehead down to his chin, weaving across the contours of his face. His skin had turned the same colour as the lights above. And on the floor next to him was a gun.

Tim wanted to vomit but fought the rising bile in his stomach. The acid pained him as it descended back down his throat.

'What the—' Tim started. He was too overcome with fear and shock to speak. 'Who – what? Who did this?'

'I don't know.' Vince walked closer to Rik's body.

'What are you doing?'

'Trying to find out what the fuck is going on here.'

'Rik's been murdered, Vince. He's been shot several . . . like five or more fucking times.' Tim reached into his trouser pocket and produced his phone. 'I need to call the police.'

'No,' Vince said, turning to Tim, his expression stern and rigid. 'Not yet. Not until we've been inside the control room.'

'Why?'

Vince didn't respond; instead he walked through the glass door into the control room and out of sight.

'Fuck's sake!' Tim said to himself. He was torn. Should he stay, or follow Vince?

Tim couldn't look at Rik's body on the ground. It was too painful on his eyes. The two of them had been friends ever since Tim started. They had spent time with one another outside of work, too. Drinking at a nearby bar every Friday night, talking, getting to know each other, trying to relive their youth. It was the first time Tim had ever had a companion, and now he was gone.

Tim stepped into the control room after Vince. The first thing he noticed was the smell. Poison. Gas. Burning? Yes, but what, and why? He cautiously approached the control panel, paying attention to where he was stepping.

'Jesus . . .' was all he could manage. The knobs and dials and levers and switches had all corroded and dissolved in on themselves, leaving nothing but a mixture of metal and melted plastic.

Tim rotated his head to the rest of the room. The metal pipes running along the right-hand side of the wall were split in half.

'This is bad, Vince,' Tim said. 'This is really bad. I don't care what you say, I'm calling the police.'

Tim removed his phone from his pocket and dialled. He glanced at Vince, who was preoccupied with the pipes on the wall, his fingers running along the sawn-off metal.

'Hello, 999 – what's your emergency?'

24

Splash Back

December 2, 2017, 12:44

Ciara Reed felt sick. She hadn't felt like this in a long time. Her body was still feeling the effects of the night before. She and the rest of dispatch had been celebrating someone's leaving drinks, and she had less than two hours' sleep. Usually, as soon as her head hit the pillow, she would black out. But last night had been different. She had lain there, on her bed, staring into the ceiling. Her mind was awash with confusion and conflicting emotions. She didn't know what to do. She had missed her period. It was three weeks overdue, and her body was already beginning to feel strange. She knew who the father was, but was too afraid to tell him. It was her flatmate, and they had slept together after another night of drunken idiocy. It was just a fling, and it meant nothing. But there was someone else. The guy at work she had had a crush on for ages. Liam. He was the one she had wanted to be with ever since he joined the team a few months ago, but had always been too scared to do anything about. And then, last night, their relationship had progressed to the next level. They kissed. And she wanted everyone to know about it. She wanted to be with him, she was sure of it. But did she want to keep the baby? She didn't know. She was in her late thirties and was running out of time. And, if was she pregnant, should she tell the father? He had a right to know. He was a genuine, attentive man who, she knew, would do anything to support her.

All she wanted was someone she could love unconditionally – someone who would love her unconditionally, too. And she wasn't sure who offered the best solution.

Ciara stared blankly at the Metropolitan Police Service emblem on her computer. Her thoughts were brought to an abrupt stop by the sound of her telephone ringing in her ear.

'999, what's your emergency?' she said automatically, answering the phone.

'Someone's been shot! My friend. He's been shot several times and – and – we don't know what to do. Please! Help us!'

'What's happened, sir?' Ciara asked, struggling to focus.

'I just told you. Someone's been shot. They're dead! Send help quickly.'

'Sir, please calm down.' The man's voice was making the pain on the side of her head worse.

'I'm trying, but you're not listening to me.'

'I am, sir. I just need you to remain calm so I can help you.

What's your name?' She spoke softly, clearly and slowly. Not for the other person's benefit, but her own.

'Tim. My name is Tim. I'm one of the security guards.'

'Hi, Tim. My name is Ciara. Where are you a security guard, Tim?'

'The Shard.'

'Tim?' Ciara repeated. 'Rik's colleague?'

'Yes?' Tim said slowly. 'How do you know Rik?'

'I'm . . . I'm his housemate. Is Rik OK?' Ciara swallowed hard, fearing the worst.

'He's dead, Ciara. Someone came in and shot him at point blank.'

The world around her went quiet, and her body went cold. She stared at the screen, zoning out of her surroundings. The potential father of her child had just been murdered in cold blood. Now she would never get the chance to tell him.

'Ciara? Are you there?'

'I . . . I don't know what . . .'

'Please. You have to send help. The killer might still be in the building. The power's been cut. We can't do anything.'

Ciara kept zoning in and out. Her mind wandered to images of Rik, and to that night.

'Ciara!' Tim screamed in her ear, snapping her back to attention. 'Please, you have to help us! There are thousands of other people in this building. We need to get them out of here.'

'Yes. OK.' Ciara stopped. Something to her right caught her eye. Liam. After the news she had just received, she couldn't bear to look at him.

'Ciara!' Tim called again. 'Can you hear me?'

She hesitated. 'Is he really dead?'

'Yes, Ciara. I'm sorry, but he's gone. I didn't know you two were close.'

Ciara looked at the computer monitor. She moved the mouse on her screen. Her body shook with fear. As she hovered the cursor over the large button that muted the call – so she could organise an emergency response unit to the building – her wrist jolted and pressed the button next to it.

The line went dead, and Tim, one of Rik's colleagues, was gone. She had just hung up on him.

'Fuck,' she whispered.

She searched the call history on her computer, trying to find Tim's mobile number and dialled. The phone went to voicemail straight away. She hoped it was because Tim was trying 999 again, but a part of her knew that wasn't the case; there were no other phones ringing beside her or in the centre.

The feeling of nausea rose in her stomach and throat. She couldn't hold it in anymore. If she didn't go to the bathroom now, she would vomit on herself and her computer

Ciara rose, clutching her stomach, and sprinted towards the toilets. She vomited into the bowl of water, grimacing as the contents splashed back onto her face and arms.

25

Hurried

December 2, 2017, 12:46

The line went dead. Tim stared ahead into nothing.

'Hello?' he shouted into the microphone, his voice echoing around the landing. 'Hello?' When no response came, he said, 'I don't fucking believe it. She's gone.'

'Try again?' Vince suggested. 'Someone else will answer. They have to.'

Nodding, Tim dialled. Before the phone connected the call, the line went silent.

'Shit!' he said, crushing the mobile in his hands in frustration. 'My signal's just gone. I don't believe this.'

'Here, try mine.' Vince reached into his pocket, removed his phone, and said, 'No luck. Battery's dead. I knew I should have charged it last night.'

They were running out of options.

'What are we going to do?' Tim asked, ignoring the blinking lights overhead.

And then it struck him. It was simple and so obvious that it could have saved them plenty of time, but he had been so caught up in the furore of the moment, it'd slipped his mind.

'CCTV,' Tim said, thinking aloud. 'All we have to do is check the CCTV to find out what happened in here and who killed Rik.'

'Right, yeah. That makes sense. But – wait. Won't it all be erased? The power outage would have knackered everything.'

Tim shook his head. 'It backs up to the cloud, mate. That's where all this money's gone – instead of our pay cheques. If we can get one of the computers working, then we can access the footage. It shouldn't be an issue.'

'I hope you're right.'

So do I, Tim thought.

Vince spun on the spot, starting towards the stairwell. Before following him, Tim glanced behind. He held out a hand to stop Vince. 'Hey, hold up.' He pointed to the gun on the floor. 'Maybe we should take it. You know, just in case we need to defend ourselves.'

'Don't be stupid, Tim. You'll get your fingerprints all over the bloody thing. Besides, have you ever held one before? And no, shooting your little thirteen-year-old mates on a video game doesn't qualify.'

'Fine. Let's go.'

Vince started off first again, but Tim stayed back, rushed over to Rik's body, apologised as he picked up the gun, and put it inside his blazer pocket. Something told him it was a good idea. That he may need it in the near future. Even though he hoped he wouldn't.

He was out of breath by the time he caught up with Vince at the top of the stairs. Together they headed down.

The security room was located on the ground floor, hidden behind a series of doors and corridors. It was a small room, only large enough for two people, with a desk and two chairs at one end and a back wall covered in television monitors displaying both The Shard's internal and external CCTV footage. There was so much artificial light and infrared in the room that someone could only spend a couple of hours in there before having to pause to relax their eyes.

Tim entered the cramped space first. 'Seems the money hasn't been a waste,' he said, bringing the computer to life.

Feeling grateful that the systems were still active, Tim pulled one of the office chairs from the desk, sat on it and typed furiously on the keyboard. He located the correct camera angle on the thirtieth floor, rewound the video playback and waited.

A few seconds later, he watched the killer slice through the pipes on the wall, pour liquid over the control panel, and kill Rik in reverse. Tim paused the footage as soon as the killer turned in the camera's direction. The image was grainy and pixelated. Identifying the killer was going to be difficult, considering it could have been any one of the several hundred employees or civilians within The Shard at that particular time. Tim pressed the 'Print Screen' button and the printer at the other end of the room burst into life.

'Grab that for us, would you?' he said to Vince.

Vince turned and grabbed the piece of paper and examined it.

'I don't recognise him. Do you?'

Tim looked at the printout. 'Jesus. Yes,' he said, suddenly recalling the man with the striking green eyes. 'But I can't remember where from. His face is ringing a few alarms in my head.'

Tim typed on the keyboard again. This time he found the CCTV footage based at the entrance to The Shard, a few doors from where he was sat right now. He started the playback from 9 a.m. that morning. The beginning of his shift. The attacker must have got into the building somehow, and if it was under Tim's watch, he would never forgive himself.

As the tiny digits rolled past on the bottom left corner of the screen at triple speed, Tim leaned closer, his eyes inches away from the artificial light. He wasn't going to let the unnamed attacker slip away again.

By the time he reached 10:00 a.m., he'd lost hope. There was no one that even remotely resembled the blond-haired man with luminous green eyes.

Tim increased the speed. Tiny figures paced around the reception area like they were in some cartoon or video game. On the screen, he saw himself leaning over the desk and talking to the girls behind it, his arms gesticulating wildly. Then he moved back to his station by the X-ray machines, at the bottom of the image.

Tim stopped the playback.

A man dressed in casual clothes with a large gym bag dangling over his shoulder had just walked in behind a group of women. And then it all made sense. Tim remembered what had happened perfectly.

The man on the screen wandered up to the X-ray machines, his bag bouncing against his hip. He placed the bag on the conveyor belt and walked forward, away from view.

Tim knew the rest. He scanned the bag, saw the suspicious contents, lifted himself out of his seat and approached the man, asking him to open the bag. But he never got that far. The woman at the reception desk collapsed, and Tim watched it unfold again in front of his eyes: the woman fell to the ground and Tim rushed to her side, allowing the man with the bag to go through unattended.

It was his fault. He had let the killer enter the building and kill Rik and who knew how many others. The death toll could be greater than just one, and Tim was responsible for it.

But who was that man with the bag? Tim rewound the video and played it again. The man entered the building, removed an ID card from his pocket and scanned it through the turnstiles. *He's an employee. Someone who works in The Shard, who has access to all the floors, is now going around killing people.*

'Oh fuck,' Tim said, voicing his thoughts aloud.

'What?' Vince said.

Tim pointed to the figure on the screen and explained what had happened.

'How could you have been so stupid? What were you thinking?'

'I – I don't know. I wasn't. I was trying to help.'

'Do you know who he is? If he works here, then you must recognise him.'

Shaking his head, Tim said, 'How can I? This was my first shift down here in a long time.'

'Find out who he is. Check the sign-in records with the

time he entered.'

Tim spent the next few moments in silence as he called up the log of employees who had signed in at the exact time of 10:14. Only one hit came up.

'Charlie Paxman,' Tim said, reading the name aloud. 'That's who this son of a bitch is.'

'Good work,' Vince said, congratulating him with a pat on the back. 'In the meantime, we need to send this footage to the police somehow. Can we email it to them?'

'Maybe. I'd need to find an email address. The Wi-Fi's still running.'

'OK, do that. How far away is Scotland Yard?'

Tim hesitated. Searched his memory. 'Westminster. That's a good half-hour run, especially with your fitness. Why?'

'I'll get the Underground.'

'What about a cab?'

'Still too long. It could take them too long to find the email, or it might not have even sent by the time I get there. I'll show them the footage myself. Explain the situation. They'll have to listen. The Counter Terrorism department is there.'

'It's a Saturday,' Tim said.

'Terrorists and mad gunmen don't take fucking weekend breaks, Tim. This is the prime time to do it, when everyone is out and about with their families, not locked inside their offices.'

Tim nodded and reached into the drawer next to him, fished through the messy contents - pens, pencils, stapler, calculator, notepads, a hole punch - and found what he was looking for. He unclipped the USB stick's cap and plunged it into the computer. He stored the video footage of the man entering the building and killing Rik on the external drive, yanked it from the socket and handed the memory stick to Vince.

'Go on, then. Hurry!'

'What are you going to do?' Vince asked, squeezing the drive in his hands.

'Find out where Charlie Paxman is now. Put the place on lockdown so he can't get out. Come back here once you're done, OK? I might need you.'

Vince nodded before he turned his back on Tim and slammed the door, the noise of wood splintering and hurried footsteps echoed down the corridor.

26

Mum

December 2, 2017, 12:46

The cold reached past Mamadou's scarf, coat, jumper, shirt, and skin, and attacked his bones. It was nearly zero degrees, and the last place he wanted to be was outside. It had been four months since his mother's death - she'd died of a heart attack the same day as the 01/08 terrorist attacks - and he hadn't been to see her since. The only reason he had chosen to visit her grave now was because he was feeling guilty. Jake had been to visit Tyler every month, and he hadn't even bothered to visit his own mother. What sort of son did that make him? In fact, coming to her grave this once was already more than he'd ever visited his father's. Perhaps it was because the man he used to call Dad had left him when he was a child. Or perhaps it was because he used to assault and victimise both his mum and him. Either way, Mamadou didn't care. His father was where he deserved to be: six feet under. In the ground, where he was unable to harm or upset or torment anyone ever again.

His father's abuse had allowed Mamadou and his mother to grow closer, bonded by their victimhood; when Mamadou's father had finished abusing his mother, he would turn his attention, and anger, towards him. Sometimes it was a slap. Sometimes it was a beating with a chopping board. Sometimes it would be that his cigarette needed extinguishing, and Mamadou's arm was the ashtray.

Mamadou involuntarily touched his left arm, his fingers caressing the smooth lumps and bumps in his skin that still stung with the vivid and visceral memories of the past.

There was a lot of anger in his father, Mamadou knew that. And some of it had transferred to Mamadou and manifested itself during his twenties, when he was in a bar. The alcohol had been flowing all night, and an unfortunate drunkard had mentioned something to Mamadou about his mother. At that, he saw red and repeatedly beat the boy until he was unconscious and fighting for his life.

It took a lot of counselling after that. Anger management. Therapy. Breathing and stress-relief exercises, all designed to calm him and make him think of better, more relaxing times. But the problem was there weren't any. It was all shit.

There had been some light: the police service, which he inadvertently found himself falling into after graduating from Oxford University. Thanks to his mother. She put in his application, and within a few months he was a member of the domestic abuse team. He never questioned his mother's choice for him to be there, but deep down he knew. Deep down, he knew it was a cry for help, eighteen years too late. And an opportunity for him to make sure the same thing wouldn't happen to someone else. Since then he had never looked back.

He had a lot to be grateful to his mum for, and he wished now he had thanked her more often when he still could.

'Funny, isn't it, Mum?' Mamadou said, placing a bouquet of flowers by the grave. 'How we only realise the things we should have appreciated when it's too late.'

Mamadou didn't wait for a response before turning and heading back home. It was his day off and there was nothing else he had planned. Days like this were a rarity. In recent months the stresses and constant pressures of his job were beginning to fatigue him, in both body and mind. He was too committed. That's what Lori, his ex-wife, had told him. And now that she wasn't there, he finally realised what she meant. He had thought about throwing it all in. Packing it up and beginning a new life for himself. But the thought had been fleeting and was instantly dismissed. What would he do? He had nothing after the service. Nothing.

No, he wouldn't leave. He was too obsessed with the job to pack it in. There were people relying on him. And he had worked too hard to leave it all now. They wouldn't even be able to force him out.

Wrapping his scarf tighter around his neck, Mamadou left the graveyard. He'd just made it to the gate when his phone vibrated. It was work. He answered.

'What do you want, Tanner?'

Mamadou made it as far as the pavement when he realised something was wrong. Jake didn't speak, but Mamadou could hear something in the background. He sensed something serious was going on. An emergency. He listened intently. The voices on the other end had confirmed it for him. There had been shouts and screams, and then one person yelling above the noise, telling everyone else to do what he wanted.

Mamadou left the graveyard, sprinted up the street to his car, and stopped. Standing beside his unmarked X5 was a traffic warden, looking obnoxious and smug.

'Hey!' Mamadou said, running to the man placing a parking ticket underneath his windscreen wiper. 'What do you think you're doing?'

The warden looked at him. 'Giving you a ticket. What does it look like?'

'It looks like you're about to lose your fucking job, that's what.'

'You can't talk to me like that.'

'I can do whatever I want.' Mamadou removed his ID card from his back pocket and held it under the man's chin. 'And there's nothing you can do about *that*.'

The warden looked at his ID card ambivalently. 'Are you on duty?'

'What? What's that got to do with anything?'

'If you're on duty, and you're here for policing purposes, then you can appeal. If not, then you have to pay, just like the rest of us.'

He shook his head. 'You know what – I don't have time for this. Get out of my face.'

The man stepped to the side, onto the kerb. Mamadou barged past him. His hand caught the warden's arm and his phone dropped into a puddle, splashing ice-cold water onto his ankle.

'Oh fuck,' Mamadou said, staring at the phone in disbelief. He bent down, picked it up, rinsed the water off, and inspected it. It was damaged beyond repair. The Met's budget hadn't extended to water-resistant handsets, something he had campaigned for since the beginning of the year. 'Now look what you've done!'

'That wasn't me,' the warden replied defiantly.

'Yes, it was. You don't know what you've just done, do you?' Mamadou swung the car door wide into the oncoming traffic. He had every right to ask for the man's name and ID so when he got back to the office, he could file a complaint, but he was in a hurry, and he needed to speak with Frances to find out what was happening with Jake; there was no time.

Mamadou hopped into the car, started the engine, pulled out and drove towards New Scotland Yard. He was more than ten minutes away. He reached into his blazer pocket, produced his personal phone and dialled. Dame Frances Walken, assistant commissioner of the Metropolitan Police Service, answered on the second ring.

'AC.'

'Ma'am – it's Mamadou.'

'I know. I have caller ID. What are you calling me on the personal line for? What's happened to your work phone?'

'It's occupied.'

'What with?'

'It doesn't matter,' Mamadou snapped, tearing through traffic, the sound of the sirens blasting overhead. His patience was wearing thin, and the day hadn't even started yet.

'Excuse me?' Frances sounded vexed.

'I think we have an emergency. Where are you now?'

Frances hesitated. 'My office.'

'I thought it was your day off?'

'Things to do, Mamadou. What's the crisis?'

'I'll give you the details when I see you. I'm on my way now.'

Mamadou hung up the phone before Frances had a chance to argue.

27

Setting Examples

December 2, 2017, 12:48

Charlie Paxman lifted the gun in the air and aimed it at everyone in the crowd, starting from the right and moving along to the group of scientists at the other end. Charlie entered the pen, advancing towards Jake. Jake stuck his arms out to protect his girls behind him. He felt Elizabeth cling to his shoulder. Maisie dug her nails into his back in fear. Meanwhile, Ellie spread her arms around his waist.

Behind him he could hear Mamadou's voice on the phone, muffled underneath Elizabeth's dress and leg.

'What is all that screaming?' Mamadou said.

Jake and everyone else in the restaurant remained quiet. *Please don't hang up,* Jake thought to himself. *And please stop talking, you'll give us away.*

'I didn't want to have to do that!' Charlie shouted, pacing up and down the length of the tables and chairs Jake had overturned. 'But I had to set an example. If I let her get away, what sort of precedent would that have set? And I can't be having that. I can't allow any of you to leave here for the next few hours.'

Jake felt Elizabeth's grip release on his shoulder and stroke his right hip. He hazarded a glance down there and saw her cupping his mobile phone in her hands. *Clever girl,* Jake thought. She was making it easier for Mamadou to hear. Hopefully all the superintendent would need was to hear a few more seconds of Paxman screaming to realise something wasn't right, something terrible was happening on the thirty-second floor of The Shard.

'You – Edgar! And you – Filipe!' Charlie said, pointing to two men in tuxedos to Jake's right. 'I want you to pick her body up and put it on the other side of this table, so she can join the rest of you.'

Without hesitation, for fear of getting shot, the two men, who Jake recognised as members of the World Health Organisation party, jumped to their feet, hopped over the table, and picked up the dead body. Blood and bits of brain matter soiled one of the man's white shirt and hands. The men clambered back over the table. The one carrying the woman's legs caught his foot on the table leg and stumbled to the floor. The body landed in a heap as both men fell over like dominoes. Some within the crowd gasped in horror; Jake shielded Ellie and Maisie's eyes by keeping his daughters hidden behind his back.

A man at the other end of the room jumped to his feet and moved the two men aside. He bent down by the woman's head, cradled her neck in his hands, and began weeping. Soft sobs resonated through everyone around him. The two men returned to the rest of their party, sitting beside Jake and his own.

Charlie wandered over to the distraught man, knelt down, and said, 'It was her own fault. She was stupid and reckless. Shame, though. She did this population a great service. It's people like her the world needs more of.'

The man Jake presumed to be the woman's husband or partner kept his head down, rocking her dead body in his arms. He was in his own state of contemplation, which Jake knew he would never be able to escape.

Charlie stepped over to the other side of the barrier. 'Right, ladies and gentlemen,' he said. 'What I want you all to do now is remove your mobile phones and place them here by me.' Charlie pointed to a small opening in front of him inside the enclosure. 'One at a time, please. I know what world we live in today, so don't lie to me and tell me you don't have one, or that you left it at home, because I'll call bullshit and shoot you for it. That includes tablets as well for all those mindless children who spend their time using them. If anyone tries any funny business . . .'

Charlie gestured to the dead woman on the floor. Silence fell. He didn't need to say any more; everyone was painfully aware of the consequences.

Jake had a decision to make: act now or wait for another opportunity.

The dead woman's partner rose to his feet, fished out his phone from his trouser pocket and placed it on the ground. Gradually, one by one, everyone else in the row followed suit. Some surrendered one phone, while others gave up two, until eventually a small pile had built up inches away from the wall of furniture.

'Come on, Benjamin,' Charlie said as Benjamin Weiss stood. 'Don't be afraid. I won't hurt you. Yet.'

Benjamin dropped the phone to the floor. The screen cracked on the hard ground.

'What are you doing? I know you have two phones. I know all of you have two phones, including Marianne. Don't think you can protect her by hiding hers. Need I remind you what will happen if you double-cross me?'

Benjamin remained silent. Stared at Charlie. Shook his head. 'No, you don't.' There was fear in the man's high-pitched voice, as if someone had grabbed hold of his testicles and squeezed.

'Very well. Sit back down.'

It was Jake's turn. Keeping his eyes fixed on Charlie, he removed his personal phone, then swivelled to face Elizabeth and the rest of his party. He looked down at Elizabeth's hands, saw the phone he had given her, relaxed as he saw the call was still in progress, and mouthed to her, 'Keep it. Hide it.' Elizabeth nodded and hid the mobile underneath her dress. Aloud, Jake said, 'Give me your phone. Ellie, Maisie – can you pass Daddy your iPad? Alex, Ethan, everyone, yours as well, please. I'll take them all up.'

Seconds later, Jake held four mobiles and two tablets in his hand. He had given Maisie an instruction to keep hers on her person; Paxman wouldn't suspect her of having one – she was too young.

Just as he was about to stand and wander over to the pile of technology, he felt a cold, hard, blunt object pressed against his head.

Charlie's AK-47.

Jake froze. Any movement now would result in a bullet in the back of his head, and the shocked expressions of Elizabeth and his family would be the last thing he ever saw.

Charlie's free hand moved down Jake's back towards his trousers.

Fuck!

Charlie removed the steak knife from Jake's waistband. Jake held his breath. It felt like an integral part of him was missing. How could he have been so foolish as to forget that it would be on show? How could he so easily sacrifice whatever chance he had of saving everyone?

'What do we have here?' Charlie asked. 'Did you think you were going to stab me with this? Were you going to try to save these worthless human beings? Admirable.'

Jake didn't respond. He looked at his family and friends in front of him, his eyes darting between Elizabeth, Maisie, Ellie, Karen, Ellen, Ethan, Alex.

He had let them down.

He had let them all down. He was supposed to protect them. It was what he was paid to do. What sort of father was he if he couldn't protect his own children?

Charlie removed the blade from his pocket and pressed it against Jake's back. Now Charlie had a two-pronged attack. Gun and blade. From experience, Jake knew his odds of surviving an attack from either weapon were slim. One was close range, the other long. But when they were both pressed against his back, he stood no chance.

He would have to wait.

'Stand,' Charlie ordered, digging the blade deeper into his skin.

Jake rose, kept the phones and tablets in his hands, and sidestepped to the right. He gave one last look at Elizabeth that said, *I'll get you out of this. Keep the phone safe.*

Jake wandered to the spot where he needed to drop the devices to the floor. He bent down, piled them carefully on top of one another and waited. And waited.

'What are you doing?' Charlie asked. He released the knife against his back.

Element of surprise. Element of surprise, Jake repeated in his head, closing his eyes, preparing himself.

Jake's muscles went taut, his fists clenched, and he shifted his weight onto his front foot. He counted down.

Three.

'I'm talking to you. Don't ignore me.'

Two.

Charlie grabbed Jake's shoulder. He could feel the other man's sinewy fingers around his bones and muscles.

One.

Jake planted his right foot into the ground, swivelled on the soles of his feet, thrust himself upwards, taking Charlie by surprise, and buried his right fist into the man's solar plexus. Charlie doubled over. The gun fired a single burst. The bullets narrowly missed Jake's ear and carved into the ground. Rubble and pieces of granite spewed into the air.

Charlie swore out loud; Jake swore internally. That had been close. If he'd been two inches to the left, he would have been dead. Charlie stumbled backwards and Jake advanced, fist raised. As Jake swung a right hook, Charlie came to and shielded himself using his assault rifle. The sound - and pain - of metal on flesh made Jake grimace. His knuckles and thumb throbbed, and he felt a jolt under the strength of the weapon. He wondered if his hand was broken.

There was no time to stop and find out.

Jake clenched his other fist. It was a game of hand versus gun, and Jake knew the outcome if he didn't detain Charlie now.

Charlie caught him by surprise. A sweeping leg knocked Jake to the ground. Despite his malnourished and deprived look, Charlie was proving to be an experienced fighter. Something Jake hadn't give him credit for and now wished he had.

Jake landed on his back and felt the air from his lungs disappear. The back of his head cracked on the hard surface, and stars danced in his vision.

Rising to his knees, Jake grabbed hold of Charlie's legs, lifted him from the ground and threw him over to the other side of the table, the other side of the pen, as far away from everyone else as possible. The gun came loose from Charlie's grip and it rolled away towards the bar. In the background Jake could hear screams, but they were blocked out by the adrenaline that surged through his body and the sound of his pulsating heart.

Jake scrambled for the gun amidst the other tables and chairs in the restaurant. He grabbed a chair and threw it across the room behind him in a desperate attempt to catch the gun before Charlie recuperated and was back on his feet. But it was too late.

The gun was within an inch of Jake's grasp when he felt a foot kick him in the small of his back. The momentum sent him crashing forward through the restaurant. Shards of glass and cutlery rained down on him, slicing his skin. A table landed atop him. Delirious and disorientated, Jake staggered to his feet.

'Stop!' Charlie shouted in front of him. In his hands he held the gun.

Jake froze. Time seemed to stand still. Why hadn't Charlie pulled the trigger? Why hadn't he shot Jake just as easily as he had done that poor woman who'd tried to flee? What was holding him back?

Jake took in his surroundings. He was in the belly of the restaurant. The bar was to his left. A wall of glass to his right. Behind him: the exit. He was too far from his family now. There was no place left to run, except backwards.

Something over Charlie's shoulder caught Jake's eye.

'Don't shoot,' Jake said, holding his hands up. He tried to sound as afraid as possible. 'Please.'

Charlie opened his mouth. Before the words came out, a short but stocky bald man tackled Charlie to the ground. The waiter yelped. The impact of the blow set the gun off again, and a bullet collided into Jake's left shoulder as the two men crumpled to the ground.

A blinding pain swam around Jake's upper body, and a blanket of white and black draped over his vision, combined with the carousel of gold and brown of the restaurant. He screamed and stumbled backwards. Instinctively, his hand grabbed the wound. He was covered in blood. Jake watched the waiter and the man writhe on the floor, struggling, tussling for control. Jake wanted to step in, but he couldn't. He was afraid. Held back by an invisible force that kept him rooted to the spot.

Moshat. Adil. Tyler.

What was he going to do? He couldn't just stand there and wait to find out what would happen . . .

And then he had his answer. A single shot fired. A deafening silence fell on the restaurant. Charlie struggled to his feet. He had shot and killed the hero, the man who had saved Jake's life.

And now he's coming for me.

Without thinking, Jake turned on the spot and hobbled out of the restaurant. Gunfire rained down on him, narrowly avoiding his head and body. Spent casings dropped to the floor and echoed around the restaurant as he threw himself into the same door the other patrons had exited through – the same door Charlie had used to enter the restaurant before shooting it up. He forced it open, dived into the stairwell and started down the stairs.

Blood stained his clothes and the banisters. Droplets fell onto the floor and formed small puddles on the concrete.

Jake was alone and wounded. An innocent man had lost his life for the sake of Jake and everyone else. Jake had deserted his family and friends and left them with a crazed gunman. And to make things worse, he was having an anxiety attack. His head throbbed. The stairwell spun.

A few seconds later, he collapsed to the floor.

28

Explain

December 2, 2017, 12:53

Jake felt cold. Afraid. Weak. Claustrophobic. Out of breath. Like he was locked in a chamber tied to a chair, with the sound of a leaking pipe driving him insane. The stairwell spun as he stumbled down the steps. His stomach softened the blows, but it wasn't enough to avoid the pain in his shoulder. He landed on it hard and cried out. Blood seeped through the wound and by now, thanks to his exasperated breath and pumping heart, it had stained his left arm and the left side of his body.

He felt sick.

He needed to get help, and fast. He needed to staunch the bleeding before he lost too much. Jake remembered his training. Using his right hand and whatever strength he had left, he removed his coat and yanked the sleeve of his shirt from his left arm. He grimaced and gritted his teeth as the movement jerked the wound, sending another waterfall of blood down his bicep. Jake flung the garment over his left shoulder, grabbed it from under his armpit and tied a knot over the bullet hole. Tight. His fists clenched to fight the pain as he fought against the delirium of unconsciousness.

As soon as he finished, he scanned his surroundings. Where was he? Where could he go to get help? At the top of the stairs, a large number 32 had been painted on the wall. The Oblix restaurant. Elizabeth. Ellie. Maisie. They were all on the other side of that door, waiting for him, expecting him to protect them. He wasn't going to let them down. A part of him wanted to go back, to surrender to Charlie and his gun, just so he could be with them, by their sides. But he knew it was a bad idea. He was going to have to hope Elizabeth and the girls stayed out of trouble. Not knowing what was happening to them was going to kill him inside, he knew that. But there was no other option.

Jake stood still for a beat. Listened.

Silence. There was no encore of gunfire. No screams. Nothing.

Satisfied that his family was safe for the time being, Jake headed upstairs, his jacket dragging against his heels. He remembered the Shangri-La hotel was on the thirty-fourth floor. He had read the floor guide downstairs in the building's entrance as they arrived. *They'll have a first-aid kit. Come on.*

Jake staggered up the stairs, growing more and more fatigued as he climbed higher. He arrived at the door to the thirty-fourth floor. Using all his strength, Jake leaned into it, hoping it would give way and allow him entry. It didn't. After multiple attempts, he slammed his fists on the door, angry and frustrated. Less than a second later, it opened. A confused civilian stood on the other side, terrified at the sight of Jake's blood-covered body. Jake ignored him and stumbled into the lobby.

The Shangri-La hotel was busy. Clients carrying suitcases meandered along the marble flooring. Reception staff and bellboys tailed one another, sprinting across the entrance, pandering to their customers' every need. There was a certain atmosphere that Jake enjoyed about hotels. He usually felt comfortable in one because it was busy, satisfying his need to be doing something. It relaxed him, knowing the world was constantly in motion. That everything was as it should be.

Today's trip to a hotel, however, was different.

With blood dripping down his arm and onto the concrete, Jake stopped at the reception desk. A man dressed in shirt and waistcoat, his hair slicked back and greased like it had been dipped in an industrial tub of hair gel, looked at him aghast. His mouth opened and his eyes widened; the lines on his forehead increased.

'Oh my God,' was all the man could manage. Jake looked at the name badge on the man's breast pocket.

'Nathan – I need a first-aid kit and a first-aid room if you have one. This is an emergency. I'm a police officer,' Jake said, too tired to show his ID card to the young man in front of him.

Nathan looked around him desperately. He dropped to his knees and fumbled for a first-aid kit. When he popped back up his hands were empty.

'I – there's nothing here,' Nathan said, his voice weak.

'Then find something.' Jake winced in pain. His patience was growing thin.

'Yes. Right. I'll . . . I'll be right – hang on!'

Nathan's colleague, someone else dressed in the same uniform, approached them. In her hand she held a folder containing documents and, by the sound it made when she dropped it to the floor, something made of glass.

'Oh my God,' she said as if she were a carbon copy of Nathan.

'Kayla,' Jake said, reading her name tag. 'Calm down. I just need a first-aid kit and some alcohol. That's all. And I need someone to call the police. Let them know there's been an attack in the Oblix restaurant. Tell them it's urgent. Tell them DC Tanner requested immediate backup.'

Kayla nodded, absorbing the information. 'Do you need an ambulance?'

'I don't, but others will. All I need is a first-aid kit – do you know where it is?'

Kayla turned to Nathan and said, 'Call the police. I'll take him to the medical room.' She faced Jake. 'Follow me.'

They sped across to the other side of the lobby, past a lounge area where hotel guests were sitting, and through a nearby door. They entered a large hospital-white corridor. Jake looked down the other end. It was so far away, and as he stood there, the walls and hallway began to pulsate, as if it were a beating vein in the building's body.

Jake's legs felt weak. He was losing a lot of blood, and soon he was going to pass out.

'Sir?' Kayla asked, grabbing his arms. There was no pain when she touched him. 'Sir? Are you OK?'

'Hurry,' Jake told her. There was no time to waste by

speaking in full, coherent sentences.

With fear and uncertainty in her eyes, she extended her hand. Jake took it. Squeezing his fingers, Kayla dragged him down the corridor. They stopped at a set of double doors. She led him into an emergency first-aid room. Two hospital beds were in the middle, with medical equipment either side. Jake assumed this was the place to go if someone in the seventy-plus storey building suffered an injury or had a cardiac arrest.

'Tweezers. Bandages. Alcohol,' Jake said, in between breaths. His eyes scanned the room in search of the objects. And then one last item came to mind. 'A towel.'

Kayla looked at him perplexed, as if to say, *What do you need one of those for?*

Jake ignored the look she gave him and searched the right-hand side of the room while Kayla searched the left. Jake opened drawers, cupboards, trays, plunged his hand inside them and knocked everything out. He was getting dizzier by the second. If he didn't stop the bleeding and remove what was left of the bullet, he was going to pass out for sure.

Yes! There it was. The alcohol solution and tweezers. Now all he needed was a bandage and a towel. Jake turned around to find Kayla holding those items in her hands.

'Thank you,' he mumbled.

Moving across the room, Jake sat down, landed with a heavy thud, and placed the towel in his mouth. Using his bloodied fingers, Jake tried to undo the knot he had made using his sleeve, but he was too weak. Kayla helped. She removed the sleeve from his shoulder and opened the packet of bandages. Jake unscrewed the lid from the alcohol solution and doused the wound with it. An immense pain consumed his body, made it tingle, shake. He screamed into the towel, his teeth biting hard on the fabric until his jaw hurt. Waves of nausea battered him like a tidal surge against a cliff face. His head lulled back and forth.

Kayla tapped him on the face and shoulder repeatedly.

'Sir? Sir?' Her voice was plagued with distress. 'Come on. Stay awake.'

Consciousness returned. Jake bolted upright. He wiped the blood clean from his shoulder, then thumbed inside the wound to locate the bullet. But it wasn't there. It never had been. It was just a flesh wound – the bullet had only penetrated the top of his trapezoid, chipping away some of his flesh and bone. It had felt more painful and serious than it was.

Without wasting any time, Jake dressed the wound with a bandage and wrapped it tightly. The pain subsided, but it still throbbed. Jake eased back, his chest heaving.

Delirious and in shock, he mumbled, 'Phone.'

There was no answer. He looked up; Kayla had left him and was at the other side of the room, pouring him a glass of water. She returned and handed it to him.

'You're not going anywhere just yet. Drink.' Kayla forced the cup to Jake's mouth.

The water descended his throat and cooled it. It sent a chilling sensation across his entire body. Jake downed it in one.

Feeling invigorated, he started out of his chair.

Kayla pushed him back down.

'No. You're staying here. You can't go anywhere yet. What happened?'

Jake shook his head. 'Phone first. Explain second.'

29

Only Time Will Tell

December 2, 2017, 12:53

Elizabeth's heart pounded. Her body went into a hot flush and she felt faint. She had just watched her husband get shot in the shoulder. Her mouth was open, but nothing came out. A fear so maternal and loving paralysed her. Behind her, clasping tightly against her hips, were Maisie and Ellie. Both sobbed into Elizabeth's dress.

She sat there evaluating Jake's actions. He had endangered all their lives. He had run away, and now no one was there to protect them. Of course, there was everyone else in the restaurant, but none of them had taken a stand yet, so why would they now? And they had already seen what would happen to someone when they did. There was no chance of that happening.

No – Maisie and Ellie were easy targets, and now she would have to protect them. The heavily pregnant mother. The mother who could barely sit down for a second before everything hurt. The mother who needed to pee every five minutes.

Charlie, the deranged waiter, returned. His lip and nose were bloody. He walked with a slight limp and was out of breath. The afternoon light reflected off his face and cast ominous shadows over his cheeks that danced up and down as his chest heaved with every breath.

As Charlie came to a stop, there was a loud thud. Behind the overturned tables, it was difficult for Elizabeth to gauge what had caused it. But it didn't take her long to work out. Charlie bent down, grabbed the bald man by the collar and dragged his body along the length of the tables, around the side and into the pen next to the pile of phones. Everybody screamed. Elizabeth stared in horror.

She glanced down at her legs, lifted her dress slightly and looked at the ground. The phone was still there. But Mamadou's name and number had gone. Elizabeth froze. The world around her went blank. Her only contact with the outside had disappeared.

She closed her eyes. Prayed that Jake or Mamadou or someone else would come to their rescue. How long would that take? She didn't know, but she couldn't afford to wait. Their lives were hanging in the balance, at the whim of this maniac. She was going to have to do something. Anything.

Jake once told her it was important to get the person on the other end of a gun talking. It relaxed them, he said. Calmed them.

Sheltering the girls behind her, Elizabeth cleared her

throat. 'Why are you doing this?'

Charlie stopped dead.

'What did you say?' he asked her.

'Why are you doing this? None of these people here have done anything to hurt you.'

Charlie chuckled. 'Wrong,' he said. He walked over to her. 'Many of the people in this room have betrayed me in a former life. And now they're going to pay the price. All of them. Not to mention your husband – he assaulted me, and if I'm not mistaken, he's the one responsible for causing this.' Charlie pointed to his nose and mouth. His teeth were stained red with blood as he smiled.

Elizabeth said nothing.

'Now that he's gone, what does that mean for you? Does it mean I should get my revenge on you, your friends, or the rest of your family?' Charlie peered at either side of Elizabeth.

Another maternal instinct overcame her, and she pushed Ellie and Maisie away with her arms towards Karen.

'Don't you dare touch them.'

'Or what?' Charlie grimaced again.

'I'll make you suffer a painful and horrible death. No one touches my children and gets away with it. They've tried and failed in the past.'

'Scary. Really scary. You should be an actress.'

Elizabeth opened her mouth to speak, but no words came out.

Before she could do anything, the floor vibrated, and the phone rubbed against her thigh. She looked down into her lap. The small screen cast a vague rectangular shape underneath the dress. Someone was trying to ring her. And they had just blown her cover.

Charlie looked at her crotch. His eyes widened. He grabbed for the phone and observed it in his hand. His pupils dilated. He dropped the phone to the ground, stood up and stamped on it. The phone shattered into a dozen pieces, the damage irrevocable.

'Who the fuck is Mamadou? How dare you think you could outsmart me!' Charlie bent down to Elizabeth's level, slapped her across the cheek with the back of his hand and grabbed her by the hair. Elizabeth screamed as her hair was ripped from her scalp. She had no other choice but to oblige and follow him to her feet, holding her stomach as she was lifted into the air, ignoring the pressure her bladder placed on her body.

'Charlie!' a voice to Elizabeth's right shouted. It came from the booths. 'Stop this at once!'

As if on cue, Charlie stopped. Elizabeth had her eyes closed; the pain was too much. But in that moment, she could feel Charlie's grip around her hair loosen.

Opening her eyes, Elizabeth searched the crowd for the source of support. Whoever it was had just saved her from potential death. She recognised her as the woman who was sat at the table next to them during lunch.

Charlie laughed. It was evil, insane, insidious. It echoed around the restaurant. He threw Elizabeth to the ground sideways, and she landed on the floor by her daughters' feet, her hands absorbing most of the impact. She clambered over to them and huddled them against her chest, ignoring the pain in her stomach. Her cheek throbbed as the blood rushed to it. It was over. Now Mamadou and everyone else back at Counter Terrorism Command would be stranded with no one to contact.

'Marianne,' Charlie began, moving to the wall on the right, 'that used to work before. It won't anymore.'

Marianne shifted herself to her feet. As she left the protection of her colleagues, she swatted away their hands that were trying to hold her back.

'Please, stop. Put the gun down. I'm sure there's something we can do. I'm sure there's something we can discuss. Give us some time and we can work it out. All of us.'

'I wish that were true.'

'Why isn't it?'

'Because this needs to be done, Marianne. It has to take place.'

'Why?'

'Because I need you to listen. You and everyone else who used to call themselves my colleagues. The cunts who betrayed me.' Charlie lifted the weapon. Elizabeth wasn't sure if her eyes betrayed her, but she was certain she saw a thin watery film form over Charlie's eyes. 'Now, get the fuck back down before I shoot you.'

Marianne inched backward, raising her hands in defence.

'Your time will come, Marianne. As will all of yours!' Charlie addressed the rest of the members of the World Health Organisation, holding the gun out with his wide-open arms. 'Only time - our greatest friend - will tell us when.'

30

In Safe Hands

December 2, 2017, 12:55

Ciara needed fresh air urgently. She needed to clear her head and make sure she was capable of functioning properly. She had just spent the last ten minutes in the bathroom, filling the toilet with the contents of her stomach. Her body and throat ached, and every time she tried to inhale, the smell made her feel worse. She had never seen so much of her stomach lining. After she had finished, she had spoken with her manager, explained the situation and organised an emergency response team to The Shard. She had decided to skip the fact that the person who had been killed was her housemate.

The cold air outside Scotland Yard was refreshing, and it helped calm her down. In the distance, conquering over everything else in the skyline, was The Shard. She thought of

Rik. How they had only spoken with one another last night. How he had told her to have a nice time and to be safe. She thought of how she was never going to see him again, and she was hit by a wall of grief. A part of her wanted to smoke to alleviate the stress, to take her mind off everything. The other part told her not to go anywhere near that filthy habit that had dominated her life for so many years – the yellow-stained teeth and hands, the painful cough. She knew it would be bad for the baby, but she didn't care right now. She needed to clear her head.

She reached for the emergency pack of cigarettes that she had kept in her desk. She rolled the cigarette in her hand and contemplated. The smell rose up her nostrils. She sniffed hard, already feeling the effects of the nicotine on her brain.

A loud noise in front of her distracted her. A man had just fallen to the ground in front of her, colliding with a runner and knocking both of them to their hands and knees.

'Oh my God,' she said, pocketing the cigarettes in her loose jacket and rushing to them.

She bent down to the ground and dropped her coat on the concrete. She hadn't been wearing it. She was too hot.

'Are you OK?' she asked the well-dressed man, who looked vaguely familiar. Beside her, another woman who had been on her cigarette break tended to the runner. 'Are you hurt?'

'No. I'm fine,' he said, shoving her from him. 'You can get off me now.'

Ciara did as she was told, deciding it was against her better judgement to offer more aid to the man. He was clearly pissed off about something, and she was in no fit mental state to get herself involved in an altercation.

The man jumped to his feet. Ciara joined him, picking up her coat as she went, placing it under her armpit. As she was able to ask for a final time if he was OK, two police officers arrived.

'Where is it?' the man asked, frantically frisking his chest and pockets and jeans. 'Where's it gone?'

Ciara took that as her cue to leave.

Vince's heart leapt into his mouth.

The memory stick – it was gone. The only thing he needed to be in charge of had disappeared. Where was it? He looked to the ground, searching the dense mass of black concrete and puddles. A forest of legs and shoes were in the way. He crouched down, placing his hands and knees on the concrete, and crawled around the area.

It was no use. It was nowhere to be seen.

'You all right, mate?' another person asked him. This time it was a police officer, dressed in uniform.

A police officer!

'Thank God!' Vince said, becoming hysterical. 'Help me. I've lost something. A memory stick. It was in my hand and then I fell over. I can't find it.'

'What was on it?'

'A video. A video of a man shooting someone inside The Shard. Look' – Vince pointed towards the tallest building in the skyline – 'there's a terrorist attack going on over there. You have to help me. I was trying to deliver the memory stick, but—'

The officer's hand silenced Vince.

'Calm down, sir. I need you to speak slowly.'

'There's a man. Inside The Shard. Killing people. No time.'

'And what was on this memory stick you had?' the officer to Vince's left said, making notes in his small pocket notebook. Passers-by shot Vince menacing and confused looks as they strolled past, keeping well clear of the scene he was causing.

'A video of one of the employees shooting my colleague in the head.' Vince was out of breath. He was dumbfounded. Why was it taking so long for them to understand what he was saying?

'And the supposed shooting took place in the building itself?'

Annoyed, feeling like they were going around in circles and getting nowhere, Vince slapped the notebook from the officer's hand. It fell to the floor and landed in a puddle. Water climbed up the pages and the ink ran.

For a moment, nothing happened. The officer looked at the sodden notebook, and then at Vince, his expression shocked.

Then everything changed.

Vince shoved the officer nearest to him; the man staggered back.

'Come on, we have to go! We have to let someone—'

Before Vince was able to finish his sentence, both officers grabbed one of his hands each, twisted them behind his back, and cuffed them.

'You're not going anywhere,' the officer Vince had just pushed said. 'You just assaulted a police officer, and you're a danger to the public. You're under arrest. You do not have to say anything . . .'

One of the officers – Vince didn't know which; he was too bewildered to recognise the distinctive speech inflections – told him his rights and carried him into the back of a police vehicle and drove to the nearest station at Charing Cross.

As they drove further and further away from Scotland Yard, the gravity of what Vince had just done dawned on him. The ramifications of his actions. What would happen now? He wasn't thinking properly. He wasn't acting normally. And how he had no memory stick. No evidence to prove he wasn't insane. No way of contacting Tim and letting him know he was in the back of a police car on the way to a detention. No way of saving the rest of the people in the building.

Entering Charing Cross Police Station, his body welcoming the warm air inside, he couldn't help but feel responsible for anything that may happen to Tim. He should have just stayed in The Shard and helped his friend from the beginning. Leaving for Scotland Yard was a terrible decision.

Vincent couldn't help but feel that the woman who had helped him to his feet looked familiar.

Like a friend of Rik's he had met a while back.

And that she might have taken the memory stick.

Vince hoped it was in safe hands, wherever it was.

31

Busted

December 2, 2017, 12:56

Monitoring and combating terrorism in the UK were twenty-four-hour operations. The atmosphere inside Room 1430 was buzzing. The hours and shifts were gruelling, and in the aftermath of Operation Tightrope, employees were worked to the bone, with only sixty-one hours a week spare time they could spend with friends and family. For Mamadou, it seldom made a difference; he had no one to go to. His wife had left just over a year ago and he was still dealing with the consequences, so he spent many of those sixty-one hours in the office, examining evidence and gathering intelligence on known terrorists around the country. It offered him the perfect opportunity to escape the grief and mourning.

Mamadou knocked on the assistant commissioner's office

door on the fifth floor in Scotland Yard. It opened two seconds later. Before him was the second in command of Specialist Operations within the Metropolitan Police Service. She had more power in her little toe than he did in his entire body. She was his superior, and for the past twenty-two years they'd been working together – albeit in different capacities – they had always maintained a strictly professional relationship. They both worked like dogs and had signed their souls to the service.

'Mamadou.' Frances nodded and stepped aside to allow him to enter.

'Frances.' Mamadou sat down. In his hands he held both of his mobile phones.

'This better be quick,' Frances said, sitting opposite him on the other side of the desk. 'What's the issue?'

'I'm worried about Tanner. I think he's in danger.'

'Of himself?'

What? 'No.' Mamadou shook his head. 'Yesterday he told me he was going to The Shard. He should be there still, but he called me on my work phone . . .'

'And . . . ?'

Mamadou placed the damaged phone on the table. 'He didn't say anything, but I could hear noises. Shouts. Screams.'

The assistant commissioner hesitated. 'Perhaps he pocket-dialled you without realising it.'

'That doesn't explain the screaming.'

'I don't know. Maybe it's the other people around him – maybe they're afraid of heights. Or they were enjoying a good joke, and they were just being loud. I'm sure there's a perfectly good explanation for it.' Frances stared at Mamadou, her eyes unrelenting, her derision apparent in her expression.

'No, Frances. It's not like that. There's something more sinister going on here. We need to work out what it is—'

'Mamadou – I'm busy. I don't have time for speculation.'

'Gunshots.'

'Excuse me?'

'I heard gunshots. When you've been in the service as long as us, you learn what they all sound like. I think it was the sound of an AK-47,' Mamadou said.

'Are you serious?' Frances asked, her brow furrowed. 'I find it hard to believe someone would be able to storm through the skyscraper with a machine gun undetected! The Shard has one of the highest levels of security in the country.'

Evidently not.

'What is it you want me to do?' Frances asked. 'Shouldn't you be speaking with Simon?'

Mamadou fell silent. 'I'd rather not.'

Shaking her head, Frances said, 'For heaven's sake, Mamadou. The two of you need to put your personal differences aside.'

'I'm not promising anything.'

Frances looked at her computer, clicked a few buttons, and said, 'I have a meeting in ten minutes. I'll go with you to speak with Simon – he's working at the moment – but if the discussion runs over that, then you're on your own.'

Mamadou nodded. 'Thank you.'

Frances rose out of her chair and glided to the door in silence. They headed to the fourteenth floor of New Scotland Yard, to Mamadou's second home. Simon's office was at the far left corner of the room, nearest to the canteen. Frances entered without knocking. Simon was busy typing away into his computer.

'Ma'am,' Simon said, startled. 'Is everything OK?'

'Not quite. Mamadou is concerned for DC Tanner's safety. He thinks something is going on at The Shard.'

'What sort of thing? Concert? Musical?' Simon shot Mamadou a scowl, and Mamadou returned it with just as much malevolence.

'No. A terrorist attack.'

Simon's ears perked up. 'Explain.'

Mamadou repeated what he had told Frances.

'Are you willing to entertain this, Simon? I have a meeting with the Home Secretary I need to attend.'

'What? Oh, yes. Come on, let's get the team on it.' Simon started out of his chair, barged past Mamadou, and headed to the focal point of the operation room. The fluorescent light from the wall of televisions cast a dark shadow over his body. 'Can I have everyone's attention, please? We think we may have a situation with Tanner.'

Simon repeated what Mamadou had told him.

'I want red team to confirm the validity of this claim. See if there's anything that's been reported to 999. Speak with the temporary switchboard downstairs and ask around the borough. That'll be the first port of call. If there is something going on up there, someone in that building must have called it in. If that doesn't work, then I want green team to request the CCTV footage from in and around The Shard. That way we'll be able to determine precisely what the threat is. As soon as one of you has something, let me know.'

At once, everybody dipped behind their computer screens and set to work. Frances checked her watch, looked to Mamadou, nodded, then headed off back towards her office.

Mamadou started towards the kitchen area when he heard someone calling his name.

It was Simon.

Reluctantly, Mamadou stopped mid-step. 'What?'

'A word. My office.' Simon shouldered past him again and left his office door open for Mamadou to follow him through.

'What do you want?' Mamadou asked, leaving the door open. There was no way he was going to spend any longer than necessary in this room.

'I want to talk about Jake's exploits.'

Mamadou swallowed deeply, felt his larynx bounce up and down in his throat, and stretched his shoulders backward.

'What exploits?'

'I know about his little adventure the other day.'

'What adventure?'

'Don't play dumb with me.'

'I'm not.'

'Yes, you are.'

'I don't know what you're talking about. What did he do?'

'Obtained a warrant to search the premises of Reliance Autos.'

'Did he? Seems unlike Jake.'

'Perhaps because it's so unlike him, it's the perfect excuse. The perfect cover. Perfect opportunity to get away with it.'

Mamadou nodded. 'Last time I checked there wasn't anything wrong with obtaining a warrant. I assume he progressed it through the various channels.'

Simon slammed his fist on the table. 'Mamadou, for fuck's sake, take this seriously. This is a very serious matter. You and he both need to be worried about what's going to happen next.'

'And what's that?'

'If I think there's been some unlawful wrongdoing, then an investigation is most likely going to be launched by the directorate of professional standards. Maybe the IPCC if it escalates that far. I hope you understand that this is a big problem, Mamadou.'

'Do you have any evidence?' Mamadou asked, knowing full well that Simon didn't; after Mamadou had had his meeting with Jake, he had found the phone recording of Jake and Lucy's conversation, and erased it from the records.

Simon ignored the question and moved on. 'It could seriously damage Jake's reputation, yours, mine – everyone's. Don't you care? He's a member of your team and you will face the consequences of your inaction as much as he.'

Mamadou leaned forward, resting his palms on the table. 'Did you face the consequences of your actions?'

'Excuse me?' Simon said, taken aback.

Mamadou repeated himself.

'Look – what happened with Lori was a mistake. I should never have done what I did. It will live with me for the rest of my life. But you can't blame me forever. She was the one who decided she didn't love you anymore.'

'No thanks to you.'

'I only progressed her decision. I'm only responsible for her relapse, nothing else. Besides, that's a personal matter, and this is work. You need to forget about it. It was eighteen months ago.'

'How can I? What you did lives with me every day. Every time I see your face, I want to destroy it. Every time I think of her, I think of you. The images I have in my mind of finding her like that on the bed, nearly overdosed like that in my own home, will haunt me forever. And what have you done about it? What's happened to you? Nothing. So, don't you fucking talk to me about facing the consequences of my actions. You never faced yours. You've still got your cushy job, your cushy pay cheque, your cushy fucking wife and kids at home. And I've got nothing. I'll never forgive you.'

'I'm not asking you to. I'm asking you to act professionally.'

Mamadou chuckled. At first it started soft, but then, as he found it funnier and funnier, his pitch amplified throughout the room. 'You fucking hypocrite. I think you need to take a leaf out of your own book.'

'What are you talking about?'

'Does your wife know you're here on your day off?'

Simon's face dropped. His body became tense. 'Yes, why?'

'What reason did you give her?'

'I don't see how it's any of your concern.'

'I'm making it my concern, Simon. Answer my question.'

'I told her there was stuff that needed doing.'

'So, it's safe to assume she doesn't know the real reason you're here when you're not scheduled to be?'

'What real reason are you talking about?' Simon's voice went soft. He shifted in his chair, obviously growing more uncomfortable with each passing second.

'How do you think she'd feel if she found out? The kids as well? They'd be distraught, upset. That their daddy was a drug addict and an adulterer. Imagine how ashamed they'd feel after they learned their daddy was having an affair with someone at work.'

'What? How? How?' Simon was blabbering like a child. He had just given away his hand and lost.

For the past few weeks Mamadou had noticed the deputy assistant commissioner acting suspiciously around the office. Coming in on his days off, disappearing to the toilet frequently. At first, he thought Simon was experiencing marital issues at home. Arguments, disagreements - the lot. Either that or he had some sort of infection. At one point, Mamadou believed Simon had been kicked out of the house; he spent the night in his office and washed in the gym showers.

But then Mamadou had found the real reason Simon Ashdown was spending so much extra time at work. DCI Ashley Rivers - one of Jake's former colleagues from when he worked in the Criminal Investigation Department. He had stumbled across them one evening. Everyone else in the office had left for the night, and on his way out, Mamadou saw Ashley and Simon enter the bathroom cubicles on the fourteenth floor. That was when he knew.

Mamadou smiled at Simon, said nothing, and left the room. He didn't need to do or say anything more.

If Simon knew what was good for him, he would leave Jake's exploits alone.

32

One Done

December 2, 2017, 12:57

It was time to act. Everyone inside The Shard's reception area was counting on him for answers, and he couldn't give them if he continued to shy away in the CCTV room. Even if he didn't know the answers, he would still help. It was his duty.

Tim stepped out of his chair and exited the room. When he arrived at the reception desk, he was greeted by a barrage of questions and shouting men and women. Employees from the companies within the offices in the floors above had accumulated and were waiting for him.

'What's going on?' one of them pestered.

'We've lost all communications internally and externally. We demand to know what is happening!' screamed another.

Tim waded through the sea of people. He could feel their

scathing looks boring into him, as if it were his fault the building's power had gone. Adrenaline, combined with unprecedented fear, surged through him.

'Could I please have your attention?' Tim climbed atop counter, clapping his hands together. He hoped it would signal for everyone to stop talking. His voice carried through the large space. 'I appreciate and understand your concern, however, I need you all to listen to me. The sudden electrical outage has been caused by a power cut. I do not know when, or if, the power will return. The situation is a little more complicated than we first thought, so if you could please evacuate the building as soon as possible, that would be great.'

'What are you talking about?' a man wearing an expensive suit asked. 'Why do we have to evacuate if it's just a power cut? That's ridiculous.'

Tim ignored the remark and looked around him. No one moved. No one was doing what he told them. He didn't want to tell them the real reason they all needed to evacuate, that there was a maniac with a gun in the building who was going around shooting people. That if they did nothing, they could be next.

An idea popped into his head. The gun. The gun in his pocket. That was the answer. That was how he was going to evacuate the reception.

Tim's breathing increased. He'd never been under this much pressure before. He reached into his pocket, gripped the handgun that had been used to kill Rik, removed it from his blazer and held it triumphantly in the air. Almost as soon as it was on full show, the entire room panicked and bolted out of the building. The revolving doors moved at an all-time high, and within thirty seconds, the lobby was empty.

Placing the gun against his chest in his breast pocket, Tim jumped down from the counter, and walked towards the stairwell. The gravity of what he had just done didn't kick in immediately. It would be a few minutes before it did.

As he climbed the steps, satisfied that he had done the right thing, a depressing thought occurred to him: one floor done, another seventy to go.

33

Precious

December 2, 2017, 12:57

Charlie Paxman felt alive. The events of the past thirty minutes had felt like a reawakening in his soul. For too long, he had been depressed, moping around, resenting everyone and everything around him. Doing nothing about it all.

But now he was finally doing something.

Inside, he laughed. It had been so easy. Those people hadn't deserved to die. He was sure they were innocent human beings. But they had needed to. They stood in his way and he needed to make a statement. Needed to let everyone else know not to fuck with him, that he was serious about seeing his mission through to the end. That he was looking forward to slaughtering those who had wronged him.

So long as no one else gets in the way.

Charlie cleared his throat. It was his time to tell all the frightened men, women and children a story. And he was going to tell it as truthfully as possible.

'Listen up,' he began, 'there are a few things you all need to understand. In a previous life I was a scientist. In fact, all my life I've been a scientist, dedicated to the research of human genetics. Recently, I was part of a team that worked towards the prevention of noncommunicable diseases. And you see, what I learned was that the population on this earth suffers from one fundamental flaw.' Charlie hesitated for maximum effect. 'There are too many of us. It's as simple as that. This planet cannot function with so many individuals reducing its resources at an increasingly alarming rate.

'The human species is on the brink of destruction. Thanks to nothing other than itself. And if we do nothing about it, then we will all suffer the consequences. That's what I aimed to combat at the World Health Organisation. Yes – that's right. Some of these people in front of you are my former colleagues.' Charlie waved the gun at Benjamin, Marianne and everyone else from the WHO. 'And some of them have pretended not to know me ever since I was forced out of the organisation nine months ago by my old pal, Benjamin Weiss, and the woman I considered to be the mother I should have had, Marianne.

'They saw me as a threat to their careers, and the company. They didn't like what I was doing, so they forced me out. I was just a scapegoat, so they could make themselves look good. And I will never forgive them.' Charlie paused. His throat was dry. He needed a drink.

Charlie turned, went behind the bar and poured himself some tap water. The water felt good – so much so, he drank three glasses consecutively. Killing people was thirsty work.

'Can we have some of that?' a voice from the crowd of distressed hostages said, taking him by surprise. He hadn't been expecting someone to address him so soon.

Charlie craned his neck in search of the person who had spoken. The brunette woman. The one who was sat next to Jake's wife. In the middle of the crowd. She was the one who had spoken out of turn.

'Excuse me?' Charlie asked, placing the glass down on the bar.

The woman adjusted herself on her knees.

'I'm not asking for me. I'm asking for her.' The brunette pointed to the blonde, the wife. 'She's pregnant. She needs to keep herself hydrated and away from as much stress as possible.'

Pregnant. The word sent alarm bells ringing inside his head.

'Why?' he asked.

The brunette woman's face looked abashed. 'Excuse me? Why does she need water? I've just told you. She's pregnant.'

Charlie shook his head. 'No. Why is she pregnant?'

'What?' the wife asked.

'Why are you pregnant? Have you not got enough children? Have you not put this country under enough strain with your two offspring already?' Charlie said. He could feel the excitement building within him. There was nothing more pertinent to his cause than a pregnant woman, and this one just so happened to be the partner of the man who'd attacked him. Slowly, he wandered towards the two women. Addressing the pregnant woman again, he said, 'What is your name?'

'Melissa,' the woman said quickly. Too quickly. As if rehearsed.

'Don't lie to me.'

'I'm not.'

Turning to face the brunette, he said, 'What is your name?'

'Ka – I mean Jenna.'

Classic, Charlie thought to himself. One of them knows what she's doing, while the other has no clue.

'I'll ask both of you again – what are your names?'

Charlie's question was met with silence. Rolling his eyes, he pointed the rifle at them and said, 'Show me some ID.'

The two women looked at one another. Neither responded. Rapidly running out patience, Charlie grabbed one of the children from the pregnant woman's side, fought off her punches, and aimed the gun at the small girl's head, retreating to a safe distance.

'I said show me your ID.'

The two women fumbled in their purses and threw their driving licences to him. Charlie picked them up and read the names.

Karen Jenna Tough. *We'll see how tough she really is.*

Elizabeth Jane Tanner. Tanner. *Tanner.* Where had he heard that name?

And then he had it. Jake Tanner. The unlikely hero who saved thousands of passengers during the terrorist attack in the summer. The one televised almost every day afterward. The one who had appeared modest, reserved, shy. *Just like me.*

Charlie remembered something he had read in one of the news articles online shortly after the attack. How Jake Tanner loved his family more than anything else in the world, especially his two girls. Maisie. And Ellie.

A smile grew on Charlie's face.

'Elizabeth,' he began. 'I wonder how your husband is getting along? How do you reckon he would feel if he found out I had one of your precious daughters under my control? Which one do I have here – Ellie or Maisie? I'm sure he'd love to hear them scream his name.'

34

Shard Syndrome

December 2, 2017, 12:57

Christina placed her foot in Neil's palms. He absorbed all the weight as she reached for the ceiling of the lift. They had found a small hole in a panel overhead. And she had seen too many Hollywood movies to not give it a go. She wasn't holding out for much, but it was the only option they had for an escape.

'You've got to dig your fingers in,' Neil said as Christina stuck her index finger through the small hole in the panel overhead. She grunted and groaned as she tried to pry the panel free. 'Bet you wish you didn't get that manicure now, don't you?'

'Shut up, arsehole,' she said involuntarily. She didn't even feel bad for saying it.

'I will if you do.'

Christina pulled hard, and the panel shook away from its place.

'Yes!' she screamed. 'I did it!'

'Well done. Now the hard part. You've got to climb up and get out that way.'

Christina's face dropped.

'How?'

'Your guess is as good as mine.'

'Why can't you do it?'

'I'm too big. I won't fit through the hole. You will – you're just the right size.' Neil hesitated. 'I might call you Goldilocks.'

'A Latina Goldilocks? Now that's something I never thought I'd hear.'

Neil smiled, bearing his incandescent white teeth. 'Come on. Stop stalling and get up there.'

Christina pulled herself up through the hole in the ceiling, got her shoulders through fine, and supported herself using her elbows. The air inside the elevator shaft was cold and icy, and it was darker than she had expected.

'What can you see?'

'Black. A lot of black.'

'Good. Helpful. Anything else? Any signs of a way out?'

Christina cast her eye over the pitch dark.

'No. Nothing. I know we're at the sixty-third floor, though.'

'You can count as well,' Neil said.

Christina adjusted herself, placing all her weight on her right elbow to create a small gap under her arm to see beneath her. 'Are you going to constantly undermine me, or . . .'

She faltered. A lump grew in her throat. The world around her spun, sending her into a vortex of darkness. She lulled in and out of consciousness, and a knot formed in her stomach. She wanted to be sick. As she allowed her body to enter the vortex, her arm slipped, and she fell through the hole. She landed on top of Neil and onto the floor. She screamed in pain; she'd twisted her ankle and bruised her shoulder, Neil's soft body somewhat cushioning the rest of her fall.

'Oh my God, Christina – are you OK?' he asked. Within seconds he was on her, helping her sit up, attending to her ankle.

'I'll . . . I'll be fine. I just fell.'

'I know. I felt most of it. What happened?'

'I lost my footing,' she lied. She didn't need to tell Neil she had been feeling that way for a long time now. The nausea. The vomiting. The fatigue. The heavy sense of dread. The chemo that wasn't working. The short time she had left on earth.

He didn't need to know.

'So long as you're OK. Let me check this for you.' Neil held her foot in his hands, massaged it, rotated it, assessed it. 'I don't think there's too much damage. Just a bit of a tear in one of your muscles. Some bruising. Give it some ice when we get out of here and you'll be fine,' Neil told her, but she wasn't paying attention. Her mind was too preoccupied with the man in front of her. How handsome he was. His dark features. And his dark, unassuming eyes – just what she liked. A man who probably had charisma and charm in a normal environment. But this wasn't a normal environment, so what did that mean? Was this some sort of new strain of Stockholm syndrome whereby people who are locked up with one another in an enclosed space behave like wild animals and revert to one of their most basic human instincts: sex?

Shard syndrome.

The thought made Christina laugh.

'What's so funny?' Neil asked.

'Nothing. Honestly. I was just thinking this place is going to make me go crazy.'

'Perhaps we're safer in here than we are outside.'

The smile on Christina's face grew. 'Could think of worse people to be with.'

Neil shuffled closer to her. 'Nobody can touch us in here.'

Christina looked into his eyes. 'I hope you're right.'

Before Neil could respond, Christina's phone vibrated in her pocket. She read the message. It was from her husband.

Won't be able to make dinner tonight. Something's come up at work. Shouldn't be home too late. Speak soon. Xx

Christina's eyes fell over the words on the screen, not really taking them in.

'What's that?' Neil asked, applying more pressure to her ankle to grab her attention.

'What? Oh, nothing. It's nothing. Just one of the many mistakes I've made in life. This particular one made me realise life is really, really short.'

Christina locked her phone and placed it back in her pocket.

35

Admission

December 2, 2017, 12:57

Ciara returned to her desk. Flustered. Out of breath. The man outside had riled her up. He was incredibly rude, and she was only trying to help him. What was wrong with him? No – what was wrong with people nowadays? They never wanted help when it was given to them. Everyone was too proud to accept it when they needed it. She couldn't tolerate it anymore.

She threw her coat over the back of her chair. As she patted down the arms, something dropped and fell to the floor. It landed with a clang and bounced over her feet behind her colleague's chair. Curious, she bent down to pick it up.

It was a memory stick.

Where did that come from? she thought as she inspected the small device. And then she remembered. The man. He had lost something. He had been acting erratically and, she had seen, it had led to him getting arrested.

What was on the memory stick?

Ciara inserted the flash drive, waited for the computer to register it, and opened the most recent file. A video played. A man, dressed casually, gunned down a security guard in cold blood, shooting him multiple times. Ciara paused the video instantly. Her mouth fell open and her skin went cold. *Rik*. She had just witnessed her close friend get shot. Her tongue turned moist, tears welled in her eyes and the sensation of nausea returned, this time with a vengeance. She couldn't believe what she was seeing. She needed to get the footage to someone important, and fast.

Wiping her eyes dry, she unplugged the memory stick from her computer and rushed over to her manager's office at the corner of the room. She repeatedly slammed her fist on the door, and entered without waiting. He was sat at his desk, typing on his keyboard.

'Ciara,' he said, shocked. 'What's the matter?'

'There's something you need to see.'

Ciara moved around the desk, leaned across her manager and plunged the memory stick into his monitor. She loaded the video and pressed play. On the second time of watching it, Ciara averted her gaze. It was too hard to watch again.

Her manager pressed the space bar to pause the video.

'Where did you get this?' he asked.

'I found it on the floor. Someone was trying to bring it to us. They worked in The Shard as one of the security guards, I think.'

'Where are they now?'

'Police station. They got arrested for assaulting an officer. That's not the point, though, guv. This happened an hour ago, after I received the call about it. The attacker is still in the building. He might be killing more. What did the emergency response team find?'

'Nothing,' her manager said. 'The building's reception had been evacuated. The building's lost almost all of its power.'

'So, what? They just decided to leave it and come home? Someone's fucking died in that building, guv. And they're doing nothing about it.' Ciara's pulse raced as she thought of the man who had killed her friend. She imagined him suffering as painful a death as Rik's. And she was the one to inflict it.

'I'll speak with SO15,' her manager said, picking up the phone on his desk.

Ciara waited on the seat opposite while her manager explained the situation.

'Yes,' he said. 'Certainly. I understand.' He looked at Ciara, and said, 'It's DCS Kuhoba. He wants to speak with you.'

Ciara's eyes widened. DCS Mamadou Kuhoba. She had heard the name float around the office over in Waterloo, and the rumours that came with it. DCS Kuhoba was a tyrant, a beast that had the power to invoke fear in even the strongest of souls.

Her manager passed the phone across the table. Ciara took it and held it to her ear.

'H-Hello?'

'Who is this?' Mamadou asked, pacing around his office.

'Ciara Reed, sir.'

'Who are you, Ciara Reed?'

'Someone who seems to be more determined about finding out what is going on at The Shard than anyone else,' she said.

Mamadou stopped in his tracks. He stared out of his office window. The Shard was in view in the distance.

'What makes you think we're not working on it?' he asked.

'Because there's nobody there. Emergency response units pulled out.' Ciara hesitated. 'We need armed response vehicles surrounding the entire building. We need to find out what's going inside.'

'You don't need to tell me how to do my job, Ciara Reed,' he said. 'I've been doing it long enough.'

'Evidently I do.'

'What makes you so close to the case?'

'I . . .' Ciara paused again. 'I know someone in there.'

'So do I. One of our own. His name's Jake Tanner. He's got his wife and kids in there. His little girls are ten and seven. And you don't think we're doing anything about it? I would advise you to use your words carefully, in future, Ciara Reed. You might come to regret the things you say. Now, I want you to run me through what happened when you received the initial call this morning,' Mamadou said. He kept his voice neutral and calm. But deep down he was seething with anger. It was pointless shouting at her; it would only aggravate the situation further.

Ciara spent the next minute explaining to him what had happened. He nodded and made acknowledging noises through the phone.

Once she'd finished, he said, 'How long did it take you for to call the emergency response team?'

'I . . . er, I don't know.'

'Five minutes? Ten? Twenty?'

'Ten minutes. I don't know! I didn't time myself.' Ciara was becoming more irate with every passing second.

'Ten minutes is a long time in situations like this. It can be the difference between life and death. You of all people should know that. If anything's happened to Jake, I will hold you responsible, Ciara Reed. Your inactivity may have cost him his life – and the lives of countless others.'

There was a prolonged silence on the phone. 'That's . . . Ridiculous. I . . .'

'Nigel said you have a video of the attack. I want it sent up to my office within the next five minutes, or you'll be receiving another call from me shortly.' Mamadou hung up the phone. He was fuming. His breathing was heavy and he clenched his left fist.

He put his phone his pocket and started out of the room. By the time he reached the door, his phone vibrated.

'Boss, it's me.'

36

Bigger Picture

December 2, 2017, 13:00

Jake felt euphoria travel through his body as he listened to Mamadou's voice. It made him feel safe, protected, invigorated – like he could conquer the world.

'Thank fuck you're safe, Tanner!' Mamadou shouted through the phone.

Mam's excitement almost made Jake smile. Beside him, Kayla continued to apply pressure to Jake's wound, wrapping it tighter and tighter around his shoulder, whilst feeding him water. Now and then he would rotate his arm to gauge the mobility in his shoulder. He wanted to see how effective it would be in combat. The answer: useless. There was more damage he could do with his heel than he could the whole left side of his body.

'It's good to hear you're OK, boss. I'm glad you heard the message all right. Sorry for ruining your day off. But I knew you'd want something to keep you busy.' It was difficult for Jake to speak. His chest and lungs hurt. Hyperventilation caused by shock and sudden blood loss had wreaked havoc on his body. He coughed, and the drastic movement flared the pain in his shoulder.

Mamadou chuckled. 'I can't keep away, you know that. Jake, you've got to tell me what's going on. We need to get you and everyone else there out as fast as possible, but first I need to know what we're dealing with.'

Jake told Mamadou everything. From start to finish. From the moment he and everyone else sat down at the table to where he was now, sitting in an emergency room inside the Shangri-La. Jake left no details behind. Kayla stared at him as he spoke, absorbing his every word.

'And you're sure Paxman's working alone?'

'Almost positive. When he charged the restaurant, it was just him in his one-man band.'

'OK. That makes things a little easier to manage. I'll get someone to investigate him, Weiss, and the director general of the WHO. As soon as we've built up an image of him, I'll let you know. Has he made any demands yet, or suggested any reason behind this sudden attack?'

'No. I got out of there before he had the chance.'

'Right.' Mamadou hesitated, as if he were planning in his head. 'We'll get in contact with the security teams in the building and start an emergency evacuation. We'll send them up to the top floors, then they'll make their way down. The stairs will be busy. So right now, I want you to stay put. Don't go anywhere.'

'No.'

'Jake, you have to. You've just been shot. You've lost a lot of blood. You'll only be putting yourself at more risk. Do you really want that to happen? What if the girls watch you get shot while you're trying to protect them?'

'That's not going to happen. They need me and they're waiting for me,' Jake said through gritted teeth. 'It's non-negotiable. You can contact me on this number. I'll be using this mobile from now on. I'll be in touch if I find anything.'

Jake hung up before Mamadou could attempt to dissuade him.

'I hope that's all right?' Jake asked Kayla, looking at her. He waved the phone in his hand.

'Don't have much of a choice now, do I? The passcode is 1066.'

'Any reason?'

'History fan. The Battle of Hastings was my favourite battle in British history. It changed our nation.' Kayla smirked smugly.

Jake lifted himself out of the chair, stopped, looked around him and said, 'I don't suppose you have anything in the way of energy, do you? Sugars. A drink? Fuel bars? All of that stuff?'

Kayla considered for a moment and then nodded. 'Yes, one of my colleagues will. Imran. He cycles to work every morning. He'll have some in his locker for sure.'

'Great. When you're there, can you bring back some tobacco and Rizla?'

She looked at him, aghast.

'Your hands. They're stained. I just need one sheet.'

'What for?'

'It doesn't matter. Just bring what you have. I'll get my coat.'

Confused, Kayla nodded, said she would be right back, and disappeared. In the time he had alone, Jake strolled over to the corner of the room, picked up his bloodied coat, fished inside his pocket, searching for the leftover bag of weed, and picked it apart with his fingers on the surface. By the time Kayla returned, the small nugget of cannabis was nothing more than a fine pile of dust.

'What are you doing?' Kayla asked, closing the door behind her. 'You can't do that in here.'

Taking the pouch of tobacco from her, he said, 'Watch me.'

Jake removed a Rizla from the packet, rolled the cannabis into a joint, and ignited the end using Kayla's lighter from the same packet. He hated what he was doing. He hated that he was relying on this drug to make him feel better, but he knew the sensation would alleviate the pain, clear his mind, make him more alert and focused. He convinced himself he was doing it for the good of his children.

'You really think it will make a difference?' Kayla said, holding him by his right arm and the left side of his waist.

'I do. Give it some time to kick in,' Jake said, stopping in the middle of the room. 'This, and the sugar, should help.'

In her hands, Kayla held a handful of small banana-flavoured tubes of glucose gel. Jake ripped off their heads and squeezed every last drop into his mouth. They tasted disgusting, but he could feel the energy flowing through his bloodstream.

'Thank you,' Jake said, throwing the final wrapper on top of the others.

'You're welcome.'

'I mean it,' he said. 'Thank you for helping me. But I need to go. Where's the general manager?'

Kayla smiled, snatched the phone back from him and dialled a number. After she had passed the phone to Jake, he explained to the GM what was happening and what he wanted to happen.

Jake hung up, pocketed the phone, thanked Kayla, bolted for the exit and left.

He used whatever of his memory he had left to guide him towards the lift. He stopped after he entered the foyer. By now, at the reception desks, clients and hotel visitors were queuing behind one another, bombarding the staff with panicked, angry questions. It was mayhem. Just under a half hour had passed and the building still hadn't regained its power. The patrons were becoming irate with every passing minute.

Jake needed to get their attention. Make sure they listened to him. But how? He could hardly hear himself think over everyone else. He scanned the horizon. Nothing. All he needed was a platform.

His answer was right in front of him. The reception desks.

Jake strode towards them, limping and holding his shoulder, compressing the wound. He barged past members of hotel staff and a few guests. They shot him dirty looks, but Jake ignored them all. He was determined, full of energy again, and nobody was going to stop him. Eventually, he reached the desk, clambered atop it, and called out.

'Ladies and gentlemen, can I have your attention, please? My name is Jake Tanner. I'm a detective with Counter Terrorism police.'

Before he could continue, he heard clapping. Then the clapping turned into a round of applause.

What is going on?

'I know who you are!' one person standing by his feet shouted. 'You're that guy who saved everyone on those trains.'

Jake understood. They must have seen him on the television or in the newspapers during the aftermath of 01/08. And now they were showing him their appreciation. He had hated the attention then, and he hated it even more now.

'Thank you,' he continued. 'I'm flattered. But I need you all to listen and to listen carefully. We believe there may be a potential hostage situation in the Oblix restaurant two floors beneath us.' Murmurs and cries came from the crowd. 'Listen to me, please. It is imperative you do exactly as I tell you.

'We need to conduct an emergency evacuation. I need you all to head towards any of the four stairwells in this building. Leave your possessions in your rooms. You can retrieve them later. If you have any loved ones or friends left in their rooms, the hotel staff are conducting a thorough sweep of the entire hotel. You are under no circumstances to go back to your room and grab what you think may be important. You will endanger countless lives if you do – including your own. In addition, you are under no circumstances to use any of the lifts, only the stairs. So, please, do as I say and get moving!'

Jake coughed, the remnants of the marijuana playing games with his lungs. But as he stood there, he grew increasingly annoyed. Nobody moved. Nobody took it upon themselves to take the lead and follow Jake's orders.

'What are you doing?' Jake asked, throwing his hands in

the air. 'Move! Move now!'

It was then that everything Jake had said sank in. The massive sea of people before him turned and started towards the exit. They pushed past one another like a pack of hungry hyenas fighting over the next piece of meat. As they funnelled into the double doors that led into the stairwell, Jake saw the people who had been left behind. Many were standing there, defiant, waiting for the front desks to free up so they could be first in line to ask their incessant questions. Meanwhile others headed back towards their hotel rooms.

Jake sighed heavily. He didn't have time for this. He was going to have to evacuate the rest of the building. He couldn't waste his time here; it would be up to the hotel staff to sort it out. He had his family to save.

Jake clambered down from the reception desk. There were two members of staff who had remained behind.

'Kayla,' he said to the young girl who had helped him. 'Where can I find the electricity control room? The place that supplies the entire building with its power?'

Kayla put her finger to her lips, deep in thought. 'Floor thirty, I think.'

Jake embraced her as a way of saying thank you for helping him, told her to continue evacuating the Shangri-La hotel and to be safe, and then said goodbye. As he hobbled towards the control room on the thirtieth floor, Jake was already feeling better. The pain had subsided, and his mental capacity felt good, open, clearer. He was beginning to see the bigger picture – how Charlie Paxman had cut the power to the building. And as a result, a plan was forming in Jake's head.

37

Creation

December 2, 2017, 13:01

The Oblix restaurant fell silent. Elizabeth's face had dropped at the mention of her family's name. How did Charlie know who Jake was? Who Maisie was? Ellie? Was this another relative of Moshat or Adil Hakim? Or was it another survivor of the Detson tower fire, seeking revenge? She didn't know.

'Give her here,' Elizabeth said, holding her hand out.

Maisie was standing to the side of Charlie's legs, hostage. He had grabbed her from Elizabeth as soon as he'd identified them all. Since then, Charlie had been tending to her, making sure she was safe. He gave her a glass of water and some snacks from behind the bar. Everything about what he was doing concerned Elizabeth. She hated not being by Maisie's side.

'I don't think so, Elizabeth. I'm not going to hurt her, don't worry. She could prove valuable to me. You've still got the little one with you. And I wouldn't want to harm a precious, gorgeous little girl like this, would I?' Charlie bent his knees, stroked Maisie's face and smiled. Looking to Elizabeth, he said, 'You didn't answer my earlier question.'

'What was it?' Elizabeth asked.

'I asked why you were pregnant. Are two children not enough for you? Have you not wasted enough of the planet's resources as it is with your existence and your children's existence?'

Elizabeth didn't reply. Not because she was afraid or pretending to act defiant, but because she didn't know what to say. She hadn't even considered the impact her baby would have on the environment. And anyway, why should she care? It didn't affect her, and it wouldn't affect her unborn baby, either. There was enough income to feed the soon-to-be five of them, and if there wasn't, Jake and Elizabeth would look into their options. They had discussed Elizabeth's potential return to a salaried job, whereby she could earn enough to compensate for the newborn, and then, once they were more financially stable, she could return to freelance photography.

'Elizabeth,' Charlie said, taking her by surprise. 'I'm talking to you.'

'No,' she said instinctively.

'No? You don't think having another baby is a problem?'

'Should I?'

Charlie hesitated for a moment.

'Did you plan them?'

'Yes. And no.'

'Do you feel like they're the biggest mistake you ever made in your life? Do you look at them every day and regret their entire existence? Do you wish you could wind back the time and kill them while they were in the womb?'

Elizabeth stared at her daughters. 'Please, you're scaring me. I love them.'

'This country – and the rest of the population – is wrought with poverty, undernourishment, and depravity. The rich stay rich while the poor stay poor, and then they're just left to die without a National Health Service that can afford to look after them. Tell me, Elizabeth Jane Tanner, how much do your children mean to you?'

Elizabeth fell silent. Was this a trick question? Was he going to make her choose between Maisie or Ellie?

'They're my entire world,' she said finally.

'Do you love them more than you love your hero husband?'

'It's a different kind of love, something I reckon you wouldn't understand.' Elizabeth shifted uneasily on the floor. Her back and stomach were hurting. The baby could sense her distress, and she felt a wave of fear and regret crash over her after she made her final remark.

'Excuse me?' Charlie said. 'I knew love once.' He turned to face Marianne. 'But then it was ripped from me. And I never even considered having kids. I do not want them. I have been around enough to know they are not the future; I am. They have become too thick, too unintelligent to change this world. I have seen where our education systems – and the rest of the establishments across the globe – have failed. Which is why it is up to us to make that difference, to protect our species from harm's way. Why it is up to *me*.'

'How are you going to do that?' Elizabeth asked. The rest of the restaurant was profoundly silent.

Charlie grinned. His yellow-stained teeth flashed.

'I'm glad you asked.'

He bent down, reached inside his gym bag that was a few feet behind him, and removed something. A tube of green glass with some kind of transparent liquid inside.

'I'm going to change the world with this.'

'What is it?' Elizabeth's interest had been piqued.

'This, my darling Elizabeth, and the rest of you – especially those from the World Health Organisation – is a virus, a genetically engineered virus that has the capabilities to alter the genetic strands of human DNA.'

Charlie's face beamed. He looked proud of himself. Too proud. It was evident to see that months, if not years, had gone into the manufacturing of the virus, and now here he was, ready to showcase it to the world.

'You created it, then?' a voice asked. Elizabeth recognised it as Benjamin Weiss's, the one she had heard belittle Charlie at the beginning of their meal.

Charlie nodded to the scientist. 'Yes. Even without your help. You all discouraged me, said it couldn't be done, said it wouldn't be possible for at least another ten, fifty, hundred years. Well, look at it now. It's only taken me a matter of months.' Charlie held the object in the air and shook it. The contents spilled around inside.

'How can you be sure it works?' Benjamin asked.

'Because I'm a scientist. A much better one than you, that's for sure. I've tested it on myself.'

'And?'

'Conclusive. It works. Do you really think I would be

doing this today if it didn't? Do you really think all of this was just a coincidence? Us being together again after so long. I told you that I would stop at nothing to succeed, didn't I?'

Elizabeth cleared her throat and raised her hand. 'Succeed in what?'

Charlie's head bolted towards her, and she felt afraid. His gaze was unrelenting, his cavernous eyes boring into her soul. 'I won't stop until the vector virus has been released.'

Elizabeth raised her hand again. 'Forgive my ignorance, but what is a vector virus? What does this particular one do?'

Charlie opened his mouth to speak but was cut off by a soft voice next to Benjamin.

'It's a virus that is transmitted through the air,' Marianne said. She spoke calmly and softly, her voice demanding the attention of the entire room. 'Once airborne, there is almost nothing that can stop it. It can spread exponentially and populate the entire earth within a matter of days.'

'Precisely,' Charlie echoed. He shook the vial in front of his face. 'And this one will stop rapid population growth indefinitely. You see, everyone, Benjamin and I started this process at the same time, together. We graduated from the same classes, with the same grades, from the same university, and both found the same job as deputy directors of Noncommunicable Diseases and Mental Health at the WHO. We were equals. Except for one vital thing. Together we studied the genetic composition of animals and the human body and how to adjust nucleotides to benefit medical procedures and healing. Together we were responsible for altering your DNA so you could defeat cancer, eliminate AIDS, become immune to malaria, or even the bubonic plague.' Charlie paused for dramatic effect. He held the room's attention. He swallowed before continuing. 'But I took it a step further. I experimented with genetic recalibration, something nobody has ever attempted before. And it was a success.

'There are seven billion people on this planet. Billion. Not million. It's inconceivable. Compare this number to just over two hundred years ago – the number was at one billion. Two hundred years before that: five hundred million. Since the nineteenth century, the human population has grown exponentially, and it is continuing to do so. Most of you already know this, but it's not something you bother thinking about.

'And there are more and more people every day being born into poverty and depravity, that there is not enough soup to feed everyone around the table. There are only so many animals on this planet. There's only so much oxygen we can consume before suffocating on our own carbon dioxide. A finite amount of natural resources before we use them all up. Not to mention, there is only so much space we can occupy before we get on top of one another and kill everyone. You see, as soon as there are too many of us on this planet, wars will wage and bouts of extreme violence will take place on our streets. I mean, look how close we are to a nuclear war already. We're just too afraid to press the trigger right now. Something in our brains is beginning to switch to primal survivalism, a lack of empathy for each other. But what if the population growth stopped? What if it was stunted?

'What if I could genetically engineer a virus or a disease or a plague that would alter everyone on the planet's DNA so that some became infertile, while others remained reproductive? The virus would attach itself to a particular strand in a third of the current population's DNA – so that approximately 2.5 billion people are able to reproduce and sustain humanity. As for the rest of the five billion people on the planet, nothing will happen. They will die out due to natural causes, and there may be some who will become susceptible to more serious, life-threatening side effects. But those numbers are in the millions. Nothing compared to what it could be.' Charlie coughed, and wiped his hands on his trousers. 'Sure, people like Benjamin will work towards prolonging life extensively, but it will be no use. It won't be a match for my virus.

'The number of us on this planet is too great. I believe it is selfish to produce so many children nowadays. It has become glorified to have families of four, five, six, and live off the state, when not a single shred of consideration is taken as to the effect it will have on the planet. More mouths equal less food. It is only a matter of time until we all press that big red button on ourselves, whether it be inadvertently or done with intent. Nobody said it could be done. And now, today, you will be the first to experience the full wrath of my creation.'

38

Warrant

December 2, 2017, 13:03

Mamadou hung up the phone. Pocketed it. Charged to the head of Counter Terrorism Command by the wall of television screens displaying images of the news and rolling CCTV footage from across the city. He stopped by Frances and explained to her the call he had just had with Jake.

'Charlie Paxman? That's who's behind this?' Frances asked. Because of the validity of Mamadou's suspicions, she had postponed her meeting with the Home Secretary.

Mamadou nodded.

'And Tanner's certain?'

'Yes. Paxman works as a waiter inside the Oblix – the restaurant he's taken hostage. There's video footage of him killing a security guard – it's coming up to 1430 now. And

Jake said Paxman's killed two other people already. He doesn't know if there have been any more murders since.'

'What about demands? Do we know anything about that yet?'

Mamadou shook his head.

Frances looked to the ground in deep thought. Mamadou joined her and tried to piece all the information together. First, they needed to build a profile around Charlie Paxman. Get to know his habits, his daily routine, any family, kids, pets, friends, hobbies – anything that would suggest he had gone off the rails to commit this act of terrorism.

'Is it a copycat?' Frances asked, taking Mamadou by surprise.

'What? Copycat to whom?'

'Moshat and Adil Hakim.'

Over the weeks succeeding Operation Tightrope, there had been a sudden insurgence of terrorism and potential terrorist threats. The Joint Terrorism Analysis Centre had raised the nation's threat level to critical, and the staff at SO15 had been at full capacity. Most of the new terrorist attacks had been conducted by single cells who had been inspired by the Hakim brothers. Fortunately, due to these new-wave terrorists' short-term planning and lack of experience with anything explosive, they were quickly caught and imprisoned. That didn't reduce the amount of paperwork, though, and since then, Mamadou had heard through the grapevine that there would be new legislation coming into force to combat the threat that Moshat and Adil Hakim posed to British society.

The two brothers had changed the face of terrorism forever, and nothing would be the same.

'No,' Mamadou said. 'I don't think this is a copycat. It seems too organised compared to the others we've had over the past few months. I mean, he destroyed The Shard's power supply. He knew where it was, and he did it all on his own. No, I think this is a statement, a display of his prowess and intelligence and drive. We won't know more until we profile and investigate him.'

Frances agreed. She walked to the front row of desks and called into the room, 'Listen, team. Tanner has confirmed a positive ID on the suspect: a Mr Charlie Paxman. I want to know everything about him. Where he works, what he does for fun, where he lives. I even want to know where he shits. In the meantime, I need magenta and blue teams to organise all emergency response vehicles to the base of The Shard – X-Ray One. They must start full evac support.' Frances turned to face the wall behind her. 'Where's this CCTV footage, team? It's been too long, and we've not had a single still come in.'

As soon as she had finished talking, a man with a wide jaw wearing glasses stood up.

'Memory stick has just been dropped off now, ma'am. Coming on the screens for you in three . . . two . . .'

Within seconds, the top-left quadrant of the six-by-four screen wall changed. The time stamp on the bottom showed footage from almost three hours ago. The most prominent images that caught Mamadou's attention were in the centre: a man he presumed to be Charlie Paxman wandered up to a security guard, fired a bullet into his head, multiple more into the rest of his body, and then moved into a large room where, moments later, he poured a liquid onto a control panel. Mamadou charged forward towards the wall of televisions, his eyes glued to the screens.

'Stop it right there!' he yelled, holding his hand in the air behind him.

The CCTV footage froze. A still, pixelated image of Charlie Paxman's face appeared on the screen. Was that a smile? Mamadou was sure of it.

'Send the image to the top right. We'll use that until we get an official image of his face.'

Someone behind him enlarged the pixelated image onto the top-right quadrant of the wall. Over the next few minutes, Mamadou and Frances stood there watching the running playback of the CCTV feeds from the entire building. Mamadou's eyes darted from left to right, right to left, top to bottom, and bottom to top in a mad frenzy. It was like he was watching a magic trick, trying to locate the ball hidden underneath one of a dozen cups.

On the screen, Charlie Paxman strolled from the control room up the stairs to the restaurant and unleashed his assault rifle. Mamadou watched chaos descend upon the Oblix.

'Oh my God,' he said, after he had just watched Jake and Charlie Paxman wrestle on the floor. Mamadou turned to Frances. 'He's definitely working alone.'

Frances agreed and addressed the room. 'Come on, people. Where are we with his profile?'

At that moment, DC Edwards, a skinny woman who wore too much make-up, wandered up to Mamadou and Frances. She walked with a slight skip in her step, and in her hand, she held a tablet and dossier.

'Charlie Paxman,' she began as she approached them, 'DOB December 1, 1987. Child prodigy. Studied biomedical science at the University of York. Completed his PhD in the same field and then went into teaching at a small school in the north. Signed off for a period of time due to stress, returned, and then eventually joined the World Health Organisation somehow as one of their most senior representatives. A few months ago, he was released and then found full-time work at the Oblix restaurant inside The Shard.'

'Why was he signed off for stress?'

'Intelligence says he wandered in on a pupil who had hung himself in his classroom. One of Paxman's top students.'

'Jesus Christ.'

'He had a series of consultations after that, and the weird thing is, he'd had a brief romance with the boy's mum before he committed suicide. But it didn't last long. Charlie could see they were struggling, and offered her money and support, for both of them. She said no. Said she didn't need charity. That she could provide for herself fine, and that the boy would have to learn to do it on his own. They split up just before the son killed himself. The mum was interviewed extensively by representatives from the Department of Education and the NSPCC and police over the years, but Charlie's relationship with her only came out after the boy died.'

'What was the boy's name?'

'Reece Alexander.'

Mamadou absorbed the information. 'Anything else? What happened at the WHO?'

Edwards shuffled through the pile of papers she was currently juggling in her hands. 'He was there for two years, right until April this year. Considered one of the most intelligent people to have ever become part of the team. His appointment was rejected by many. They saw him as too young, too naive. There are transcripts of him at a convention talking about trying to change the world with a virus or a weapon of some kind. His views were widely unpopular as well. He did, however, win many awards and accolades. He took the field of genetics to a different level, apparently.'

'Jesus,' Mamadou said, lost for words. 'What more do you know about this virus he talked about?'

'Nothing yet,' DC Edwards replied. 'Everyone else in the organisation said it was impossible.'

'Well, I get the sneaky suspicion it is possible, and that's what this entire fucking thing is about.'

'I'll find out what I can,' DC Edwards said, making a note on her tablet.

'Good. Why did he leave the World Health Organisation?'

Edwards took a moment to read through the notes. 'He was removed from the company. Reports say he . . . he made a move on the DG, Marianne Evans. One of their colleagues, Benjamin Weiss, found Charlie on top of her, undressing her.'

'Consensual?'

'According to the reports, no.'

'And what do you think?'

'In all honesty, yes. There's nothing I've found so far to suggest he was sexually violent, or violent at all.'

Nodding, Mamadou moved the conversation along. 'What happened after he was found undressing her?'

'She filed on grounds of sexual harassment and got him sacked. Benjamin, a long-term friend and colleague, backed her up. Said he saw Paxman forcing himself upon her. Paxman had no chance.'

'Who is this Benjamin Weiss?'

'Descended from royalty, long way down the line. The distance hasn't stopped him owning a lovely mansion down in Surrey and flaunting his family's wealth and status everywhere he goes.'

Mamadou nodded. He ran his fingers through his thin beard. 'Sounds like Paxman's had a hard time. First, he finds a kid dead in his classroom, then he's shunned from an organisation for something he potentially didn't do by one of his closest allies. Seems like he's out for revenge. Anything about his family life, personal life?'

'We're working on it.'

'Don't get back to me until you do.'

Mamadou was heading back to his office when he was accosted by DS Monroe. His face was flustered and his cheeks red.

'Sir,' Monroe began. He was a thick man with wide shoulders, arms and chest. His clothes were so tight it was almost as if he were bursting out of them. 'I've got something.'

'What is it?'

'We've just got a confirmed address via both Paxman's passport and driving licence.'

'Give it to me.'

DS Monroe repeated Charlie Paxman's address to Mamadou.

'Thanks. I want you to send everything you find to my inbox – all of you. No matter how small. If you think it's important, I want to know about it.'

Without saying anything, he started towards the lift.

'Where are you going?' Monroe asked.

Mamadou stopped mid-stride. Frances was right behind him.

'To COBRA,' Frances said, speaking before him. 'The PM's called it.'

'What about you, guv?' Monroe said, nodding past Frances to Mamadou.

'To get a search warrant. Paxman's property could tell us everything we need to know. And more.'

39

Collapse

December 2, 2017, 13:12

Tim was on the bottom step of the thirtieth floor when he heard a door slam open, and the sound of hundreds of shoes pounding above him. He had just ventured up the first thirty floors, hurrying everyone out and evacuating them. And now he was having a break. There were only so many steps his legs and body could handle before he needed to take a rest. His thighs ached the most, and then as soon as his chest began to tighten, he decided it was time to stop.

His physical fitness was abysmal. He had been single for over ten years, and because he had never found anyone since, he'd descended into a spiral of depression. It wasn't through lack of trying. No – he was signed up to various online dating websites, and he'd try to pick up girls at bars. But there was only so much rejection he could take. A part of him hated himself for it. What was wrong with him? Why didn't anyone love him?

His previous relationship had ended badly. She had left him so distraught and broken. She said it wasn't because he was infertile and unable to give her children, but Tim knew that was bullshit. He remembered the look on her face every time she saw – or even mentioned – one of her friends' babies. Now he had nothing left. No one to fight for. No one to welcome him home every night. No one to wake up next to.

No one.

The sound of footsteps grew louder. It sounded like a stampede heading straight towards him. Tim steadied himself. He tensed his muscles and flexed his wrist. He was unarmed and outnumbered. He didn't know who, or what, was coming down those stairs, and his best form of defence was going to be himself.

Seconds later, the source of the noise revealed itself. A flood of people charged down the steps, each of the individuals in the first few rows trying to get ahead of one another, their arms flailing. It reminded Tim of videos he had seen on social media of Black Friday shoppers in the USA, fighting over televisions and other discounted products.

Tim pressed his back against the wall. He allowed the stampede to pass him. They were headed to safety, and he wasn't going to stand in the way.

Just then, as the crowd flowing past him reached halfway, a woman tripped and stumbled to the ground. She rolled down a few steps and landed heavily near Tim's feet. She screamed out in pain as the rest of the civilians trampled over her in a desperate bid to escape. It was their lives or hers, and they had taken the selfish route.

'Hey! Hey!' Tim called out as he stepped into the torrent of bodies. One man collided with him and almost sent him into the wall.

After steadying himself, Tim formed a barrier around the felled woman, lifted her to her feet and brought her to the wall. She clung to him like a newborn baby in its mother's arms.

'You're OK now,' he said, shielding her.

'Thank you.'

'What happened?' Tim asked. She felt light in his arms, delicate, precious.

'Someone - someone pushed me in the back and I fell.' She whimpered in pain.

'What's your name?' Tim asked.

'Samantha.'

'Hi, Samantha. I'm Tim. I'm going to help. Where does it hurt?'

'My ankle. I think it's broken.'

Tim looked down the woman's leg and enjoyed the view, until his eyes fell on her ankle. It was swollen and red and hanging to the side slightly.

'You won't be able to walk on it anymore. I'll carry you down.'

'No,' she said, taking Tim by surprise. 'I'll be OK. I can do it.'

Samantha shifted her weight onto her good foot, attempted to walk on it, but stumbled against the railing that ran the length of the wall.

'Here,' Tim said, jumping after her. 'Let me help you.'

Tim took Samantha under the arm and supported her weight. By now the flurry of people had disappeared. It was just the two of them. At that moment, Tim wanted to hold her and never let go. It had been so long since he'd last felt the tender touch of a woman, and he felt protective in a way he hadn't in a long time.

Tim looked at her. She was so pretty. Her hair long and flowing. Her figure relatively trim and healthy. Strong grip. Plus, she was in a pencil skirt and button-up shirt. His Achilles heel.

Just as he was realising now was not the time to compliment her outfit, he heard a noise from above echo down, distorting the relative calm on the thirtieth floor. *Paxman*. Tim panicked. In an instant, he threw both his arms over Samantha, protecting her like he would have done if she were Amy, his ex-partner.

'Hey!' a voice called from above. It sounded weak and feeble.

Tim said nothing and hoped the person had neither heard nor seen them. Eventually, a man came into view. His shoulder was bloodied and his face pale.

'Oh my God,' Tim said, standing there, staring at the bloodied man, his mouth agape. 'What the hell happened to you. Are you OK?'

The man smiled. 'I've been better. Last time it was just a stab wound.'

Last time? Stab wound? Already Tim was brimming with questions, but this was neither the place nor the time to ask them.

'Do you work here?' the man asked.

Tim nodded.

'What do you do?'

'Security guard.'

'Great. What's your name?'

'Tim. Tim Keane.'

The man extended his hand. 'DC Jake Tanner. You and I are going to be spending a lot of time together. I need your help.'

'But I . . . I was helping Samantha.' Tim looked at her, realised he must have been coming across as afraid and impudent, and swallowed hard, breathing deeply. Speaking more sternly this time, he said, 'She fell and twisted her ankle. She can't get down.'

'Find someone else to take her. I need you to come with me.'

'No. I need to help Samantha first—'

'Tim,' Samantha interrupted, placing her hand on his chest. 'It's fine. I can manage.' She smiled and struggled down the stairs. Before she left, she stared into his eyes. It was only for a brief moment, but he was sure it was there. He was sure he had seen it. The look in her eye that said, *Thank you, my hero.*

'Be safe, OK?' Tim said, feeling elated.

'Only if you will.'

'I'll come and find you once this is all done,' Tim called down.

'I'd like that.' And then Samantha was gone.

Tim looked to DC Jake Tanner. He was smiling.

'You two just met?' he asked Tim.

'Yes, why?'

DC Jake Tanner laughed, slapped him on the upper arm and said, 'Nothing. Smooth, that's all.'

For someone who had been shot, he was in a surprisingly chirpy mood.

'Now listen up. We're facing a new threat today. There's a man—'

'I know. I know what you're talking about. I was the one who let him into the building. His name's Charlie Paxman. I've spent the past fifteen-twenty minutes trying to evacuate the building.'

'Legend,' Jake said. 'You've saved me an entire job. That's what I was going to get you to do. Is there anyone else who can help us?'

Tim shook his head. 'No. Rik's dead; Paxman killed him. Two others called in sick. And Vince . . .' Tim checked his watch. It was 13:14. 'Vince was supposed to be back by now.'

'Where did he go?'

'Scotland Yard.'

'What for?'

'To show them the footage of the terrorist killing my friend. We caught him on CCTV. Vince was going to give it to them as evidence.'

Jake Tanner looked into the stairwell, deep in thought. 'Maybe Vince is still at New Scotland Yard.'

Tim shook his head. 'I told him to come back.'

'He wouldn't be permitted. The police and emergency response teams would have set up a perimeter. There's no way he'll be allowed back in - not unless he knows the Prime Minister. There's nothing either of us can do about him, so it's up to us - we'll continue without him or anyone else. We need to get the rest of the people in this building out of here safely without raising an alarm. We don't know how Paxman is going to react to anything, so we need to remain as inconspicuous as possible. He's already killed two people in the restaurant – both unprovoked. Three, counting . . . Rik, right?'

'Yes. Jesus. I don't believe it.' Tim glanced down at the floor. He spared a thought for the dead and their families.

'I need to speak to Paxman. Make contact. Try and calm him down. Find out what he wants. Talk him out of this. But I need to be careful. He's got my wife and kids hostage.'

'Shit.' Tim gasped. 'That's heavy. What's your plan?'

Before Jake Tanner answered, he swayed from side to side and then collapsed to the floor.

40

Collateral

December 2, 2017, 13:15

Jake opened his eyes. Light filtered in and he tried to blink it away. His entire body felt weak, and as he lifted himself to his feet, he felt a pair of hands grapple his arms.

'What happened?' he asked, thinking out loud.

'I don't know,' the owner of the hands said. 'You fainted, I think. Are you OK?'

Jake looked up, saw the man in front of him and then remembered. His name was Tim. He closed his eyes and breathed deeply, allowing his entire body to fill with oxygen before dumping carbon dioxide back into the stairwell.

'I'm fine. It must be the blood loss,' Jake said, deciding it would be better not to tell Tim that the last thing he saw before passing out was Moshat Hakim's face.

It had been another anxiety attack. A powerful and sudden one. With the added fatigue of reduced blood in his body and the effects of the cannabis, Jake had experienced the full wrath of Moshat and the explosion and Martha's dead body swimming in his mind.

And now he was still feeling the aftermath.

'You can't carry on like this, man,' Tim said. 'It's not good for your health.'

'I don't care. I've got a family up there that needs me.' Jake lifted himself to his feet, reached into his pocket. Dialled. The phone answered almost immediately. 'Mam? It's Tanner. What have you got for me? How is Elizabeth? The kids? My friends?'

'They're fine, Jake. For now. We're getting the live feed come through on the CCTV. We've got enough power to tap into it. Paxman's making sure nobody's going anywhere.'

Please stay like that, Jake thought. There was no knowing what might happen to them in the next ten minutes. Twenty. Thirty.

'What else? Anything on Paxman?'

'Yes. It's good, too. Jerome and Matilda did some digging into Charlie's history. When he was a child, social services were always calling.'

'Why?'

'His parents didn't want him. They hated him. Wished they'd never had him. But the catch was, they enjoyed the benefit cheque at the end of the month. So they kept him. Abused him. Tormented him. His mum was worse. She'd usually do stuff to him while his dad was passed out on something. There was no mention in the social services report, but I wouldn't be surprised if his mum used to molest him based on notes from a primary school advisor.'

Jesus. 'Anything else?'

'That's all we've got now, but I'll let you know if something new comes up.'

In the background, Jake heard sirens. 'Where are you?'

'En route to Paxman's flat.'

'Be safe, please.'

'You too.'

Jake rung off. His mind processed what Mamadou told him before he opened Kayla's address book and dialled another number from memory. Elizabeth's.

Nothing.

He tried Alex's.

Nothing.

And then, in one final attempt, he tried Maisie's. Jake and Elizabeth had given her a hand-me-down phone with a pay-as-you-go SIM inside earlier in the year. All her friends had one, and she was feeling left out. Although, they had told her it was to be used explicitly for emergencies only when she was on the commute to and from school.

It rang. And rang. And rang.

'Hello?' Charlie Paxman answered; Jake recognised his voice at once.

Jake breathed a sigh of relief; Charlie had answered. But why? Did he have Maisie captive? She hadn't handed in her mobile phone earlier. Paxman must have heard it and taken it from her. Jake's body filled with dread. He couldn't bear to see or hear anything happening to his first little miracle.

'Is this Professor Paxman?' Jake asked.

'Hello, Detective.'

Jake paused. How could Charlie have known his

occupation?

'Jake?' Charlie asked. 'You still there? Or has the cat got your tongue?'

'No,' Jake said, swallowing. 'I'm still here. As are my family and friends, I hope?'

'They are, alive and well. For now. How's the shoulder?' Charlie's tone seemed jovial, as if they were good friends who hadn't spoken to one another for a while.

'It's been worse.'

'Excellent. How can I be of assistance?'

'I want to know what you want. What are you going to do with my family, and with everyone else up there?'

Charlie sniggered. 'It's all about you and your family, isn't it, Jake? Well, there's been a slight change in plan. My original idea was to take an old compatriot of mine as my insurance package, but now I've learned that the great Jake Tanner, defeater of terrorists, is among us, and his family is here with me – well, I realised it's too good an opportunity to miss. You're going to spread the popularity of my name.'

'What are you going to do?' Jake asked, his breathing steady.

'I'm going to change the course of history.'

'How?'

'You'll have to be patient.'

'What are your demands?'

'That you stay well clear of me. And you can tell your little friends back at Scotland Yard to stand down any armed officers they might have coming up here. I've seen how trigger happy they can get – and we don't want anyone you love being caught in the crossfire. If they do, I shoot one person every five minutes. I've got some unfinished business to attend to, and some friends to get reacquainted with, and I don't want you jeopardising that.'

'What will it take for you to stop?'

'For me to get what I want.'

'And what do you want?'

'You'll have to wait and see.'

Jake became infuriated. Charlie Paxman's constant undermining showed who was in charge here. And Jake didn't like it.

'Why are you doing this, Charlie? Why this building? Why now?'

Charlie hesitated. Jake could hear his soft breathing in his ear. 'It's better than doing it in the Underground, wouldn't you agree? Or is that too fresh in the memory for you?'

Jake ignored the remark. 'Let the people in the restaurant go, Charlie.'

'I can't do that, Jake. There are some very important people here who need to be taught a lesson.'

Jake took a moment to consider what Charlie meant. 'You mean Benjamin Weiss, and the rest of the World Health Organisation?'

'Ah, so you're familiar with their names?'

'Only Benjamin's.'

'Yes, he is famous, isn't he? I could have shared a similar notoriety—'

'What happened between you two?'

'Excuse me?'

'Why is he famous when you're not? What happened?'

'I'm not famous, yet - but I'm going to be.'

'Stop ignoring the question and answer. Why did Benjamin succeed where you didn't?'

'Because he ruined my career. He snaked me out of my position and threw me off the edge. He destroyed any chance I had of salvaging my reputation as a respected scientist.'

'What did he do?' Jake asked, easing the tension in his voice; if Charlie started trusting him, he might just be able to reason with him.

'You don't need the specifics.' Shit, Charlie had just thrown him off completely. 'Listen, Jake. I don't think you realise who's in charge here. I've got you wrapped round my tiny little finger, more than you know. So, I want you to listen to me, or you will regret it. Nothing will ever be the same again, not when I'm finished.' Charlie coughed down the phone. It sounded harsh, violent, wet. 'This is my time to prove everyone wrong, and I want to see everyone's faces when I do, just before I kill them all. I want them to see the powerful, merciless human being I have become – the one *they* created – all for the greater good.'

'Why does everyone else need to suffer?'

'They're collateral, Jake. Give me one good reason why they shouldn't. Especially your dear wife, who seems to be bringing yet another creature into the world, putting this planet under more strain.'

'Because I love them,' Jake said. 'And I'd do anything for them.'

41

Trigger

December 2, 2017, 13:17

Charlie Paxman hung up the phone.

A few hours had passed since he planted the bomb in the bathroom on the sixty-eighth floor. He hoped there were still people up there. Clueless. Meandering around the small enclosure, looking out at the city of London beneath them. Unaware of what lay in their way. The device that was rigged to blow in less than an hour's time.

But there was an issue.

Tanner.

Jake had shown irritating perseverance and tenacity. He had become the cancerous thorn in his side, eating away at him, immobilising him, putting him under pressure to carry out his mission quickly. But Charlie didn't want to. He wanted to take his time with it. Enjoy it. Savour it. Soak up every ounce of excitement he would get from it, so he could live with it at the forefront of his mind for the rest of his life. And Charlie knew Jake was close behind, inhibiting his plans.

Jake would return soon, and when he did, Charlie needed to be prepared. But for now he needed to mix things up. Stall Jake long enough for the bomb to go off. Make Jake believe he still had a chance to stop it. And if Jake died in the aftermath, then so be it. It was one less person for Charlie to deal with.

Charlie needed the explosion to go off. He needed to plant the seed to the outside world that his virus was in the air. That it was airborne and making its way around the millions of citizens and tourists roaming the streets three hundred feet below. That there would be nothing any of them could do about it. That, as soon as it was in their lungs, their DNA would be altered.

Charlie coughed. Convulsed. His abdomen and chest hurt. He moved his hand away from his mouth. Blood. Dark red, lined with a hint of black. His organs were rotting at an alarming rate. He didn't know how long he had left, but he was certain he'd make it to the end of the day, at least.

His thoughts turned back to the present.

The bomb.

The countdown.

Then he had an idea. Pushing Maisie Tanner back to Elizabeth, Charlie scanned the room, searching for his next victim. He was bored with Tanner's children. He wanted to test Jake, give him something fun to do.

The answer presented itself a moment later. *Perfect.*

'You,' he said, pointing at a young boy, the blood in his hands running over his fingers and dropping to the ground.

The little boy looked up. 'Come here.'

At once the child was protected behind his mother.

'No!' she screamed. 'I won't let you take him.'

'I don't care what you're going to let me do, Karen Tough. Your son will do as I say.'

Karen pulled the boy closer to her chest. Protected his eyes with her hands. Cradled him like he was a baby. The way Charlie's mother would never have done to him – even if it meant he was about to be taken into the arms of a terrorist; she didn't love him enough to object.

'Give me the fucking boy, now!' Charlie said, pointing the gun at Karen's head.

Karen shielded the child more tightly. She looked to her husband. 'Alex – do something!'

The man sat there, wide-eyed. Frozen.

'Alex!' Karen cried again.

Charlie had had enough. He rushed over to Karen, tucked the AK under his armpit, and reached for the boy. Karen fought as much as she could. She clawed. Scratched. Slapped. Elizabeth, to Charlie's right, tried to fend him off, but it was no use; he pushed her down, and she hit the back of her head on the windowpane.

'Elizabeth!' the man named Alex cried. 'Are you OK?'

One adult down. Two to go.

'Alex, please! He's taking Ethan away from us! Our son!' Karen called.

Alex steadied himself to his feet, left Elizabeth on the floor and started towards him. Charlie swung the butt of the gun from under his arm and smashed it against Alex's head. Alex fell faster than he had stood. Blood streamed from the incision in his forehead. The man was incapacitated.

Charlie gripped Ethan's arm. Karen fought harder. She dug her nails into his forearm and drew blood. He ignored the pain – it was nothing compared to what he had been through in his life.

'Give me the fucking child,' Charlie said again. 'This is your last warning.'

Charlie pointed the gun at Karen and pressed it against her temple. He cast a quick glance behind him to see if anyone had tried to make an escape, or if there was anyone trying to attack him from behind. Two individuals were on their feet, hiding behind the piano to the right of the lounge area.

He needed to take control of the situation.

'Don't you fucking dare move another muscle, or so help me God I will shoot her in the head!' Bits of spittle and blood were expelled from Charlie's mouth as he spoke, and it rained down on Elizabeth next to him who fervently rubbed the back of her head.

Everyone in the restaurant froze. The couple returned to their place on the floor, and just like that, with a loud shout that hurt his throat and body more than he cared to admit, order was restored.

Turning back to Karen, he said, 'I promise nothing bad will happen to him.'

'I don't believe you.'

'Whether you do or not, I don't care. It doesn't make a difference. Now, hand him over and I'll make sure I can protect him for as long as possible.'

Karen stared at Charlie. Her son. Back at Charlie. Tears welled in her eyes, and the light glistened in them. Eventually, she nodded, releasing her grip on Charlie's arm.

'What's going on, Mum?'

'Look at me, Ethan.' She pulled his head away from her chest, stroked his hair and cheeks. 'Everything will be OK. I promise. This man just wants to speak to you for a little bit.'

'Is that it?'

Karen nodded.

Ethan turned his attention to Charlie. 'What do I have to do?'

Charlie smiled as appealingly as he could manage. 'Follow my instructions and wait. Come.' Charlie extended his hand; Ethan took it and the two of them moved towards Charlie's gym bag.

Reaching into his bag, Charlie removed his suicide vest. Strapped to the fabric was a series of plastic boxes encircling the waist. Each box contained dummy explosives. Different-coloured wires protruded from the boxes and connected to the others, in a network of plastic and copper. At the front was a countdown timer. The digits read 00:00:00. It was a fake vest he had made himself, intended to be used only as a last resort, if he needed to escape with a hostage. But the dynamic of his operation had changed, and so would his plans.

Charlie placed the vest around Ethan's small body and tightened it. The vest hung low, swallowing him, making him look stupid, but it would have to do. There was no other option.

'What's this for?' Ethan asked, his eyes looking into Charlie's.

'It's just a little vest I need you to wear for the next ten minutes or so.' Charlie reached inside the bag, grabbed a dummy detonator, and placed it in Ethan's hands. 'Keep the lever pressed at all times, OK? Because if you let go, bad things will happen, and you'll never get to see your mummy or daddy again.'

Ethan said nothing. Charlie reached into his back pocket, found the pen and paper he had used to write customers' orders earlier in the day, and scribbled a note. His hand shook as he attempted to inscribe the message. Physical and mental fatigue, and the virus, were getting to him.

It read:

> *Inspired by your old friends Moshat and Adil. I'm sure you know how it works. You do it wrong, and the child dies.*

Charlie folded the note, grabbed Ethan's free hand, and wrapped his fingers over the paper.

'You keep that safe as well, yeah?' Charlie said. 'Only adults can read it. You understand?'

Ethan nodded. Charlie faced him so they were square-on. He gave the vest a once-over. He needed to make sure it looked as legitimate as possible. He was nearly done, but there was one final piece, which he wanted to leave until the last minute.

'I'm scared,' Ethan said, tears now forming in his eyes.

'Don't be, OK? You'll be fine. Man up. Be a bigger man than your father is.'

Charlie grabbed Ethan's arms, and at that moment, it felt as if he were sending his fictional son away on their first day of school. It was an alien concept, one he didn't like and tried to remove from his mind as quickly as possible. Rising to his feet, Charlie ushered Ethan to the side of the bar. He tried the door, using his shoulder. It was locked. He tried again. Nothing. It was still jammed from the earlier power outage. Growing impatient, Charlie raised the gun, fired at the door handle - and the electrical system operating it - and recoiled as the door swung up. After the excitement of the gunshot had died down, he bent to Ethan's eye level and told him to go to the stairwell on the other side of the door and wait there.

'I'll call Jake so he can help,' Charlie said as he clicked the button at the top of the countdown timer. The digits flashed red and counted down from ten minutes.

00:09:58.

Charlie waved Ethan away and turned his back on him before the child went through another set of double doors that led to the stairs.

As he returned to the Oblix, Charlie used the concealed phone he had grabbed from Maisie Tanner and dialled the last number. The person on the other end answered almost immediately.

'Tanner? It's Paxman. There's a little present waiting for you.'

42

Confirmed Suspicions

December 2, 2017, 13:19

Alex Tough didn't know what to feel; he didn't know what to think. All he did know was that his forehead hurt like fuck, and that the streaming blood down the side of his face was increasing with every passing second. He grabbed for a napkin on the floor and held it against his skin. He couldn't feel anything. His body was numb with pain. Fear. Cowardice. Regret. Guilt.

He had just watched - and allowed - his only son to be kidnapped and taken away by a bioterrorist. And what had he done about it? Nothing. He had been selfish. He hadn't wanted to get hurt and instead had risked the lives of the ones he loved.

Karen and Ellen were locked in an embrace. He had left it

up to her to protect their daughter from the reality of what was going on. Tears streamed down both of their cheeks.

Alex extended his hand to Karen's shoulder. She shook him off and glared at him.

'Don't touch me,' she said. 'You coward. You could have protected him. You could have saved him. If you had acted like a man – like a father – then none of this would be happening. Jake wouldn't let that happen to Ellie or Maisie. He would have done everything in his power to make sure they were safe. Just like he's doing now.'

Karen hissed her words at him, and they were laced with a venom that poisoned him as far as his soul.

But it was that word that piqued Alex's interest.

Jake.

At first, Alex had thought Karen's casual flirtatious behaviour with Jake was just that – casual. Elizabeth had brought it to his attention at first, but he hadn't believed her – he hadn't wanted to believe her. But as it happened more and more frequently, and as the signs became more opaque, so did his suspicions. Karen had feelings for Jake, it was clear to see. And her words just now were all he needed to confirm her interest in him. The leg touching at the table, the laughing at his unfunny jokes, the checking him out, staring at him, giving him the eye – even when she thought nobody else was looking – all the other advances she made at him were there, too.

And now he knew.

Alex had used Elizabeth as a confidant. Someone he could speak to about it. She tried to reassure him, but they both knew it was pointless. She had nothing to worry about; it was all Karen, of course. Jake was a good husband. Jake was loyal.

Jake neither acted on nor instigated any of it.

Jake, the role model.

Jake, the stand-up guy.

Jake, the hero.

Jake, the one everyone looked up to.

Alex hated it. He hated being made second best to someone Karen didn't even really know – someone she hadn't spent the past fifteen years building a life with.

Alex sat there, on the floor inside the Oblix, contemplating, reflecting, considering. How would Karen react if he died? How would he react if she died? How would things be different if they weren't together anymore? Would he mind? Would he care? He didn't think so. But maybe time would tell.

43

Outbreak

December 2, 2017, 13:20

On the other side of the city, in Greenwich, Mamadou stepped out from his unmarked BMW. Behind him, a group of Trojans, members of the Met's specialist armed division SCO19, jumped out of armoured Land Rovers. Each of them carried standard issue Heckler & Koch MP5s round their shoulders and Kevlar vests and helmets to protect them from whatever lay ahead.

'Guv,' one of the armed officers said. 'We'll enter first. Only come in when we give you the OK.'

Mamadou nodded. The officer spun on the spot and sprinted towards the door to the block of flats where Charlie Paxman lived. His address had been confirmed and his neighbours had corroborated he still lived there. The last time someone had seen him was this morning.

Mamadou watched the Met's elite team enter the building, storm the stairs and enter Charlie Paxman's flat through a live feed on a tablet. In the surrounding area, cars slowed down as their drivers' curiosity got the better of them, eager to see what was happening. Mamadou ignored them all. There was a job to do, and he needed to be totally focused.

'Guv,' the Trojan in charge said on the radio a few minutes later. 'All clear. Come on up.'

Mamadou placed the radio receiver back on the dashboard of his car and shut the door. He left two police constables in charge of the area until he returned.

Charlie Paxman's flat was small, barely large enough for one man. The kitchen was the first thing Mamadou saw. Leftover pots and pans and plates and forks and glasses sat in the sink and on the counter. Two men, no longer wearing their helmets, stood resting against the kitchen surface, apparently content there was no immediate threat.

Mamadou moved through the apartment. The kitchen and living room were open-plan. Patio doors at the back end of the room led onto a small balcony where a plastic garden chair rested upside down. The bathroom was narrow, only just wide enough for Mamadou's shoulders to fit through. On the right-hand side of the corridor stood two officers, waiting outside Charlie Paxman's room.

'Guv, you're going to want to see this,' an AFO wearing protective goggles said. Mamadou recognised the voice as belonging to the man in charge: Dean Smith.

Saying nothing, Mamadou peered his head through the door. A hand touched him on the back.

'No, guv, not this one.' Dean thumbed to the door on the

other side of the corridor.

Charlie Paxman's office, his laboratory. The room he had spent months cramped inside concocting his evil plan. Mamadou knew straight away before he even entered the room. An acrid stench hung in the air and stuck inside his throat. It made him gag.

'What the fuck is this?' Mamadou asked, his retching turning into a cough.

In front of him was an iMac computer. Next to it was what looked like a science experiment gone wrong. A large tray of glass vials ran along the table, along with some liquid that had spilled over onto the oak-like finish. There were three holes in the vial tray, and the middle hole was empty.

'Nobody touch a fucking thing. I need his computer unlocked,' Mamadou ordered. 'I want to know where he got all of these chemicals from. Forensics – get them in. Tell us how volatile this stuff is, what the threat level is, and whether . . .'

Mamadou trailed off. A concerning thought occurred to him. There was no knowing what the chemicals inside the tubes were capable of, especially the one that was missing, at least not until the forensics team arrived.

Mamadou ordered someone to get on the phone to the forensics department.

'Get this entire block sealed shut. I want everybody to stay here. Close all the windows, doors, blinds – whatever. No one else in or out. Not until we find out what we're dealing with. We're going into quarantine,' he said.

'What you saying, guv?' a man behind him asked. 'That we got to stay here because there might be something in the air?'

'Yes,' Mamadou said, his attention focused on a large metal box on the desk. It looked like an incubator.

'And if there is something in the air, then you saying we've got to stay in here?'

'Yes.'

'So we might catch it?'

'I fear we already have, fellas. That's part of what a quarantine is. I think we've got an outbreak on our hands.'

Mamadou made a call.

'Frances? It's Mamadou. We've got a situation.'

44

Bite

December 2, 2017, 13:22

COBRA, the acronym for Cabinet Office Briefing Room A. The place where the country's most powerful and senior members of staff meet in times of threat to national security. Frances's worst nightmare.

It was her fifth time there this year while the commissioner was on sick leave, and she was beginning to think she would have to set up a small office for herself in the corridor. There had been multiple attacks in the space of two months earlier in the year. The first during the London Marathon, then around the royal wedding, and then a callous attack in a football stadium. In the summer, the 01/08 attack had taken place, and Frances had led the entire operation, placed all the burden of blame on her shoulders, and had come out victorious. With the threat of a new terror attack increasing every day, COBRA meetings grew in intensity and frequency.

The door opened and the Prime Minister stepped in. She was the last to arrive, and the room fell silent as soon as she entered. In her hands she held a large dossier. Placing it on the table, she began, 'Thanks for coming, everyone.'

The Prime Minister sat down and placed her elbows on the table and knitted her fingers together. Her voice was calm and neutral, yet commanding and authoritative. Everyone knew where they were and who they were in the company of.

'I trust you have all had time to read through your very brief summary of notes?' The Prime Minister looked around the room; her eyes fell the longest on Frances.

Great, she thought. *The ridicule begins.*

'The team are working on it, ma'am,' Simon Ashdown said beside her, defending SO15. He was the national coordinator for terrorism, and his face was becoming increasingly recognisable to the other members of COBRA as the threat to the nation's security worsened.

His sudden outburst took Frances by surprise – he seldom spoke in any of the meetings, and the only time he did was when he was spoken to where he would always rely on Frances to bail him out from any holes into which he'd dug himself. In recent months she had taken a keen disliking towards Simon, but had never thought to tell anyone about it. She knew what he'd done to Mamadou, and she would never be able to forgive him for it. But she couldn't punish him – because Mamadou had asked her not to, and because he was good at his job. She thought Simon Ashdown should step down as deputy assistant commissioner if he had any sense of pride and remorse. So far, eighteen months on, he hadn't. And, in short, Frances thought he was a bollockless twat.

'How is it taking so long?' the Home Secretary said. 'How long have you been sitting on this information?'

'Not long enough, evidently,' the Foreign Secretary added.

'The attack this morning at The Shard was brought to our attention early on; however, there have been delays in gathering the intelligence we need,' Frances said.

'Why?'

'Because of cuts, Home Secretary. We are understaffed as it is at the moment down in SO15, and this attack has stretched us incredibly thin.' Frances had been in the job long enough to know when to stand up for herself, and she wasn't about to be intimidated by someone just as incompetent at their job as a hamster working behind a cash register. Although, in this instance, Frances supposed the hamster would do a better job than the Home Secretary at keeping the country safe from threat.

'Don't start with this again, Frances. You've seen the numbers. You know full well that SO15 can function as it is.'

'Ladies!' the Prime Minister interrupted. 'I don't care who has more money than who. That's a discussion for another day. What I want to know is, how come Charlie Paxman hasn't been picked up before?'

The room fell silent. Frances hated this part of the meeting. The part where she would embarrass herself and prove how adept the country's response to terrorism was. The part where she would tell them she and her team knew nothing about what was happening. It had happened five months ago on the first of August, and it seemed almost poetic for history to repeat itself now.

'It's a domestic attack, ma'am,' Frances replied, seeing as no one else would. 'They are harder to defend against.'

'Have you not learned anything since Operation Tightrope? Isn't this what you've been spending the majority of your time since the attack coming up with – a contingency plan to minimise the threat of these risks?' the Home Secretary said.

'Excuse me, Amanda. I wasn't aware we had switched roles. Last I heard, it was the Office for Security and Counter Terrorism's responsibility to govern all of us. If you can't do your job properly, then don't pass the fucking blame onto the rest of us.' Frances was furious; she hated swearing, but she hadn't signed up for this shit, and she wasn't going to let anyone tell her how to do her job.

Simon Ashdown cleared his throat. 'I think what the assistant commissioner is trying to say is that we are working flat out to come up with the information necessary for you. Regardless of whether or not this is a domestic attack, and only one cell, the Metropolitan Police Service – and by extension SO15 – will do everything it can to stop it.'

'Are you sure it's only a single-cell attack?' the mayor of London entered the conversation. Until this point, he had sat there silently, nearly at the point of twiddling his thumbs.

'Positive. We've got a confirmed sighting of Charlie Paxman on the CCTV footage inside the building, and he doesn't appear to be accompanied by anyone.'

'Doesn't appear to be?' the Foreign Secretary interrupted. 'We don't want fucking hypotheses. We want the facts, Simon. How long have you been in this job?'

Simon sat back in his chair, defeated. Frances couldn't

help but stifle a smile; whatever his hidden agenda was – trying to get one up on her, she presumed – he had failed. It was a bittersweet victory.

Frances cleared her throat. 'What Simon means is that, with the details we have now, and the incoming stream of intelligence, we can confirm there are no other attackers. From what we've learned so far, Paxman led a very isolated life. He had no friends, no family. The only people who would ever speak to him were his colleagues. No email correspondence with anyone. No one on his social media profiles. It's almost as if he's never existed.'

'I agree.'

Frances turned to her left. Sat immediately next to her was Martin Ball, the new director general of MI5. Martin was a big man with even bigger legs. His hair was receding on the top, and he wore glasses that hung low on his crooked nose. All in all, he was an unattractive human being, but there was something about him – something mysterious – that Frances liked. Maybe it was his personality. Maybe it was his generosity, his kindness, the fact he was one of the few people she trusted enough to tell about her family and her husband.

The thought made her feel a morsel of warmth, a welcoming change to the cold and terse atmosphere of the room.

'Is there anyone from the World Health Organisation who can give us more information about Charlie Paxman? Someone who knows – knew – him well?' the Prime Minister asked, shuffling the papers on the desk. Her voice remained as calm as it had when she'd entered the room.

Frances shook her head. 'They're all locked inside The

Shard with him. It's their annual convention. Delayed several months because of an outbreak of illness amongst the most senior members. And this year they decided to have a change of scenery. All the people he worked with during his time there are currently being held at gunpoint.'

The Home Secretary shook her head. 'What are we going to do?'

Ignoring Amanda's question, the Prime Minister asked, 'Do we know what sort of threat we're dealing with yet? Do we know what Paxman's demands are? His motivations?'

Frances opened her mouth to speak but was interrupted by Martin. As they both modestly allowed the other to go first, Frances's phone vibrated in her pocket. She answered.

'At this current moment in time, we don't—' Martin began.

'Wait,' Frances said, holding her hand in the air. She hesitated. Absorbed the words Mamadou had just told her in her ear and then hung up the phone. 'It's a virus.'

'Excuse me?' the PM asked.

'It's some sort of virus. In liquid form. DCS Kuhoba is at Paxman's property now. They've found glass vials containing a liquid, but one of them is missing.' Frances paused a beat. 'One of the reports we found earlier stated that Paxman's opinions and views were rejected. They mentioned something about him wanting to change the world. To release something into the atmosphere. I think he's going to release a virus into the air at the top of the city's tallest building.'

Expletives echoed around the room in whispered tones.

'This is just guesswork, Assistant Commissioner. We need concrete evidence,' the Prime Minister said.

'I'm on it,' the Home Secretary replied, starting out of her chair, making a phone call.

The Prime Minister turned to address the rest of the room. 'What is our response to a CBRN threat?'

CBRN stood for chemical, biological, radiological and nuclear threats – and on the scale of severity, they stood at the top.

'First things first,' Frances said. 'We need to deploy all officers within the vicinity to the base of the building. Prepare them with suits. Evacuate the area.'

'Where to?' the chief constable of the British Transport Police asked.

Frances considered for a moment.

'The Underground.'

Silence fell on the room.

'What? You can't be serious. How is that going to work?'

'Close down London Bridge and every other station nearby. It's the safest and quickest route for people to evacuate. Think about it – Paxman and this liquid are situated about five hundred feet in the air. If he's able to release it into the atmosphere, it will infect everyone in the surrounding area. But if they're underground, they've got a better chance of getting out unaffected.'

Heads nodded around the room. She glanced to her right at Simon, who glared at her. Smiling facetiously, she turned to Martin and felt her smile turn into a real one. Martin's approval was the one she valued more.

'Right, fine.' The Prime Minister made a note of what Frances had said on her pad. 'Ian – I want you to get on that straight away. Same for you, Simon – organise the uniformed officers and Trojans in and around the area. Prepare them for immediate evac.'

Both men nodded, said, 'Ma'am,' and left.

'Next objective,' the Prime Minister continued, 'is how the bloody hell we're going to get Charlie Paxman out of that building before he releases his virus – or, worse, shoots everyone inside and then releases the virus.'

'Send in the armed officers,' the Foreign Secretary said.

'The armed forces,' someone suggested.

'The SAS,' suggested another.

'They will have little time to prepare and familiarise themselves with the plans of the building,' Glen Strachan, the head of the Ministry of Defence said. Until this point, it had almost been as if he weren't there, sitting quietly in the background of the room, waiting for the opportune moment to raise his voice.

'Isn't that what these guys are trained to do? Adapt to different surroundings quickly? If they can't, then why are they in that role? If all it takes is to familiarise yourself with some stupid blueprints, anyone could do it,' the mayor of London scoffed.

'Don't you dare insult my men, Christian. I'd love to see you even shoot a gun. You don't know your arse from your mouth, and as soon as you pressed that trigger, the only thing you'd put an end to is sperm coming out of your balls.' The head of the MOD was a proud man, especially with his soldiers. If there was one thing Frances had learned from her experiences in COBRA, it was to not insult his team's capabilities.

Frances shook her head. This was getting out of hand. What were they thinking, sending in the country's finest, most elite shooters to combat an almost invisible man with over a dozen hostages and a potentially deadly virus? No. All it would take is for one thing to go wrong and the virus would be released. It was too large a margin for error.

'I have a better idea,' Frances said. She paused a beat until she commanded the attention of everyone in the room. 'Jake Tanner. He's in The Shard as we speak. He's able to get close to Paxman, to reason with him, to get him to hand over whatever is in the contents of that glass – and himself. He's our only hope.'

45

DMS

December 2, 2017, 13:23

'Good luck.' Charlie Paxman's final words to Jake before he hung up were filled with malevolence.

He had just been told that Ethan was the next victim in Charlie's detestable game.

'What did he say?' Tim asked, leaning against the banister of the thirtieth floor.

'A boy. He's strapped an explosive vest to a young boy. There's a timer on it, and a note.'

Tim's mouth opened wide. 'What does the note say?'

'He wouldn't tell me.'

'Where's the boy?'

Jake didn't respond. Instead, he looked upwards at the dozens of steps that stood between him and Ethan.

'Come on,' Jake said, already starting up the stairs.

Tim followed closely behind. As they ascended the stairs, Jake called Ethan's name. After a few attempts, Ethan responded.

'Jake? Is that you?' Ethan cried down, his voice hoarse and weak. His words filled Jake with happiness.

'Yes, buddy, it's me. We're coming up, OK? Stay where you are – we'll be there in a minute.'

Twenty seconds later, Jake and Tim arrived on the thirty-second floor of The Shard. Ethan was sat awkwardly at the top of the stairs. The vest was too big for him and looked uncomfortable. His small face beamed at the sight of Jake.

The two of them embraced.

'You're OK,' he said, pressing Ethan as tightly against his chest as he dared. 'Thank God you're OK.' Jake released him. 'How is everyone else?'

'They're fine.'

'Any of them hurt?'

Ethan shook his head.

Thank God. Thank God. Thank God. A lump swelled in Jake's throat, and he swallowed hard to keep it down.

'It's so good to see you,' Jake said. 'There's someone I want you to meet.'

Jake turned to Tim and introduced them to one another. Tim ruffled the boy's hair and smiled at him.

'We're going to make sure you're all right, OK?' Jake wasn't going to have a repeat of August. No way. He wasn't going to let someone else dear to him die at the hands of a terrorist. Not if he could help it. He would do anything.

Ethan nodded.

'Good. Now, let me see the note the man gave you.'

Ethan opened his left hand and passed the scrap of paper to Jake. Jake's eyes fell over the words, and inside him fury burned.

Inspired by your friends . . . Moshat . . . Adil . . .

What inspiration? Jake looked over the vest. The explosives. The countdown timer. They were all there, but what made it the same as Moshat's or Adil's?

Ethan raised his other hand.

The detonator. It was exactly like the one Moshat had held during Operation Tightrope. Small. Compact. Black. Wireless.

Jake grabbed Ethan's fist. 'Whatever you do, buddy, don't open this hand. Don't let the trigger go, OK? Because if you do, then something bad will happen. And we don't want that, do we?'

'No.'

Jake screwed the piece of paper in his hands and threw it down the stairs, erasing its words from his mind. He needed a clear head. The time on the countdown flicked to 00:08:43.

'We've got a little under ten minutes to defuse this,' Jake said to Tim.

'OK . . .' Tim bent down to Jake and Ethan's height. 'Any idea how?'

'Can't say I do, no. Is there anyone you can call who can help?'

'Surprisingly, I'm not acquainted with many bomb-disposal experts,' Tim said.

Jake knew it was a long shot, but he didn't appreciate the sarcasm. He considered his options for a moment. Who did he know that could help him defuse a bomb?

00:07:58.

'There's no one,' Jake said, admiring and studying the

intricacies of the wiring. 'Unless . . .'

Jake removed his phone and dialled. Ten seconds later, Frances Walken responded.

'Jake – is that you?' she asked. She sounded surprised to hear him.

'Yes. I don't have a lot of time,' he told her. 'I need your help, quickly. Or I need you to get me in touch with someone who can.'

'What's wrong? What's happening?' In the background, Jake could hear various officials discussing a plan of action.

Jake explained the situation.

'Ethan? Is that the boy's name?'

'Yes,' Jake said.

A pause on the other end.

'Frances? Frances, are you there?' Jake asked.

'Yes. Yes . . . I . . . I'm sorry. I—'

'Is there anyone who can help us?' Jake hurried her along.

'Hold on,' Frances said, 'I'll ask.'

Jake waited patiently on the phone. In the meantime, his eyes followed the wires around Ethan's body. As his gaze met Ethan's, he smiled to reassure the boy that everything was OK.

'Jake,' Frances said a few seconds later, 'Jake – are you there?'

'Yeah.'

'Right, we've got someone who can help. We're just trying to get hold of him. As soon as we do, we'll put you on speaker, so we can all communicate with one another.'

'Do what you have to,' Jake said, 'so long as you hurry. We don't have long.'

Less than a minute later, Jake heard Frances's voice in his

ear.

'Jeremy,' Frances said, 'Jake's on the line with us now. We've got a vest with five cells on it, all of which are connected to a main cell in the middle by a series of wires. Any suggestions?'

Jake put the phone on speaker. A moment of silence passed.

'How many wires?' a man's voice said.

Jake made a quick count. 'Fifteen.'

'For five cells?'

'Yes.'

'So, three each?'

'This isn't a maths lesson.'

'Is there anything else I need to know?' Jeremy asked.

'There's a detonator. Similar to the one Moshat Hakim used a few months ago.'

'How can you be sure it's a similar device?' the unfamiliar voice asked.

'Because Paxman left me a note, and it told me so. It's using a dead man's switch.'

00:06:14.

A sound of disturbance and distorted chatter filtered through the microphone. Talking to so many people at once was a bad idea, and it was beginning to run his patience thin.

'Jake,' it was Jeremy speaking, 'if it were the same setup as the Hakim brothers', then there would be no wires connecting the explosives.'

'What makes you think that?' Jake asked, keeping one eye on the time and the other on Ethan.

'I was part of the bomb-disposal unit tasked with removing the devices on board those trains. There were no wires on any of them. It was all remote-controlled. Wireless. They were all separate entities. As soon as one went off, the others would have in a chain reaction.'

'So, what does that mean?'

'That I think you're dealing with a hoax. Those explosives on that vest aren't live. Nor are the wires. There are too many of them for it to be legit.'

'Are you sure?'

'Yes.'

'How sure?'

'Ninety per cent.'

Jake shook his head. 'No, no, no. I'd prefer if you were a hundred.'

'Well, I'm not. But you have to trust me on this one. If anything is going to be active, it'll be the DMS. It might be connected to something else in the building. So, whatever you do, just keep that lever depressed.'

00:05:46.

'You hear that, Ethan? Keep your fingers down on that thing in your hand and don't let go,' Frances said through the phone.

'OK,' Ethan replied. He appeared the calmest out of everyone, and Jake admired the boy's bravery.

'To clarify,' Jake said, 'you are advising that we remove the vest, but keep the detonator with us?'

'Yes,' Jeremy said.

'Fine.' Jake bent down on both knees and untied the knots and buckles strapped around Ethan's chest. The entire thing came loose freely. Jake let out a heavy sigh as he placed the vest on the floor. There had been no explosion. No sign of initiating the cells. It had been a success. He said as much into the phone.

'Thank goodness for that,' Frances said. 'Now, Tanner, you need to get the boy to a safe distance and the vest well out of the way of everyone.'

'Yes, ma'am. We'll be in touch if we need anything else.' Jake hung up the phone and looked at Tim. 'You take him downstairs. Find some Sellotape or something – stick the lever to the device. It's wireless, so even if you let go the tiniest amount, it could detonate. I don't know what the range is – if any – but I'd rather not find out.'

'And what are you going to do?' Tim interrupted.

'I'm going to get the vest out of harm's way. I'll put it upstairs somewhere, in one of the empty floors. I'll make sure it doesn't kill anyone if it goes off. Just don't kill me in the process.' Jake looked at Ethan. 'After you've done that, take him down to the bottom and get him some help. Do not let him go. Do not let him out of your sight. He's your responsibility. I'm entrusting you with him.'

'Will Paxman mind if he's missing?'

'I don't care. So long as he's safe.' Jake nodded at Ethan discreetly, his paternal instinct overcoming him all at once.

'Are we all agreed?'

'Agreed.'

Jake shook Tim's hand, then bent down to hug Ethan. As soon as they started walking away, Tim called back to him.

'Wait,' he said, reaching into his pockets, 'you're going to need these.'

Tim produced a key card and a handgun. Jake didn't recognise it for what it was at first. The light reflecting off the dark surface of the SIG Sauer P220 glistened. Then, after Jake eventually realised what he was looking at, he stared at Tim in disbelief.

'What's that for?'

Tim looked at the key card, bemused. 'Well, it's so you can get in and out of the floors. After the power outage, some of the doors work and some don't. This will help you get to where you need to go.'

Jake shook his head. 'That's not what I meant.' He pointed to the gun. 'Where did you get *that*?'

'That's not important. You're going to need it more than I am. Besides, you know your way around guns better than I do. I'd probably shoot someone by accident. Or myself.'

Jake smiled. He took the gun and card from Tim, tucked the handgun in his trousers in the small of his back, and placed the card in his pocket, alongside his wallet. The two of them shook hands again as if for one final time. Jake grabbed the vest, started climbing the steps to get the hazardous explosives as far away from his family as possible, and as he ascended the building, he couldn't help wondering what the use of dummy explosives was for.

46

Airborne

December 2, 2017, 13:32

Jake stopped on the fifty-second floor inside the Shangri-La. It was empty, desolate. It was surreal to think that not long ago he had been in the hotel amidst the furore of the power outage, when the lobby was packed.

Jake had climbed the steps leading to the hotel's Skypool, western Europe's highest swimming pool.

'This'll do,' he said to himself as he looked over the shimmering crystal-blue water.

Jake checked the time on the vest. 00:02:04. Without thinking about it, he lobbed the vest into the water and sprinted out of the spa room. Heading back to the stairwell, his chest heaving, he made a call. He tried to force the ticking countdown from his mind.

'Did you save him?' Charlie asked, a moment after answering the call.

'Yes. Why was it a dummy? What else is going on here?'

'It was to stall you.'

'Stall me from what?'

'The bigger picture.'

'What bigger picture?'

'The one that makes you look fucking inept at your job, and the one that makes me look like a hero.'

'A hero to who?'

'Friends.'

'You've got some, then?'

'More than you do, Tanner. I can see that much right in front of me. These guys are the only friends and family you've got.'

Jake ignored the comment.

'Tell a lie, you do have friends . . . Did you appreciate the homage to them?'

'Fuck you,' Jake hissed.

'Be careful what you say, Jake. One of your children might accidentally be on the receiving end of a bullet if you're not careful. How ironic would that be – you can defend someone else's child, but not your own.'

Jake clenched his fist. 'Tell me what else is going to happen. Tell me what else you've got planned.'

'What's the best way to release a virus, Jake? I didn't think I'd have to spell it out for you, but perhaps I overestimated your abilities. Disappointing, really, considering the media painted you as some sort of deity.'

The air. The cogs in Jake's exhausted brain began turning. *The virus. It's in another bomb. It's going to be made airborne . . .*

and that's what the dead man's switch is for.

'I judge by your silence you've worked it out.' A pause. 'You best hurry, I don't think you've got long to find it.' Another pause. 'Go on, Jake. Be a hero. Save everyone.'

'I will,' Jake said.

'I'd like to see you try.'

'Watch me.'

Jake hung up the phone before Charlie could respond. Something he had seen earlier rose to the forefront of his mind. Something that piqued his interest then just as much as it did now. Something he should have acted upon as soon as he saw it.

The View From The Shard. The bathroom.

With a solid purpose in his mind, Jake started climbing higher and higher, deeper and deeper into the depths of the building, to the sixty-eighth floor of The Shard. Running against an invisible clock, he pushed his body to an unprecedented level of endurance.

47

Sudden Death

December 2, 2017, 13:34

The air inside the flat tasted toxic. Since the outbreak, the armed officers, and Mamadou himself, had all struggled to calm themselves. The forensic scientists had arrived less than five minutes after Mamadou called Frances. They had been ordered to take samples of the liquid on Charlie Paxman's office table, and only three officers had remained. Everyone in the room was tense, and the level of stress was made worse by the severe claustrophobia of fitting fifteen people into such a small enclosure.

'How long is this going to take?' one of the armed officers asked.

'Shut up, Craig,' said another.

'As long as it needs to.' Mamadou glared at Craig; the

man's questions had been non-stop – he was behaving like a child on a car journey – and Mamadou's patience had reached the end of its tether. 'So sit down, find something to do, and be quiet for a minute.'

Craig shot Mamadou a scowl, furrowed his brow, and moved into the living room adjoining the kitchenette. He sat on the sofa and sulked.

Growing annoyed, Mamadou made his way into Charlie Paxman's office. The computer was unlocked, and sat in front of it was a computer scientist who had been sent down along with the forensics team. He wore a hazmat suit like the rest of the scientists, and was searching through Paxman's files.

'Found anything?' Mamadou asked, standing to the man's left.

'Nothing yet. Nothing that lets us know what's inside those glasses.' His voice sounded robotic coming through the microphone inside his suit.

'But did you find anything else?'

The computer scientist said nothing. He clicked the mouse a few times, searched for a document, and loaded it up.

'This makes for an interesting read.' Without being told to, the man moved out of the chair and made way for Mamadou.

Mamadou sat, leaned forward so he could see the screen better, and read the Word document open in front of him. It was an itinerary. A list of Charlie's plans for the day.

'I don't fucking believe it,' Mamadou said after reading the first line. 'This is a gold mine. And I thought he was supposed to be a genius.'

He continued reading.

11 a.m. — World Health Organisation meeting begins.

12 p.m. — Convention finishes. Seat them furthest away

from the exits.

12:30 p.m. – Destroy the power.

12:40 p.m. – Take the Oblix hostage.

1 p.m. – Shoot and kill everyone in the Oblix, including BENJAMIN WEISS and MARIANNE EVANS.

1:10 p.m. – Escape in the–

Before Mamadou could read any further, a noise distracted him in the other room. He jumped out of the seat and moved quickly into the living room.

'What are you doing?' Mamadou asked, pointing at the television. It was resting atop a stack of books and organised files. 'Who said you could put that on?'

Nobody replied; they were too afraid to admit to it and feel the extent of Mamadou's wrath. As he made his way over to the television, he stopped. The colour red caught his eye. *BBC News* was playing. An aerial image of The Shard filled the entire screen. It switched back to the news reporter live at the base of the building. Camera crews surrounded the correspondent.

'There has been little information released yet, Vanessa,' the reporter said.

'Turn it up!' Mamadou ordered.

Whoever held the remote control behind him complied.

The news reporter continued. 'We are still getting images coming through of the man thought to be behind the attack. Our sources are naming the attacker as a Charlie Paxman, estranged biogeneticist formerly of the World Health Organisation.' At that point, a photo of Charlie occupied the top right of the screen. It wasn't the same image Mamadou had seen earlier, and he noticed the men in the two photos looked completely different. In the one Mamadou had seen,

Charlie looked old, weak, beaten; in the on-screen photo, Charlie looked youthful and full of drive. He even wore a smile on his face.

The reporter continued, 'This is the first attack The Shard has seen since its construction finished in 2012. The number of casualties is unknown, and at this moment in time there are still dozens of people filtering out of the building. Many unharmed, but most of them suffering shock.'

The live feed cut back to the BBC studio, and Mamadou quickly lost interest. At least now he could keep as up to date as possible on what was happening without having to call Frances or someone else back in the office every five minutes.

Mamadou turned to face the sofa. Three men sat on it with their elbows resting on their knees, and one lounged on the armrest.

'Hey,' Mamadou said to Craig, 'good idea putting that on.'

Craig nodded, started to speak, and then coughed. It was a violent cough. It was the first time Mamadou had seen Craig show any sign of illness.

Craig pulled his hand away from his mouth, and his eyes widened at what he saw. Blood. Lined with what looked like tar.

'What the—' he started but was interrupted by another coughing fit.

This time he rose to his feet. Blood spattered everywhere, over his hands, forearms, chin, and face. His body convulsed and, immediately after he'd finished coughing, he vomited on the floor. It was a dark, thick ooze.

'Craig!' one of the officers next to him said, rushing to his side. 'Are you OK?'

Craig said nothing. He was in too much pain and too busy trying to keep the contents of his lungs and stomach inside him.

'Shit, shit, shit!' another officer said.

Craig collapsed to the floor. He lay curled up on the ground in a foetal position, his body writhing. Foam frothed at his mouth, and blood ran down his nose, over his lips, joining the rest of the blood and mucus on the carpet, and spread across his neck. He said nothing. Made no noise. He lay there silently, as if the suffering and pain he endured was only on the inside, and it was too great for him to voice.

Mamadou looked on in shock, as did everyone else in the room. No one knew what to do. No one had ever seen anything like this before. They were only trained up to a certain point for administering first aid, and Mamadou suspected the recovery position would have little to no effect on Craig now.

'Someone do something!' a forensic scientist said behind him.

Mamadou watched in horror. A grown man was dying in front of him, and he felt helpless. Craig's eyes had turned bloodshot, and now a stream of blood seeped through his tear ducts. Foam and mucus continued to flow over his mouth and stain the carpet.

Within seconds, Craig was dead.

Just like that. No warning. No preamble. Gone.

Everyone in the room stared at Craig's lifeless body. Some ran their fingers through their hair in disbelief. Some screamed, cried, cowered down to the floor. Some threw up in the kitchen and bathroom sink.

Mamadou had seen a lot of things in his time, but never

something as horrifying and grotesque as this. He turned away, tried to force the image of Craig from his mind and think rationally. What had happened to him? How could he have died so abruptly – and, more importantly, how could he have died so violently?

'How many of you knew him?' Mamadou asked, looking around the room. Most of the armed officers who remained nodded. 'Did he ever say he was ill? Did he ever mention anything about not feeling well over the past couple of days?'

The officers shook their heads collectively.

Christ.

Mamadou joined up the dots. There was only one thing everyone in the room had in common, and that was the contents of the lab in Paxman's office.

'It's been weaponised,' Mamadou whispered.

'It's been what?'

'The liquid. It's been weaponised. That's what's going to happen. Paxman's going to kill billions of people. Craig's the first victim.'

Silence fell on the room.

'What – what are we going to do?' the man nearest to Craig asked. He shuffled away and protected his mouth with his hands.

'There's nothing we can do. The virus stays in here, and so do we. The scientists who came earlier will be able to prevent a breakout. Nobody leaves until it's been removed from the air and it's safe to evacuate,' Mamadou replied.

'And how long is that going to take?'

'It could be hours. It could be days. Weeks. Who knows.'

'And what – we're just supposed to accept we may all die in here?'

Mamadou nodded. 'I don't like it any more than any of you, but it's what we have to do to protect everyone else in the world.'

'Fuck them! Fuck all of them.'

'Hey,' Mamadou said, pointing at the man's chest. 'What's your name?'

'Darren.'

'Well, Darren. Shit happens in life you have no control over, so the best way to deal with it is to accept it and move on. So, I'm asking you to accept the fact we're going to be here for a long time, and that some of us may never see our families or loved ones again. I know it's not what any of you signed up for – I'll be fucked if I did – but we've got to bear in mind that if this virus gets out and we're responsible, your families may suffer the same fate as . . .' Mamadou couldn't bring himself to say Craig's name, and instead nodded at his body.

'Is there nothing we can do?' Darren asked.

Mamadou considered this for a moment. 'Yes. I want you to search through Paxman's things. See if there's anything in there that suggests there's an antidote or a way to stop the virus. Something that will help us better identify what we're dealing with scientifically.' He paused to breathe. 'I don't care if we contaminate the scene – Craig's already done that, so there's no going back. And someone needs to place a towel or a sheet over his body. I don't want us trampling all over him. Let's pay him some respect.'

Everyone in the room nodded and got to work. Mamadou watched them all split up into their various roles about the flat.

He moved to the front door, out the way of everyone else,

removed his phone, and called Frances.

'Hello? Frances. It's Mamadou. There's been a development. The virus – it's been weaponised.'

48

Working On It

December 2, 2017, 13:42

A lump caught in Frances's throat, and it made her want to vomit. In all her years of experience, she had never encountered a threat as devastating and terrifying as this. She placed the phone on the desk, her hands shaking with fear.

'What is it?' Martin Ball asked, his hand touching her arm. She felt cold.

Frances opened her mouth, but the words wouldn't come out. Her tongue was dry, and her mind surged with thoughts and fears and concerns. She reached for a cup of water on the desk and drank.

'That was Mamadou,' Frances said, placing the cup back and struggling to find the strength to say the words. 'The situation has just got a lot worse. One of the Trojans has died in Charlie Paxman's flat.'

'Died?' the room echoed.

Frances nodded.

'How?' the Home Secretary asked.

'The virus. Charlie Paxman's plague.' Frances paused, finding that the strength in her voice had returned. 'The virus has been weaponised. One of the Trojans collapsed and started coughing. He was dead within a minute. If we don't contain this thing . . . I don't even want to think about the consequences. I mean, if it's already killed one person who's been exposed to it, then who knows how many more it can kill? Who knows the extent of what we're dealing with?'

'I can tell you that.'

Before anyone could respond, there was a knock on the open door. A man wearing thick glasses with a chain around his neck peered his head into the room.

'Ah, brilliant. You're here,' the Home Secretary said, rising to her feet. 'This here is Professor Grisham from the Earlham Institute. My team have asked him to run tests on the possible outcomes of the outbreak. They got their hands on a sample from Paxman's apartment when the CSI arrived. Please, Louis, take a seat. Might I remind you that whatever is said here goes no further than these four walls.'

'Oh, yes. Well understood, Home Secretary, I assure you.' Louis sat beside Frances, filling Simon's vacant seat. She grimaced as his body odour assaulted her nose.

'How have your investigations been going?'

'Fantastic! My team and I have found out so much. It's been quite startling how quickly we've uncovered results.'

Frances sighed heavily. 'Well, stop blabbering and get on with it.'

'Your suspicions in thinking it was a virus have been confirmed. We analysed the structure of the DNA pattern found in the sample from Paxman's flat, and the results are alarming—'

'We don't need to know how great a job you think he's done. What's the impact it's going to have?' Frances interrupted.

Louis cleared his throat before continuing. 'Well, if the virus gets out, then it will render two-thirds of the entire population infertile. They will no longer be able to repopulate, and therefore, millions of family lines will die out.'

A moment of silence fell on the room. Everyone looked at one another. Nobody knew what to say, and nobody wanted to be the first to speak. They were dealing with something unprecedented, something none of them had ever seen in their careers. And in all likelihood, it was something they would never see again.

'What are the defining characteristics of the genes that will be affected?' the Home Secretary asked, snapping everyone's attention back to the present.

Shrugging, Louis said, 'It's difficult to say. I should mention Paxman once bragged to some of my colleagues about something like this at a local genetics conference a couple of years ago. He didn't mention a virus, mind you, but he said he would one day create something that would favour more intelligent human beings for the so-called betterment of society. From some of the complexities we're seeing with this virus's design, it appears he may have tried, and even succeeded, at doing just that.'

Another wave of silence descended on them. Everyone

looked at one another, aware of what the words meant but afraid to ask for clarification.

Frances bit the bullet. 'What are you saying? That this is some sort of intellectual genocide where only the most intelligent survive?'

'As I said, it's difficult to be certain.'

'And what about the weaponisation of the virus?' the Prime Minister stepped in, her eyes wide with curiosity. 'How is that possible? And how will it affect *us*?'

Frances didn't like how much emphasis the Prime Minister placed on the final word. It was as if she were only looking out for herself while the rest of the world suffered.

Fucking politicians, Frances thought to herself.

'Prime Minister,' Louis began, 'if you can create a disease that will change the face of the human planet, you can almost certainly manipulate it to serve a more sinister purpose. My team and I have done some simple extrapolation in the short time we've had the samples in our possession, and from our early investigations, it doesn't seem that the virus is intended to kill. Possible death is a side effect – like the pain you receive every time you knock a bruise. There does not seem to be a defining characteristic for who the virus kills, either. My team believe it attaches itself to a particular code in our DNA, and that's what destroys the host. It's completely random. And it catches victims completely unaware. However, from our data and experiments, we believe at least fifty million people worldwide will suffer the same fate as the officer in Paxman's flat. It's just a matter of who and when.'

'Fifty million?' the room echoed.

'That's the biggest mass killing in the history of humanity. That's almost the entire population of this country,' Glen

Strachan said, slamming his fists on the table. 'This man has to be stopped.'

49

Developments

December 2, 2017, 13:47

'How come you know so much about ankles?' Christina asked.

'In a former life I was a physiotherapist for a local leisure centre.'

'Wait. That's an actual job?' Christina laughed. 'Did you rub down the old men after they'd finished their morning swim?'

Neil scowled at her. 'Fuck off. It was a different sort of leisure centre.'

'Did it have slides and ball pits and fun things you could play on?' Christina was enjoying herself. For the past fifty minutes, both she and Neil had been getting to know one another. Not once had she looked at the time, at her phone, or even at the lift doors, hoping they would open. She had completely forgotten about the outside world. And there was only one man responsible. Neil. He made her feel comfortable. Relaxed. As if there was nothing in the world that could harm her.

'I won't talk to you anymore if you keep being a dickhead,' Neil said, struggling to suppress a smile.

'I'm sorry, I'll stop.' Christina hesitated. 'If you did that in a former life, then what do you do now?'

'I've been a salesman for about five years now,' the man said.

'Selling what?'

'Selling shit nobody wants to people who have no need for it – that's the basic story behind my life. But I believe in what I sell – and say – and so do most of the people I talk to. And the commission is gorgeous when it comes in. Although the bastard tax man takes most of it.'

'What are you doing here, then?'

'Oh, I was having lunch with a client, and I thought I'd check out the view. I've never seen it before. Doesn't look like I'll get to, either. Why are you here on your own?'

Shrugging, being careful of how much to disclose, she said, 'It's on my bucket list. I work in the city and I thought, "Fuck it! Why not?" And now here we are.'

She wasn't telling a complete lie. It *was* on her bucket list, and she did work in the city. But she wasn't on her lunch break. The real reason she was there was because she needed time to think. Time to clear her head of all the turmoil that was building inside it. She didn't have long to live, and she wasn't going to let herself become dormant. Besides, Sebastian wasn't going to join her – he seemed occupied with other things – so she decided she would go alone. And now here she was.

Neil didn't say anything. A moment of silence – the first they had experienced together since they began talking – passed through the lift shaft.

'What about your love life?' Neil asked.

'I've made a few mistakes.' Christina rubbed her ring finger involuntarily.

'Haven't we all? Are you still making that same mistake?'

'The mistake always remains the same. There's no changing it.'

Neil placed his hand on her knee. 'There's a first time for everything. I'll tell you my mistake if you tell me yours.'

'Is it any of your business?' *Yes, it is,* she answered for herself.

'You know, they often say women who don't talk about their husbands are ashamed of them.'

'Who says that?'

'Everybody.'

'Bullshit.'

'Prove them wrong, then.'

Christina inhaled deeply and considered her options. Sure, she could confess all of her personal and marital issues to a complete stranger, or she could not. The options were that simple. But if she did share, what would happen? Nothing, she decided. She would have nothing to lose. *Besides, it'll get some stuff off your chest.*

'Fine. You got me. My ex was a yoga instructor—'

'Wait.' Neil held his hand in the air.

'What?'

'That's an actual job?'

Christina slapped him on the arm playfully.

'Let me guess,' Neil said. 'You slept with him, fell in love and then he ran away to the next girl he laid eyes on?'

'We were married,' Christina said. Her eyes fell away from his and landed on the ground. 'For a few years. At first it was great. You know, the honeymoon period. We'd spend all of our time together. Laughing, chilling, wrapping ourselves under the blankets. And then he got bored of me. He started coming home late, cancelling our meetings. He got paranoid when I went near his phone or any of his social media accounts. He gave me a reason not to trust him, so I didn't.'

'What happened?'

'I found him messaging a girl late at night. He denied it at first. Said she was just a client who kept flirting with him. I gave him the benefit of the doubt, but then it persisted. It became more and more frequent. So I ended it with him. I haven't spoken to him since.' Christina paused. She felt a heavy weight lift from her shoulders as she told him the half-truth about her broken marriage, embellishing a few of the plot lines. She blinked and turned to face Neil. 'Not all men are the same, are they?'

Neil shook his head. 'No. There are a few of us good ones remaining. But we are a dying breed.'

His words made her smile. A warm sensation travelled through her body. 'What makes you so good, then?'

'I know when a good thing is staring me in the face. Unlike your ex who was willing to throw it all away for some piece of flastic.'

'Flastic?'

'Fake plastic. Superficial.'

'Is that a salesman saying?'

'I thought I told you? I speak two languages. English and bullshit.'

Christina laughed until her eyes teared. And then: 'I hope what you just told me about you being a good guy wasn't bullshit.'

Neil's hand touched her thigh. 'Of course not.'

'Good. I wouldn't want the dying breed to be a man down.'

Neil stared into her eyes. Leaned forward. Caressed the back of her head with his fingers. 'I'm not going anywhere.' Pulled her close. 'And neither are you.'

The sound of something on the other side of the door distracted them. The tingling sensation coursing through Christina's veins dissipated.

'What's that?' she asked, pretending as if *that* hadn't just happened.

'I don't know.' Neil jumped to his feet and placed his ear against the door. 'I think someone's out there. Someone's come to save us!'

Elated, Christina joined him and listened. The sound of heavy panting and calling steadily increased. Overcome with emotions, Christina slammed her fists on the door and started screaming, 'Hello? Help! Help! Get us out! Can you hear me?'

Neil joined in.

Three seconds later they heard a voice.

50

Time To Think

December 2, 2017, 13:49

The cold air chilled Ciara Reed's face as she exited New Scotland Yard. She was mad. Worse, she was furious. It seemed like nothing was being done - nobody gave a fuck - about what was happening in The Shard. Nobody seemed to be doing anything about the fact that a terrorist was in the building. And she had been the one who was burdened with the blame. Her! *Fuck Mamadou*. How dare he? She had tried to help the case; she had been the one to give him the hard drive of the terrorist killing Rik. And this was how she was thanked? No. It was unacceptable. If the police weren't going to do anything about it, then she would.

She stood at the top step outside The Yard. She gave one last look at The Shard before heading towards Westminster station. As she rounded the corner to the Underground, she reached inside her pocket for her Oyster card, and her fingers fumbled on her emergency packet of cigarettes. She came to an abrupt halt, ignoring the people she cut off who scowled and sighed in disgust at her. Ciara pulled the pack out of her pocket and removed one. The sight of it made her sick; it was worsened by the smell. Once, a long time ago, it would have excited her, but now, things were different. She had a baby to prepare for. Even if she wasn't going to keep it, that didn't mean she should try and kill it while it was still inside her. It was murder.

Ciara stepped out of the station's entrance and threw the cigarette pack in the bin. She turned her back on them and returned to the station. As she descended the steps into Westminster, she saw a large sign that read, 'Jubilee service suspended until further notice.'

Ciara rolled her eyes. The Jubilee line was her only direct route to London Bridge. She couldn't get a bus or a cab, either, because the streets were heaving with the backlog of traffic as everyone in the city was beginning to evacuate from The Shard. Ciara checked her watch, and decided she would run to the skyscraper. It wasn't that far away. Besides, the journey gave her ample time to plan what she was going to do to the son of a bitch who murdered Rik when she found him.

And if there was only one person she was going to kill today, she knew who it was.

51

Skyward

December 2, 2017, 13:50

Jake felt exhausted. He had stopped at each of the apartment floors from the fifty-third up, making a quick sweep of the inside, confirming they were completely empty. He wouldn't be able to forgive himself if he made the mistake of leaving someone behind, especially if someone was on the same floor as the explosives.

He didn't stop until he got to the sixty-third floor. He needed a break. His body needed a break. His mind needed a break. Fatigue was beginning to plague him, and the effects of the combination of adrenaline and energy liquid and cannabis were starting to wear thin.

Jake entered through the double doors that led to the landing. He pushed the door so hard it smashed on the wall and ricocheted into his leg. He bent double to catch his breath and let out a deep groan of exasperation.

And then he heard it.

Screaming. Banging. Shouting.

But from where? He didn't know. He felt disorientated, and the noises only made it more difficult for him to focus. But he knew they were there. The voices were distinct. A woman. And a man. He was certain of that.

And then he realised. The lift. There were people stuck inside. They needed his help. Urgently.

Jake rushed to the doors.

'Hello?' he shouted, pressing his face right against the metal. 'Can you hear me?'

'Yes!' a unanimous cry came from inside. 'Get us out of here, please. Help us. Hurry.'

'Remain calm, OK? I'll get you out. I'm a police officer. You're going to be OK.' Jake didn't believe what he was saying. In fact, he had no idea what would happen to any of them. How big was the bomb? Did it contain enough explosives to destroy the whole building and send it crumbling to the ground like the Twin Towers on 9/11? Was it going to kill everyone inside, including Elizabeth and Ellie and Maisie? Was it worth him saving these people here, or were they already doomed?

Of course they aren't.

'Are you OK?' Jake asked through the small line that ran down the middle of the doors. He could feel a draught blowing against his skin.

'Yes,' the woman replied. 'We're fine.'

'How many of you are there?'

'Two.'

Two, Jake repeated to himself. His thoughts darted to Tyler and Martha, and how there had been two that he had failed to rescue before.

'Have you tried opening the doors from your side?' Jake asked.

'Yes. But they're stuck. They won't budge,' the man said.

Wedging his fingers through the thin crack, Jake tried to part the doors. It wouldn't move, and as soon as he felt the resistance in his left shoulder, he knew his efforts were futile. He knew he wouldn't be able to do it. His right arm was not strong enough to do it alone, nor his left. Annoyed, Jake slammed the wall with his palm. It was too late to ask Tim to come back up. By the time he arrived, the bomb could have killed them all. He would have to do it alone.

Think, Jake. Think. He needed to open both sets of doors on his own. His eyes searched for something – anything – that could help him now.

But there was nothing. Not even a long, thin piece of metal he could use to leverage the door. Jake swore aloud.

'What's the matter?' the woman behind the door asked, their words laced with dread and disappointment.

Jake ignored her. He couldn't afford to be distracted. Turning to face the rest of the sixty-third floor, his heart raced. Desks and chairs littered the vast reception area of the penthouse suites.

The chairs. Office chairs. Their legs were metal poles. Jake rushed over to one, overturned it, and stamped on a leg. The thin piece of metal bent under his immense weight. He repeated, stamping harder each time, until eventually it gave way and sheared off completely. The broken end was sharp and rigid.

Slamming it into the crack in the door he had wedged wider with his fingers, Jake leaned into it using his back. The door slid an inch. Jake groaned as he exerted all his remaining strength into opening the door. There were people inside there that needed him. They needed him now more than ever, and he wasn't going to let them down. He wasn't going to let anyone down ever again.

It was at that moment Tyler and Martha's faces appeared in his mind again. Hiding behind the door. Screaming. Clawing at the metal. Begging him.

'No!' Jake yelled, 'It won't happen again. I won't let it!'

Jake let out a shrill caw as he gave one final push into the metal pole. To his amazement, the door opened, and he fell backward, slamming his head on the concrete. The two bodies from inside the lift spilled out on top of him, using his body as a soft landing.

They rushed to their feet. They embraced. Kissed. Stared at one another for a moment, before realising where they were.

The woman turned to him, grabbed his arm and helped him stand. 'Thank you, thank you, thank you!'

Next thing he knew, he was being hugged. Her body felt tight against his, warm. Like home. Like Elizabeth.

'I could kiss you!' she said, throwing her hands into his face. 'You're my hero!'

'Please,' Jake said, shaking her away. 'I'm flattered. But I need you to get out of here. I need you to head down as soon as you can. A bomb is about to go off.' Jake paused a beat to catch his breath. 'Please.'

Jake and the lady shared a moment. Her eyes widened in horror, disbelief. It wasn't until the man accompanying her touched her on the arm that she finally came to.

'Christina, come on – we need to get out of here.' The man dragged Christina away.

'No, Neil,' Christina said. 'We can't leave him here. I'm going with him.'

Jake stopped her, and held her sides with both arms, despite the pain in his shoulder.

'I can't allow that. I've made that same mistake before. I can't let it happen again.' Jake smiled at her. 'It'll be fine. I promise. Now . . . go! Get out of here.'

Neil and Christina didn't need telling a third time. They turned on the spot, sprinted across the hallway, out into the stairwell, and out of sight. Christina gave one last look at Jake before disappearing behind the door.

He was alone. As he had been for much of the day. A part of him wanted them to stay. But he knew that wouldn't be feasible. It would have been a mistake to think they could handle what he was about to go through.

Realising he was being stupid, and that the time on the invisible clock was running out, Jake followed them, stopped on the stairwell landing, listened for them, and heard their sounds disappearing further and further down the building.

Jake looked skyward. Only five more floors to go.

52

Estimates

December 2, 2017, 13:51

Charlie Paxman was enjoying himself. The restaurant felt calm, tranquil. And the noise of the wind wheezing past the windows relaxed him. He had given himself a window of opportunity. By now, Jake Tanner would be staggering around the building, searching for a virus that didn't exist, hoping he would be able to save the entire planet. In the end, Charlie hoped Jake found the explosives moments before they were about to detonate. That way, he wouldn't have to worry about Tanner returning. That way, he could have a little more fun with Benjamin and the rest of the World Health Organisation. After all, that was the reason he was still inside the restaurant. The reason he hadn't wanted to take them outside, or to the top of the building. No, he had wanted to enjoy this until the very last moment, right up until he put a bullet inside Benjamin's skull, and put an end to his own misery. Benjamin Weiss was the closure he needed.

He wasn't too worried about the virus. That was a by-product of the day. He had a contingency plan in place for that, and he would only use it if it was absolutely necessary – a final resort. He would cement himself as one of the most prolific scientists in the history of humankind.

Before he did anything else, he wanted to play a little game while he still had the opportunity.

Charlie wandered to the edge of an overturned table and rested his knees against it. The hard wooden surface pained his frail, brittle knees.

'Ladies and gentlemen,' he began, 'you've been very patient, and I commend you for that. But now it's time to mix things up a little bit. I'm sure you're worried that I'm going to kill you all today. Well, you'll be pleased to know that isn't the case. In fact, only some of you will be dying today. And can any of you guess who that "some" might be?' Charlie kept his eyes fixed on Benjamin, Marianne and the rest of the team from the WHO. In his peripheral vision, he didn't see a single hand rise. 'Come on, guys. Someone must have an idea.' Charlie moved his attention away from the people who had betrayed him and turned it to his gun. He counted the bullets inside. Twenty-three left. Plenty.

Charlie paced up and down the length of the table wall. 'Anyone? No one want to have a little guess?'

Then, just as he was about to continue, he saw the hand. Thin, delicate. Wearing a bracelet. No, three. Too many. And four rings, one on one hand and three on another. Too many again.

'Yes?' Charlie said, coming to a stop. 'Do you have something you want to say?'

The jewellery-wearing woman put her hand down, afraid. Charlie smiled. He pointed to her.

'You. Stand up,' he ordered. For a few seconds the woman didn't respond; it wasn't until Charlie pointed the gun at her head that she did. 'Come here.'

Reluctantly, the woman obliged. Charlie got a strong whiff of her perfume as she neared him. It smelled like she had been part of an industrial explosion at a Chanel factory. It was horrible and made him want to cough.

'I want you to pick one,' he said.

'For what?' she asked, her voice trembling.

'You're going to elect one of them to die.'

Saying nothing more, Charlie held the trigger down for a beat and a half. A few bullets tore through the floor-to-ceiling windowpane above the WHO members' heads to the left of the room. Shattered glass sprinkled down on them and scattered across the floor. Everyone surrounding them shifted out of the way for fear of getting cut by the shards of glass.

Screaming. Crying. Hugging. Protecting.

Charlie loathed it all.

The members of the World Health Organisation who were closest to the edge of the building clambered over one another to a safe distance, a few feet from their deaths. Some climbed over the booths nearest to them, stumbling to the floor as their momentum carried them forward. A harsh breeze billowed through the restaurant, buffeted, and then stilled, making the hairs on Charlie's skin prickle.

The restaurant immediately fell silent.

'What are you doing?' the woman next to him wailed.

Charlie rolled his eyes. 'I want you to pick one of them. And fast. I don't have a lot of time to be messing about.'

'Pick them for what?'

'I want them to get a special view. One they've never seen before. I want them to go flying out of this building.'

The woman shook her head. 'No, I won't do it. You'll have to kill me instead.'

Charlie shrugged. 'OK. It was you or them, anyway.'

Charlie aimed the gun at her, pulled the trigger and fired.

By his estimate, there were approximately eighteen bullets left in the AK's magazine.

53

I'll Be Waiting

December 2, 2017, 13:53

Ethan felt heavy in Tim's arms. His back ached, and his biceps burned. His legs shook with every descending step. They were still five floors from the base of the tower, but it felt like they were at the top, facing an insurmountable task ahead.

'How you holding up, buddy?' Tim asked the young boy dangling round his neck. Ever since they left Jake, Ethan had been silent. Tim could hardly blame him; he had just had a decoy explosive vest strapped around his stomach. Tim tried to make the boy feel comfortable as much as possible.

'OK,' Ethan said, his voice weak and shy.

Tim smiled. He was just glad to get a response.

'That's good to hear, bud. Not long now. Only a few more

floors and then we'll be safe and sound on the bottom.'

'What about my mum and dad? Will they be OK?'

Tim lost his footing on one of the steps and stumbled. Ethan slipped out of his arms, letting out a little yelp. The boy dropped the detonator on the ground as Tim stretched and clawed for a grip around Ethan's shirt. The detonator clattered and bounced to the bottom of the steps.

'No!' Ethan cried, frantically trying to squirm free from Tim's grip.

'What's wrong? What are you doing?' Tim let Ethan climb down him and pick up the device.

Holding the detonator in his hands, Ethan teared up. Tim bent down to his side and attended to the small boy.

'The thing. It's stopped working. I let go of the switch.'

'That's OK,' Tim said. 'That's all right.'

'No, it's not!' Ethan shouted in his face. 'The man in the restaurant told me that if I let go bad things were going to happen to my mum and dad.'

Fuck, Tim thought. What was he supposed to say? What could he? He didn't want to tell the boy what that really meant, and he definitely didn't want to scare him.

Tim played it safe.

'Everything's going to be fine,' he told Ethan. 'They're going to be OK. Nothing's going to happen to them.'

'You promise?' Ethan asked.

'I promise.'

Content with his response, Ethan climbed back into Tim's arms, and together they descended another seemingly never-ending flight of stairs. A few minutes later, Tim stopped. Listened.

A noise came from below. It was the sound of heavy

breathing, whimpering. He recognised the soft tones at once. Samantha.

'Hello?' he called down.

'Hello?' came a reply. 'Who's that?'

Tim showed his face. Samantha beamed. She was sat down, resting her head against a step. She looked fatigued, her skin pale, her body weak.

'Fancy seeing you again, stranger. You come to rescue me?'

'I'm afraid I can only do it the once,' he said, 'otherwise I have to charge.'

Tim stopped by her side, placed Ethan on the ground, and helped Samantha to her feet. She struggled, and her weight felt dead, like she was devoid of all energy.

'What's happened?' Tim asked.

'My foot. I twisted it again. Smashed my head.' Samantha turned the side of her face to show Tim a gouge in the top of her temple.

'Oh my God. Are you OK?'

'Yeah,' she said. 'I'm fine. I just want to get out of this bloody building. And I'm afraid if I go alone, I might pass out. Stranger things have happened today.'

'It's fine. I'm here. I'll help you. Come on, you're safe with me.'

Tim wrapped his arm around her waist, burdened the weight of her body on his shoulder, and carried her down the stairs. They made it as far as halfway when Tim felt something touch his leg. He stopped. Spun.

It was Ethan, his bulging childish eyes glaring at him.

'What about me?' he asked.

'Don't worry, bud. You're coming with us. Come on, take

my arm.' Tim extended his arm for Ethan to take it. The boy retreated further up the steps. 'What are you doing, Ethan? Take my hand and we can go down together, the three of us.'

'No. I don't want to.' Ethan paused; Tim stared at him in bewilderment. 'Jake said you're supposed to stay with me at all times.'

For fuck's sake. Not now. Please.

'I'm not. You'll be coming with us. You won't be left alone.'

'No.' Ethan folded his arms. 'I want to go on your back again. Jake told you to look after me. He told you to take me to the bottom of the building.'

Tim sighed. 'And that's what I'm trying to do, buddy. But you're not helping me. I have to help this lady here.'

Saying nothing, Ethan turned his back on Tim and Samantha, and started up the stairs. Tim swore aloud, heedless of whether Ethan heard. He placed Samantha on the step, raced up to Ethan, picked him up, and threw him over his back.

'Don't run off like that,' he said. 'Otherwise I'll have to tell your mum and dad you misbehaved. Do you want me to do that?'

Ethan made a noise. He felt Ethan's hair stroke against his neck as the boy shook his head. Tim stopped and took a moment to think. He now had two people he had to rescue, but there was only one of him.

'I'm sorry,' he said to Samantha. 'I can't take you both down. If I could, I would.'

'It's fine, I understand.' Samantha looked to the ground. 'Do what you have to.'

'Hey, hey. I'll be coming back, OK? I promise. I can't

ignore the fact we've run into one another twice already. We just have to make it third time lucky.' Tim bent down and kissed her on the cheek.

'Hurry,' she said, a smile beginning to break out on her face. 'I'll be waiting.'

54

Floor 68

December 2, 2017, 13:58

Nearly two hundred metres above Tim was Jake. He had just got to the sixty-eighth floor, and he was beat. His feet, ankles, calves and thighs cried out in constant agony. They throbbed with each pulsing beat of his heart.

He stopped against a wall and bent double to catch his breath. The air this high up seemed different, thinner, like he was up in the mountains. He checked his watch. It was 13:58, and on his invisible countdown he had spent too long climbing the steps. However, to his surprise, there had been no explosion. Yet. He just hoped he was in the right place. He had been adamant Charlie Paxman had placed his explosives on the sixty-eighth floor. There was something peculiar about what he had seen earlier that day which didn't sit right with him. It was the detective intuition in him, the ability to notice something barely visible that appeared out of place and treat it as suspicious. But he hadn't been allowed to focus on work – Elizabeth's orders – so he had ignored it and carried on with his day.

And now look where I am.

The View From The Shard viewing platform was empty. It felt eerie. Quiet. Isolated. Desolate. Yet oddly frightening, as if there were someone else there with him. Invisible. Silent. Taunting him. Teasing him. Waiting for him to make a mistake before attacking him. Beating him. Killing him.

Moshat.

An apparition of Moshat lurked behind a pillar, his breath nothing but a passing breeze, his footsteps no louder than a leaf falling to the ground. Jake closed his eyes, attempting to force out the bald man who stood there, grimacing. The outside world – the buildings, the blue sky, yellow sun, grey clouds – had all turned to brown and green, illuminated orange by the blazing ruins of the Heathrow Express. Jake could feel a gun strapped against his chest. Moshat remained standing where he was, toying with Jake, bearing that smile, tempting him into doing something foolish, something he would later regret.

So that's what Jake did. That something foolish, that something he had never done before in any of his previous altercations with Moshat, that something he knew he would never regret, because he knew no matter how long he bore the guilt, it would soon pass.

Jake grabbed for the gun in his breast pocket, unclipped it from its holster, aimed it at Moshat and pulled the trigger. The noise of his enemy's body slamming to the ground awoke him and startled him back to the reality of the sixty-eighth floor; the sound of the bullet firing echoed in his mind.

Jake started towards the men's toilets. Inside, he opened the door to the cubicle he had used not so long ago. Inching closer to the tiles on the wall, Jake reached inside his pocket and retrieved his set of house keys. He ran his finger along the edge of the dismantled tile he had spotted earlier. The air still smelled of glue and other chemicals. Was this it? Was this what the virus smelled like? Was it really in here, ready to change the face of the human race?

Jake dug his keys into the sealant that had been used to stick the tile on. The adhesive chipped away and floated to the floor.

After two long minutes, the tile came loose, and Jake placed it on the ground. He'd found what he was looking for. A narrow hole that was dug deep into the wall. A cylindrical tube that contained a transparent liquid.

And then he saw it. The digits on the clock attached to the countdown timer on the end. The numbers that represented how little time he had left to succeed. How little time he had left to do anything.

Ten seconds remained.

What could he accomplish in those ten seconds? Nothing. He couldn't disarm arm it, dispose of it, or even flush it down the toilet and let the building's irrigation systems take care of it. There was only one other thing he could do, and that was to hobble away as fast as possible.

Ten.

Jake placed the bomb delicately on the toilet seat, lest he drop it and inadvertently detonate it.

Nine.

He turned. Jumped out of the toilet cubicle.

Eight.

His legs carried him out of the bathroom and into the vast expanse of open flooring.

Seven.

Jake burst through the emergency exit and into the stairwell.

Five.

His foot caught something on the floor.

Four.

He tumbled down the top half of the steps. His body landed hard on his right shoulder.

Three.

Jake swore out loud, his voice echoing up and down the staircase.

Two.

He counted the final seconds, his body too worn out to move any further.

One.

55

Cut Off

December 2, 2017, 14:00

The bomb exploded.

The fire doors burst from their hinges and rolled down the stairs, narrowly avoiding Jake.

The first of Jake's senses to be affected by the explosion was his sight. A harsh light, brighter than the sun, blinded him as it erupted through the door. Then his hearing. The sound was deafening, piercing his eardrums, filling them with a tinny ringing sound. It was closely followed by the sensations on his skin. An intense burning swarmed the naked hairs on his arms, legs and face as giant balls of flame scorched the walls. Plumes of smoke filled the air and rose to the ceiling. Jake coughed in the acrid smoke. Overhead the fire alarms sounded, and the water sprinklers started.

Within seconds the floor was covered in a film of water, his clothes were sodden, and his body shook with cold.

Jake lumbered to his feet, ignoring the pain that consumed his entire body. He couldn't sit around and feel sorry for himself. He needed to see the extent of the damage, even if it meant he inhaled whatever toxic gas had been expelled into the air by the explosion.

The sixty-eighth floor was carnage. Shrapnel and debris littered the floor. Glass. Rubble. Metal rods. Destruction everywhere.

The windows had been blasted open, and a torrent of wind billowed in, chilling Jake to his bones. Over the ringing noise in his ears he could barely hear the wind buffeting around him and the hubbub of London a thousand feet below. Jake stepped deeper into the area, his feet getting wetter with each passing second. The building's internal structures had withstood the blast and were keeping The Shard upright. Jake felt grateful for the engineering work that had gone into creating the skyscraper.

He returned to the bathroom and stopped outside the door. What had once been the bathroom was now nothing more than a pile of charred ceramic and plaster. A large hole in the ground had been created by the explosion. Standing there, his chest heaving, he allowed the sprinkler water to rain down over him. As he caught his breath, he gave himself time for his thoughts to recuperate before the numbing water froze them.

He had failed to stop the bomb from exploding, and the virus from being released, but that didn't mean he wouldn't stop Paxman from escaping. There was still his family to protect.

Jake reached for Kayla's phone and dialled.

'Tim? I—'

'Jesus Christ, Jake,' Tim said, interrupting him. 'What happened up there? The sprinklers and fire alarms are going crazy down here. I swear the whole building just shook.'

'I know,' Jake said. 'The bomb went off. I couldn't defuse it in time. But we've got something else we should worry about.'

'What's that?'

'Paxman. I think he's going to try to escape.'

'Shit.'

'Where are you?'

'I'm coming into the lobby now.'

'Is Ethan OK? Is he all right?'

Tim started to speak, but he was cut off by the sounds of shouting.

'Put your hands in the air!' a deep voice called.

'Put the boy down, now!' another cried.

The line went dead.

56

Caught

December 2, 2017, 14:02

Tim had never felt so scared in his life. So far, in all his thirty-four years on earth, he had never experienced what it felt like to stare down the end of four MP5 submachine guns. In fact, his life had been pretty tame. Nothing out of the ordinary. Simple. Easy. Exactly how he liked it.

And now he faced his biggest test: not shitting himself in public.

'Drop the phone and put your arms in the air,' one officer aiming a gun at him shouted. It was the third time they'd told him, but he wasn't paying attention. His mind was elsewhere: He had Ethan to protect.

'I won't ask you again! Put the phone down or we will be forced to shoot you.'

Tim remained frozen to the spot, but the phone just slipped out of his grip. It smashed as it landed on the ground and bounced away beside an overturned chair, instantly soaking up the thin layer of water that now covered the floor.

Methodically, instinctively, the armed officers approached him, their guns still raised. As they surrounded him, they placed his hands behind his back and cuffed them. Saying nothing, as if speaking telepathically to one another – the result of countless hours' worth of training – they led him out of the building.

'The boy!' Tim shouted. 'What are you going to do to him? I need to make sure he gets to his parents safely.'

'Don't worry about that, mate. We'll take care of him.'

The officers stopped at the revolving doors, affording Tim one last look at Ethan. The child was being wrapped up in a jacket and towel to keep him warm and protected from the sprinklers. He looked up at Tim; there was a slight smirk in his expression that disconcerted him.

'Is this him, guv?' the officer holding Tim's left arm asked.

'Yes. It's him,' the one holding the right said.

'What are you talking about?' Tim found himself saying; the words hadn't communicated from his brain to his mouth properly. 'What's going on?'

'That little stunt you pulled earlier. We received reports of you wielding a firearm in public. Where did you get it from?'

Tim fell silent. And then the gravity of the situation came crashing down on him. The gun. The reception team. The evacuation. *Fuck!* Why hadn't they listened to him? Why had he felt it sensible to reveal the weapon and use it as a motivating factor to get them to evacuate? He had been so stupid.

And now he was suffering as a result.

'No, you've got it wrong. Honestly. I didn't mean anything by it.'

'And I suppose you didn't mean to kill anyone else either?'

'Kill anyone? What are you—?' Tim hesitated. He stopped resisting. 'Wait. You think I did this? You think I'm the terrorist?'

The armed officers said nothing.

'Oh, bloody hell. You can't be serious. You've got the wrong guy. I just used the gun to evacuate the building – not shoot it!'

Silence. The officers forced Tim outside. To his left was the set of escalators that led to a small ring road around The Shard. To his right was London Bridge Underground station. A thin stream of people continued to flood through the Underground.

He felt the officer pulling him to the right.

'Where are we going?' Tim asked.

'This way.'

'Why?'

'It's a CBRN threat. The Underground is the safest route. It's where everyone's being evacuated.'

Tim swallowed.

'What's going to happen to me?'

'We just need to ask you a few questions.'

57

Last Resort

December 2, 2017, 14:03

'I don't believe what I'm seeing!' The Home Secretary slammed her fist on the table.

The tension inside COBRA had reached critical. They had just seen the top of one of the most coveted, prestigious and expensive buildings in the country explode on national television. They had failed. Charlie Paxman was taking over the entire building and highlighting the government's ineptitude. He was mocking them from several hundred feet in the air. And there was nothing any of them could do about it. And to make matters worse, he had potentially just released his virus into the air.

'This is ridiculous,' the Prime Minister said. She turned to Frances. 'Your man has let us down. Again. I should never have let you convince me it was a good idea. We can't continue to allow Tanner to solve this himself. We need a new plan.'

'Hopkins,' someone in the room called. Frances didn't know who it was, but they sounded near; she was still thinking about little Ethan, the boy Jake had helped save. She had observed him a few months ago in the park with Alex and his family, and she had wanted to say hello, but hadn't, because she had an important meeting to attend at the time.

Frances's skin prickled.

'No,' she found herself saying.

'I'm sorry, Frances, but we've gone past the point of listening to you. Your suggestions aren't helping anyone,' Ian said.

The words hurt, and she reclined in her seat.

'I say we send in the SAS,' Glen Strachan added, resting his arms on the table.

'It's too late to send the SAS in now,' the PM replied.

Glen rose to his feet, marched to the television screen at the other end of the room, and pointed to the top of the building. 'It would be too late to launch an aerial assault – he'd see us coming from a mile off – but we could send them in from the bottom. Get them to swarm the restaurant, stun Paxman, take him out, and save the hostages. Nice and simple. The boys practise it in training all the time.'

'It won't work. He told us not to go in there, armed. And so far, we've honoured his wishes. We don't know if Paxman's lined the entrance to the restaurant with more explosives, or if he's just sat there ready and waiting with a gun for someone to enter. And there are lives in there we can't afford to lose,' Frances said.

Glen turned to face her. 'My men know what they're doing. There's a reason they're in this job. They've dealt with countless hostage negotiations. This isn't the first, and it certainly won't be the last.'

Frances shook her head. 'This isn't a hostage negotiation, Glen. Not at any point has Paxman come to us with demands. It seems clear that what he wants is inside that restaurant with him. You go storming in there, with your flash bangs and your weapons, who knows what will happen.'

'How is it any different to your boy, Jake, going in on his own?'

'Because Jake's done it before. He's been in a similar situation. Plus, he's got his family in there. He won't let anyone jeopardise their safety. Not you, the SAS, or Joe Bloggs from off the street.' Frances paused, swallowed and caught her breath. 'Hypothetically, if you go in there, and one of Tanner's family – or even his friends – gets killed in the crossfire, he will hold every one of you accountable. Think about it this way: If you were in his situation, Glen, and your family were held hostage, would you want their lives in someone else's hands, or would you want to save them yourself if you knew you could?'

No one said anything for ten seconds. Everyone in the room glanced at one another sheepishly. Again, Frances had raised a valid point, but no one was willing to admit she was right.

'Frances, listen,' the Prime Minister began, 'I know you have some kind of affiliation with Jake Tanner, but we need to resolve this as soon as possible. We can't "wait to see what happens."' She used her fingers as air quotes. 'Before Paxman kills anyone else, we need to remove him. We will have to assume he has already released his virus. And if that is the case, there is nothing we can do about that. We will have to adapt and discover an antidote. For now, we must manage the damage to the rest of the hostages inside that building. We have to use our last resort.'

'What are you saying, Prime Minister?'

'Hopkins,' Charlie Brent, head of MI6, said again.

'Yes,' the Prime Minister agreed, looking around the room. She averted her gaze from Frances.

'Jesus Christ,' Frances whispered.

The Prime Minister turned to Martin Ball and said, 'I want you to line Hopkins up. Ready him.' Directing her words towards Frances, she continued, 'It will be a covert operation. No one need know a thing. We can't let what happened with Moshat and Adil Hakim happen again. This country has already been brought to its knees by one attack – we can't let it happen a second time.'

Just like that, Frances had been overruled. Everything she'd suggested was shot down. Everything she believed to be true about the way the government worked had been a lie. And Martin. What was he about to do? He didn't understand the gravity of the situation. Or his actions. Not one bit. None of them did.

Martin nodded, accepting the Prime Minister's instructions.

Frances stormed out of the room without saying anything. It felt like a betrayal, and she was already on the phone to Jake by the time the door closed behind her.

58

Target Practice

December 2, 2017, 14:05

The helicopter blades rotated as the aircraft landed on Kieran Hopkins's four-acre property hidden in the depths of Surrey Hills, buffeting the air around him. His upcoming mission should have scared him, but it didn't. Just another terrorist that needed killing. Another bug that the British government needed to squash without the rest of the world knowing.

Kieran Hopkins was ex-SAS. He had served for twenty years, becoming an expert in killing targets from hundreds of metres away, using the world's top sniper rifles. And then he moved to Counter Terrorism where he was SCO19's top marksman. Now retired at the age of forty-two, and doing his best to remain under the radar, he was the government's last resort. They called upon him when there were no options left, and when they weren't looking for an inquisition into the official squads if something went wrong. It had been just over a year since they last needed him, and now he was going to be back in the zone, this time with a sniper rifle in his hands. Where it should be. And with a bullet lodged in the top of someone's skull.

Where it should be.

'I understand, Martin,' Kieran said into the phone just as he was about to set foot inside the helicopter that had been sent from Gatwick airport. Climbing into the backseat, he disabled the call.

The director general of MI5 had explained the situation. There was a biological terrorist inside The Shard. He had taken a group of individuals hostage and was holding them at gunpoint. His instructions: shoot to kill.

Charlie Paxman, he repeated the name of his target in his head. It always helped him visualise the target. It helped him to consider them before he killed them. Sometimes he liked to imagine their lives: what they did for a living, where they grew up, where they fucked it up so bad they resorted to killing large quantities of people.

Kieran sat in the helicopter and looked at his phone in his lap. Martin Ball had emailed him a dozen snapshots of Charlie Paxman, along with a brief biography of the man.

Kieran skimmed through, absorbing all the information on the screen. He came away with the same conclusion he always did: for all intents and purposes, Charlie Paxman was a loner, a nobody, a shadow in the darkness who wanted nothing more than to bring himself to light, in whichever inconceivable and inhumane way possible.

And it was Kieran's job to stop him before he had the

chance.

The helicopter rose from the ground, jostling against the southern winds of Reigate. Kieran's house, buried deep within the hills and fields, quickly disappeared as the chopper climbed altitude. He stroked the side of the five-foot case next to him. Inside was the Accuracy International AWM. The acronym stood for Arctic Warfare Magnum. It had a five-round detachable magazine that housed .300 calibre bullets and, with the addition of a suppressor, came in at 1.5 metres in length.

Capable of firing bullets at a target over a kilometre away, it had been Kieran's friend for nearly ten years. It had killed approximately fifty individuals, and his greatest achievement was gunning down two targets with one bullet. In his entire career, Kieran had never missed a shot.

And he wasn't about to start now.

59

Warning

December 2, 2017, 14:06

Jake descended the stairs, stumbled, rolled, knocked his shoulder, and lifted himself back up again, ploughing through the dizzying pain. He was in a blind state of fury, consumed by a dangerous sense of rage. He was in a hurry. He needed to get Charlie Paxman's attention before he did anything stupid. He needed to divert his focus from Elizabeth, the kids and the rest of the hostages and direct it towards himself. It was the only way if he was going to save them.

And there was only one way he would succeed.

Jake reached the fiftieth floor. Halfway. He stopped for a break. He needed to conserve whatever energy he had left. Jake bent down, placing his hands on his legs and pushing his shoulder blades back to open his chest. Oxygen soared through his bloodstream and reinvigorated his red blood cells. It wasn't much of a recuperation, but it would suffice. He hadn't realised it, but the physical exertion had warmed his body, and he no longer felt the icy cold of the water pouring overhead. But as he stood there, he could feel the cold creeping back in.

His phone rang, distracting him.

'Hello?' Jake answered.

'Tanner? It's Frances.' She sounded relieved to hear him.

'How did you get this number?'

'Mamadou.'

'Where is he? Is he OK?'

'He's at Paxman's address. Quarantined.' She hesitated. 'Jake, I can't disclose too much; this isn't a secure line.'

'I understand.'

'We don't have much time, so I'll make it quick. Are you out of earshot of anyone?'

Jake looked around. Up and down. There was no one in sight.

'I'm clear.'

'Good. I've stepped out of COBRA. I need to make it brief so listen carefully: an ex-SAS field agent is on his way to you now. He's flying in a helicopter, and he's armed with a sniper. He's been given his orders to take out Paxman cleanly and quietly.' Frances spoke in hushed tones.

'What? How is that possible?'

'He's the guy they call in when they want something done fast and easy. No one will know it was him. The government will swing it so it was the brave, fearless hostages who overthrew Paxman. They'll say they lodged the bullet in his head. They'll call it self-defence, but it makes them a scapegoat for what the government is about to do.'

'Who authorised it?'

'The PM. I argued against it, said you were capable of dealing with this situation yourself, but they ignored me.'

Jake sighed heavily. It wasn't the first time he had been undermined and under appreciated, and he was certain it wouldn't be the last. For a moment he would have to put his ego aside, or else it might cloud his judgement; there were lives that needed saving. 'What do you want me to do?'

'Protect Paxman, Jake. I know he doesn't deserve it, but make sure Hopkins doesn't assassinate him. I won't let this nation sink to that level of vengeance.'

Shit. Shit, shit, shit. Jake paced up and down the stairs. He recognised the name. Hopkins. Kieran Hopkins. The man who had assassinated a small boy right in front of Jake's eyes inside the London Eye eighteen months ago. The man Jake had never forgiven. Highly decorated. Veteran. A force within the force. Never missed a shot. Fifty-six bullet casings spent. Fifty-six kills. He was just another weapon in the government's terrifying arsenal.

Frances spoke again: 'It's vital you save him, Jake. Paxman holds the answers to a potential antidote to this virus. He might be able to reverse its effects on the entire population. If nothing else, that's reason enough to save him now.'

'I'll do what I can.'

'Thank you. Hopkins's ETA is less than fifteen minutes. If he fails, they're sending in the SAS. Please, hurry.'

'What's the other helicopter that's already outside the building for?' Jake asked. Moments after the explosion, he had heard a helicopter hovering outside somewhere; at first, he hadn't been sure whether it was real or if he was delirious, but then as he paid closer attention, he realised what it was.

'The news. The BBC have been flying around the city for hours. They might have to refuel soon, but we can't rely on that to deter Hopkins from taking his shot. With any luck, it'll slow him down. The government won't want footage of the assassination going viral. Anyway, I've got to go. Be careful, Tanner. For Tyler's sake.'

Her final words hit Jake hard. Hit him right in his centre of mass. Right where he knew they would stick and remain for a long time. Tyler. That name. The images, memories, happiness associated with it – all appeared in his mind. A lump swelled in his throat.

For the first time in a long time, the blissful memories of Tyler outweighed the monstrous memories of Moshat.

With the embryonic stages of a new idea forming in his head, Jake started down the stairs. There were lives to save. And Charlie Paxman's was one of them.

60

Trap Door

December 2, 2017, 14:06

'Pick one!' Charlie screamed at another woman he had selected from the crowd. This one was different, quieter, shy. Tears streamed down her face, and she wrapped her arms around her body. 'They all have to die – you'll be hurrying the process along.'

The woman remained still, defiant. Afraid. Charlie grabbed her by the hair and forced her down to her knees. He was getting angry. He didn't like it when people disobeyed him. He didn't like it when people ignored him. Delayed him. Belittled him. They had done his entire life, and now it was time to show them how serious he was. It was time to teach them some respect.

'I told you, didn't I?' he hissed in the woman's ear. 'If you don't do as I say, then you will suffer the same fate as her.'

Charlie nodded at the petite woman he had killed moments earlier. He removed the steak knife Jake Tanner had kept in his back pocket and held it against the throat of the woman beside him. It wasn't the sharpest blade he'd ever held, but it would do. It would be enough to convey his sincerity.

Charlie leaned forward. His eyes met the hostage's, moved further down her body, and noticed a small bump in her dress she had been hiding with her arms. It was something he hadn't noticed before, and she had done well to conceal it from him. It was circular, too solid to be excess fat. Which could only mean one thing: she was pregnant. Another one. *Another fiend who cares little for the amount of suffering they're causing the planet.*

Charlie's hand touched her stomach. The woman's reaction confirmed his suspicions: she startled and slapped his hand away, trying to wriggle free from his deathly grip. He smiled and lowered the knife.

'OK,' he said. 'How about I put it this way? You choose one of them to die, or I will kill your unborn child.'

The woman's eyes bulged, and they glistened with an uncertainty that Charlie savoured. He was going to remove any hope she may have of getting out alive unless she did as he ordered. The woman's hair rustled as the wind picked up outside, flicking her in the face, covering the horror in her expression.

'Please, no!'

Charlie ignored her.

Three, he counted in his head.

'I . . . I . . .' The woman looked around the crowd of

revered scientists. 'I . . .'

Two.

Just as the woman opened her mouth, Charlie plunged the blade into her stomach.

One. Too late.

The woman screamed. Her hands flew to her belly and she shouldered Charlie aside. A crimson flower of red spread across her lilac blouse. A man from the crowd rushed to her side. He held her body in his arms. Charlie stepped back to let the man attempt to rescue her and her unborn baby.

'Someone give me a coat!' the man shouted, his hands pressed firmly against the woman's stomach, applying pressure to the wound spewing the fountain of blood that pooled around her.

A few other members of the crowd jumped to their feet and attended to the dying woman. Charlie knew that if she didn't get immediate medical attention, she would be dead. By his estimation, she had only minutes to live.

Charlie's attention waned and returned to Benjamin Weiss and the rest of the people responsible for his dismissal from the World Health Organisation. He readjusted the AK-47 on his shoulder and aimed it at one of them.

'Lucas,' he barked over the sound of the woman screaming. 'Get the fuck up, now.'

Adrenaline surged through him. It felt exciting, elating, alien. Something deep within him – the desire to burn everything to the ground – blew up. He didn't know where it came from, but now that the locks had been ripped off from the trapdoor, there would be no one that could stop him.

Luke rose to his feet, his body trembling with fear.

Charlie aimed. Steadied his breath. And pulled the trigger.

61

Nightmare

December 2, 2017, 14:09

The stairwell was quiet save for the sound of Jake's heavy breathing and his tired, aching feet on the steps. His blood pumped through his body. By now the bleeding from his bullet wound had staunched; the cloth wrapped tightly around his shoulder was damp and warm. Jake stopped on the thirty-second floor. On the other side of the security door was the Oblix restaurant.

Jake untied the knot around his shoulder and inspected the wound. The gouge at the top was large, and clumps of flesh dangled from where the metal had lacerated his skin. He lifted his shoulder straight up and then outward in a circle, testing its manoeuvrability. It felt stiff, tight, and he could only raise it sideways; moving it in front was too painful. But there wasn't anything he could do about it; it was too late to fix it now. Jake folded the cloth in half and tightened it again, this time with a clean piece resting on the wound.

Standing in front of the double doors, he exhaled deeply. He prepared himself for the horror that lay on the other side.

Jake prepared Tim's security card, but he soon realised he didn't need it. The door was ajar, and the handle had been strafed with bullet holes. He leaned closer, trying to peer through the gap, but he could see nothing. A draught flew in by his feet and hands and set the hairs on the back of his arms on end. He was startled by the sound of an ear-piercing scream. A lump grew in his throat. As soon as he heard the noise, his instincts should have taken over; under usual circumstances, he would have rushed towards the sound and attended the situation. But this wasn't a usual situation. This was far worse.

The scream continued, and now it was harmonised by a series of deep, baritone shouts. Jake tried to work out what had happened: there had been no gunshot, yet a woman was screaming.

Through the cacophony of noise emanating ten yards away from him, Jake heard someone scream, 'My baby! My baby!'

The words harrowed Jake, filling him with a paralysing sense of dread. He listened intently to the hysterical woman's accent, tone, and intonation. Jake concluded it wasn't Elizabeth screaming; after witnessing her give birth twice, he knew what she sounded like when she was under immense pain and stress.

And then everything stopped. A gunshot echoed around

the room like a balloon exploding. The tiny explosion from the gun commanded entire silence.

Jake feared the worst.

Elizabeth. Maisie. Ellie. Karen. Alex. Ellen. Had any of them died? Had Charlie shot one of them? Or were they already dead and now he was just finishing up the rest of the party?

And then his mind made a U-turn. Was it Hopkins? Was he here already? Had he shot Paxman in the head and ended today's nightmare? Jake could not help but feel that he would have preferred that option. Despite what Frances had said, he wanted Paxman to suffer in unimaginable ways - ways just as horrible as the kind he had enforced upon those he had shot. Charlie was evil, inhuman, and, Jake knew, he would not stop until he succeeded.

Swallowing hard, Jake stepped into the restaurant and revealed himself to the man he was going to save.

62

Calling Bluffs

December 2, 2017, 14:10

'Paxman!' Jake shouted.

His voice carried further than he expected. A group of people were huddled together to Jake's right, yelling and shouting. They surrounded a woman clutching her stomach. He had entered through the north side, where the two restaurants met – the same door Ethan had been ushered from. Beside the group, a few feet to the left, was Charlie, standing in the middle of the pen. His tall, wiry frame twisted and turned towards Jake. He moved slowly, gracefully. He had an air about him that suggested he wasn't afraid, that he was in control. Charlie Paxman had colonised the Oblix restaurant and made himself invincible.

Jake saw a smile stretch over Charlie's face.

'Well, well, well,' he said, 'if it isn't Detective Tanner. Hero of the day. Hero of the summer. Hero of the year. I wasn't expecting you back so soon. In fact, I wasn't expecting you back at all. Did you like my little present for you upstairs?'

Jake said nothing at first. He ignored the deliberate attempt to antagonise him and calculated what he was going to do next.

'How quickly does it spread?' Jake asked, jumping straight to the point.

'It infects four million people an hour. And you were the first person ever to be infected – how does it feel?'

'What does it do?'

'It stops stupid people being able to do stupid things.'

'What's the antidote?'

'What do I get in return for that information? A cash reward? A lifetime supply of everything I want?' Charlie smirked and lowered the gun.

While Charlie had been speaking, Jake cast his eyes around the restaurant, darting left and right, in search of Elizabeth and the rest of his family. Where were they? For what he had planned, he hoped they were as far away from Paxman as possible.

'I'm sure we can work something out,' Jake said, focusing his attention back on Charlie.

'Are you going to talk me out of this? Is that how this is going to work?'

'Something like that. I'm going to save your life.'

Charlie laughed again, his demonic, hoarse voice filling the room. 'Please, satisfy my curiosity and tell me how.'

Jake stepped forward. Checked his watch. Stopped.

'In approximately four minutes, a helicopter will arrive. On the helicopter is one of the government's finest sharpshooters. He's got his instructions, and so do I.'

Charlie's face dropped. He twisted his neck to look behind him out the window.

'He could be here out of sight a very long way away. I think his furthest recorded kill was over twelve hundred metres. Now, with today's conditions, I don't think he'll risk that trajectory alteration, so I'd say you're trying to find someone who's at least six hundred metres away. Give or take.' Jake stepped further forward while Paxman had his back turned. It was then that Elizabeth and the girls, and Alex and the rest of the Tough family, came into view. They were hiding in the corner, just over Charlie's shoulder, where the two window edges met, a few metres away from where they were sat during lunch. The tension in his shoulders and hands eased as soon as he saw they were all safe.

'You're bluffing,' Paxman said. Jake observed him; he wasn't looking at the same man that had served him his drinks a few hours ago. He seemed almost evil, as if he gone off the chains, and there was no chance for retribution.

'I wish I was, Charlie. But are you really willing to find out?'

The question hung in the air like a bubble delicately floating in front of them, waiting to be popped. Charlie looked at Jake. There was something in his eyes – his expression – that filled Jake with dread.

'Charlie? We can help you.'

'Nobody can help me now.'

63

Escape

December 2, 2017, 14:11

Charlie stared out of the window. He couldn't believe it. He had seen a helicopter way off in the distance, which meant Jake Tanner was right. So why was he helping him? Why didn't Jake just let him die?

Unless it's all a diversion to get me talking, to get me standing still, so I become a target in plain sight for the sniper.

Charlie didn't like the sound of that. He didn't like the sound of being betrayed so easily. It had happened before, and he wasn't about to allow it to happen again. He still needed to complete his mission and kill Benjamin and Marianne, and if there really was a sniper on their way to assassinate him, he would have to act quickly.

Decision made, Charlie turned. He was going to kill them

all. He raised the gun. Pointed it at his former colleagues pressed against the window on the north side and held down the trigger. Bullets burst from the end of the gun and lodged themselves in their targets, killing some of them almost instantly, bursting through the other side of their heads and bodies. Charlie spread the fire across the whole group so as to kill and injure all of them. It was a massacre. Blood, intestines, organs, and a little brain matter flew into the air, showering everyone else in the restaurant.

As Charlie held down the trigger, the hammer inside the weapon smashed bullet after bullet. Each shot, each ignition, sent mini shock waves through his body. But he remained focused. He enjoyed it, seeing their faces – the people he had once enjoyed the company of, and now hated – explode with shock and horror as bullets penetrated their abdomen or chest or shoulder or leg or skull.

But there was a problem. Benjamin and Marianne weren't visible. They were hiding amidst the dead bodies, protected by their inferiors. Those bastards! Still trying to evade justice, even now. How had he missed them? In the furore of the execution, some of the scientists had attempted to clamber over one another instinctively, and in the process had stumbled and, with the impact of the bullets, fallen out of the open window. If they weren't dead, then they would be in seconds' time when they became a part of the concrete.

His eyes scanned the horizon. Still no sign of Benjamin or that bitch Marianne. He was getting angrier by the second. He didn't know how many bullets he had left, but he needed to make sure there were two reserved for them.

And then he felt it.

A jab in the back, like the one he had experienced earlier

when the bald hero had rugby-tackled him to the ground. This time it was a similar pain. But he had little time to react. He felt someone against him. A head. Shoulders. Hands.

Charlie rolled to the ground, the gun flew from his grip and landed by the pile of phones, and Jake Tanner stumbled on top of him. There was menace in the detective's dark brown eyes. Jake punched him in the face; his head recoiled, and the back of his skull bashed onto the solid flooring. Stars swam in his vision. Charlie blinked them away and blocked everyone else out of the room. Struggling for strength, he threw his opponent from him onto the floor.

He staggered to his feet, dazed. In front of him, at the far end of the room, Benjamin Weiss was making his way towards the exit.

64

Momentum

December 2, 2017, 14:13

Jake felt weak. His body had been depleted of all energy, and the punch he had just landed on Charlie Paxman's face was half-hearted at best. He had received worse from Elizabeth when they argued playfully. But Paxman was no better at this point; his exhaustion was starting to show. His bone density and wiry frame meant they were equally matched. It was just a case of who could outsmart whom. And who would be the first to do it.

Jake rolled onto his back. Paxman was in front of him, headed towards the gun on the floor beside the pile of phones. Jake lifted himself to his feet and jumped on Charlie's back. He carried too much weight and slipped, falling to the floor. Charlie turned and jumped on him, pinning Jake to the ground with his knees straddled either side of him. He moved his hands to Jake's neck and wrapped them around it. Jake lashed out with his fingers, clawing at Charlie's face, nose, and eyes. Anything he could get a grip of.

'Give it up, Charlie!' Jake gasped, coughing as he felt his windpipe crushing under Paxman's weight.

'Make me.' Charlie shifted his position atop Jake so that his right knee was pressed firmly into Jake's bullet wound.

Jake screamed in agony. He faded in and out of consciousness as a barrage of nausea crashed over him. In the distance, the sound of a helicopter approaching grew louder. Jake knew he didn't have long until Hopkins arrived and assassinated Charlie Paxman. He needed to protect the man from imminent death, even if he didn't deserve it. Paxman was his best shot at providing an antidote for himself and for his family - and the rest of the planet. He could not let the man die. He could not fail. Again.

Charlie applied more pressure to Jake's wound, bringing him out of his state of reflection. The pain spurred him on. Jake punched Charlie's arm with the palm of his right hand, nearly snapping the elbow, and hooked him round the face with his injured left. It was a clean hit even if it pained him to do it. Charlie held his nose as blood ran down his shirt. Jake pushed Charlie from atop him and clambered to his feet.

'Get out of here!' he screamed to everyone else in the restaurant, surprised to learn most of them already had. Jake quickly scanned his surroundings and noticed Benjamin Weiss was nowhere to be seen. He hoped the man had been able to avoid death. 'Get down to the first floor. You'll be safe there! Be as quick as you can.'

Charlie regained his senses and tackled Jake to the floor again. The two of them tussled, throwing one another across the pile of dead bodies until they landed by the floor-to-ceiling window next to the mountain of corpses. At once, those who had remained hiding behind the bodies jumped to their feet and sprinted towards the exit on the east side of the building, nearest to the toilets. Soon after, it felt like nobody else was in the room. Just the two of them. Jake and Charlie. But there were survivors still. The idiots! He couldn't make out who they were; he was too dazed and focused on his opponent.

Jake and Charlie both jumped to their feet, fists raised. Jake paused a moment, feeling the wind of the open window against his back; the adrenaline surging through his body had warmed him, and his fist was numb to the pain of punching Charlie in the face. Jake gauged his opponent's stance, position, distance - everything he would need to know to floor the man and pin him down in such a way he wouldn't be able to get back up again.

Then Charlie did something that surprised him: he glanced out of the window, then turned and sprinted towards the exit. *He's escaping.* And then Jake realised in what direction. Elizabeth. The girls. They were still there - they were the ones he had seen - hiding behind the wooden surface of the bar, frozen solid, watching in disbelief. Karen, Alex and Ellen were with them. They were all safe.

For now.

Jake's first instinct was to chase after Charlie, but when Charlie stopped and bent down to the ground, he realised there wasn't anything he could do.

In his arms, Charlie held the AK-47, pointed directly at

him.

Fuck.

'Jake!' Elizabeth screamed, her voice topping every other sound in his head.

'Daddy!'

Jake froze, unable to think, unable to calculate his next move. Slowly, he raised his hands, surrendering to Charlie's trigger finger. Outside, he heard the helicopter near.

Charlie swivelled on the spot, raised the gun, held it in the nook of his shoulder, aimed down the sights and fired. Jake watched in disbelief. Paxman wasn't firing at him. Instead, he was firing at the helicopter in the distance.

Kieran Hopkins, one of the country's most prolific shooters, dangled from the open door of the aircraft, his feet discernible against the grey-blue canvas of sky. Charlie's crazed gunfire seemed ineffective in deterring the assassin. Jake saw the reflection of sunlight on Hopkins's scope as he raised it for the shot.

Holy shit.

Jake couldn't fail again. He couldn't let another person die. First it had been Martha. Then Tyler. And he had only just avenged Moshat in his mind for their deaths. He couldn't let more innocent people be killed. He turned and faced Charlie.

'Everyone, get down!' Jake screamed, looking at Paxman but directing his words to his friends and family.

Jake started towards Charlie, who had flames spitting from the end of his machine gun. Ten feet separated them. But it was already too late. Alex Tough, Jake's recent friend – the one who had almost begun to fill Tyler's position – got to Charlie before him. Alex had hopped an overturned chair, and was sprinting towards Charlie by the time Jake realised what was going on. His friend rammed into Charlie's behind, knocked the gun from Paxman's grip and pushed him forwards, tumbling towards the open window.

Before Jake could do anything, everything around him seemed to move as if in slow motion. In front of him, Alex stopped, stunned, frozen in a moment of confusion and then realisation. A cloud of fine blood and skin and bone exploded behind him as the bullet from Kieran Hopkins's sniper ripped through him. Alex collapsed to the ground. He was dead before he hit the floor.

Then it all happened so fast.

Karen rose her head from behind the sheltered bar. She screamed. All of them did. Elizabeth, Ellie, Maisie, Ellen – their lives would never be the same.

As Jake watched Alex's body crumple to the ground, something to his left caught his eye. Charlie. He was heading straight for the edge of the building. Alex's momentum from charging into Charlie had been too strong and sent him cascading forward. Charlie fell over the lip of the building, unable to stop himself.

'Charlie!' Jake screamed.

Jake sprinted a few steps and jumped, his arm outstretched, reaching after him. He was determined not to let Paxman fall. Jake's body landed halfway out the window, skidding to a halt against the metal divide that separated the window panels. He dangled over the edge of the window, reaching for Charlie, hoping for a touch, a sign, anything to let him know Charlie was holding on to him.

Then he felt Charlie's hand clasp around his, several hundred feet in the air.

65

Disappear

December 2, 2017, 14:15

Kieran Hopkins had missed a shot for the first time, ever. He had failed to even hit the target. His record of the best sharpshooter in the country was in tatters. He didn't know what had happened. He should have seen the civilian charging towards Paxman, but he didn't. He had fucked it.

And there was no going back from it now.

Except he had another opportunity. Charlie Paxman was hanging out of the window. A sitting duck. Kieran could redeem himself. He could salvage his career statistics and shoot the man before he plummeted to his death. He could discard the original bullet casing; nobody else need know about his failed shot.

It was the perfect opportunity.

Kieran readied the sniper rifle once more, steadied himself and his breathing and secured Paxman in his sights. His finger hovered over the trigger. He pulled. The trajectory was thrown off. The helicopter veered to the right, and the bullet smashed into the windowpane beneath Paxman, shattering the glass; Kieran had missed his shot. Again.

'Fuck!' he screamed, his voice inaudible over the din of the rotary blades.

He threw the weapon inside the cabin and put on his earphones.

'What the fuck are you doing?' he said to the pilot. 'I had a clean shot.'

'Following orders, mate. They told me one shot, one kill. And that one shot, no kill, meant we turn around and come home.'

Kieran slammed his fist on the pilot's chair in front of him.

'Besides,' the co-pilot continued, 'the BBC News heli was nearby. They were getting suspicious. You'll be lucky if they don't have footage of you. Of us.'

Even if they do, it will never make the headlines, Kieran tried to console himself.

'You fucking idiot. You ruined it,' he said, speaking to the pilot.

'No, mate. That was you.'

Kieran ignored him. As they flew away, he kept his eyes fixed on The Shard until eventually it disappeared from view.

66

Tinted Windows

December 2, 2017, 14:16

The choked atmosphere inside COBRA was tangible. Frances could feel the tension seeping through the air. They had just watched Kieran Hopkins fail. An innocent civilian, a bystander, had lost his life. And it was the government's fault. The Prime Minister's fault. Frances would never be able to forgive the country's leader for it.

Frances was heartbroken, crushed. She froze and went silent for a moment, deaf to all sounds around her. Time seemed to slow down as she came to terms with what she saw, and as she drowned out the muttered conversations, her emotions turned to anger, disgust.

Enraged, she stormed out of the room.

'Assistant Commissioner,' Martin Ball called behind her.

'Wait.'

Frances swivelled on the spot, scowling. 'What?'

Martin came to a slow stop. 'Where are you going?'

'Back to the Yard, where people listen to my expertise. I told you all it would be a bad idea to send Hopkins in, but no one listened. She didn't listen. You didn't listen.' Frances spat as she enunciated every word. She seethed with anger.

The innocent civilian's death meant more to her than anyone could have known. She had seen his face clearly through the high-definition camera on board the helicopter and the CCTV footage inside the Oblix.

His name was Alex Tough. At least, that's what he had been brought up as. A Tough. A man born into a wealthy family in the south-west of the country. Except he wasn't a Tough – he was a Walken. His birth name had been Alex Frank Walken. And he was Assistant Commissioner Dame Frances Walken's first and only child.

She had just watched her son get assassinated.

Before Martin could say anything, the Prime Minister entered the hallway behind him. Frances could hear her heeled stilettos clanging through the corridor before she saw her. That noise. Those shoes. That murdering bitch who had the biggest hand to play in Alex's death.

'Assistant Commissioner,' the Prime Minister said, stopping beside Martin. 'Where are you going? You can't leave. We require your presence.'

'Why? So you can ignore me again? So you can pretend that you're going to listen to me and then when my back is turned ignore me?' The Prime Minister said nothing. 'I won't have it. I won't stand for it. Not anymore, Hilary.'

Calmly, the Prime Minister replied, 'Please, let us finish

this and then we can discuss your options afterward. There is still a lot of work required.'

Frances looked around her. A crowd had formed at either end of the corridor, and the heads of the country's most powerful establishments hung outside the COBRA doorframe. She could feel their judgemental looks boring into her.

'No.' Frances turned. 'That's it. I'm done.'

Frances stormed out of the underground corridors, into her unmarked bulletproof Land Rover, and headed towards The Shard, where she could be closer to her dead son and where she could help Tanner. These people certainly weren't going to, so she would have to do it herself.

On the drive there, hidden behind tinted windows, the assistant commissioner sobbed. Nothing could stop her tears.

67

Inside All Of Us

December 2, 2017, 14:15

'Don't let go!' Jake screamed at the top of his voice. Charlie was on the other end of his arm, clinging to him for life. The wind shook Charlie against the side of the building.

The helicopter had gone. Hopkins had gone. But Alex was still dead on the floor behind Jake, his face ripped in two by the .300 calibre bullet that tore through him. Elizabeth, Karen, and the children behind him continued to scream, their shrill cries buffeting against the wind.

Jake looked into Charlie's eyes. They were filled with sympathy, a willingness to live and recompense for what he had done.

'Please, Jake,' he said. 'Don't let me fall. I don't want to die.'

Jake gritted his teeth and ignored him. He didn't like what he was doing, saving a terrorist – it was working against every instinct in his body – and the man deserved to be several hundred feet below, but it was a necessity. Jake held on to the window frame with his left arm. The metal dug into his shoulder, and shards of glass lacerated his skin. A blinding pain now and then lowered a blanket of white across his vision. He forced it back, determined not to be consumed by the fear that had plagued him for so long in his life. Howling through the pain, Jake tried to life Charlie higher up the building. But it was no use. He was too weak, and Charlie too heavy.

'It's not working!' Jake looked down, saw how high he was and closed his eyes. The likelihood of falling out of the window and plummeting to his death increased with every passing second.

'Jake!' Elizabeth screamed behind him. She rushed over and bent down by his side. Her hand fell on his back; it was bliss, the first touch of hers he had felt in what seemed like an eternity. 'Jake, what are you doing?'

'Must. Save. Him.' Jake paused with every breath.

'What? You can't. He's a murderer, a psychopath. He doesn't deserve to live.'

Jake didn't need reminding – the body of the dead World Health Organisation employee next to him was a constant reminder of the fact.

'Elizabeth,' Jake said. 'Trust me. We can't let him die.'

'Yes, we can.'

'If we do, then are we any better than him?'

Elizabeth said nothing.

'Liz, he might be able to create an antidote. This is about

more than just morals. This is about saving as many people as we can.'

'Fine,' she whispered, her voice barely audible next to Jake's ear. 'What do you need me to do?'

'Hold on to my legs.' Elizabeth grabbed his ankles. 'Charlie – climb up me. Climb up my arm!'

The sound of sirens and screams from below cut into Jake's words. Charlie pulled on Jake's arm, which felt like it was going to pop out of its socket. His fingers dug through Jake's clothing and into his skin. Jake closed his eyes, blocking out the searing pain. He swayed in and out of consciousness like a Newton's cradle.

He yelled out in agony.

Charlie's weight had completely dislodged his shoulder joint, pulling it out of its socket. Now both of his shoulders were injured. He would be unable to do anything. Not even arrest Charlie and keep him pinned to the ground until the rest of the Metropolitan Police Service arrived.

He had a decision to make: let Charlie slip and fall to his death, or let him clamber up the rest of his body and escape to the bottom of the building.

His decision was made for him.

Elizabeth's hand dangled beside his face. Another hand joined it. Charlie's. Jake's body had been so numb with pain and cold, he hadn't realised how far Charlie had climbed. Elizabeth hefted the man into the building, and for a moment, all three of them laying on floor, catching their breath.

As Jake struggled to lift himself, Charlie rolled over, and climbed to his feet and rushed over to the gym bag on the floor.

'Charlie, stay where you are,' Jake said, struggling.

Elizabeth rushed to his side and helped him stand. He embraced her with what little energy he had left, held her close to his chest, ignoring the pain. He had lost all control of his right arm and couldn't move it.

'I can't do that, Jake,' Charlie said, picking up the bag. They stared at one another, suspended in a moment of uncertainty. Charlie's expression was unassuming, giving nothing away. 'There are things I still need to do.'

Charlie reached inside the bag.

'You're evil!' Elizabeth shouted, leaning against Jake's shoulder. 'You won't get away with this.'

The geneticist smiled slowly and removed a glass vial from the bag. He looked directly at Jake as he spoke. 'There's evil inside all of us. I learned that a long time ago. It may lie dormant for most of your life, but it's there. You and I both know it. It's just that I'm not afraid to realise it.' He wiggled the glass tube in the air. 'This virus is just the beginning. Overpopulation will always be an issue. Many will agree with me. I can see it in your eyes, Jake – you do, too. What's your evil?'

Just as Jake opened his mouth to respond, Charlie bolted. He cleared the overturned table by a few metres, clutched his large duffel bag in his arms, and sprinted out of the restaurant, heading towards the back end, nearest to the kitchen.

Just like that, Paxman had gone. Jake didn't know whether he wanted to laugh or cry.

In the end, he stopped paying attention to Paxman and focused on everything else in the room. Everything good in his life. Everything that made him feel whole.

Ellie and Maisie had all survived unscathed and

unharmed, save for Elizabeth who had a slight graze on her face. They hugged him. They made him feel warm and powerful, as if there was nothing in the world that could stop them. He felt so much blood and love coursing through his veins at that moment, that he didn't want it to end.

'Are you OK?' he asked her.

She nodded. 'I'm fine.'

'The baby?'

Her hands fell to her stomach. 'OK, I think.'

Jake smiled, kissed Elizabeth on the forehead, and turned his attention to his other children. 'How are my girls doing?' Jake bent down to their height. He cradled his dislocated shoulder with his left arm. Movement in both agonised him.

'Daddy! I'm scared,' Ellie said, rushing to him. 'Has the bad man gone away now?'

'Yes, Darling. He's gone. Don't worry. He won't hurt anyone anymore.' Jake pulled Ellie away from his body and looked her in the eyes. 'He didn't you, did he? Either of you?'

Both girls shook their heads. Strands of hair flicked their tear-laden faces.

'Good. You were so brave out there. I'm so proud of both of you.' Jake embraced them and kissed their heads. The smell of their shampoo wafted through his nose, and a warming sensation coursed through his body.

Jake released and looked to the distraught and broken woman on the floor lying next to her husband, cradling what was left of his head in her hands. Ellen sat on the other side of her dad, holding his hand.

He felt sick. The gravity of Alex's death crashed down on him like a plane into the ground. He was mad. No, he was furious. Kieran Hopkins had brutally murdered his friend.

Jake didn't care if it was an accident. There was always a chance that Hopkins would have hit a civilian, and given that risk he shouldn't have pulled the trigger; it didn't matter if he was the finest shooter the nation had ever had.

Jake rose to his feet, wandered over to Karen, bent down and embraced her with his bloodied left arm. That was when the tears came, the point when the barriers of Karen's emotional strength were finally worn away, and the torrent of turmoil came flooding out.

'Why did he have to do it?' Karen yelled through her tears. She began to hyperventilate. 'Why did he have to be so stupid and try to stop it from happening?'

'Everything's going to be OK,' Jake told her, even though he knew it was a lie. Nothing would ever be OK again. Nothing would bring back Alex. 'He's a hero. He died protecting you and his family. He put you before himself, and don't you ever forget that.'

'He was stupid.'

'No, he wasn't. He was doing what he signed up to do all those years ago when you married him and started a family. He signed up to protect you and the kids, no matter the cost. He always put you before himself. That's one of the terms and conditions,' Jake said. Somehow, he managed a smile. Karen couldn't meet his eyes.

Jake held her as tightly against him as he could manage for a moment more, then let go and helped her to her feet.

Brushing himself down, his face and clothes and hair sodden with water, he said, 'Right, I need you to stay put—'

'Where are you going?' Elizabeth interrupted.

'I've got to go. Charlie's still got the virus. God knows whether he released another vial with the bomb or if that was just a decoy all along. Either way, I think he's going to release it now. If I stand any chance of stopping that from happening, now would be it. I just needed to know you were all safe first. This isn't over yet.'

Nobody said anything. Jake reached inside his pocket for the phone Kayla had given him.

It wasn't there.

Fuck! Jake frisked his pockets, front and back, searching for it, knowing he wouldn't find it. And then he realised something else: the weapon Tim had given him had fallen out as well. They must have fallen out when he and Charlie wrestled on the floor.

'Jake?' Elizabeth said, touching his arm. 'What is it? What's the matter?'

'Find me a phone. I need to make a call. And a gun. I had one. It fell out of my pocket. Find it.'

While Elizabeth scanned the floor in search of a phone, Jake walked over to the massacre by the window. His eyes searched for Benjamin Weiss or Marianne Evans, Charlie Paxman's nemeses. They were nowhere to be seen amongst the dead. They had escaped. And he had saved them.

'Hey,' Elizabeth said, returning by his side. In her hand, she concealed the SIG Tim had given him, and passed it to Jake. He thanked her and put it in his waistband against the small of his back.

He turned and started towards the centre of the pen. As he reached halfway, Maisie raised her hand, holding a phone. 'Daddy,' she yelled. 'I think I found it. Is this yours?'

Jake took the phone and examined it. The home screen illuminated, revealing an image of his three girls: Elizabeth, Ellie, and Maisie.

'That's my princess,' Jake said, giving Maisie another kiss on the forehead.

He unlocked the phone, scrolled through his address book and dialled.

'Frances, is that you? Frances – it's Tanner.'

68

Sidelines

December 2, 2017, 14:17

In Greenwich, Mamadou watched the news. The live events of what was being dubbed the 'Shard Attack' played on the television screen in Charlie Paxman's quarantined flat. The news helicopter had been right up close to the action, which meant that, for that precise second, Mamadou - and the entire world - had seen everything that had happened.

It was a disaster. Britain's media had just shown a civilian being shot in the head on live TV. There was nothing anyone could do about that now - not even the country's most intelligent cyber-security analysts. The footage was there on the internet, and it would never come down. Sure, they could wipe what they believed to be every trace of the video, but it wouldn't be enough. It would still exist, and damning evidence such as that would only thrive on the black market. And sooner or later, Mamadou knew, it would come back to haunt them all.

'Jesus fucking Christ,' he said, his hands flying to his mouth.

The situation down at The Shard was deteriorating rapidly; Mamadou could see that. And it pained him to be stuck inside the confines of Paxman's flat. Fortunately for him, and not so fortunately for the rest of the human population, the news helicopter had also shown the explosion that occurred right at the top of the building. Which could mean only one thing: Paxman's virus had been released into the air. Quarantining Mamadou and the team of armed officers from the rest of the city was pointless now.

Lifting himself out of Charlie Paxman's sofa, he said, 'I'm out of here.'

'Where do you think you're going?' one of the armed officers said to him.

'I just told you. Out.'

'No, you're not. No one is allowed out of here.'

'None of you can stop me.'

The Trojan stepped in front of him.

'Listen,' Mamadou continued, 'I'm not in the mood to be pissed about like this. You really think us being contained in here will make a difference to anything? The virus has already been released. It makes no sense for the city's most experienced armed officers to be cooped up here for the next couple of hours. Not while the person responsible is still alive and moving. Now get out of my way before I make you.'

The Trojan stood strong. Mamadou tried to walk through her as if she weren't there and managed to knock her back a few paces. Then the officer grabbed Mamadou's trailing hand, twisted it behind his back and lifted it towards his shoulder blade. His entire right arm ached and he felt another arm grapple his neck.

He was in a chokehold. Locked with nowhere to go.

'I said no one is going anywhere,' the officer hissed through her teeth.

'What makes you think I'm going to sit down and pay attention to you?' Mamadou asked.

'I could ask you the same thing. I don't care what title you have, you are not in a position to release this virus to the outside world regardless of whether or not it has already been expelled elsewhere. I don't care who you are, it's not happening.'

Mamadou remained silent. He could hear whispers coming from behind him.

'Damn, she got him good,' one of the officers said to another.

'I know, right? She's always had a temper on her.'

Mamadou had tried and failed. He was stuck inside Charlie Paxman's flat for the foreseeable future, only able to watch from the sidelines.

69

Exit

December 2, 2017, 14:20

The sound of Charlie's footsteps echoed up and down the stairwell, with the sound of his exasperated breath trailing behind. His body shook with adrenaline. He couldn't believe he was alive. He should have died. His body should be impaled on the concrete. But it wasn't. He had been offered a second chance. But there was an issue. Benjamin and Marianne. They were still alive, still out there, having narrowly escaped death. Now there was no way he would be able to assassinate them. He had missed his chance. And he would never be able to forgive himself for letting them get away.

Charlie stopped on the twentieth floor, darted to the bathrooms, and placed his bag on the sink. Inside was an inconspicuous grey T-shirt, a pair of jeans, and a Primark AC/DC hoodie to cover the claw marks on his arms. In total, it had cost him a tenner, and it was the perfect disguise. Not to mention the brown wig he had in the bag, too. And the glasses and coloured contact lenses.

The lights flickered overhead. He flung his old clothes off into the cubicle and pulled the new ones over his skin. They felt clean, the smell of fresh cotton rising through his nostrils. By now the sprinkler systems had stopped, and the fresh clothes reinvigorated him. After he finished, he removed the contact lenses from the bag and leaned forward until his face was within a foot of the mirror. Placing the first lens in his eye, Charlie blinked, and the colour of his iris changed from green to blue. It was a subtle yet very effective change. He did the other eye, then placed the wig on his head and, finally, the glasses. His disguise was complete, and he had managed it in less than three minutes.

He put the small vial of liquid in the front pocket of his hoodie and left the gym bag behind. Before leaving, he washed his face free from dried and running blood. He tore a sheet of toilet paper free and dabbed at his skin.

As he approached the doors leading into the stairwell, Charlie listened intently and peered through the gap in the doors. He was waiting for footsteps, the soldiers, the enforcers, the people who were going to come and take him away. But he was met with complete silence.

Charlie exhaled. Now that he was alone and without a weapon, he was on edge. He opened the door, ignored the squeaking hinges, and hurried down the stairs.

Soon he would be in the Underground. If he couldn't kill the people he hated most, then he would release the virus. He couldn't let today become a complete failure. It saddened him to think his work and ingenuity wasn't appreciated. That he hadn't been able to convince anyone to side with him.

When Charlie came to the fourth floor, he heard a cry for help. He stopped, his body consumed with a paralysing fear he hadn't felt since Benjamin had stumbled across him and Marianne in her office that day.

'Help! Help me, please!'

It was the sound of a woman in distress. *Beautiful,* Charlie thought. It was all he needed to complete the disguise.

'Hold on,' he called down, 'I'm coming. You're safe. No one's going to hurt you.'

Charlie skipped the steps two at a time, holding on to the railing to keep his balance. At the sight of a middle-aged brunette with blood running down the side of her face, Charlie slowed. He bent down by her side.

'Are you OK? What are you doing here?' he asked.

'I'm fine. I tripped and fell.'

'You've been on your own all this time?'

The woman nodded. 'Someone was supposed to come back, but he never did.'

'What did he look like?'

'Tall. Brown hair. Slim. And he was carrying a little boy with him.'

'Have you seen anyone else? An elderly woman and a man?'

The woman looked at him suspiciously for a moment, dismissed whatever concern had arisen in her head, and said, 'No. Nobody's come down this way. I've been on my own all this time.'

Shit. Benjamin and Marianne must have taken a separate

route through the building. They could be anywhere by now. The small hope he had left of finding them had been diminished.

'Nothing to worry about,' he said, returning his attention to her. 'I'll help you get out of here. Together – we're going to get out of here. How does that sound?'

'Please. Everything hurts. I need to see a doctor.'

'I'll get you to one. Just hold on. What's your name?' Charlie asked, helping her to her feet. He placed her arm over his shoulder and started down the stairs.

'Samantha.'

'Nice to meet you, Samantha. I'm Charlie.'

He gave her a smile before continuing. They made their way down the building slowly, pausing every five minutes for Samantha to take a break, when he was the one who needed the respite. He was the one carrying her. He was the one burdening himself with her weight on his weak and feeble knees.

But he couldn't get rid of her. He needed her for the next part of the operation. If he were to safely get out of the building, he needed all the alibis he could get. She was his blessing in disguise.

Eventually, they stopped behind the reception door. He hesitated, steadied his breathing and steadied himself.

He would need to be perfect to pull this off. Nothing could go wrong; or his cover would be blown. He closed his eyes and exhaled deeply, then shoved the door open wide. It slammed against the adjacent wall. Lumbering with Samantha in tow, he tentatively crossed the threshold into the reception area.

'Help!' he screamed. 'Please, we need your help!'

The lobby was swamped. Armed police officers carrying weapons populated the entrance. They were in the middle of escorting some of Charlie's hostages out of the building; at the sight of them, he lowered his head. Upon hearing his voice, the unoccupied officers twisted on the spot and aimed their firearms at them both.

'Stop! Armed police!' they shouted. 'Stay right where you are.'

Charlie and Samantha complied. Within seconds they were surrounded.

'What are you . . . ?' one officer began. He hesitated to inspect Samantha's face, while another spoke discreetly into the radio on his chest. 'Samantha?'

Charlie could feel his blood pulsing in his temple.

'Samantha, is that you? Oh my God. What happened to you? Are you OK?' the officer asked, reaching out to her.

Samantha didn't respond. She had her eyes closed, and as the time passed, her weight increased on Charlie's shoulder. He needed to get them both out of there now.

'She's suffered a head injury and hurt her ankle. Possibly minor concussion. We need to get her to a paramedic as soon as possible.'

The officer who'd recognised Samantha lowered his weapon, stepped aside, and said, 'Let them through. They're clear.'

Charlie started towards the exit, leading Samantha alongside him. As they exited the building, a woman dressed in dark green overalls came rushing over. She wore a mask over her face, and at the sight of it, Charlie smirked. 'Are you OK?' she asked.

'I'm fine,' Charlie said, 'but she's not.'

'Never mind,' the paramedic said, stepping to the other side of Samantha. 'I'll take care of both of you. Come with me.'

The paramedic led Charlie towards an ambulance to the left of the train station. As they walked, Charlie realised how desolate and quiet it was. Glass and other bits of debris littered the ground, and it made him smile. This was his work – his reward for all his efforts. He wondered how many people the shower of glass had injured. He hoped a lot. In the distance, a thin perimeter of officers wearing hazmat suits had been set up, but the area was scarcely populated. He had succeeded. He had managed to invoke fear into the entire population, and now they were paying attention to him. His name would become synonymous with overpopulation, he knew. And he would have tarnished everyone within the World Health Organisation's reputation.

The paramedic sat them both down – Samantha inside the vehicle on a stretcher, and Charlie on the edge of the van. She attended to Samantha first, flashing a light in her eyes and throwing a space blanket over her.

'How do you feel?' she asked Samantha.

'My ankle. It hurts to move it.' Samantha flinched as the paramedic dabbed the side of her face with a cotton pad, wiping away the blood.

Charlie had had enough. He'd already wasted too much time standing in the open, and he was beginning to feel vulnerable.

He started off towards London Bridge train station.

'Where are you going, Charlie?' Samantha mumbled to him. She looked at him with tired eyes.

'You don't need me anymore, do you?' he asked.

'Yes,' the paramedic said. 'I need to check you over. We've been so thin on the ground because there have been so many injured people evacuating the building. For now, it's just me who can look after you, so you'll have to be patient.'

'I'm fine. Honest. Just a little shaken up.' Charlie placed his hand in his hoodie pocket and made sure the glass vial was still there. He relaxed as he felt his fingers caressing the solid cylinder.

'It doesn't matter. You still need to be seen.'

Before Charlie could do anything, the sound of footsteps rushing towards them distracted him.

'Excuse me,' a small woman said, flashing an ID card. 'PC Ciara Reed. I was just wondering if I could ask you a few questions?'

70

Loose

December 2, 2017, 14:25

Ciara was out of breath. She had seen two injured civilians meandering to an ambulance with the help of a paramedic and just sprinted over. She had ignored the police officer standing behind the cordon calling after her, beckoning her to come back. She had ignored the team of forensic officers hovering around a dead body that had been flattened on the concrete. She had ignored the blood everywhere. Brain matter everywhere. Organs and limbs everywhere. The worst thing she had ever seen in her life. She had ignored the deep feeling of regret and guilt she had in her stomach.

As she arrived at the ambulance, the man standing on the outside looked shocked, taken aback. He went pale as if he had just seen the sight of his hollow face in a mirror.

'Can I ask you a few questions?' she asked, brandishing her ID.

The man stared inside the van at the two women, and then back at Ciara.

'How long will it take?' he said. As he moved, Ciara caught sight of something glass-like glimmering in the man's front jumper pocket.

She observed the minutiae of his face. The hair. The glasses. The eyes. The eyebrows.

The eyebrows. They looked familiar, like she had seen them recently, but she had never met this man before. She had once read online that the most recognisable features on a human's face were the eyebrows. There was something about this man's that made her feel uneasy.

Was this him? Was this the man who had murdered Rik? She didn't know. She needed more time to figure it out.

'It will take as long as it needs to.' Ciara removed a small notebook and pen from her coat pocket and began writing. 'What's your name?'

'Kyle.'

'Kyle?' Ciara repeated.

'Kyle?' the woman on the gurney said. 'You told me it was Charlie.'

'I . . . it . . . I . . . ,' the man stuttered.

Before Ciara could ask a follow-up question, or even ask him to clarify his name, the man lunged inside the ambulance, grabbed a small Automated External Defibrillator loose on the vehicle's floor, and swung it at Ciara's face. The impact made her nose bleed and sent her head spinning. She toppled to the ground in a heap, smashing the back of her head on the pavement. The world around her went black for a split moment. Screams and shouts came from within the ambulance, worsening the ringing in her ears.

As she came to and felt the paramedic's hands on her face, she realised the man named Charlie – the man she believed to be the terrorist who had slaughtered her friend – had escaped.

71

Passing Seconds

December 2, 2017, 14:30

For what felt like the hundredth time that day, Jake clambered down the stairs. He had just got off the phone with Frances after informing her that Paxman was on his way out of the building, that he still had the virus with him, that there had been approximately thirty casualties, that Kieran Hopkins had missed the shot and killed an innocent civilian instead.

'I know,' Frances had said on the phone. She sounded more saddened than usual by the news. 'I watched him do it in COBRA.'

Frances was going to make her way towards the terror scene so she and he could have a full debrief in person. Jake was just grateful she was coming. He needed someone there.

A familiar face. Someone he knew and could trust. Someone with authority who could take control of the situation on the ground.

But first, he had to get his shoulder fixed. The pain was killing him. Jake reached the base of the skyscraper, and he felt a wave of relief descend over him. He had made it. And he had managed to protect the most precious thing in his life: his family.

But it wasn't over.

As soon as he stepped out of the heavy fire doors into the reception, he exhaled, almost collapsing to the floor.

'Gentlemen,' Jake said weakly. He looked out at the armed officers. Admired them. Envied them for having protective clothing and a weapon that they could legally use if the circumstances demanded it.

The men who weren't facing him now turned and aimed their MP5s directly at him.

'Get down on the ground, now!' they said in unison, rushing over to him.

'Fuck's sake,' Jake whispered under his breath.

In an instant, the armed officers surrounded him, shouting at him, making the hairs on his arm stand on end.

'Spread your arms and legs wide!' one of them screamed in his ear.

Jake did as they told him. A series of hands searched his body, moving from top to bottom, patting him down, looking for any surprise devices. As the hands moved lower down his body, he heard one of them say, 'What the fuck?'

Before Jake could react, they jumped on him. A knee pressed firmly into his back. Meanwhile, two others pinned his legs to the ground.

'Hey! Hey!' he cried. 'What are you doing? Are you mad? Do you know who I am?'

'Be quiet.'

One of the searching hands touched the small of his back and removed the handgun.

'Fellas, please!'

'I said, be quiet!' The man he assumed to be the commanding officer – according to his authoritative and powerful voice – stepped in front of Jake's face. 'Arrest him.'

At once, Jake's hands were twisted behind his back, and he was lifted to his feet. He wanted to scream, but there was no oxygen or energy left in his body to do so. As he was dragged to and bent over the reception desk, everything – and everyone – stopped.

The Shard's entrance opened. The sound of sirens fleeted in and then disappeared just as quickly. Jake craned his neck to the door, but two officers were in the way. Who was it? What was there? Was it Paxman? Had he come back?

'What is going on in here?' a voice asked.

'Ma'am!' the officers shouted simultaneously. They stepped away from Jake, standing to attention.

The mysterious person came closer, the sound of soft shoes on the tiles the loudest noise in the entire room.

'Tanner – what's going on?'

Jake craned his neck. Frances.

'Ma'am!' Jake said. He tried to lift himself from the desk, but his body collapsed.

'What are you doing to him, you idiots? Get off him, now!' Frances ordered.

Before the last word had left her mouth, Jake felt the grip on his shoulders release, and the handcuffs were removed from his wrists.

'What are you doing?' Frances asked the commanding officer.

'He . . . We . . .'

'What?'

'We . . . He had a gun on him,' one said shyly.

'I don't care. You should have known who he was before you bullied him. It's a good thing he had the gun, anyway. He'd be able to put it to better use than the lot of you.'

'Frances, it's fine.' Jake shuffled towards the revolving doors. 'It was an honest mistake.'

Frances's face didn't budge. She wasn't happy, and he knew any attempts at lightening the mood wouldn't work, either. She snatched the firearm from him and gave it back to Jake. He looked at her confused. 'Just in case,' she said. 'I trust you more with it right now than I do anyone else.'

Jake took the gun from her and placed it in his back pocket again, out of sight. 'Has anyone else come out in the last five or ten minutes?' Jake asked, changing the subject.

The commanding officer nodded. 'Yes. We had a flurry of people and then these two came out.'

'What two?' Jake asked.

'There was a guy and a girl. He was supporting her.'

'What did this person look like?' Jake's voice went weak.

'Glasses. Dark hair. Wearing an AC/DC hoodie, I think it was.'

'What did you do with him?'

'Got him out of here.'

'What did the woman look like?'

The man shrugged. 'Brunette. Her face was bleeding. She couldn't walk very well – I think she'd sprained her ankle or something.'

Samantha.

'Where did they go?' he asked.

'From what I saw, a paramedic dealt with them.'

'Which one? Which paramedic?'

The officer said nothing and pointed to an ambulance outside the building. Jake didn't need to be told twice to realise what it meant. He said nothing and started out of the revolving doors, his body feeling weaker by the second. Frances followed him, and as they neared the closest ambulance, something caught Jake's eye. Two women, one dressed in paramedic's uniform and the other dressed in smart clothes, acting erratically.

'Where's he gone?' one of the women was asking.

Already Jake's paranoia and fear were growing. And it was made worse by the increasingly stressful behaviour of the two women.

Deep down Jake knew his window of opportunity to catch Paxman was shrinking.

72

Believe Me

December 2, 2017, 14:42

'Excuse me,' Jake said, 'what's the issue here?'

Both women's faces dropped. One of them had blood gushing from her nose, pouring into her mouth and spreading across the width of her neck. She was the first to speak. She removed her ID card, flashing it. 'A guy. I was gathering a statement. He assaulted me. Ran off.' Her words were filled with blood, and with every syllable she tried to enunciate, small droplets of red fell to the floor.

Fuck.

'Did you get a name?'

'Charlie.'

'Kyle.'

The paramedic and woman in front of him both spoke at

the same time.

'He told us different names,' the paramedic said.

Nodding, Jake asked, 'Which way did he go?'

The officer pointed towards London Bridge. 'The Underground.'

'What was he wearing?'

The officer described Charlie's appearance.

'Who are you?' Frances asked the officer.

The woman's face dropped. Her eyes danced between Jake and Frances. Eventually, after swallowing hard, she began, 'Ciara Reed, ma'am. Dispatch.'

Frances froze and her face turned pale.

'I don't bloody believe it,' she said.

'What?' Jake asked.

'Mamadou told me. This is the idiot who answered the original 999 distress call this morning and did nothing about it. If she'd have done her job properly, we'd have known about this attack sooner. We would have been able to save countless lives. And we wouldn't be in this fucking mess!' Frances's chest rose and fell heavily. Jake could hear her breathing through her nostrils from a few feet away. What was happening? She was acting out of character, and he didn't like it. He had never seen her behave like this.

'That's not true,' Ciara said, defending herself.

'I don't want to hear it.' Frances dismissed her with a wave of her hand.

Jake stood there silently, on the outskirts of the argument. He didn't know what to say. He didn't know who to believe. It didn't seem fair to place the blame on one person, especially if she was here right now. Jake could only assume, if she had made the mistake Frances accused her of, that she was here to atone for her error. She was there to fight back, and help them capture Charlie. Because, after all, that was all that mattered: Paxman. He was still out there, and he still needed to be caught.

'Please,' Ciara said, her voice still muffled with blood. 'It's not like that at all. You don't understand.'

Frances said nothing. Her brow furrowed, increasing the lines on her forehead and at the sides of her eyes; the complexion of her skin changed to pink. She tried to glare through Jake.

'Frances!' Jake said. The old woman's arms felt stick thin in his grasp. 'Pay attention. Put your differences aside. Paxman's the real reason we're here. He's the real reason this has all happened. He's missing. And he's still got the virus. We need to find him before it's too late.'

Jake's words made Frances come to; after a few seconds, she blinked back to reality and removed her phone from her pocket.

'Simon,' she said almost immediately. 'Paxman slipped away. Order an emergency cordon for a mile radius. He could be anywhere by now. I want CCTV, facial-recognition footage working overtime. Be advised, he is wearing a disguise. Description is dark wig, glasses, AC/DC hoodie. That's all we've got to go on. Better find him ASAP, Simon – I'm not in the mood to be delayed.'

Frances hung up the phone and put it back into her pocket. She turned and started towards London Bridge station.

As Jake followed behind, he felt a hand touch his left arm, pulling him back.

'You believe me, don't you?' Ciara Reed said.

'I hope what she says isn't true. I watched one of my friends die up there.'

73

Release

December 2, 2017, 14:48

Huge blasts of air hit Charlie in the face as he entered the London Bridge station. An eerie silence drifted in and out of the station. It looked like a scene from a Cold War movie. Or Chernobyl. The desolation. The isolation. The loneliness. The despair of knowing that no one would come and save you.

It chilled him. But also excited him.

He was so close to finishing his mission and putting into place the result of countless hours of work. Even if it meant he couldn't kill Benjamin and Marianne. Perhaps it was a good thing they were alive. Now they could see the effects of his virus first-hand. Now they could realise how formidable a geneticist he was. Give him the credit he was well overdue.

Charlie walked with a Transport for London employee.

The man had been positioned at the entrance to the station, funnelling people through the turnstiles, and onto the train tracks. He explained that he had been drafted in due to his extensive knowledge of the network. Apparently, escorting people through the Underground was the quickest way to get people into the safety of another station outside the perimeter of the attack. But Charlie didn't care. He had other things on his mind.

'The live lines have been switched off,' the man said, 'but we need to be quick. They're starting to turn some of them back on to reduce the backlog of stationary trains in the tunnels. There are so many, they're having difficulty getting them into the nearest station.'

Charlie grunted in acknowledgement, even though he was only half paying attention. The rest of him was focused on what he was going to do next: how he was going to get rid of this person.

Then he had it.

He stopped abruptly and bent down to tie his shoelace. The TfL employee stopped and hovered beside him.

'Look at this,' Charlie said, pointing to a blank spot on the floor.

'What is it?' the man asked, bending down.

As the man reached Charlie's level, he delivered an uppercut to his throat, dazing the man, and threw his body into the walkway that led to the eastbound platform. Charlie searched the felled man's pockets for a security card. A second later, he found it, kicked the man in the ribs and stomach and sprinted onto the eastbound platform. It was empty and silent, save for the sound of his heavy breathing. He glanced up and down the platform. Posters and pieces of rubbish littered the walls and floor. Charlie moved towards the glass safety doors on the edge of the platform. He scanned the card at the top of the doors. They parted seamlessly, and he peered through. So far, this had been the easiest part of the entire operation.

He looked down at the tracks beneath him. Remembering what the man had just told him, he jumped down. The Underground network was Charlie's playground, and he was going to make full use of it. Charlie jogged precariously along the tracks, being careful not to stumble. After a while, he stopped to catch his breath. His chest was heaving. He coughed and spurted the black and red liquid onto his hands. Time was running out.

Today could not be a failure. His mother used to tell him he was one. That he should never have existed, and that nothing he did would ever amount to anything. She would abuse him, ridicule him, chastise him. Bully him, starve him, molest him. Beat him for the smallest things. For being alive. His parents felt it was justified because Charlie had been an accident, a stain on their lives. And they reminded him of it daily.

Now they were both dead, he could live freely, and he would prove to them he wasn't a failure. He would prove it to everyone.

Charlie began to walk again, the wind buffeting through the tunnels whipping around his ears. He could only just hear the sound of his feet stumbling over the stones underfoot. He glanced behind him. There was no one there. His pulse raced with adrenaline. He had been treading a fine line with the officer by the ambulance – hanging around for so long, giving the wrong name. It had almost cost him entirely.

A few metres further and then Charlie stopped in front of a curved door buried deep into the tunnel walls. A lightning bolt symbol stared back at him. The acronym 'AC' was written underneath.

Charlie's skin prickled, raising the hairs on the back of his neck.

This was it.

The final stage.

He grabbed the handle and pushed it down. The door didn't budge. He stepped back a few paces, bent his knee, steadied himself and then kicked the door. The ancient hinges gave way, and the door blew in, slammed against the wall on the inside and bounced back to the doorframe.

A loud, monotonous humming emanated from the room.

Charlie stepped in and was hit by a wave of warm air. He was inside one of the Underground's many air-cooling units that supplied the network with circulated oxygen from outside. He was inside the room that would spread the vector virus through the air at an unprecedented rate, reaching millions within hours, altering their lives and the face of humanity one molecule at a time.

The machine dominated the room. It was wider than Charlie's single bed, more than double his height, and as long as the corridor in his flat. Charlie walked to the long side of the AC unit and ran his hands along the metal, feeling the grooves on the casing beneath his fingers. A series of tubes, each of them the size of a football in diameter and covered in a material that looked like tinfoil, protruded from the top and disappeared into the ceiling.

Charlie examined the machine, searching for a foothold.

He found one. Removing the glass vial from his pocket and keeping it in his hands where it was safe, Charlie climbed to the top of the unit. When he pulled away the tinfoil tube, a blast of air smacked him in the face so hard it nearly knocked him to the floor. He straddled the machine. The air continued to blow through the gaping hole at the top. Charlie held the vial in his hands. Looked at it. Reminisced.

Oddly, he felt sad. Sad that he would leave it behind. A part of him wanted to keep it as a memento, the only one of its kind. But another, bigger part of him wanted to use it, let it flow through the air-conditioning system in the Underground, infecting everyone on the planet.

Charlie unscrewed the lid. With his right hand, he grabbed the tinfoil tube and pulled it close to the hole so it was only a couple of centimetres from the vial. Using his left, Charlie flipped the lid of the vial, hovered it over the hole, breathed slowly, said his goodbyes, and then poured the liquid in. The warm air coming from the machine shot it upwards, and some contents spilled over the side.

Within minutes, the temperature from the cooling unit would turn the liquid into a vapour, which would fill the air and then the lungs of every human on earth. It would take a few weeks for it to take full effect across the globe, but Charlie was prepared to wait. A second in the grand scheme of time and history. Future generations would thank him for his efforts even if the current population wouldn't.

Charlie exhaled heavily. He replaced the tinfoil seal round the hole, making sure it was stuck tight. He leaned back. Relaxed. It was done. Years of preparation. Years of working out the logistics, the chemical balances during his shifts at the WHO. Years of hatred for his mother and father festering in the back of his mind like the liquids in his setup at home.

All done, just like that.

He lay there a few minutes, his spine and ribs moulding to the shape of the air-conditioning unit. In his mind, all was good with the world. He was feeling euphoric. Elated. Nothing was going to stop him from riding this high.

Not even Jake Tanner could fuck this one up.

74

Late

December 2, 2017, 14:50

Jake stopped and thought. Hard. He considered everything he had done today. Everything he had learned about Charlie Paxman. Yes, the man was a bioterrorist whose hatred was aimed at the entire world. But there must have been something Charlie had either said or done that would lead Jake, Frances and Ciara to him. Something. Anything.

He drew blanks.

Both his body and mind had been so shocked and distorted, he couldn't recall anything.

Think, Jake. Think. He closed his eyes, blocking out the world. Had Charlie said anything suspicious? Where would he have gone? He had mentioned nothing about his home life, or his flat in London. He had not mentioned any family or friends or intimate partners. He had not mentioned anyone – or anything – at all. In fact, it dawned on Jake that there was little Charlie Paxman *had* said. Jake's hostage negotiation training had completely slipped through his fingers.

What would have happened if he had remembered his training? How many more lives would he have been able to save? Probably none. Paxman seemed intent on releasing the virus into the air, killing as many people as possible in the process.

And then it hit Jake. Hit him harder than the bullet had when it entered his body.

'He's in here somewhere. On one of the lines.'

'What? What makes you so sure?' Frances asked him.

'It was something he said.' Jake hesitated as he tried to recall Charlie's words exactly. '"It's better than doing it on the Underground, wouldn't you agree? Or is that too soon?" – that's what he said. He was trying to antagonise me, but he also gave me a clue. The clever bastard.'

'I need you to be one hundred per cent sure on this one, Jake,' Frances said. 'This will be the only chance we'll have of finding him.'

'Why would he have gone down there? There's no escape for him. The Jubilee and Northern lines are closed both ways,' Ciara interrupted.

'He's not looking for an escape. He's looking for a way to release the virus.'

'How?'

'Through the Underground.' Jake looked at their dumbfounded faces.

'It's an airborne virus—' Frances began.

'Which means that it spreads via inhalation. All he's got to do is filter it into the air-conditioning system, and in a matter of minutes, he'll have infected thousands of people.'

Jake stopped speaking. Frances looked at him, said nothing, and as one they turned on the spot, sprinting deeper into the station. As they descended the steps to the nearest platform, on the eastbound Jubilee line, Jake hoped they weren't too late.

75

Unafraid

December 2, 2017, 14:52

'Which way do you reckon he went?' Jake asked, looking up and down the platform.

'I need to make a call,' Frances said beside him. She held her phone to her ear and walked to the side. A few moments later she returned. 'Simon's gathering the CCTV footage of inside the station. It'll show us which way Paxman went. He's also organising SCO19 to come down here. They should arrive soon. They shouldn't be too far away, considering they're filtering the rest of the civilians out of the building.'

Jake was grateful Frances was with them – she had a direct line to anyone superior enough to do anything almost instantly, no questions asked.

'What do we do now, then?' Ciara asked. She sounded

both eager and afraid. Curious. Like a child entering a haunted house with their friends. By now, most of the blood flow from her wound had been staunched, but now and then she wiped her face clean with the back of her sleeve.

'Wander up and down the platforms. See if we can find any sign of him,' Jake said, descending a small ramp.

'What are we going to do when we see him?'

'Arrest him,' Jake said. His mouth stopped moving, as did the rest of his body.

On the floor, curled up in a ball, was a TfL guard, whimpering, crying out for help. Jake rushed over to him.

'Sir, are you OK? What happened?'

The man's voice was raspy, and he clung to his throat. 'Some bastard attacked me. Stole my key card.'

'Did you see which way he went?'

The man pointed to the nearest platform. Jake and Frances looked at one another, nodded, and started off. As they left the man on the floor, Jake ordered Ciara to stick by his side and wait for SCO19 to arrive.

'No. I'm coming with you,' she said defiantly.

'You're staying here until they arrive,' Frances ordered.

'Fine.'

Just as Jake and Frances made it to the platform, her phone rang. 'Yes? OK. All right. And you're sure? OK. Yeah.' Frances hung up the phone. 'Simon confirmed Paxman's disappeared through a door in the tunnel. They're monitoring the live feed, and he hasn't come out yet. Although they've said some trains have started to reverse on the tracks – something about there being no space at any stations. We don't have a lot of time.'

'But he's still in there?' Jake said, feeling full of optimism and a renewed sense of hope.

Frances nodded. 'Remember, Jake, he needs to be taken into custody as soon as possible. If he has released his virus, he's our best hope of a fast antidote.'

'I understand. The fuck are we waiting for?' Jake turned on the spot and headed towards the end of the platform—

A wall of darkness stopped him dead in his tracks. His body went cold. The pitch-black tunnel reminded him of the day five months ago when he chased after a District line train containing Lucy Sanderson and Adil Hakim. Jake remained frozen, gripped by fear.

'Jake – Jake, are you OK?' Frances asked. He felt a hand on his back.

Snapping out of his dark thoughts, Jake said, 'I'm fine. Come on, let's get after him. Where are SCO19?'

'I don't know. They'll get here when they get here. Simon's keeping them updated of our position.'

Jake and Frances sprinted towards the end of the platform. As they arrived at the open doors in the glass barrier, Jake skidded to a stop, his fears multiplying. This was no mistake. There wasn't a technical malfunction on the doors. This was the work of Paxman. Realising he was wasting time, Jake jumped down onto the tracks. His legs absorbed his weight, and they gave way slightly. Frances joined him. Silently, they moved forward, descending deeper into the darkness. It felt as if they were walking into a cave, a horror scene, never to return. Jake hoped that wouldn't be the case.

They made it ten metres into the tunnel, hopping over the drainage pits that intersected the floor, when a noise echoed around them. The walls amplified the noise and deafened

Jake. The hairs on the back of his neck stood on end. Frances came to a stop, but not Jake; he continued forward.

A rectangular light burned a hole in the tunnel wall on the left-hand side. A silhouette stepped out from the light and into the darkness. Twenty feet separated them. Jake couldn't see his face, but he knew who it was. He and Frances both did.

Paxman.

Charlie stood still as soon as he caught sight of Jake. Unfazed. Unmoved. Unafraid. Then he started laughing. His callous, cold cackles cascaded down the tunnel.

'Detective Tanner,' Charlie said. There seemed to be a second's delay before Jake heard his words. 'It's too late. The virus has been released. There is nothing you can do.'

Jake ran his fingers through his hair. His body felt tired, weak, and now it had completely deflated. He had nothing left to give.

'Do you know what it does?' Charlie asked. 'I mean, do you *really* know?'

Jake looked at him for a moment, contemplating his next move and anticipating Charlie's. 'Enlighten me,' Jake said.

'Thick people won't be able to reproduce. Those who don't know what they're doing. And those who have a complete disregard for the effect their consumption is having on the planet. We need to keep the intelligent people alive to preserve it.'

'So, you're going to kill off the "thick" people?' Jake used his fingers as air quotes.

'There's no killing involved. It's natural selection at its finest.'

'If you've just released the virus, then why did the bomb

on floor sixty-eight explode?'

'Because it was a decoy – something to keep you occupied while I slaughtered the rest of the people I once knew. I needed you and the rest of the world to know what I was capable of. Believe me when I tell you I could have put the virus in the bomb and infected everyone there and then.'

'Why didn't you?'

'It was more fun this way. Plus, it wouldn't have been as effective from within The Shard. I figured by the time you arrested me, the virus wouldn't have reached maximum impact. And nobody would have known; the more serious side effects can lie dormant for many years to come. Festering inside you. Waiting for the opportune moment to strike and immobilise you. But by doing it this way, the incubation of the virus in the air-conditioning unit, especially during winter time, will hurry the process along, meaning I can watch everyone descend into a panic just before I'm sent away.'

'What if you never made it down here? What if we caught and arrested you before you released it?'

Charlie shrugged. 'It was a risk I was willing to take. Besides, I had a backup.'

'What?'

'My house. I knew you'd break into my flat, tear through my things, overturn everything in sight. Which is why I set up a device there that initiated the gradual release of the virus. It was in the toilet, the place where no one would think to look. It would have taken longer to reach maximum impact, but the damage would still have been done. I just enjoyed it more this way.'

Jake thought of Mamadou. He had been exposed to the

virus sooner than anyone else in the world.

'You were right, we did send someone down there, and we did initiate the virus, but it's locked down. No one in, no one out,' Jake said.

'It doesn't make a difference.'

'How about you come with us?' Jake said, conscious of the rapidly passing time. 'We can discuss this on the train platform where it's safer.'

Charlie mimicked a child's voice as he spoke. 'Aww, is Jake getting scared? Getting worried about a train coming towards him? Afraid it might run him over. Run his family over. His mother-in-law. His best friend. Afraid it might blow up and kill everyone he loves?' Charlie adjusted his voice to normal. 'You know, I didn't get to have as much fun with you as I would have preferred, Jake.'

'Perhaps you'll have to save that for another day.'

Charlie shrugged.

Jake stepped forward, slowly. He gauged Charlie's reaction; the man didn't move. Jake took another step forward. 'You're under arrest, Charlie. You're coming with us. There's nowhere else for you to go.'

Charlie stepped backward and his face came into the light. His pronounced cheekbones cast dark shadows over his cheeks and jaw, and the dark lines under his eyes increased.

'No, Jake. There's always somewhere else for me to go. You're just standing in the way.'

'You know I can't let you go.'

'Why not? You did Moshat Hakim.' Jake froze. 'What has he got that I haven't? What separated him from me? He and I are very similar.'

'You're coming with us.'

'Only if we can work out a negotiation. I want to continue making my experiments from the comfort of one of Her Majesty's finest prison cells.'

'What do we get in return?'

'An antidote.'

Jake listened intently.

'It's in your best interests to keep me alive. Perhaps that's what I'll work on in my experiments. Assuming the virus doesn't kill me first.'

'I thought it wasn't intended to kill?'

Charlie chuckled. His demonic laugh echoed up and down the tunnel. Shortly after, the laugh turned into a cough, and as Charlie finished, he pulled his hand away from his mouth, revealing a black-red liquid. Charlie wiped his hand on his trouser. 'When you've been exposed to as much of the chemicals as I have, it begins to have adverse effects on your body. It begins to shut down your immune system. Rapidly. It will affect some in the same way, but not everyone. It's difficult to say how many.' He paused a beat. 'It's funny, isn't it? I've created something that even I don't know the potential of. I don't know how many will die. I don't know when. All I know is that I have changed the face of humanity forever.'

'Is that so you could show off to Benjamin, Marianne and the rest of the World Health Organisation?'

Charlie's demeanour changed at the mention of their names; his face dropped. 'They'll suffer. Especially. Don't worry.'

'How?'

'I created the virus, Jake. Their exposure will be different to many others'. Their DNA is encoded in the virus. There is no escape from the horrible, violent death they deserve. That I'm sure of.'

'I don't think you're smart enough to pull that off.'

'Don't insult my intelligence, Jake. Do you want me to come with you or not?'

'Yes.'

Charlie's head dipped forward in an admission of defeat. It was a moment before he spoke. 'I'll join you, but on my own accord. Keep your distance until we get to the platform. And then we can discuss something.'

Jake smiled, and there was laughter in his voice as he said, 'That suits me fine. I've not got any handcuffs. Not that I'd be able to use them anyway.'

Jake stepped backward, placed his feet together, and waited until Charlie stepped forward the same distance. They were on the same page, understanding one another. Glancing over his shoulder, Jake nodded to Frances before walking backward. He kept his eyes glued to Charlie, lest the terrorist flee in the opposite direction, disappearing deeper into the Underground.

When Jake approached the platform, Frances was already up there. He turned to face her and considered how he was going to climb up. The top of the platform came level to his chest. He couldn't use his arms because the day's events had rendered them almost obsolete.

Charlie stopped beside him.

'Need a hand?' he said, humour lacing his words. A smile grew on the skinny man's face. It felt strange being so close to him.

Jake scowled. 'Funny. Give me your leg.'

Charlie bent down on one knee, placed Jake's foot atop it,

and gave him a boost. Jake used what strength remained in his left arm to lever himself over the ledge. He was on. Safe. And he felt better for it.

But there was still one person missing.

Charlie.

Jake rose to his feet and looked down at the person who, only hours ago, had fired a bullet into his shoulder. 'Come on, Paxman,' Jake said. 'Now your end of the bargain.'

The sound of an approaching train echoed around the station. Jake leaned forward. It was an eastbound train headed straight towards them, reversing slowly.

'Charlie. Charlie! What are you doing? Get up here!' Jake screamed, peering down the tracks.

Charlie said nothing. He stood still. His eyes fixed on the train rolling towards him. Why wasn't he moving?

Jake shot out his left arm to grab Charlie and pull him up, but he was too slow, and Charlie ducked out of the way. The bioterrorist stepped into the centre of the tracks.

'Charlie!' Jake said, his body overcome with adrenaline and fear. 'Don't do anything stupid.'

He didn't know what to do. He couldn't jump down there and rescue Charlie because it would mean death for both of them.

'Charlie, what are you doing? Get up here now. It's not going to stop!'

Charlie said nothing. Did nothing. He looked at Jake and put his hands behind his back. At first Jake thought he was going to reveal something – a gun, bomb, machete, a bunch of bananas, anything. But he didn't. And then Jake knew it was a sign. Charlie had decided at the last minute to give up, concede defeat. Charlie Paxman had decided he was going nowhere with them.

76

The Last Thing

December 2, 2017, 14:59

Ciara sprinted down the platform. She had heard the armed officers descending the escalators and decided to leave the man on the floor. There was a terrorist she wanted to capture.

As she reached Jake and Frances, she watched Charlie Paxman stand in the middle of the tracks. A thousand thoughts raced through her mind. But then she settled on one. She wasn't going to let Charlie Paxman take the easy way out. He wasn't going to get run over by a train. She needed closure, to avenge Rik's death. Because of Charlie, her future child wouldn't ever get the chance to meet their dad.

The train was two hundred yards away, moving at a reduced pace, but with each passing second, the gap was steadily closing.

She estimated she had less than thirty seconds to stop him.

Lunging forward onto the balls of her feet, she reached for Jake Tanner's back pocket, grabbed the visible gun tucked in there, and jumped down. Her body felt as if she were functioning on autopilot. She ignored the screams coming from behind her.

She needed to do this. Right now, she was the one with the gun. And she was angry.

'Ciara! What are you doing?' she heard Jake say. 'Put the gun down!'

She ignored him. A smile spread over Paxman's face.

'Is that mine?' he asked. 'The same gun that misfired a few hours ago, after I shot what's-his-name?' He reached into his jean pocket and produced the key card he had stolen from the security guard earlier. 'Yes, there it is. Rik.'

'Don't you dare say his name!' Ciara yelled, her body shaking with hatred. 'He was my . . . He was my . . . He was going to be the father of my child, you sick bastard! You – you murdered him!' Tears formed in her eyes as she spat a mouthful of blood mixed with saliva onto the tracks.

'Good.' Charlie said. 'I enjoyed it. I'd do it all again if I had the chance to. He's responsible for bringing in yet another fucking cancerous cell to this fucking planet. And I'd kill you if I had the chance.'

In a state of blind rage and vengeance, Ciara pulled the trigger.

Nothing happened. The world went silent. The only thing she could hear was the sound of her breathing, and the deafening echo of the gun's hammer hitting nothing.

Charlie Paxman smirked at her. That same smug smile she had seen on the CCTV footage.

She'd had enough. Throwing the gun to the ground, she grabbed for his shirt and tugged. He unwrapped his arms from behind him, shoved her and pushed her backward. She fell over the railway line, smashed her head against the brick platform and landed on her elbows. She looked up; Paxman was making a dash for it in the opposite direction, heading away from the train. She ignored the pain, rose to her feet and, using all her strength, chased after him.

'Ciara!' Jake called. She heard him, and saw him sprinting alongside her on the left, on the other side of the glass partition.

Ciara lunged and pulled Charlie to the ground. They landed in a heap on the tracks. His body cushioned her fall and she clambered atop him. She looked behind her. The bright lights of the train were growing larger with every passing second. And that was when she realised SCO19 had arrived. An officer, clad in Kevlar, with his face and body hidden from view, had jumped down from the platform using the same entrance she had. He raced along the tracks, the weapon in his hand swinging from side to side.

'Get up!' he shouted. 'Get back.'

A bang on the window beside her distracted her attention. She was becoming disorientated from all angles. On the other side of the glass was Jake and the rest of the armed officers. One of them held a metal bar in his hands and was trying to force open the nearest door.

'Come on!' the officer's voice echoed up and down the tunnel.

The armed officer rushing towards Ciara arrived and he pulled Paxman to his feet. Charlie writhed in the man's embrace, trying to break free. Ciara's head darted from left to right – at the door, then at the train, back at the door again. It was close now. She estimated twenty feet. If they didn't open the door immediately, they were all going to—

The door opened, and Ciara felt herself scream in relief inside. The armed officer was standing in front of her, still holding Charlie. He locked his arms around Charlie's waist, bent down, and heaved him over the platform's edge. The rest of SCO19 on the other side of the partition pulled the terrorist to safety

Time was running out.

'Quick!' the officer said, holding his hand out for Ciara.

She took it, placed her right foot in front of her, and then stumbled. She twisted her ankle on a stone underfoot that had come loose. The officer caught her as she fell, but it was too late. She had wasted her only opportunity at surviving. She never saw the wall of black and white hitting her, trampling her, killing her.

Detective Jake Tanner's face was the last thing she ever saw.

77

Recollections

December 2, 2017, 15:03

Jake couldn't breathe. It felt like the air in his lungs had been forced out of him by a knockout punch. As if he were being suffocated inside a plastic bag, and the asphyxiation was causing his body to wobble.

He had just seen an innocent soldier and police officer get run over by a train. Their bodies had disappeared beneath the carriage. Even when the train had passed through to the other side of the tunnel, Jake couldn't bring himself to look at the mangled and disfigured remains. He had only seen the impact for a second, and the image would forever be ingrained in his memory.

'I'm going to be sick,' he said, feeling a load of bile rise from his stomach to his throat. It had come out of nowhere.

He turned to the right, away from everyone else, and vomited on the concrete. Bits of stomach lining and breakfast landed on the floor and spattered onto his feet. Frances's hand touched his back.

Wiping the leftover vomit from his lips, Jake said, 'I'm fine.'

The acidity stung his throat and mouth, and it left a disgusting aftertaste. He turned and saw Paxman pinned to the floor. Three men were on top of him, holding him down, pressing his face into the concrete. There was no resistance, no fight left in Charlie. He had given up and was just lying there, waiting for his hands to be tied behind his back. Jake thought he looked broken, beaten, devoid of all hope. In a bizarre sort of way, Jake felt sympathetic towards him. Deep down, he admitted to himself, Charlie's intentions had been just. Overpopulation was an issue, and the government – and everyone in the country – was suffering. Something had needed to be done a long time ago, and Paxman had had an answer. If only this man's brilliance hadn't been twisted towards the barbarism of eugenics.

'Bring him here,' Frances said, her voice demanding the attention of the entire station.

Three Trojans lifted Charlie to his feet and shoved him towards her. She told him his rights, grabbed his arm, and started for the exit. 'Jake – with me.'

'But . . . what about . . . ?' Jake asked, his body already following Frances.

'They'll deal with it.'

As the three of them ascended the escalators, a torrent of police officers rushed the other way. Accompanying them were a group of individuals dressed in white scrubs. They would be there all night. Jake didn't even want to imagine how many pieces of both Ciara and the soldier there were on the floor.

He forced the thought from his mind and considered the positives. The day was done. And he couldn't wait to hold his family again; he was grateful that this time he wouldn't be in a hospital bed with only a vague recollection of what had happened the night before.

78

Pint

December 3, 2017, 18:00

The tobacco entered Tim Keane's lungs. It felt great. Made him feel alive – like all the tension and the stresses of the past twenty-four hours could disappear with one deep inhalation.

Tim's shoulders and back and neck muscles relaxed. He exhaled. The smoke filled the air and lingered close to his face, meaning he could inhale more of the toxins and chemicals that would one day kill him.

Months ago, if the virus had been released then, he would have hoped it was the virus that killed him. He had been bordering on depression, and after hearing about the horrific death in Charlie Paxman's flat, he would have said he would like to go the same way. For it to be over in an instant. No warning. No preamble. No cure. Just death. Just like that.

Now, however, things were different. There was someone in his life worth caring for. Samantha. Even if he had known her less than a day, he could sense they were going to be lifelong partners. They shared a closer connection than anyone he had ever met before in his life. And if they were both affected by the virus, and if neither of them could have kids, then so be it. They had each other, and that was all that mattered. Just one step at a time.

But for now, they were enjoying their brief time together. They were standing outside Charing Cross police station in the cold, waiting for Vince.

'How long will he be?' Samantha asked, juggling the cigarette in her hand with the crutches she had been given for her injuries. The cigarette made her look like Marilyn Monroe – a personal favourite of his. Except this one had different-coloured hair and was much better-looking.

'Hopefully not too long. They're still running up his charges. They wouldn't tell me much, but he's been in there since yesterday, so go easy on him. He's going to be fragile.'

Samantha smiled and kissed him. Her lips and mouth felt warm. He didn't mind the taste of nicotine on her tongue – it only made her more arousing. While they waited, they grabbed a seat on a nearby bench, and less than ten minutes later, the station doors opened.

Vince, wearing the same clothes as the day before, looked left and right, up and down the street, his face a portrait of confusion and aggression. In the end, he turned right.

'Vince!' Tim called after him, jumping off the bench and dragging Samantha along with him. 'Wait up, mate.'

Vince spun on the spot. 'There you fucking are! I was waiting inside for you. The police told me I had visitors coming to pick me up. But when you didn't show, I thought you'd died.'

'You're lucky I came at all,' Tim said, shaking his friend's hand.

Tim looked behind him at Samantha; Vince must have followed his gaze because he said, 'Who's this, then?'

'Samantha,' she said, extending her hand to Vince.

'Pleasure.' Vince turned to address Tim. 'Is she with you? Christ, how long was I in there?'

'Funny. You and I have a lot to catch up on.'

'Come on, let's walk and talk. You can tell me about it in the pub,' Vince said, starting off down the street.

'Which one?'

'Any. I don't care. I need a drink.'

They found a small pub called The King of Egypt stationed outside the north side of Charing Cross train station. It was busy - heaving with holidaymakers - and warm, and had a genuine pub feel to it. Tim had never been there before, but after he took his first sip of beer, he decided it would become one of his regular haunts. They found a table upstairs and sat next to a window.

'So, what did I miss?' Vince asked, wiping his top lip free of beer.

Tim and Samantha looked at one another. 'Where should we begin?' he asked her.

Together, sharing the story between them, they told Vince everything that had taken place the previous day. There were things Tim didn't know, but that hadn't stopped him trying to grind answers out of people who did. Like what happened down in the Underground. What happened to Detective Tanner. What happened to Charlie Paxman. He embellished some of the things he had been unsuccessful in uncovering.

'Bloody hell,' Vince said, after Samantha and Tim had finished. 'I can't believe Ciara's dead as well. I thought I recognised her when I lost the memory stick.'

'I've heard she was pregnant,' Tim added.

'Right?'

'With Rik's child.'

'Fuck.' Vince's mouth fell open.

'One of her friends said they'd slept together a few weeks back, but it was just a fling.'

'I don't know what to say. How did you manage to find this out?'

'I'm good at finding out information, it would seem.'

'You should be a detective,' Vince took another sip of beer. Placing the glass on the mat, he turned to face Samantha, and said, 'You're lucky to be alive. Although, I'm surprised this mug didn't save you sooner. He could have stopped you from being picked up by that crazy terrorist.'

Samantha chuckled softly and touched Tim's arm. 'He did what he had to. He saved me in more ways than one, trust me.'

Vince rolled his eyes. 'What about you, mate?' he asked. 'How did you get out?'

Tim swallowed his mouthful of drink and said, 'After I'd explained who I was and what I was doing with the gun, they released me. Obviously, they wanted to know what happened, and they spent hours taking my statement. They wanted it in audio, video, and written format. My wrists never hurt so much in my life.'

'At least they won't have to anymore.' Vince winked at Tim, nodding to Samantha.

'After they let me go, I headed straight to the nearest hospital. I needed to find Samantha. I wasn't going to let her go for a third time. Fortunately, I didn't have to look too far – she was admitted to Guy's Hospital. Her and a dozen other patients. And now here we are.'

On the other side of the room, a group of middle-aged men dressed in shirts and suits, laughed deeply, filling the entire room. Tim glanced at them. At their happiness, their enthusiasm.

At that moment, he was filled with a tingling warmth.

'It's crazy, isn't it?' he said.

'What's that?'

'How the human race is going to change forever, but most people don't seem to care. They're living life as it goes on.'

'Death,' Samantha said, 'it's out of our control. It puts things into perspective for us, but there's no point worrying about it. Might as well appreciate the things you do have while you've still got them.'

Tim faced Samantha, kissed her on the forehead, and said, 'I plan to. If it's the last thing I do.'

79

Home

December 4, 2017, 12:00

Jake entered Frances's office and sat down. Mamadou was beside her. He had been summoned there by phone call only a few minutes ago.

'Morning, Tanner!' Mamadou said, his white teeth looking illuminated against his dark skin.

'Mam.' Jake nodded. 'How you feeling? You're looking pale.'

'Threw up twice yesterday, but nothing I can't handle. The scientists reckon the effects will wear off in a couple of days. They said my exposure to the virus wasn't that concentrated – not as concentrated as Paxman's, at least. I'm just as infected as you are, apparently. Nothing to worry about. Yet. I'm counting myself lucky that I'm not one of the ten thousand who have already suffered the same fate as Craig.'

'Yes, it's horrible – truly, truly horrible. But enough of that.' Frances turned her attention to Jake; it was clear to see she did not like to talk about the effect Charlie Paxman's virus was having on her colleagues and friends. 'How's the arm?'

'Arms,' Jake corrected.

'Apologies. How are they?'

'Ruined, still.' Jake lifted his right in the air. It was in a sling. 'This one won't heal for another two or three months, and then I'll have to do loads of physio with it.' He lifted his left arm and nodded at the bullet wound. 'And as for this one, the doctor fished whatever was left of the bullet out of there, gave it a good clean, sterilised it, bandaged it, and sent me on my way.'

'Can you write with them?' Frances asked.

'I'm afraid I can't. Not for some time. Sorry – doctor's orders.'

'We'll look into getting you signed off for a couple of weeks. Come back after Christmas. Spend time with your family. They'll need you right now. I would have done it sooner, but I've just been swamped down here.'

'It's fine,' Jake said. 'I know how it is.'

Frances leafed through a pile of notes on her desk. She placed one on top of the file and read. 'I've scheduled weekly meetings with Dr Hamzah for your return after your break, Jake. I know you've spoken with him before.'

'Trouble has a way of finding me.'

'Be that as it may, your mental and physical well-being is my top priority, even if it may not be your own. I want to know how you're getting on and the progress you've made. I don't want you coming back to work too soon if you're not ready. You did an excellent job up there. You're one of our most experienced and gifted detectives, and we can't afford to lose you.'

Jake felt happy, and his body swirled with warmth. It was funny how words could have that effect on you. So why were they so hard to say? Why had she never made these comments before when he'd needed them most?

'Even if you did it without my help,' Mamadou said, chuckling.

'What do you mean?' Jake asked.

'While I was inside Paxman's flat, I found a manifesto – an itinerary.'

'What did it say?'

'It said he was going to kill every member of the World Health Organisation by one o'clock. And then he was going to release the virus in the Underground about half an hour later. He had floor plans for London Bridge station buried deep on his hard drive.'

'But the explosion didn't go off until two,' Jake said.

Mamadou shrugged. 'It was probably a distraction, to divert our attention away from him while he escaped in the Underground.'

'It would have been nice if someone could have told me that beforehand,' Jake added.

'Hey, hindsight's a wonderful thing. There were delays. Something came up. If I could have, I would. But that's not my point. What I'm trying to say is that you delayed him, Jake. You stalled him for long enough to make a difference.'

'But it didn't make a difference, did it? Those scientists

still died, and he still released the virus.'

'There were survivors. Benjamin Weiss and Marianne Evans. They escaped. You saved them, Jake. The ones Paxman detested the most, according to his manifesto. You didn't give him the luxury of killing them. He didn't win. Not to mention, you saved others in the restaurant as well. If it hadn't been for you, everyone inside that place would have died. Including your family. You saved a lot more lives than you give yourself credit for.'

A moment of silence fell on the room. Jake absorbed Mamadou's words. At this point in his career, he knew when Mamadou was lying to make Jake feel better about himself, but this wasn't one of those times. Mamadou was being genuine, honest, and, more importantly, a friend – someone who was truthful and faithful to him.

Frances cleared her throat. 'Next on the list: your family. How are they?'

Jake hesitated. Swallowed hard.

'I'll be honest with you, not good. Maisie and Ellie can't sleep. They've spent every night since the attack with us, and neither myself nor Elizabeth can sleep, either. They've seen things no one should ever have to see. And it's going to stay with them for a very long time. The kids especially.'

'We can get them help as well,' Mamadou said, his voice soft and endearing.

'Thank you. And not to mention the amount of stress this has caused Elizabeth. She pretends she's OK, but deep down I know she isn't. And she won't admit it to me, either – she's stubborn like that. We went to the doctor's yesterday, and they said the baby was fine, but I'm still paranoid about it. It's a miracle we can even have another one, and I don't want anything to happen to her or the baby.'

'Have you found out the sex yet?' Frances asked.

'We're having a little boy.' The words filled him with raw happiness.

'Oh, Jake, that's fantastic! I'm so pleased for you both.'

'You have my permission to name him after me,' Mamadou said.

Jake chuckled. 'I'll try to get that one by Elizabeth, but I can't promise anything.'

There was something burning in the back of Jake's mind. In the days following the hostage situation, the news had been inundated with information and video footage of Charlie Paxman and Kieran Hopkins hovering several hundred feet in the air. But Jake had heard nothing about Charlie's trial. Nothing about his interview progress. Nothing.

He felt obliged to find out.

'What's going to happen to him?' he asked.

'To Charlie?'

Jake nodded.

'We don't know. He's pleading guilty, but also playing the insanity and suicidal card, which, if it goes ahead, will mean he's going to be locked up in one of the most secure prisons in the country, where nobody can hurt him. Not even himself.'

'What about the cure for the virus?'

'If he goes down the insanity route, then there will be no cure. They wouldn't let him anywhere near a drop of water if they thought it meant he might kill himself with it, let alone a bunch of chemicals that can alter strands of human DNA.'

Jake hung his head low.

'Paxman is a very dangerous, intelligent man, Jake, who deserves to go down for the rest of his life. He planned all of this – I'm telling you. There are things not right in his head.'

'There are some who respect him.'

'And they're all insane.'

'What about me? Am I insane?'

Frances's eyes widened. Her lips opened a little. And she leaned back in her chair.

'You support him? You think what he did was good?'

Jake considered carefully what to say next.

'I think his motives hold some merit, yes, even though he did some horrific shit that vastly overshadows his original aims. But overpopulation is a massive issue which no one seems to be addressing. At least not now, because Charlie's already done it for everyone. I don't agree with his methods at all, but I can understand where he was coming from. But when thinking about the virus itself, it wasn't designed to massacre a third of the world's entire population – he tried to reduce future population growth as humanely as possible.'

Silence. Jake didn't care; he felt a weight lift from his shoulders. He hadn't told anyone else his opinions, and it relieved him to reveal them.

'You're about to have another child,' Frances said. 'How can you say something like that?'

Here we go, Jake thought. 'It's different. We were told we could never have another. It makes our baby boy even more special.'

'Have you been smoking something, Jake?' Mamadou asked, smirking.

It was then that Jake remembered what he had done a few nights ago and during the attack. How he had relied on the marijuana so heavily. How it had helped him sleep. How it had helped alleviate the pain of his gunshot wound. Both he considered to be out of necessity. But not anymore. He hadn't touched it since that night, and he never wanted to have another drag. He didn't want to rely on it to help combat his issues, his night terrors. He would find alternative methods.

'Not quite, no,' Jake said eventually.

'I don't know what to say,' Frances said.

'I presume you don't feel the same way?'

'No, I do not.' Frances enunciated every syllable.

'Is that why you treated Charlie with so much contempt, or is there another reason?'

'What do you mean?'

'When I saw you at the base of The Shard, you were angry. Worse, you were fuming. About something in particular. I've never seen you behave like that before.'

Frances said nothing, keeping her gaze fixed on Jake.

'It was about Alex, wasn't it? Alex Tough. My friend.'

Frances remained silent. Her complexion turned pale. Her eyes didn't leave Jake's until she was just about to speak, then she looked down at her desk. He couldn't be certain, but he thought he had seen tears resting at the bottom of her eyes, building up, waiting to be released down her cheeks.

'He was my son.'

What?

Frances hesitated before continuing. 'I got pregnant when I was young. Too young. My husband and I couldn't afford to keep him. I wanted to keep him, but my husband didn't, and I was afraid that if we did, then my husband wouldn't love him – or me – anymore. And then I would have been on my own. I had no family to support me, and neither did he. We gave Alex up for adoption a few days after he was born.

'I've been watching him grow up ever since, keeping an eye on him in my own way, making sure he stayed out of trouble and moved onto a decent career path. I met him a few times in person, but he never knew who I was. I didn't want him to find out. I didn't want him to get involved in this line of work because if he did, and he died as a result, I would never have been able to forgive myself.

'Perhaps one day I would have told him. I don't know. But when I heard he met you, Jake, I couldn't have been happier. He was one step closer to knowing who I was.'

Jake didn't know what to say. A lump had formed in his throat. Frances's brutal honesty saddened him. Her son had never known who she was. And he never would. Jake had known Alex was adopted, but he had never learned the full extent of his family history. It explained so many things about Alex's personality: the stubbornness, the kind-heartedness, the intelligence, the drive, the determination to succeed.

'There was a lot of you inside him, you know,' Jake said.

Frances nodded. 'Thank you.' She sniffed. Hard. Wiped her eyes, and then said, 'Anyway, I think that concludes everything for today. But before you go, I'm telling you this personally so you can hear it from me, and you know that it's coming from above: during your time off, if you wish, you've been granted permission to pursue potential leads as to the whereabouts of Moshat Hakim. Providing Elizabeth lets you.'

'What?' Jake said, before his mind had had a chance to compute the words.

'Just don't go looking for illegal warrants this time or stealing recording devices from secure locations – it reflects badly on us all here,' Frances said, smiling.

Jake looked to Mamadou, who winked back at him.

Jake stood, hugged Frances, shook Mamadou's hand, said his goodbyes and made for the door. Before leaving the building, he made a quick detour to his desk, logged in and grabbed a few things from his hard drive. Then he headed home. Exiting the building's revolving doors, Jake felt as if he were losing another part of himself, one that was just as irreplaceable as Tyler's friendship. But, more than anything, he was excited to be spending overdue quality time at home with his family.

His girls.

His everything.

EPILOGUE

A Friend From The Past

December 4, 2017, 17:40

Stationed a few miles outside Stansted Airport, in a one-bedroom flat, Moshat Hakim stepped out of the shower, leaving the door open. Steam clawed its way up the bathroom mirror. He wandered into the living room. As he wiped himself with the towel he had been given, Rachael entered.

'How was the shower?'

'Good,' Moshat replied, sitting down on the sofa. 'Think I'm finally getting the hang of it.'

'About time. It's only taken you five months.' She smiled. Her perfect set of white teeth seemed to illuminate the rest of her face.

Moshat smirked. 'Now I've figured out how to work it, it's

time for me to leave. I suppose it was the only thing keeping me here.'

Rachael dropped her bag and raincoat to the floor, shook the umbrella free of the fine snowflakes that had been falling outside for the past few nights and dangled it over the nearest door. She wandered over to him, straddled either side of his legs and said, 'Is that so? Perhaps I'll have to give you another reason to stay.'

Her body felt cold against his freshly warmed skin. She rested her hips on his, placed her arms around his neck and kissed him. Hard. Passionately. He kissed back. Just as hard. Just as passionately, ignoring the chilling sensation that ran up and down his spine.

His penis went erect. Rachael ripped the towel from him, undressed her lower half, and rode him on the sofa. Moshat was overcome with raw energy, raw pleasure, raw desire to tear her clothes from her body and spend the rest of the night in her arms.

They moved about the flat. First the living room. Then the kitchen. Bedroom. And, finally, the office, atop the desk.

It was the longest he had ever lasted in their short relationship. And he thought it was a fitting end.

After he had finished inside her, Moshat wiped himself clean and got dressed while Rachael showered. When she was done, she joined him on the sofa.

'How was work?' he asked as she sat down next to him, placing her head under his arm. She wore her nylon bed shorts that rode up every time she bent over. As his hands moved down her body, she flinched, went over to her bag, and removed something from within. It was tiny, smaller than a fingernail. She held it in the air. Moshat recognised it as a recording device.

'I found this today. I was cleaning the office and found it on the underside of one of the desks.'

'Looks like Christmas has come early for me. You think Tanner placed it there?'

Rachael nodded.

Snatching it from her grasp, he said, 'You haven't said anything about me round the office, have you?'

'No, don't be silly. You really think I'd be that stupid? No one else knows about you.'

'What about now? Is it still working?'

'Of course not. As soon as I found it, I destroyed it. Look at it: I submerged it in water and removed the chip from inside.'

Moshat shook his head. 'I don't like this.'

'It's fine. Honest. Don't you trust me? I promise it doesn't work anymore.' She looked him in the eye. 'Scout's honour.'

'It's not that,' Moshat said. 'It means he's getting more suspicious. More tactical.'

'You reckon he's going to come back?'

'He won't stop until he finds me. I need to get out of here. It's already too dangerous for me as it is. I haven't been out of the house in months. It's driving me insane.'

'I know,' she said, moving her hand to his chest, stroking it. 'I'm so glad I picked you up that night. You were such a mess. And you know the worst thing about it?'

'What's that?'

'You should have scared me, but you didn't.'

'Well, hopefully next time you'll be the one doing all the scaring.'

'Have you heard from The Denizen?'

'He sent me an email this morning.'

'And?'

'We're good to go. He's managed to source the men, equipment and money.'

'Does he need more? I told you it's not a problem. I'll send him some of my dad's. He won't notice it's missing.'

'No,' Moshat said. 'Not yet. I've just set up the account. We don't want to deposit too much in it at once, or SO15 will get suspicious. Let me get out of the country first, and then we'll work it all out.'

'When will that be?'

'Soon, Rachael. Soon.' Moshat faced the television, oblivious to what was on. 'Jake Tanner won't even know what hit him.'

Also By Jack Probyn.

The Red Viper.
An Unlikely Betrayal.
Standstill.

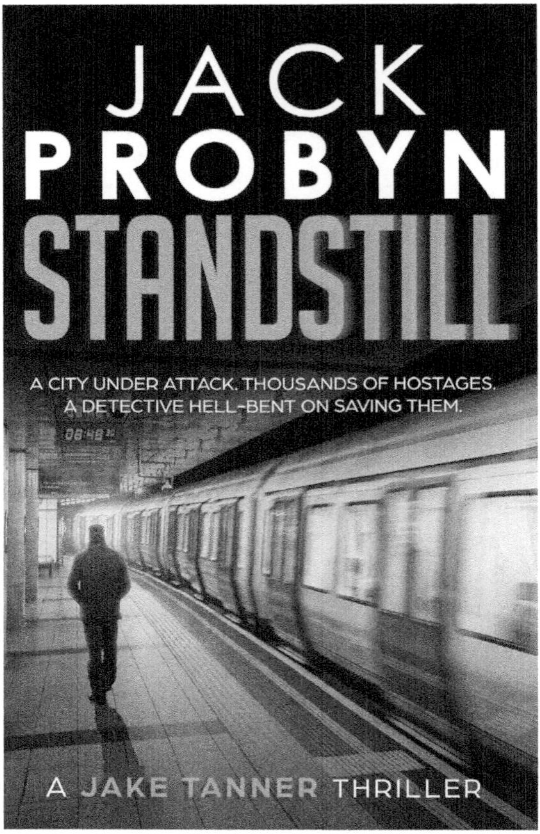

Turn over the page to read the first chapter of Standstill…

PROLOGUE

Factory

July 31, 23:50

Homemade bombs are easy to make.

All it takes is some ammonium nitrate and hydrogen peroxide. Both can be found in household items such as haircare products and fertiliser. Mix the ingredients together below ten degrees to form crystals, then combine with water, flour, and an initiator, and you've got yourself a device capable of killing dozens and injuring countless more. On the face of it, it's simple. But both substances are incredibly volatile and must be handled with extreme care. It had taken Moshat and his brother months to learn the basics, but, for Moshat, homemade bombs wouldn't do. Killing dozens wasn't enough. For their operation, they would need professional, large-scale stuff. And they had the training to acquire it.

Moshat stood beside the desk and leafed through the files in the ring binder, counting off the seconds until it was time to begin, when his colleague entered the room. 'Come on, mate. Shift's over. You coming?' Adam said.

Moshat hesitated. 'I'm just finishing up a few more things.' The light above him flickered, making the shadow he cast over the documents he held in his hands more ominous. It was important to make it look like he was busy. 'You go. I'll catch you up or see you tomorrow. I don't know how long I'll be.'

'You sure?'

Moshat nodded, keeping his gaze fixed on the papers in front of him. 'It's fine. Just go home, your missus will be getting worried. She might think you're cheating on her.'

Adam chuckled, his oversized belly and sagging jowls wobbling with each laugh. 'Chance would be a fine thing.' He turned to leave the room. 'See you tomorrow, then. Have a good one.'

Moshat grunted as a way of response. *Finally.* He let a deep sigh of exultation. *Fucking finally.*

Now he could begin.

As soon as he heard the factory shutter door close, way off in the distance, he placed his pen on the table. It was exactly parallel to the three other pens, two pencils, a small rubber and a shatterproof ruler. After a quick readjustment of the ruler, he was ready to go. Everything needed to be perfectly aligned, perfectly in order, and perfectly well-hidden.

Moshat glanced over at the red clock hanging on the wall and then at the digital clock on his desk. 23:50. Ten minutes to go. He breathed out and relaxed, allowing the tension in his back and shoulders to ease. As he arched closer to the wall, the knots in his muscles loosened. *That idiot Gardner*, he thought, shaking his head. It had been a close call; he didn't think he would shake Adam away in time, like a piece of discarded chewing gum on his shoe. It was imperative that there were no delays. Delays were costly and could lead to further mistakes – or worse, they could lead to nothing happening at all. And so far, Adam Gardner had posed the biggest threat to the operation.

Moshat sat down on his chair. The wave of pain deep in his back returned with a vengeance. The injury hadn't been kind to him. It had changed the course of his career, meant his dream was ruined, and nearly left him paralysed and in a wheelchair for the rest of his life. The discomfort and hurt was a constant reminder of those responsible and how they now lifted trophies in the youth team for West Ham with promising careers ahead of them. Tomorrow he would ignore the pain, give in to it, sacrifice himself so he could see the operation through to the end and have enough painkillers in his system to knock out a horse. He would not let any signs of weakness ruin the worst terror attack London had ever seen, the attack which he had worked so hard to prepare for.

Moshat found himself transfixed by the second hand on the clock making its long and arduous journey around the face. He let out a sigh. It was no use. He needed to focus on something else.

He jumped to his feet, wincing as a bolt of pain pierced through his entire body, and shuffled over to the office window with his hand pressed against his lower back. Moshat rested his elbows on the ledge and rested his forehead against the glass. It was cold to the touch. Dim lights illuminated the factory floor below. Stretching into the distance as far as he could make out in the gloom, were train carriages – like giant slugs all lined up in a row. Each one looked powerful, yet tranquil, and most importantly, uninhabited. To many, the stillness of the factory at this time of night would have been enough to make their hair stand on end. Not him, though; in the two years he had been working in the factory, he had grown accustomed to the eerie silence during the nights often spent on his own there, and he had begun to appreciate what magnificent feats of engineering the trains were.

Moshat marvelled in their magnificence. They had the ability to transport thousands of passengers every day. They had the power to travel at vast speeds while keeping everyone aboard cocooned in a bubble of relative calm. They even had the ability to come to an immediate halt or derail at any moment and invoke the primal fear of survival in their passengers.

As he gazed at the trains below, an odd emotion welled up in him. Like an alligator's eyes breaking the still surface of the water, it had risen from the depths of his soul and then dipped back down. Was it doubt? He didn't know. Was he nervous? Was he afraid? Was he regretting the path he was about to take? Either way, it didn't matter; he couldn't let it matter. He and his brother had invested too much of their time and life, injected copious amounts of hatred and animosity into what was going to happen in the next twelve hours. It was too late to get cold feet and back out now.

Their lives would change forever. And everything needed to be perfect for it.

The phone in Moshat's pocket vibrated. He dragged it out,

unlocked it, opened his messages, and read the most recent one.

'Adil,' he whispered to himself after reading the text, as if to not disturb the trains while they rested. He checked the time. 23:55.

He pocketed the phone, made his way down the stairs and headed towards the factory's exit. He approached the shutters and pressed a large green button on the control panel next to them. With a loud groan, the cogs and gears in the mechanism above him engaged, lifting the door and letting a torrent of cold air flood in over his feet.

Before him, silhouetted against the backdrop of the artificial light in the car park beyond, stood Moshat's brother, his features barely discernible except for the wide smile he wore on his face. Adil stepped forward into the factory. He wore a woollen hooded jumper with a leather satchel that hung off one shoulder and stretched across his body. His eyes and forehead were concealed by the low hanging hood. There was a commanding presence about Adil. Moshat's brother wasn't the biggest man, nor the most intimidating. Instead, there was something else about him: he had the aura of someone with the brains and skills that had the power to bring a country to its knees.

'You read your text messages, then?' Adil asked, pulling the hood from his face. His large, black, deep-set eyes seemed to absorb the light of the factory.

Moshat glared at him. 'You're early. Why are you early? You're not supposed to be early. You know I don't like when you're early. We have set times for a reason.'

'The sooner we begin, the sooner we can finish,' Adil said.

'What if Gardner or someone else was still here? What if

you were seen? We cannot afford mistakes. Not this late in the stage. We have less than twelve hours until our operation begins. Can you imagine what would have happened if you were caught?' Moshat said.

'Relax, Moshat. Don't you trust me? I made sure you were all alone before I made myself visible.' Adil smiled and slapped Moshat on the shoulder. 'Now, stop complaining and let's get to work.'

The two of them moved over to a small workbench next to the stairs. It was littered with the day's rubbish of wrenches, dozens of screws and a hammer. Adil removed his bag and slammed it down amongst the carnage.

'What are you doing?' Moshat asked, rushing over. 'Do not make more of a mess than there already is, please. They'll know if it's been tampered with. I don't want your fingerprints over everything.'

Adil continued, heedless of Moshat's protestations, and picked up the wrench. He bounced it in his hands, gauging the density and weight of the tool, and said, 'What are we waiting for?'

Moshat nodded and started towards the office. In the middle of the room was Moshat's desk, neatly laden with stationary and paperwork. Moshat sat in his chair, and Adil grabbed one from the neighbouring desk and sat opposite him, placing his bag on the wooden surface.

Adil appeared to observe the room, casting his gaze around and taking in its neatness and ordinariness before he opened his bag and removed a wad of paperwork. Post-Its and scribbles decorated the pages. 'I have brought all of the plans and documents with me.'

'We won't need them. I have them all committed to

memory,' Moshat said.

'Did you learn nothing in your training? Prepare, prepare, prepare.'

Yes, Moshat thought. *That old credo. The one I heard a thousand times while I sat in the mud, aiming down the sites of a sniper, rain lashing at my face.* Moshat dipped his head. The two brothers laid the documents along the table in a row and reviewed them yet again for the next five minutes. They made sure there were no mistakes, no stones left unturned, no possibility that anything could go wrong. Once they had finished, Moshat suggested they go downstairs to the car and remove the contents from the boot.

They both started out of the office and left the factory through a side door to avoid patrolling security. The air outside was warm. When they reached the car, Adil opened the boot. Inside were three black duffel bags with the zipper only three-quarters of the way done. The outline of the bags was jagged, as if they were packed full of bricks.

'I will take two,' Moshat said stoically. The pain in his back had disappeared, and he would not let his brother know he was in any discomfort.

'Be careful,' Adil said. 'We don't want anything to explode now, do we?'

As Moshat hoisted the bags onto his back, he winced. Ignoring the hurt, Moshat carried the bags to the factory, maintaining a steady but brisk pace. If one bag were to fall from his shoulder and crash to the ground, he, his brother, and everything else within the factory, would be obliterated. Moshat entered the building, beads of sweat dribbling down his forehead and into his eyes in the summer heat. With a wipe to his eyes of the back of his sleeve, he strolled through a myriad of corridors, and placed the bags on the concrete ground.

As Adil joined Moshat by his side, he turned to his brother and said, 'You ready?'

JACK'S EMAIL SIGN UP

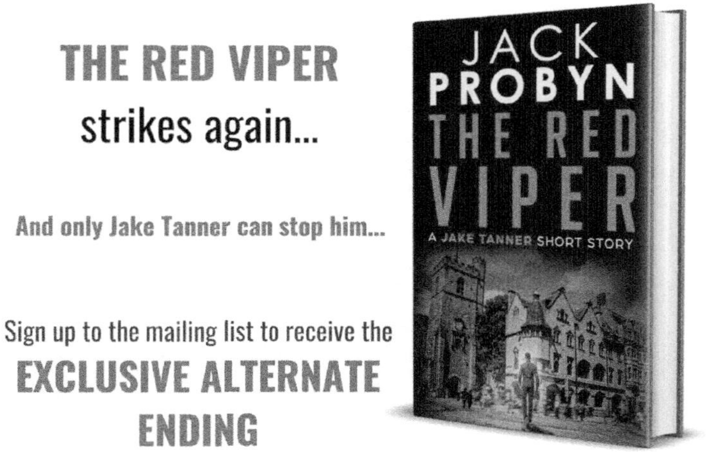

THE RED VIPER
strikes again...
And only Jake Tanner can stop him...
Sign up to the mailing list to receive the
EXCLUSIVE ALTERNATE
ENDING
JACK
PROBYN
THE RED
VIPER
A JAKE TANNER SHORT STORY

EXCLUSIVE ALTERNATE ENDING! Want to find out how *The Red Viper* could have ended? Sign up to receive the alternate ending.

https://www.jackprobynbooks.com

If you'd like to be the first to know when there's a new DC Jake Tanner book out, or if you want to receive updates on Jack's writing process, you can also receive those by signing up.

Your email address will never be shared and you can unsubscribe at any time.

ABOUT JACK PROBYN

Jack Probyn hasn't experienced the world. He's never even owned a pet. But he'd like to; there's still time. His twenty-two years on the planet have been spent in the United Kingdom, with a few excursions overseas – a particular favourite of his was Amsterdam. Or Norway. Both of which were lovely.

But what Jack lacks in life-experience, he more than makes up for in creative ingenuity. His Jake Tanner series is the birth child of a sinister and twisted mind, and a propensity to assume the worst will happen in even the most mediocre situation.

Finding himself pigeon-holed as a millennial, Jack decided to stick with the stereotype and do things his own way. After all, he felt entitled and he wanted to destroy industries.

Enter: writing.

The love of writing was rekindled in Jack's life when he (briefly) entered the corporate world, and the passion snowballed from there. No more will the millennial writer find himself working 9-5, indulging in the complexities of business life, or wearing a M&S suit.

He will take the world by storm with his pen(keyboard) and his ability to entertain and enthral readers.

Why not join him (and his future dog)?

* * *

Keep up to date with Jack at the following:
- Website: https://www.jackprobynbooks.com
- Facebook: https://www.facebook.co.uk/jackprobynbooks
- Instagram: https://www.instagram.com/jackprobynauthor

Printed in Great Britain
by Amazon

47057774R00249